# According to Their Deeds

# According to Their Deeds

Melvyn Westreich

# According to Their Deeds



First Printing: January 2022

ISBN - 978-1-7347004-1-1

Laurel Publishing
24751 Sussex Street
Oak Park, Michigan 48237

This book is a work of fiction. Names, characters, places, and incidents either are products of the author's imagination or are used fictitiously. Any resemblance to actual events or locales or persons, living or dead, is entirely coincidental. For those that are familiar with the Detroit area please excuse the geographical creativity.

Also by Melvyn Westreich

Lincoln/Lachler mystery series:

*Murder in the Kollel*

*The Kosher Butcher*

## ACKNOWLEDGEMENT

As usual I want to thank Phyllis Shapiro for her creative proof reading and for keeping both of my feet on the ground concerning male chauvinism. Well, I almost have both feet on the ground.

Rivy Gordon for her comments and advice on my early draft and final version of this book and who continues to encourage me after all these years.

Sharon and Burton Cohen and Carol and Joe Perecman my Detroit *mishpocha* and reality anchors.

I would also like to acknowledge my debt to a number of *rabbanim* who are no longer with us (listed chronologically): Rav Gershon Yanklowitz, z"l, Rav Meir Feldblum, z"l, Rav Asher Siev, z"l, Rav Moshe Tendler, z"l, Rav Henoch Fishman, z"l, Rav Aaron Soloveitchik, z"l, Rav Samuel Prero, z"l, Rav Feivel Wagner, z"l, Rav Aryeh Leib Bakst, z"l. Each of these great men – and very often their *rebbetzins* – helped form my *hashkafas olam.* If there are any gross errors in this book concerning *halacha* or Jewish concepts, rest assured that it is entirely the author's fault and not theirs.

I would also like to tell all my fans that their encouragement is what keeps me going. I love to tell stories and as long as you like to hear them, I'll continue writing. Thank you.

# DEDICATION

We, my wife and I, as children of refugees of the holocaust, are part of a generation brought up where grandparents were a rarity. Most of our elders did not survive the evils of the nazi terror that overran Europe. I was lucky, I knew my maternal grandparents because Reb Avraham Schlusselberg saw the writing on the wall in Berlin, and was able to get his family and all the families of his siblings, out of Germany. In their short periods of tranquil family life our grandparents were able to instill the love of Judaism and Torah into their children, and they were able to pass this on to us. Our Bubbies and Zeidies were dedicated to high moral standards and Yiddishkeit, and this book is dedicated to them.

Ovadiah and Maitah Westreich
Avraham and Esther Golda Schlusselberg
Yaakov and Etel Friedman
Eliezer and Hindah Katz
זצ״ל

## Author's Preface

This fun *frum* romance novel is a change of pace for me. No one gets killed or chopped up into small pieces. But Rabbi Kalmonowitz is back giving his meaningful insights, but this time to expound a bit on Jewish thoughts regarding death and dying. Kind of a downer, but it's part of life. He also helps our unlikely couple figure out their 'oil and water' relationship. She, Ayelet Weinberg, is the wonder baker from **The Kosher Butcher**, and he, Steve Lincoln, is the contractor cousin that did the house expansion for Shaindel, in the same book. I hope you will have as much fun reading this book as I had writing it. Once again, in **According to Their Deeds** all the words in *frumie-speak* (words in Yiddish and Hebrew that are liberally sprinkled in the conversations of Orthodox Jews) are not translated on the spot. Instead I have added a glossary at the end for those that need it.

## The Contradiction

**It is stated in the *Talmud*:**

*R. Samuel b. R. Isaac said: When Resh Lakish began to expound [the subject of] Sotah, he spoke thus: They only pair a woman with a man according to their deeds ...*

**But an additional statement contradicts this:**

*... for Rab Judah has said in the name of Rab: Forty days before the creation of a child, a Bath Kol (heavenly voice) issues forth and proclaims, the daughter of so-and-so is (intended) for so-and-so ...*

**The problem: How can a couple be paired according to their deeds if the decision is made before they are even born?**

**The answer:**

*There is no contradiction, the latter dictum referring to a first marriage and the former to a second marriage.*

***Babylonian Talmud - Sotah 2A***

# *Prologue*

Might as well end this three-way conference call. There was no way I was going to win. My son, David, and Rabbi Schlussel were not going to relent. "Enough already. Enough already. I'll go," I said in defeat. "Just stop *noodging* me."

"Good," said a triumphant Rabbi Schlussel. "You were a hard nut to crack, Mr. Lincoln."

"Rabbi, please call me Steve. Mr. Lincoln was my father."

David added, "Dad, we were not *noodging* you. We were just trying to show you the benefits of going."

"Yeah, just like Don Corleone made offers you couldn't refuse," I stated.

"Who is Don Corleone?" asked the rabbi.

"Rabbi Schlussel, he was talking to me. That was my father's attempt at a joke," said David. "Dad ... you know you need help."

"I don't know anything of the kind," I replied.

"Mr. Lincoln ... Steve," said the rabbi, correcting himself. "The meetings at the Jewish Center will do you good."

"Rabbi, don't start all over again. I said I was going."

My son added, "It's been two years since mom died. You have to have a positive attitude about this for it to work."

"You have enough positive attitude for the both of us and you live 700 miles away in Atlanta," I said.

"Yeah, but I'm not the one who will be going to the meetings," responded David.

"Don't I know it," I replied.

"Rabbi, tell my father how important it is for him to be positive about the meetings."

"Attitude is essential ... absolutely," said the rabbi with certainty.

"I said I would go ... but attitude is not part of the agreement. Take it or leave it."

"We'll take it!! We'll take it!!" exclaimed Rabbi Schlussel and my son in unison.

□---□---□---□---□---□---□---□

"So, Ayelet, it is agreed? You will be going to the meetings?" asked *Rebbetzin* Kalmonowitz over the phone.

I begin to protest, "But, the meetings at the Jewish Center ... men and women sit together."

"Who suggested that you go to these meetings?"

"*Rav* Kalmonowitz," I answer humbly.

"Exactly," said the *rebbetzin*. "And do you think that the *Rosh Yeshiva* does not know that the meetings are mixed?"

"Well ..."

"Of course he knows," interjected *Rebbetzin* Kalmonowitz. "So, if the *Rosh Yeshiva* suggests you go to the meetings, at least take it into consideration."

Funny, how whenever the *rebbetzin* speaks about her husband she always refers to him as the *Rosh Yeshiva* or *Rav* Kalmonowitz. She never uses his first name or calls him 'my husband'. He is the most respected *Torah* scholar in the community and had been my Rephael's mentor. If Rabbi Kalmonowitz suggests something it means I really do not have a choice.

Still it is very odd.

The *frum* community does not exactly boycott the Jewish Center, but they avoid their social gatherings because of the lax rules regarding male and female co-participation. In addition, the meetings are usually at night. That will be a problem.

"*Rebbetzin* ... aren't the meetings after dark?"

"Yes, but *Rav* Kalmonowitz will take care of that. Go down to the JCC tomorrow and register."

There is no use arguing.

"Yes, *rebbetzin,*" I respond meekly.

"Ayelet, *vet zayn gut* (things will get better)." Just before she hung up she added as a benediction, "*HaKodesh Baruch Hoo* should bless you and your children."

"Amen," I say, hoping that things would indeed get better.

# 1

# *The Grief Group*

WHAT A SURPRISE.

At precisely 9:30 in the evening, exactly one and half hours after it started, the first session of the Detroit Jewish Center's 'Loss Compensation Group' came to its end. This was quite unusual because most of the center's activities had a tendency to start on 'Jewish time' – i.e. late – and run overtime.

Punctuality was a good sign.

The session had nothing to do with stock market debacles or the recent theft of my automobile – an inconvenience I could have done without – thank you very much. Nor did it deal in articles retrieved from the 'lost and found' or finding replacements for irreplaceable pets that had gone astray. This was a therapy group set up by the social services department to help people deal with the loss of a loved one. The social workers of the JCC dubbed it the 'Grief Group'.

The psychologist in charge was Dr. Lionel Stralling – 'call me Lonnie' – and he had ended the meeting with, "Thank you for your participation. In the next few sessions I hope you will all come to see how just by verbally expressing what it is that is troubling us, we will help ourselves in the task of rebuilding and strengthening."

I thought to myself, *'verbally expressing' – 'rebuilding and strengthening'? Is he kidding?* I groaned silently. *These meetings are going to be grueling.*

Not such a good sign.

Then Dr. Stralling stood, smiled silently and dismissed the group by waving his open palm in the direction of the refreshment table at the side of the room. I, as well as the other six members of the group, rose from our chairs and meandered over to grab a cup of coffee or a piece of the JCC's generic Danish and cookies. This first meeting had been a little intense and I could sense that we were all relieved that it was over.

Funny thing about Jewish functions – there was always a refreshment table. By some profound unwritten Jewish law, there has to be something edible at the end of the meeting or it does not qualify as a Jewish anything. For those that are not well versed in Jewish gastronomy, I must explain that Jewish 'refreshments' are not of the same ilk as sumptuous Jewish meals – brisket, chicken, pastrami, stews, etc. – or the delectable after service *kiddush* fare served in the synagogue – *chulent, kugel, gefilte* fish, chopped liver etc. – both of which are birds of a different feather. Jewish 'refreshments' are what was served to participants of Jewish functions to tide them over until they got to their sumptuous Jewish meal. It probably stemmed from the harsh winters in Galitziah or the Ukraine, where you dared not venture out into the blizzards without fortifying yourself with some sort of nourishment. Funny, even the Sephardic Jews, from far warmer climates, had the same 'refreshment' rules. Perhaps crossing deserts required fortification as well.

Another aspect of Jewish 'refreshments' is their total dissimilarity from non-Jewish 'refreshments'. At a *goyish* function, the main 'refreshment' is usually served in matching glasses and has at least a 13% alcohol content. At certain specific venues and times, beer may be allowed as a substitute. If any food is served it is usually doled out on doilies or cute tiny paper receptacles or at the end of bamboo skewers. Occasionally there might be some sort of healthy salad or small quiche cups sitting on a side table.

Not so at Jewish functions.

Coffee and tea were requisite elements of 'Jewish refreshments' and they were almost always complimented by a variety of baked goods – usually store bought – all of which were served on inexpensive disposable ware. Hot water and high sugar content were essentials. A kale quiche would be useless in fighting off the ravages of a furious Russian snow storm.

Over the millennia, the consumption of refreshments at the end of any Jewish function has evolved to where it has almost become a *mitzvah*.

You had to eat something.

Theoretically, the requirement that all Jewish functions had to culminate with the serving of refreshments should have been the downfall of the Jewish race. After all, if you had to stuff your face at every Jewish meeting, lesson, outing, or get together, Jews around the world should have swelled up like blimps, sent their cholesterol into orbit, plugged their coronary arteries, and died like beached whales. However, God in his infinite wisdom sent us salvation. What saved us?

It was simple.

The baked goods proffered on the 'refreshment' table were almost always stale as last week's toast and/or tasted like reprocessed dog food. You had to be a die-hard masochist to overeat. Even so, as bad as the food was, everyone felt compelled to take something.

A *mitzvah* – remember.

So, I sipped my now lukewarm coffee from my soggy paper cup and surreptitiously looked around the room making my instant evaluations of the other participants.

Just something I do when my mind is not busy with heavy thought.

The first under my scrutiny was our fearless leader Dr. Stralling. He was about sixty years old and had a cherubic face framed by a receding silver grey head of hair and a trimmed alabaster beard. Give the man a stogie and he would be a dead ringer for Sigmund Freud. *It could be that the good doctor has some unresolved issues.* He wore a three piece grey suit, which was in considerable contrast with the informal outfits that everyone else was wearing. But, after watching the doctor for the past 90 minutes, I knew that he probably had a good reason for the dapper outfit.

Lonnie was good.

Oh yeah.

Dr. Stralling knew how to manipulate people. He certainly had manipulated me.

When it had been my turn to stand up and tell the group about my 'problem', I just chickened out. I came to the decision that I was not going to do it. Participation seemed out of the question.

I reasoned that I had not chosen to come to these sessions. If Rabbi Schlussel and my son had not double-teamed me and coerced me into attending, I would never willingly stand up in front of a bunch of absolute strangers and talk about the loss of my wife, Rebecca. The others could bare their souls like Las Vegas strippers if they wanted to, but I made up my mind that enough was enough and I was going home. I stood, smiled at the group, and instead of speaking, headed for the exit.

Lonnie surprised me.

It was only three steps to the door, but quick as a wink the shrink was able to zip across the room, and before I could react, grab on to my upper arm. His fingers latched on to my bicep like an Alaskan Grizzly sinking its teeth into the first succulent salmon of the season, "So you think this whole group thing is a waste of time for you?" he said quietly so that only I could hear.

I tried tugging my arm free but Lonnie held firm.

I had a problem.

I looked down at the doctor's tenacious grip and realized that unless I wanted to convert this little confrontation into a formal Greco-Roman wrestling match, it appeared that I was not going anywhere. I was a little – shall we say – irked with Lonnie. Somehow, I controlled my anger and said softly, "I didn't say that ... but if you brought it up ... well ... yeah. And maybe you didn't notice it ... but I'm not the only one that thinks that."

"Yes, but they haven't gotten up to leave."

"Maybe I'm just a little more convinced than they are."

"Mr. Lincoln, you lost your wife, two years ago, didn't you?" said Lonnie releasing my arm.

"Yes, that's correct." *How had he known that and why did he bring it up? Doesn't he know it hurts to talk about it? Of course he does – he talks to people about these things.*

As if reading my mind Lonnie said, "I have a basic information sheet on each of you. In your case it is from Rabbi Schlussel. He says that you went through the *shiva* and all the memorial services like a real trooper. You were a great support to your son."

"He needed me to be strong."

"But you never shed a tear. Not in public ... and I suspect ... not in private. You were a real fortress of strength. But your sheet also says that you still have all of your wife's clothing hanging in the closets and folded in the drawers. Her makeup and cosmetics are still set out where they were when she died ... *two years ago*."

Now I was really furious. The doctor and I were standing face to face at the doorway and everyone in the group was eyeing us. I felt my anger rising. "Now wait one second. I don't think you have the right to bring up those things without my ..."

"I don't? Well sue me," said the doctor emphatically. "How old are you? Thirty-eight ... Forty?"

*Why did he ask that?* "Forty-seven."

"No kidding ... you look terrific for forty-seven. So you're tall, good looking, have all your hair ... you look like you work out. When was the last time you went out on a date?"

*God!!! Could he be asking that?* I was more than peeved, "My personal business is not open ..."

The doctor cut me off by saying emphatically, "Yes, it is open to this group. That's what we do." Then added softly, "We look into personal business. I'm sorry if I just gave you a hard time or embarrassed you, but I don't want you to leave, because I think you are making a mistake. I do grief counseling. That's my business. And my professional opinion is that your grief has not been properly resolved and it is interfering with your life. You can leave if you want to, but I think you will benefit from our meetings. It's up to you," said Dr. Stralling, as he moved back to his seat.

He got me.

I did not know what to do. I realized that Lonnie had intentionally pressed all the trigger points on some of my painful raw exposed nerves and had maneuvered me expertly. *Dr. Stralling was definitely good.* I wanted to leave – to rebel – but deep down I knew that Lonnie was right. I realized that I could not hide any longer. I did need help. *Maybe Lonnie could help me.* I closed my eyes, took a deep breath, and gulped down the saliva that had somehow pooled at the back of my throat, and returned to my chair.

Oh yeah, Lonnie could manipulate people.

I took another sip of the bad coffee.

The group was made up of seven people besides Lonnie. Four men and three women.

Abe Tolwitz caught my attention. He was a slightly over-weight – five ten or eleven – fortyish divorcee, who wore worn-out-at-the-knees corduroy slacks and a flannel shirt under a shapeless grey cardigan. His long hair was unkempt and he had the kind of heavy facial hair that made him look like he needed a shave right after shaving. Best definition – he appeared to be a likeable *shlump.* He was munching on a stale cookie and mopping up some residual tears with the sleeve of his sweater. His personal grief stemmed from the loss of his son, over two years ago. This was his second year in the group and he felt he was getting better. It was slow going and he still burst out weeping whenever anyone discussed death or dying. Considering that that was all they did at these meetings he was sobbing most of the time. It would be no surprise to me if Abe collapsed from dehydration during the sessions.

Talking to Abe right now was Judith Klein. She was a short, slim blonde who was more cute than pretty. She had shoulder length – and carefully styled – hair (obviously the work of an expensive hair salon). I guessed her age to be in the thirty to forty range. It was hard to tell. Her makeup style was what my wife, Rebecca, referred to as 'au-natural'. At first glance you would think that she only had a little lipstick on her freshly washed young perfectly complexed face. But if you looked closer you could see traces of the expertly applied unguents, salves, creams, lotions, powders, and who knows what else, that hid a myriad of aging changes and gave her that healthy outdoorsy country lass appearance. This was a lady that had the knowhow, motivation, time, and money to apply those exorbitantly expensive cosmetics.

*Rebecca had never bothered to do that. She was always just naturally pretty. Why go to all the bother and expense to make up your face so that it does not look made up?*

Judith was dressed in a stylish pastel green, silky, workout suit with matching gym shoes. Expensive stuff. Her clothes were definitely not Wal-Mart knock offs – they were the real thing. For the price of that outfit – pants, top, and shoes – even at a discount – you could buy a really good used car.

Judith had revealed to the group that she was having a hard time after the loss of her mother. As she spoke, she kept her gaze up towards the ceiling. In the long intervals between her words, she clenched her rouged lips tightly together as if she was holding back tears. When she finished her story – Niagara Falls.

*Might be profitable to have the tissue concession here at the JCC.*

Standing off by himself was Harlan Jacobs nibbling on a cookie. He was about my height – six feet – but was a gaunt nerdy looking, skinny nineteen year old. His thick glasses rested on an overdeveloped nose and he suffered from terminal acne. Greasy hair hung down over his ears and he looked like he could use a shower. His physique and body demeanor reminded me of an over cooked asparagus.

His reason for coming to the group was his deep depression from the loss of his dad. He related his story in a dry whisper of a voice, while keeping his hands tucked under his behind. As he spoke he rocked forward and back continuously, like a human metronome. I immediately sensed that there was something odd about the fellow. It took a moment to realize that the style of the clothes worn by Harlan was not really appropriate for a young man. Everything was also way too big for him – simply hanging from his frame. I am willing to bet that the fellow had taken to wearing his old man's clothes. He needed help. *How sad.*

Also off by himself was the most unusual character in the group – John Langer – who was sipping Diet Sprite from a plastic cup. I put his age at thirty-six or seven and he was taller than me – six three or four. He was clean shaven, with blow dried dark brown hair, accented with blonde highlights. The guy had the rugged good looks of a younger Marlboro man. What the girls in college would have called a 'Jock'. He was dressed in a 'warning-signal-pink' long sleeved silk shirt tucked into grey slacks with Continental pleats. No tie. There was a razor crease to his pants that flowed down and draped over his spit-shined maroon Italian leather loafers. His black leather jacket was still carefully folded over the back of his chair. Everything the fellow wore screamed '*mucho dinero*' and 'look at me'. During the session he sat with his *tuchis* half off the seat and his long legs extended into the center of the group circle. He kept his head bent forward and his arms crossed over his chest as if he was bored out of his skull.

Just from his reaction to the other participant's stories – or more correctly his lack of reaction – and the way he sat in the group, I sensed that John Langer was a bit shifty. The type of fellow my late father would have called *nisht a groyseh metziah* (Yiddish for not a big find or bargain).

Bad vibes emanated from Mr. Langer and he had not even opened his mouth. Then he told the group why he was attending.

Speaking in a matter-of-fact monotone, John revealed to the group that his wife was in psychotherapy ever since the death of their little daughter, Clarisse. He was only coming to the sessions because his wife's shrink thought it would show solidarity.

I had to give Lonnie credit. As John Langer spoke, the psychologist sat listening intently and even nodded his head with concern at appropriate times. Lonnie appeared to be drinking in John's every word, while at the same time he was offering him support. If I was the guy in charge I could never have pulled that off. To me, Big John was a caricature – a joke. A bad joke.

The guy was not to be believed.

I had to control myself not to scream at John Langer, 'What the hell is wrong with you?' This guy had been talking about the loss of his daughter – his own little girl – but he had done so with a total lack of emotion. It was as if he was reading last week's weather report. This was like watching a documentary on the Nature Channel, where a female of some primitive amphibian species squirted out zillions of newborn offspring into an algae covered puddle. Meanwhile, the daddy of the primitive amphibian species was making a lunch of his own recently arrived family members. The male just gobbled down the tasty, if somewhat slimy, smorgasbord, with absolutely no emotional attachment to his own squiggly progeny.

It seemed to me that the daddy of the slimy primitive amphibian species had been sitting across the circle from me.

Intuitively I knew that John Langer only did things that were in the best interests of John Langer. I was also sure that good looking John did not personally build or create anything of substance. Nor was he associated with any manufacturing or marketing business. Those manicured hands had never ever done a single day of honest labor. My guess would be that he was probably an 'entrepreneur' – a person that made money by seizing opportunities as they arose. Most likely his work credo was 'Screw unto others before they screw unto you'. The man screamed – NOT TO BE TRUSTED.

Big John had big, big problems.

I took another sip of my tepid coffee and continued my evaluation of the group. Next in line was Alice Horowitz, who had trapped Lonnie, in the corner of the room and was now bending his ear. Her fingers were firmly clasped around her paper cup as she expressed herself Jewish style – meaning she punctuated each sentence with some sort of motion of her hands. So, whenever she said something to Dr. Stralling, the tea bag string – which was hanging from the side of her cup – would flutter about in the breeze and Earl Grey would slosh out onto the floor.

How would I classify Alice? Easy. If Steven Spielberg was ever casting for someone to play a modern Jewish grandma, he need look no further. Alice was it.

The short, 70 ish woman's face was framed by a halo

of perfectly coifed silver-blue grey hair. She appeared to have just come from the salon after a tint and a set. Not one hair was out of place. But that was only to be expected because it was quite evident that her hairdo was encased in about an inch thick layer of hair spray. The resilient lacquer would guarantee that it stayed that way even if it was suddenly attacked by a fanatic Jihadist wielding a Jack hammer. Obviously, her clothes were from the designer, or more expensive racks of Nordstrom, or some other exclusive department store.

Alice appeared to be a nice older lady, however it was difficult to look in her direction when she spoke, but it was not because of any physical imperfection. The difficulty was that Grandma Horowitz suffered from what I called – you should pardon using the expression in the JCC – the Christmas tree effect. She was like one of those mirrored balls revolving on the ceiling of a discotheque, sending flashes of light in all directions. Whenever she turned her head or moved her body her ostentatious display of jewelry sparkled, glinted and shined under the harsh fluorescent lights of the classroom and sent beams of light everywhere. Half a dozen thick golden necklaces and dozens of gem encrusted bracelets and rings, also clanked and tinkled with every change in body position. Colossal gold chandelier earrings hung down to her shoulders. It was highly unlikely that any of her gewgaws were fakes. The lady was adorned as if she was trying to impress someone at the Hadassah Women's Annual Country Club Tea and not attending a group therapy session in a multi-purpose studio/classroom at the JCC.

During the session, when Mrs. Horowitz told her story, she did so with a wad of sodden tissue pressed against her upper lip. As she spoke, she punctuated each sentence with deep breathes and loud sobbing. When appropriate she also added an expressive motion with at least one of her hands – of course. In addition she turned her head from side to side to be sure that no one missed a word. Grandma Horowitz tinkled and sparkled through the saga of her recent loss of her husband after fifty years of marriage. *The old man seemed to have left her well off.* Unfortunately, Alice's story wandered far afield. The drawn out tearful soliloquy went way off-base and began touching on her granddaughter's acceptance into Harvard undergrad. It was beyond my comprehension as to why her granddaughter's college plans should bring tears to her eyes. Lonnie finally reined her in when she began bemoaning her dog's kidney condition.

The remaining participant was Ayelet Weinberg. I left her for last because she is definitely difficult to read. All I can say for sure is that Mrs. Weinberg is a member of the Ultra-Orthodox community. She told us about the loss of her husband in a traffic accident two years before and about her three lovely children. When she spoke she did so without displaying any emotion, without body movement of any kind, and without looking up from her shoes. I had no idea what made Mrs. Ayelet Weinberg tick.

# 2

## A fish out of water

I FEEL SO UNCOMFORTABLE HERE. If *Rebbetzen* Kalmonowitz hadn't insisted, I would never in a million years come to such a place. This Doctor Stralling, he expects everyone to publically express before one and all, why they think they must come to such a meeting. And surprisingly, all these people – they agree to do this. It must be because they aren't our kind. Only the one man, the one who sat next to me, Mr. Lincoln, wears a *yarmulka*. None of the other women dress as a modest Jewish woman should. I feel so out of place.

The *rebbetzen* said that Rabbi Kalmonowitz himself suggested that I come to these meetings.

The rabbi's suggestions cannot be taken lightly.

She is right – I do need help – Rabbi Kalmonowitz and the *rebbetzen* are always right. I try to shut off the hurt that I feel for the loss of Rephael, but I cannot. When I am with people I can hide it fairly well and when I'm with my lovely children – who keep me as busy as a whirlwind – and may God protect and watch over them eternally – I function. But when I am alone – it hits me. It falls on me like a ton of sharp cutting blades. I feel overwhelmed. And it hurts. It tears me apart from within and without. And I cry. I cry and I cry and I cry. I cannot keep back the tears. At night in bed I cry until I am exhausted and I fall asleep. But when I wake I cry again. Then a new day begins. My children need me. *HaShem* wants me to stop my mourning, so I make it through the day until I have to cry again.

I know this is not normal. But I cannot help myself. It is more than two years and I'm not making progress. People say I should be forgetting, but instead I only remember him more. I miss him so. I am only half a person. I never lived until I married Rephael and now that he is far away from me, I feel as if I will never live again. Even in those first difficult years – when we could not have children – we grew close. Then – with *HaShem's* and Dr. Barclay's help – when we did have our lovely children – we grew even closer. I miss him so.

I am not well. I will stay in the group just as Rabbi Kalmonowitz requests. Perhaps it will help.

That tall man, Mr. Langer told everyone that his marriage is suffering from the loss of his daughter and has come here because his wife asked him to do so. He did not think that coming to the session will help and he spoke in such a strange way – without any feeling. How can such a person ever be helped?

I'm surprised that talking before the group wasn't as difficult as I thought it would be. I simply told the truth. I told everyone that I miss my husband. Rephael was such a great man. I hope they understood that I was so proud to be his wife and his partner in his quest to become a *talmid chochom*. But that is over. Everything is over.

I hope Lonnie – Dr. Stralling – did not forget. Rabbi Kalmonowitz said he would speak to the doctor and ask him to find someone to drive me home. I just cannot drive at night yet. I have somehow found the strength to drive during the day, but I still cannot manage in the dark. Not since that night when Rephael was running home from the *bais medrash* to take me to the hospital. The night that drunken truck driver hit him. Only when I was in the ambulance, on the way to the hospital, did they tell me that he was dead. Two hours later Racheli was born.

Perhaps I should remind Dr. Stralling.

# 3

## *Bump on a log*

MY NOSE PICKED UP the faint but acerbic smell of turpentine spirits and acrylic paint that permeated the air of the classroom, but that was understandable since this large room also served as the art studio for all the future Picassos and Renoirs of the Jewish community. There were dozens of potential masterpieces in oil and acrylic, lined up like canvas soldiers against the left side wall of the room. In addition, the gray-steel utility shelves along the back part of the room were filled with unfinished pottery and sculptures in progress. The easels – speckled with multicolored dollops of paint – and most of the tables – covered with layers of dried glue and modeling materials – were shoved over to the right side to make room for our group's circle of chairs. Two of the tables were left near the door for the refreshments. Almost everyone was munching or drinking something and making small talk.

But not Ayelet Weinberg.

That was to be expected. The Ultra Orthodox – what we call *charedi* – were exempt from the 'refreshments rule'.

How did I know she was *charedi?* Easy. She was dressed like a typical *charedi* woman, in a loose fitting baggy grey sweater and skirt outfit that covered her from her neck to her ankles. It was impossible to know if the woman was slight or stout because, as intended, her ensemble was as figure revealing as a giant burlap sack. Her facial features seemed nice, but the way she positioned her head, angled towards the floor, kept a shadow across her face, so that I was unable to determine if she was Miss America pretty or Quasimodo ugly. Every strand of her hair was tucked up into an amorphic, ash-green, super-sized beret thingee that completely covered her head. That kind of headgear would detract from anyone's looks. Once again – intentional. She also avoided eye contact with everyone in the room, including Dr. Stralling, and never took her eyes off of her shoes.

When I entered the JCC classroom before the start of the meeting and took the seat next to her, she had not reacted at all. In fact, the only obvious sign of life that she displayed was her breathing. I probably could have come in wearing a gorilla outfit and she would not have noticed. The lady was either catatonic, deep in thought, or ignoring everyone in her own aloof manner. Knowing the *charedis*, it was probably the latter.

The reason she was not partaking in the refreshments was that everyone in the holy roller *charedi* community considered all the food served in the Jewish Center to be just 'not kosher enough'. I am perpetually p... – let us say – irked by the *charedi* attitude about *kashrus*. It was as if everyone else was inferior to them. They always insisted that their meat and bread had to have extra special kosher certification. By my way of looking at things if an Orthodox rabbi says a certain food is kosher then that should be good enough. There was no need to go out of your way to see if the meat came from a circumcised bull or if the bread was made with holy water. In addition they referred to themselves as the *frum* community. The word *frum,* is a Yiddish word that means religious and they think that only their way of practicing Judaism is correct. I find that highly insulting. What were we Modern-Orthodox – second class Jews?

I just noticed that Mrs. Weinberg keeps glancing at Dr. Stralling. *If the charedi woman was not going to have any refreshments why was she still here? She must want something from Lonnie.*

I was right. When Alice finished talking with the doctor, Mrs. Weinberg quickly approached him and they exchanged a few words. Lonnie nodded his head as if he was remembering something he had forgotten and began looking around the room. His eyes latched on to me and he started walking in my direction, "Mr. Lincoln ... "

*Uh, oh, I am in trouble. What does he want?* "Steve ... please."

"Steve ... once again I'm sorry for coming down on you like gangbusters."

"Nah, that's all right," I said. "I understand what you're trying to do."

"I'm not sure you do ... yet. But we'll get to that soon enough," said Dr. Stralling. "I want to ask a favor of you."

"Sure ... if I can do it."

"It's Ayelet Weinberg. Ever since her husband's death she has trouble driving at night. A woman from the community drove her here tonight and I was hoping you could drive her back and forth to the coming meetings. She lives only a half mile from you. Would that be all right?"

My friends often told me that I had a 'thing' about always being punctual, always doing favors for people and always volunteering for community service jobs. They felt that my 'strange' behavior was nurtured by a slight touch of paranoia. I never thought my little *mishigas* was a problem. I always strived to be the best at whatever I did and that included coming on time. I feel that people that come late are not displaying good manners or proper respect. Manners and respect were an important part of my life. I hoped that most people considered me a good person. Good father, good grandfather, good worker, good boss, good neighbor, good friend. An all around good guy.

Maybe it was more than just a slight touch of paranoia.

Many times people said that folks took advantage of

me. But I never looked at it that way. I enjoy helping people. So sure, I would not mind solving Mrs. Weinberg's problem.

"I would be glad to ... but I don't think I'm going to do you much good," I said shaking my head rapidly from side to side. "I know these *charedis,* and I've got a feeling that if it is just us two in the vehicle her religious rules about *tznius* won't allow her to get into a car with a strange male. I think you better ask one of the women to give her a lift."

"I would, but Alice just had cataract surgery and doesn't drive anymore, and Judith never had a license. So that means it has to be one of the men."

I responded, "Like I said, no problem with me. But her rules won't let her."

"Her rabbi spoke with me and he said that in this case, if it's an Orthodox religious man, then he would allow it. Since you are the only Orthodox man in the group that means you've been elected."

"What makes you think I'm Orthodox?"

"That little skull cap you're wearing sort of gives it away."

"Yeah, you're right," I said, embarrassed for not realizing the obvious. "No problem, I'll be happy to give her a lift."

Wearing a *kipa* all the time, was fairly new in my life. Something I had affected during the official year of mourning for my wife, Rebecca. My life had changed during that year and this was one of the alterations. My head covering did not make me into a born again, super-holy, in-your-face, Jew. I was not any more religious than I was when I had gone bareheaded. We had always observed the *shabbos* and kept a kosher home. But the *kipa* made me feel – for want of a better word – comfortable. I do not know why – it just did.

The *kipa* brought other changes.

Some of my old friends began hinting that they were

now a bit embarrassed to be seen in my company, saying that my new headgear was not appropriate for many social situations and venues. So, I made another change in my life and started doing something else that was totally inappropriate for the old me. I – Mr. Paranoia – eliminated them as friends.

When all the participants in the group reached their tolerance of bad coffee and stale pastries, they began filing out of the room. I left the class room with Mrs. Weinberg in tow and headed slowly towards the main entrance of the JCC.

Slowly. Not running. Not even a fast walk. Slow. That was the key.

It was dangerous to run in the halls of the Jewish Community Center and there were signs galore warning people to maintain a sedate pace. The warnings had nothing to do with the normal bodily perils associated with excessive velocity.

Oh, no.

It was because of Crazy Jimmy Jameson, the night custodian.

As a past member of the JCC's Board of Directors, I knew that this just might be one of those weeks when the crotchety night janitor was not seeing eye to eye with the administration. During those confrontational intervals the old guy was suspected of surreptitiously switching the recommended safety floor wax with the regular kind. The old codger would buff up the corridors to a dangerous ice-rink slickness and send unwary JCC visitors slaloming their way to the emergency room. Try as they might they could never catch Crazy Jimmy red-handed. But if you want to stay in one piece and keep the liability premiums down – no running in the JCC.

When I got to the parking lot I hit the remote on my car alarm and my vehicle responded with its usual welcoming chirp and blink of lights. Thank God – and lazy carjackers – my new SUV was still safe. When my previous car was stolen two months ago I learned that the standard vehicle locking system was a joke. The insurance adjuster said that any crook worth his salt could disable a car lock and antitheft alarm in under twenty seconds. Apparently automobile security devices were not really intended to thwart car thieves. Their deterrent ability sort of peaked at preventing absent minded grandmothers from retrieving their keys when they inadvertently locked them inside their cars and keeping teenagers with rampaging hormones from using my vehicle as a trysting refuge.

The insurance company had been slow in allowing me to purchase a replacement vehicle and I had to use a rental for six weeks. Only when it became obvious that my previous car had gone on to the great automobile heaven in the sky, did the insurance company authorize the replacement. I usually traded in my old car for a new one every three or four years and would always special order a 'vanilla', bare essentials, pick-up or SUV for my contracting work. But it was now the middle of a model year and the dealer did not have any stripped down vehicles on the lot. So the car I had been forced to purchase was one that I normally would never order.

This vehicle was equipped with all sorts of hi-tech gizmos, doo-dads, and extras. It was a metallic blue SUV with an eight inch GPS, wrap-around surround-sound audio with giant woofers and a backseat wide screen DVD player. The seats were even covered in real leather and had a special switch that would warm my butt in winter. For me, almost all of this stuff was totally useless. I rarely had passengers in the back seat, almost never listened to music, and twenty miles was just about the furthest I got from my home. But maybe having my behind warmed on a cold winter morning was not such a bad idea.

As I opened the car door and slid behind the wheel, I

once again took great pleasure whiffing the heady new car smell. Very likely the vapors given off by the new leather and plastic interior were toxic. All those gases probably gave you cancer and rotted your brain – but it was still terrific. I remembered reading an article that claimed that only men were addicted to the smell. Something to do with an ancient caveman reflex related to a successful hunt. I knew that the smell would not last long – so for now, I just savored it.

I made a quick calculation and realized that the vehicle had been in my possession for just over a week. Officially that meant it was eight days old. Perhaps I should ask Rabbi Schlussel if there was some sort of Jewish ritual needed for eight day old cars. Maybe I was supposed to lop off six inches from the tailpipe or something.

I heard Mrs. Weinberg enter from the other side and slam her door. It took a moment for me to realize that she had gotten into the back seat. Of course – what was I thinking – I should have known she would do that. There was no way, holier-than-thou Mrs. Ayelet Weinberg would ride in the front seat with a strange man.

As I pulled out of the lot, I could just make out her dark silhouette in the rear view mirror and out of politeness I tried to start a conversation, “I'm very sorry about the loss of your husband. He sounded like a wonderful person.”

“Yes, he was. Thank you,” she said.

“Lonnie seems like a very capable fellow.”

“Yes, he does,” she responded.

“Are your kids doing OK after the loss?”

“Yes, they are.”

I was getting tired of her monosyllabic answers, “Do you think these meetings will be able to help you?”

“I don't know.”

We rode the rest of the way in silence while I contemplated whether the word ‘don't’ qualified as a two syllable word.

When we reached her home at the eastern edge of Southfield, I noted that it was a three bedroom ranch. This was the type of home that had made up the original subdivision for this part of the neighborhood. Most people that were now purchasing in this area tore down these old structures and built something new.

Mrs. Weinberg said from the backseat, "Mr. Lincoln, could ..."

"Please call me Steve."

"Could I trouble you just a bit more?"

"How can I help?" *Soft touch once again – and the word 'trouble' definitely was two syllables. We're progressing.*

"I have a babysitter, and she lives just a couple of blocks from here, but it's late and I would feel better if someone could drive her home."

"No problem."

"Thank you. I'll send her right out," she said as she hustled up the walk into her home.

After about three minutes a teen age girl came out of the house carrying a backpack and assorted books. With the exuberance of youth she clambered into the front seat slamming the door, "Hi, Mr. Lincoln."

"Oh, hi," I said recognizing the young girl. "You're Melissa Showner, aren't you?" The girl's parents were members of my synagogue and I had seen her at Saturday services.

"My name is Marissa."

As we pulled out of the driveway I said, "So hi, Marissa. You're Mrs. Weinberg's babysitter?"

"When she needs me, and I'm free. Yeah ... one of them."

I was just a bit curious about my previous passenger that had sat like a bump on a log in the back seat, "So ... is Mrs. Weinberg a good boss?"

"Mrs. Weinberg? Are you kidding? She's the greatest,"

said the teenager with enthusiasm. "The only bad thing I can say about her is that once she starts talking you can't get her to stop. She is so funny ... and so smart. And she is such a great baker. I gain two pounds every time I sit for her."

*Was this the same woman I had just dropped off?* "Are we talking about the Mrs. Weinberg that just went into that house?"

"Sure. Mrs. Ayelet Weinberg. She's always doing nice things for people. It's such a shame about her losing her husband. She really misses him."

"She talks to you about that?"

"Mrs. Weinberg? Never! She is always smiling and laughing and so full of energy and life. But sometimes when I come over to sit later in the evening, she comes out of her bedroom and I can see that she was crying."

We pulled into the drive at Marissa's house. She opened the door and said her thanks over her shoulder before she disappeared into her home.

I sat for moment in my car and thought about Ayelet Weinberg. *Could she be one of the rare individuals that I would never be able to read?*

# 4

## When spoken to

WHEN I REMINDED Lonnie about finding someone to drive me home he went over to Mr. Lincoln, the gentleman with the *yarmulka*. It's the crocheted kind so that means he isn't one of us. A *frum* Jew would never wear such a *yarmulka.* Probably he is one of the Modern Orthodox that *daven* at the Young Israel synagogue. I think I have seen him around the neighborhood. The *rebbetzen* told me that it might be a man that will take me home and that Rabbi Kalmonowitz said for this special purpose it would be allowed.

Mr. Lincoln has a very nice SUV. The kind that's really good for the heavy winter snows. Rephael always wanted to get one.

Strange, Mr. Lincoln thought that I would get into the front seat. Of course I would never think of doing something as brazen as that. A woman must show modesty at all times. That is a woman's strength and the source of her power and beauty.

He kept asking me questions.

Did Mr. Lincoln actually expect me to conduct a conversation with him? That would be inappropriate. Of course I had to answer his questions so as not to appear impolite. But no conversation.

I was relieved when we finally got to my house but I knew that I must ask his help to take Marissa home. The neighborhood is considered very safe, but Rephael always insisted that someone had to take the babysitters home.

Thankfully he agreed.

Once I got in the front door I called out, "Marissa. I'm home.".

"Hi, Mrs. Weinberg," she replied, coming out of the bedroom area. "All the kids are asleep. Chaim'l wanted to stay up to wait for you, but he dropped off about a half hour ago. Yanki and Racheli both fell asleep ten minutes after you left. So basically, other than the time Chaim'l was asking me questions about his homework ... he's so smart ... I just sat and did my own stuff."

Chaim'l *is* smart. Everyone says he is an *ilui*. He must have gotten it from Rephael. "So did you taste some of the goodies I left out for you? Can't have you starving."

"Starving? Are you kidding? Your cookies and cakes are soooooo good. I would come to sit for you for free just to eat one of your croissants."

"Thank you for coming and here's your money. A Mr. Lincoln drove me home and he said that he will take you back to your house."

"I know Mr. Lincoln," said Marissa, as she gathered her belongings. "He *davens* in our *shul*."

"He seems to be a nice man and he's waiting outside. Bye."

"Bye."

# 5

## Rosh Yeshiva's request

IT WAS FOUR WEEKS since the initial group session at the JCC and I was at morning *minyan* at the synagogue. Mortie Bartholemew was the *chazan* and he was chanting the last few prayers of the service. It looked like he was going to beat his own BPT (best personal time) of 36 minutes. Prayers usually ended at 07:40 on mornings when there was no reading from the *Torah*. But that could vary depending on the *chazan*. 'Speedy Gonzales' types – the ones on their way to a fire – got us out by 07:30. While those with molasses in their veins could drag it out almost until eight. Looks like Mr. Bartholemew had to get somewhere this morning.

The punctuality nuts – people like me – made sure to get to *shul* before the start of the morning *minyan* at exactly seven sharp. The late comers straggled – or rushed – in throughout the service. However, no matter when they arrived, everyone finished together. It was similar to a commuter train chugging its way to the big city. People got on at every stop, but when the train reached its final destination, everyone got off together.

Mr. Bartholemew finished the last line of *shacharit* at 07:34 – nice going Mortie – and the mourners began chanting the *kadish* in unison.

The *chazan* stepped away from the prayer lectern and we all became busy wrapping the black leather straps around the little boxes of our *tefilin* or folding our *talis*. The fellows that had to get out early had jumped the gun and were already well into the wrapping up process.

About fifty men made up the regulars of the morning *minyan,* and each came about 75% of the time. There was always someone that was ill, had an early morning appointment, was on vacation, or was just plain sleeping in. About a third of the regulars were business men or salaried employees. These were the ones that had their prayer accoutrements stashed away and were out the door just as the last 'amen' was being chanted. They had to get to work and – since an Orthodox man did not eat before his morning prayers – they grabbed a cup of coffee or some cookies in the kitchen before rushing to their cars.

The *mitzvah* fare – remember.

Another third were students and men in professions that allowed them to make their own daily schedule. They did not dawdle but they also did not waste much time before they skedaddled. The final third were an assortment of retired gentlemen that were not in any hurry to go anywhere. For many of them, coming to prayers was the high point of their morning and perhaps their entire day.

After the service, Rabbi Schlussel conducted a daily one hour *Talmud shiur.* His core participants were seven of the retirees; two doctors, three businessmen, a plumber, and an engineer. One or two of them actually stayed awake for the entire lesson.

I was not a member of this class, even though Rabbi Schlussel has often given me his frowning look of disappointment as I walked past his table on my way out of the synagogue. The last time I cracked a volume of the *Talmud* I was in high school, so give me a break.

I was now considered a regular at the morning *minyan* but actually I had only been attending for the last two years. Up until then I said my daily prayers at home and only came to *shul* on Saturdays. How had I – Steve Lincoln – a Saturday-only participant – changed into a morning *minyan* regular?

Hard to say.

When my dad passed away in a freak work accident seven years ago I had of course found the time to attend daily services to say *kadish,* but after that year I went back to just attending Sabbath services. However, when Rebecca passed it was expected that David, my son, would be the one to say *kadish* for the year. But he was now busy running our company and could not be sure that he would make it to the thrice daily services. Through a mutual decision it was agreed that David would try to say *kadish* whenever he could, and I, who was now officially retired from the company, would take it upon myself to say the memorial prayer for the entire year. So, once again I began attending the daily services. When I concluded the required eleven months, a little over a year ago, I found that I rather enjoyed the services and I just kept on coming. Just like the *kipa* on my head, I found it comforting.

I had been *davening* in this synagogue since I was a boy, but only of late have I come to realize that the intricate fabric of synagogue life was actually very similar to an improvisational theatre. There was even a whole cast of many special characters – each one contributing their unique part. It was an absolute blast to watch the drama that unfolded every day.

One of the most colorful characters in this daily production was Mr. Handel, an eighty year old retired lawyer, who always arrived at services freshly shaven and wearing a jacket and tie. It was as if he expected to receive a call from his old law firm asking him to come down to the office to pitch in for an ailing partner or make an emergency appearance in court. He had an important *shul* 'job' and it had nothing to do with his expertise with the law. Mr. Handel took upon himself the task of retrieving and reshelving all the orphaned prayer books that remained scattered on the tables after the service.

He was about five foot, six inches, tall and dripping wet probably did not weigh more than 120 pounds. Watching frail Mr. Handel carrying his load of books was quite a sight to behold. Like many older people he walked funny. His method of propulsion involved his sort of falling forward and then allowing his feet to shuffle quickly to catch up. Think of the Tower of Pisa sliding across the horizon – that was Mr. Handel walking. Now, imagine that someone hung a huge elephant from the upper balcony of that moving tower. That was Mr. Handel trudging back and forth with his heavy stack of books. The laws of physics say that at any moment Pisa is going to lose a famous landmark. But God works in mysterious ways and the Tower of Pisa does not topple and Mr. Handel continues to *shlep* the weighty tomes. I once made the mistake of trying to assist the old man by carrying some of the books to the shelves, but I soon learned that Mr. Handel did not take kindly to anyone encroaching on his 'book-retrieval' monopoly.

Another character of note was Mr. Aharonson, a retired gym teacher, who was the official *pishka* bearer. During the repetition of the *amidah* he would amble around the *shul* collecting everyone's donations to the charity fund. He accomplished this by stopping in front of each and every congregant and loudly rattling the coins in the chromed chalice. He would stand there shaking the *pishka* until that person anted up and inserted some cash into the little slit on the top of the cup. There was no escaping from Mr. Aharonson. From experience I can tell you that it is useless to try hiding in the restroom while he made his rounds. He was relentless. As soon as you returned he was waiting for you. Everyone had the *pishka* shoved under their nose. At the end of service he ceremoniously, and noisily, spilled out all the coins and bills on to one of the tables. He carefully counted and recorded just how much he had been able to coerce from the congregants before he deposited the cash in the strong box in the office.

There were many more characters in the *shul* drama.

Mr. Borenstein was the 'super-pious' character who yelled out his 'amens' at the end of each of the blessings so much louder than anyone else.

Mr. Katz was the 'decorum-warden', frowning upon, chastising, and shushing anyone who was in violation of proper synagogue decorum or etiquette. Do not try whispering with your neighbor if he was around.

Mr. Mandel was the 'Mr. Data-base' and had somehow memorized everyone's full Jewish name – including the names of their fathers and mothers – so that they could be called to the *Torah*.

Mr. Stein was the 'anthropologist' of the *shul* and had absolute recall of all the obscure traditions that were unique to the Young Israel. He was always saying, 'We always did it this way.'

However, the most beloved – at least by the children – was the 'candy man' character. This was the old – and sometimes not so old – Jewish man (or men - often there was more than one) that gave out candy to all the kids as a reward for coming to Sabbath services.

The current reigning Young Israel candy man was Mr. Steinberg, but years ago it had been my father.

I remember how every Friday my dad *schlepped* two pounds of assorted suckers and sweets to the synagogue to stock his private stash. He did not want to disappoint any of the starving waifs at the Saturday morning service. Whenever any of the kids got one of his treats in their hot little hands, they usually smiled from ear to ear, but my dad's smile of pleasure outshone them all.

Every day another drama.

The *minyan* was finished and the people in the weekday sanctuary were now stowing away their *talis and tefillin* or engaged in conversations with their neighbors. As I folded my *talis* I could hear Mr. Chomski's loud raspy voice – he was one of the old timers in the *shul* – making his usual complaints about this and that to anyone that had the patience to listen to him. The regulars from the *Talmud* class were setting out their books on the table near the door. I watched Mr. Handel, the Leaning Tower of Pisa, trudging back and forth with his stacks of stray books. I heard the loud clatter as Mr. Aharonson cascaded all the cash out of the *pishka* on to his table. The regular post *minyan* activities.

Then I noted that there was one unusual congregant. Someone who never ever prayed here.

Rabbi Gorrus.

He usually attended one of the *charedi shuls.* The Young Israel was just not *frum* enough – not at his level of spirituality. I had not noticed him earlier – he must have been praying in the corner. His long black frock coat and large black fedora were far different from the sweaters and slacks worn by most of the Modern Orthodox *minyan*. Even Rabbi Schlussel wore a sports jacket and a colored shirt. The *charedi* rabbi stood out like a charcoal briquette in a sack of marshmallows. Rabbi Gorrus finished putting his *talis* into its velvet bag, but instead of heading for the door he began walking straight towards me.

I quickly glanced around to check if there was anyone else in my vicinity. Apparently I was the rabbi's target. *Uh oh, what could he want?*

"Mr. Lincoln, *shalom aleichem* (peace unto you)," said the rabbi, extending his open palm.

I shook the rabbi's hand and made the formal reply, "*Aleichem ha'shalom* (unto you may there be peace)."

Straight to the point Rabbi Gorrus asked, "Mr. Lincoln, would you be free to come to the *yeshiva* this morning to speak with the *rosh yeshiva*?"

He meant Rabbi Kalmonowitz, who was the head rabbi at the *yeshiva* and his boss.

This certainly was very unusual. There had been no small talk. None of the usual – 'How have you been?' 'How long is it now ... six years since your company added on the extension to the *bais medrash*?' No beating around the bush. This was not a serendipitous occurrence. Rabbi Gorrus, Rabbi Kalmonowitz's right hand man, had come here for the sole purpose of inviting me to this meeting. I could not imagine why the *rosh yeshiva* would want to see me.

*This cannot be anything good.*

Over the years my contact with Rabbi Kalmonowitz had been minimal. When my company had done the expansion work on the *bais medrash* I met with the man twice but it had only been for a couple of minutes each time. I was surprised the *rosh yeshiva* even remembered my name, because the Modern Orthodox Young Israel crowd just did not mingle with the *charedi yeshiva* people.

"Rabbi Kalmonowitz wants to see me?" I asked warily.

"Yes, he does."

"Could you tell me why?"

"I haven't got the foggiest idea. Eleven o'clock, in his study, in the main *yeshiva* building," said the rabbi, inflecting a hint of a royal command. "Can you make it?"

I tried to rack my brain to think of an acceptable excuse for not going.

No luck.

There was no way I could make myself bend the truth and say I was busy when I was not. I had this premonition that if I lied to Rabbi Kalmonowitz, the wrath of God would come down and smite me. Without any other options I tried stalling by stammering, "Well ... well ..."

Rabbi Gorrus, like any good clergyman, could sense when he had someone boxed into a corner with no way out and said, "Good. I'll tell *Rebbi* you'll be there."

I arrived at the *yeshiva* building at five minutes to eleven and got directions to Rabbi Kalmonowitz's office from one of the *yeshiva bochurim* walking in the halls. The students were all males, since the girls learned in a separate institution. They all wore the unofficial uniform of *yeshiva* students throughout the world. Black suits, black shoes, and white shirts – ties and black hats being optional during the week. De rigueur, the fringes of their *tzitzis* hung out of their pants like Spanish moss dangling from a swamp cypress in a Louisiana bayou. A few had the long strings intricately entwined through their belt loops and I could not help but wonder if that little arrangement did not cause a bit of havoc if they had to urgently drop their trousers in the rest room. The younger students, who walked jacketless in the halls, joked and jostled each other but the older ones walked with a solemnity of purpose, never talking above a whisper. Someone must have told them that the only way to reach the status of a *talmid chochom* was to never crack a smile.

I felt an almost tangible apprehension as I stood at the door to Rabbi Kalmonowitz's study. Imagine the fear and anxiety of a high school student getting called to the principal's office or a businessman getting ready for a tax audit or a driver who had just downed a few beers getting pulled over by a police patrol car. Now combine all three and that would only be a fraction of what I was experiencing.

I knocked on the door.

"Come in, it's open!" came a loud response from within.

I pushed tentatively on the door and it swung inwards to reveal the Rabbi's miniscule study. It was a small windowless room that barely accomodated a desk and three chairs. The place smelled of the old books that filled the groaning bookshelves, which occupied every inch of wall space. There were dozens of sets of oversized tomes covered in vary hued dark leather or cloth. Almost all the gilt lettering on the spines had worn off from use, so that most of the titles were undecipherable. In addition there were books arranged helter skelter all over the place. Some were crammed into the space above the books lining the shelves or they were stacked on the table and every other available flat surface in the room. It was hard to imagine that another book could be jammed in anywhere. Even with all the books, the room did not feel oppressive or cramped. There was a feeling of intensity of purpose to the room. Like the cluttered laboratory of a scientific genius. Rabbi Kalmonowitz was seated behind his desk perusing a large well used book. I took a step into the room and said, "You wanted to see me?"

The rabbi was dressed in his shirtsleeves with his tie loosened and he wore a large black *yarmulka* instead of his wide brimmed hat, which together with his black frock coat, were hanging from a peg sticking out from one of the shelves. I guessed the rabbi's age at about 65, but the full scraggily grey beard made it hard to be accurate. I could be off by ten years or more, up or down. The rabbi looked at me with his sparkling gray-blue eyes and smiled. Then he closed the book and extended his hand, "Mr. Lincoln ... Shaul ben Baruch ... I believe that is how you are called up to the *Torah*."

*How did he know my Hebrew name?* My dad's name was Bernard in English, but his Hebrew name was Baruch. Mine, was Shaul.

I shook the rabbi's proffered hand, "Yes, it is. Call me Steve."

"*Reb* Shaul, thank you so much for coming."

*As if I ever had a choice.*

Rabbi Kalmonowitz was definitely *the* top rabbi in the community – so his request could not be taken lightly. "You asked me to come ... so I came."

"I still appreciate your taking the time," answered the rabbi sincerely.

"No problem Rabbi ... I am officially retired ... so I do have the time."

"Have a seat," said Rabbi Kalmonowitz pointing to the two chairs in front of his desk, each piled high with books.

Miraculously, the rabbi found some room on the table so that I could shift one of the stacks to his desk and sit down, "How can I help you?"

"Reb Shaul, you are already helping me."

"I am?" I asked in surprise.

"By driving Ayelet Weinberg to the meetings at the Jewish Center and then back home again. You are doing a big *mitzvah*."

I smiled and said, "No big deal. Happy to do it."

"But to me it is a big deal. Her husband, Rephael ... *zecher tzadik l'brocha* (may his memory be a blessing) was my best *talmid*. If a *rosh yeshiva* is lucky ... he has a student like Rephael perhaps once ... maybe twice ... in his lifetime. He soaked up knowledge like a sponge and remembered every word. It was a challenge to teach someone like Rephael ... but such a pleasure. I looked forward to every session we had together. But God decided that he needed him elsewhere. He was like a son to me. We all miss him greatly but it seems that Ayelet has not been able to get over the loss. So, with her problem about driving at night, she just was not getting the help she needed."

"Glad to be of assistance."

"I was wondering if there was some way I could repay you?" asked the rabbi.

*Was the rabbi thinking of giving me money?* That would not be proper. Getting paid for doing a good deed – was just wrong. In addition, you *gave* money to Rabbi Kalmonowitz – you did not take money from him. It was a one way arrangement. I shook my head from side to side, "I couldn't think of taking anything from you."

The rabbi smiled, "I was not thinking of paying you with money ... I had something else in mind."

"Like what?" I asked warily.

"How about you coming here twice a week ... say every Sunday and Thursday at 9:30 in the morning for a private *Talmud shiur* with me?" inquired the rabbi.

I was struck dumb.

It was like a lightning strike out of the blue.

I had no idea how to respond.

Having a private *shiur* with the *rosh yeshiva* was a huge *kavode.* People in the *charedi* community – or anyone in the Jewish community – would give their right arm for the privilege of getting a private lesson from the rabbi. But, I could not see myself sitting eyeball to eyeball with the most important rabbi in the city. He was probably one of the greatest rabbis in the country and maybe even the world. I stammered, "Of course ... I'm ... I'm ... honored ... I just ... don't think ... that it would be such a good idea."

"Are you saying that I don't have good ideas?" inquired the rabbi playfully.

"I'm ... not saying ... if they are good or bad. It's just ... that my level of Jewish knowledge is so far below yours that I get the bends just thinking about it. I haven't really studied *Gemorah* in almost thirty years."

"So then maybe you should get back to it," said Rabbi Kalmonowitz empathically. "You said that you are retired, so you should have the time."

"It's not a question of time ... it's just ... like I said ... my level ... is ... is ..."

"You think it's low."

"Low, Rabbi? It's none existent," I admitted sheepishly. "I don't think I could understand half of what you would say."

"Well, that would be my problem. A good teacher adapts himself to his pupil. And if you are anything like your cousin Shimon ... you should have no difficulty."

Shimon? Who is Shimon? Oh yeah ... my cousin Sy Lincoln. The former policeman and detective who chucked it all in to become a *yeshiva bocher* a couple of years ago and was now *shomer shabbos* and everything. He had learned with Rabbi Kalmonowitz in this very *yeshiva*. "That's right, you know Sy," I said, with a nod of my head.

"So I take it ... your answer is 'yes'," stated the rabbi.

Once again I paused to try and find some avenue of escape. But when I could not think of any graceful way out of this situation I capitulated and said, "I suppose so ... yes."

"Fine ... we begin next Thursday. Reb Shaul, normally I don't recommend this, but I want you to go to Silverstein's Bookstore and pick up a copy of the English translation of the tractate *Baba Basra*. Read the first two pages, so that the Aramaic won't hinder us."

I could hardly believe I had been roped into it, but there I was that very evening sitting at my desk staring at the first page of my newly purchased tractate. It was actually the first pages, because with the book opened wide, the pages on one side were the Hebrew/Aramaic text and the opposite pages held the English translation. I remembered the basic structure of the Babylonian *Talmud* from high school.

That was the version that sat in front of me now.

I have no idea how they did it, but my grade school teachers had miraculously instilled into my reluctant youthful brain a basic knowledge of Hebrew, so that I had the ability to read and phonetically pronounce the words in the text without too much difficulty – it was similar to reciting the prayers in synagogue. But the meaning of ninety percent of what was written was lost to me. It was a constant shuttle between the Hebrew text of the *Mishna* and the English translation just to make a snail's pace progress. As with Archimedes at the baths I had a 'Eureka' moment and it finally dawned on me that the legal problem discussed in the first *Mishna* dealt with a conflict between two people that wanted to build a wall at the boundary of their adjacent properties. This was a problem that I had handled numerous times when I was actively running my contracting company.

I felt pretty cocky.

Then I started the Aramaic text that explained the *Mishna* and hit a brick wall of another kind.

The words of the *Gemorah* might as well have been written in Chinese. Even though my more modern text had pronunciation symbols, commonly referred to as 'dots', I still was not sure I was pronouncing them correctly. In addition the English translation was not a big help because it translated the entire sentence and I was not sure which word meant what. I had no idea how to progress until I remembered something my son had once taught me. 'When in doubt – Google it'. Within a few minutes I found an internet site with an on-line Aramaic – English dictionary just made for this purpose. Over the next three hours – going from Aramaic to English to internet and back to the Aramaic – four cups of coffee – two visits to the can – I made it through the first page. I was not sure I understood all the concepts in the text, but I knew what the words meant.

*Again – Eureka!*

The 'Loss Compensation Group' still met regularly. Ayelet Weinberg continued to sit through most of the meetings rarely lifting her eyes from the floor and only speaking when called upon by Lonnie. The psychologist used all sorts of methods to motivate the group. He told stories and asked for reactions. We did role playing. He even had us split into pairs and perform short scenes depicting grief from famous plays. Even Mrs. Weinberg participated – if somewhat reluctantly. There was a dynamic to the group and I had to admit that Dr. Stralling was slowly getting results.

I still chauffeured Mrs. Weinberg back and forth to the sessions in almost absolute silence. About the only change was that after the third meeting, when the babysitter came out – besides her back pack and books – she also brought a small paper bag. This little sack was a special delivery just for me and contained some of Ayelet's baked goods. I sampled them when I got back to my home and found the stuff to be really terrific. *That lady can bake!!!!!* They were probably the best baked items I had ever tasted and that included pastries that had been home baked, or were from a professional bakery, or even from exclusive patisseries. When I drove her back from the next meeting I extolled and complimented her on how good they were. Her answer was a curt back seat 'Thank you.'

Just as expected.

Ayelet Weinberg remained an enigma to me. I tried to get more information from Marissa but her answers were always the same. Ayelet Weinberg was a dynamic woman and just about the most energetic, lively person she knew. In her opinion the lady was extremely charismatic, phenomenally informed, articulate, witty, and talkative. Very talkative. Could this be the same woman that I drove to and from the sessions? Yes, she was quite the enigma.

# Let's make a deal

I HOPE I SOUND CHEERFUL as I say over the headrest of the front seat, "So, Mr. Lincoln, I understand that you have a *chavrusah* with Rabbi Kalmonowitz."

My words seemed to have surprised him.

His head whipped back towards me, and that made him take his eyes off the road for a moment, and this made the car swerve. He gained control quickly and said, "Did you just say something to me?"

What a strange question? Of course it was me. Who else does he have in the back seat of his car?

I have no choice. I must speak to him.

Dr. Stralling left me no choice.

At the end of last week's session each of us wrote our names on a slip of paper and placed it in a box. Then everyone had to draw out a name and was told to keep it secret. He told us that over the next three months we were to specifically listen to that person during the sessions and then come up with suggestions as to how to help that someone get over their problems. Somehow, *HaShem* made me choose Mr. Lincoln's name. I had no idea what to do.

I asked Dr. Stralling to allow me to change names but he refused.

Mr. Lincoln, barely speaks at the meetings. He is almost as bad as I am. How will I have any suggestions if I do not know what is bothering him? I asked *Rebbetzen* Kalmonowitz what to do, and she consulted with the *rosh yeshiva.* His answer – relayed through the *rebbetzen* –

was that I had no choice but to talk with the man. He also mentioned that he knew Mr. Lincoln and felt it would not be a problem if we conversed during our trips traveling to the JCC.

"Yes, I did," I responded. "I heard from *Rebbetzen* Kalmonowitz that you are learning with Rabbi Kalmonowitz. That is a great honor." It truly was. I hope he realized this.

"That's correct. And you're responsible."

*Why am I responsible?* "Me? What do I have to do with you learning with the *rosh yeshiva*?" I asked.

"Well, I don't know if you are aware of this but Rabbi Kalmonowitz said he set up my lessons to show his gratitude for me driving you back and forth to the meetings."

*Why did Rabbi Kalmonowitz do that?* He is such a great man, one cannot always see the reason for what he does. Still, I am completely lost, "I had no idea ... he never said anything ... I really didn't ... "

"I don't know if I should thank you or blame you."

Blame me? *Why would you blame me?* "How can you say that? Don't you think it is an honor to be learning with such a great rabbi?" *Did I just say that out loud?*

"Oh, I agree that it is an honor. But I have to spend at least three or four hours ... sometimes more ... preparing for each of his lessons. I'm hitting the books now, more than I did when I was studying to be an architect."

I knew that he had been in the contracting business before he retired – but I didn't know that he was also an architect. I've learned something already. "But you enjoy the lessons, don't you?"

"Yeah ... I suppose you could say I enjoy them. It's a one of kind experience."

It most definitely is. Rephael cherished his *shiurim* with *rebbi.* "Well then, I suppose I'm happy that I was the cause for the lessons."

There was silence in the car for a few minutes and then Mr. Lincoln spoke, "Can I ask you a question?"

I guess I must answer - after all - I started the conversation. "Certainly."

"For the last few months that we have been going back and forth to the group session you hardly ever said a word. Why are you suddenly talking to me?"

I'm sure he must know that in the *frum* world men and women who are not married to each other are strictly forbidden to socialize. It is most difficult to discuss this with a man. "Do you know about *tznius*?" I ask.

"The *charedi* rules of modesty for women? Of course I know about that," he said. "No shaking hands, no long conversations. That's why you are in the back seat and I am up here."

"Exactly."

"So, why the change?"

"If Rabbi Kalmonowitz has taken you as a *chavrusah*, then you must be a good man and can be trusted more than most."

"I don't think so," he said shaking his head as he gripped the wheel firmly.

"You cannot be trusted?"

"No, that's not what I meant. I don't think that's the reason that you're talking with me. At least that's not the main reason."

"So what do *you* think is the reason?"

"I have a feeling that you drew my name out of Lonnie's box and haven't got a clue about what you're going to tell me to improve my life. So you're going fishing," he said glancing back at me.

*How did he know that? Can he read my mind?* Some great rabbis have clairvoyant abilities. Perhaps there are other men that can do that as well. I have very little experience around men. Rephael was the first and only man I ever went out with. I must answer him, "You know as well as me that even if it were true ... that I did get your name from the box ... Dr. Stralling said that I could not confirm that to you."

"I understand you loud and clear," he said. "No confirmations. Just like ... if I drew your name from the box ... I couldn't confirm it either."

*Could that be possible – could HaShem – have done something like that?* Of course he could. *HaShem* can do anything. "Did you get my name?" I asked incredulously.

"I told you, I can't confirm anything. Same as you."

This is a fine pickle I am in. "So what are we going to do?"

"Well ... without confirming anything ... we could each tell the other about ourselves and our problems."

"But at all the meetings you keep saying that you haven't got any problems."

Mr. Lincoln turned his head back towards me for a moment and said, "You say the same thing."

An impasse. "So now, what do we do?"

"I'm not saying that I picked your name ... and I'm not saying that you have any problems ... but you do have to admit that if after two years you are still crying constantly ... something might possibly be wrong."

*Ouch! Am I that obvious? How does he know about the crying?* I try not to show it. *Who told him?* Rabbi Kalmonowitz? No, he would never do that. I could deny it – but what good would it do? He's right. Something is wrong. Everyone says that I should have had my life back by now. The open gaping wound should have healed. But it has not. I miss Rephael so much. Mr. Lincoln is correct. I do have a problem, "Yes, something is wrong with me. But something is wrong with you as well."

"With me? What?"

"I cry ... but you don't. You once said you never cried. There are some heartless people in the world who feel no loss over the passing of someone close to them, but I cannot believe you are one of them. Rabbi Kalmonowitz would never learn with someone like that. In your own way you are still mourning and that is why you still have all of your wife's things in your home even after two years. Your life has simply stopped. You have not progressed. So you also have a problem." *Did I just say that?*

He seems to be considering my words. "You're right. I do miss Rebecca, very much. And I don't know why I have never cried over her. I suppose I do have a problem. My life has been put on hold. So that makes us even."

Not so even. I've learned things. I now know that you are an architect and that your wife's name was Rebecca. A name you never mentioned at the meetings. How do we move ahead? "So, without acknowledging anything, what do we do about Dr. Stralling's assignment?"

"Since you brought up the subject, you begin. Tell me about your life before you lost your husband."

Hey, that's not the way it was supposed to work. "Yes, but I was the one that had the courage to bring up the subject, so therefore you should tell me first."

"Okay, let's make a deal," he said stopping the car in front of my house. "The *tznius* business is going to make it difficult for us to talk. I can't simply come into your house and you cannot come to mine. All we have is the time in the car. Right now it's late and I still have to take your sitter home and then sit in front of the *Gemorah* preparing for my lesson with Rabbi Kalmonowitz. So, here's what I propose. On the way to the meetings you can ask me questions about my former life and on the way back I get to ask you about yours."

What a strange idea – perhaps that would work, but I have a better way to do it. "Okay, I agree ... but in reverse. I will talk about the loss of my husband on the way to the meetings." If I had to walk into my home after speaking about Rephael, I would be devastated.

"Sounds good to me."

# 7

## A silk purse

AFTER REBECCA'S DEATH I discovered that not all of our friends were created equal.

Once the *shiva* was over, most just disappeared into the woodwork. There were still a few that kept up a polite internet barrage of e-cards at the holidays and sent e-mail invitations to social gatherings. I rarely responded, but my lack of interest did not seem to faze these people in the least. Once you were on their mailing list there was no coming off. They probably did not even know they were still sending me all their e-vites and e-cards. So, their one sided media blitz continued unabated.

There were also about half a dozen couples that kept in touch with me by telephone. Actually it was not the couples that communicated with me – more specifically it was Rebecca's female friends. Apparently, each of these women firmly believed that it was a crying shame that there was a living breathing eligible man who was not under the care and feeding of some woman. I had this suspicion that they were all in cahoots. So, every few weeks, at least one of these women would call offering me a new matchmaking proposal. Each candidate was extolled as an ex-runway model and a better homemaker than Martha Stewart. I listened politely to all their exalted virtues. Then I explained to these matchmakers that I still was not dating and thanked them very much for their concern.

Even though I never agreed to go out with any of the proposed women, these modern day Yentles remained undaunted and their matchmaking attempts still continue to this day.

Slowly I came to the realization that I did not really have many true friends. I define a true friend as a person that was willing to give me support at any time, any place, and in any way or form that I needed. They were rare indeed. One of my true friends was Max Rosenstein.

It was an unusual friendship.

Our connection began four years ago when my son started taking on more responsibility at the company and I began going to the health club. Although Max is almost twice my age, that did not prevent him from becoming my unofficial exercise partner when I worked out at the gym.

He is a wiry ninety-two-year-old who is determined to fend off old age any way he can and has a *mishigas* about using/abusing over-the-counter 'fountain-of-youth' drugs and additives to stay young. I've given up arguing with the old man about the dangers of using so many untested modes of therapy. Every morning and evening Max religiously gobbles down dozens of vitamins and supplements. Each of these 'wonder-remedies' was based on a fad, a whim, or a conjecture of various media touts. He purchases non-prescription 'super duper' elixirs, pills, powders, and even suppositories at various health food stores around the city. He also gets a steady stream of other goodies from around the country via the internet and gets even more exotic stuff from abroad. Max Googles 'anti-aging' every morning and if he finds some new miraculous pill or potion, he orders them as well. The prescription medications, weird injections, and contraband 'life-giving' additives that he acquires are 'prescribed' to him by a bunch of charlatan doctors out in LA – where they seem to thrive. It is a miracle that he has not succumbed to an overdose of vitamins or monkey gland poisoning.

The old guy exercises regularly, although not excessively, and is always boasting to anyone that will listen, that he still drives his own car and can still satisfy his wife. In the old man's eyes each feat is of equal importance. I can corroborate Max's driving prowess. I have seen the old codger skillfully navigate his new Cadillac Seville around town. As to the other – I am not about to ask Esther, his wife, for confirmation. Rumor has it that the old man is worth somewhere around two hundred million dollars. After World War II he arrived in the U.S.A. as a penniless refugee and found work collecting, sorting, and selling *shmatahs*. His little rag picking business grew until it made him the 'Wiping Cloth King' of the city. His company now supplies specialized wiping rags to most of the automobile plants in the area. He began an entire industry of making brand new *shmatahs*. The business is now run by his offspring and the company's impressive trucks still crisscross the city every day.

Three years earlier, when I formally retired from running my company and I was able to start going to the gym more regularly, I discovered that my visits to the health club often coincided with Max Rosenstein's schedule. At first it was just polite hellos and nods of recognition when we would bump into each other. That led to short conversations and those to longer *shmoozes.* When we first met he proudly told me that he was 88 years old. I suspected that the old guy was embellishing his age a bit because I had seen how he moved so spryly from machine to machine in the gym. I would have estimated his age at a decade or two lower. I guess he sensed my skepticism because he whipped out his drivers license and showed me his birth date. He wasn't lying. Wow.

I guess we just hit it off, because we quickly realized that we enjoyed each other's company. Soon we fell into the habit of moving through the exercise machines together, *shmoozing* during our routines and then continuing our conversations in the health club's café afterwards.

I cannot say why I liked hanging around with the old guy. His views on life were almost directly opposite to my own, but he was a fun guy to talk to and had more love of life than just about anyone else in the gym. Then when Rebecca took sick, the only respite I had from my stressful sickroom vigil was the time I could steal to get into the gym. I was no longer able to have a set schedule and it was surprising to discover that no matter when I came, Max was there. Every morning the old man would call to inquire about Rebecca and would innocently ask me if I was going to be at the gym. If the answer was positive Max would arrange his day so that he could be at the health club whenever I was able to get free. He offered moral support right to the end. After Rebecca passed away, it was Max who helped me to get out of the house for short periods and then to return to the health club. He had been my crutch in my hour of need and I now considered him a true friend.

This morning I arrived first and was already exercising on the orbital stepper. Max came over and flipped his towel over the rail of the adjacent machine. He set the rate on the machine at about one third of what I was doing and started his routine. Between his deep gasping breaths, Max asked me in his Yiddish accented English, "So tell me ... have you ... been having ... any luck ... with the ... ladies?"

"The usual, Max. The usual," I responded, not breaking my rhythm.

"That means ... still nada ... nothing ... zilch. What's the matter ... with you? If my wife ... she should ... live to be ... a hundred and ... twenty. And I think ... she is going ... to do ... just that ... should die. I would be ... out there ... sampling ... all the fruits ... of the earth ... if you know ... what I mean."

I gave a knowing nod of my head, "Yeah, I know what you mean."

"There is ... a saying ... in the ... health club ... business ... 'Use it ... or lose it'. You don't want ... to lose it ... you might ... need it ... some day."

Max's saucy questions and his subsequent comments were no surprise to me, because this was the old man's standard mantra to signal the start of our morning conversation. "Thank you, for that piece of advice and say hello to Esther for me."

"What about ... that widow lady ... that you ... drive to those ... counseling sessions? After four months ... there must be ... something going on there."

Now I was sorry that I had mentioned her to the old man. It looks like Max was going to *noodge* me about her forever, "Get your head out of the gutter. I just drive her back and forth to the Jewish Center."

"You know ... what they say ... about ... young widows. They need ... lots of consoling ... if you know ... what I mean."

The old man was hopeless, "I always know what you mean, you old pervert."

"So how come ... you have become ... so palsy-walsy with the *frumies*?" asked Max. "I thought you were one of the Modern Orthodox."

"I haven't changed."

"Oh, really? You have a ... *chavrusah* with ... Rabbi Kalmonowitz. That's a big change."

I was surprised by two things. First how did Max know about my relationship with the rabbi? I had never mentioned it. Secondly, and stranger still, how was he familiar with the term, "You know what a *chavrusah* is?"

"What's not to know? Before the war ... until age fifteen ... I was ... a *yeshiva bochur*."

*What? Max studied in a yeshiva?* This surprised me enough so that I had to stop my machine. If there was anyone that did not fit the *yeshiva* student stereotype it was Max Rothstein. "You were a *yeshiva bochur?*"

"Yes," said Max nodding his head knowingly. "I learned ... in the *yeshiva* ... at Radin."

*Another lightning bolt from heaven.* What a revelation. Radin had been one of the truly great *yeshivas* in Europe. It was the learning center where Rabbi Yisroel Meir Kagan, known as the *Chofetz Chaim,* taught. This name was taken from the title of his most famous book and he had been just about the greatest European rabbi of the last century. Any student that had been accepted at his *yeshiva* had to have been outstanding. "Are you kidding me? You learned in Radin?" I said flabbergasted.

"What's to be ... surprised? A Jewish boy ... had to learn ... somewhere. What *mesechta* are you learning?"

"*Baba Basra,*" I answered.

"Oh yes, *Baba Basra,*" responded Max fondly.

Over the next few minutes I was witness to something unbelievable. It was more than unbelievable – it was surreal. The old man looked off into the distance and from memory began reciting, word for word, the first *Mishna* followed by just about the entire first page of the *Gemorah.* He used perfect pronunciation and inflections in the Hebrew and Aramaic indicating a complete mastery of the subject.

I was dumbfounded. Standing before me was an exception to the old adage – You cannot make a silk purse out of a sow's ear. Could this be the same Max Rosenstein I had known for the past four years? It was unbelievable. I could more easily imagine that Mother Theresa had moonlighted as a high-priced escort while she was studying in the convent. Max, the 'Old Fart' that worked out with me three times a week, had to be the most outspoken anti-religious person that I knew. The few times our conversation had turned to religion, Max told me that after what he had seen in the concentration camps he was convinced there is no God. To prove it, every year on *Yom Kippur* – the holiest day in the Jewish calendar – the day when most Jews would not allow a morsel of food or a drop of water to pass their lips – Max would dine in the finest restaurant in town. He had to go alone because Esther – much to his consternation – refused to accompany him and insisted on fasting. Max's palate naturally favored good old Jewish fare, but just for spite, for those 'special' meals, he would intentionally order pork and *tref* sea food specialties, just to challenge God to strike him down dead.

I looked at the old man incredulously, "Max ... you know *Gemorah*?"

"Don't confuse being irreligious with ignorance. Where I grew up, all the boys learned *Gemorah*."

"But how could you recite all that by heart? When was the last time you studied *Baba Basra*?" I asked starting up my machine again.

"Well, let's see. I was twelve when we studied that *mesechta* so that would make it about eighty years ago."

"You just blew me away," I stated in awe. "You have got to come to my next lesson and meet Rabbi Kalmonowitz."

"I don't have to do anything of the sort and I certainly don't want to go see any black-hat rabbi. The modern ones with the crocheted *yarmulkas* are bad enough."

"But Rabbi Kalmonowitz is different, you'll like him," I said beseechingly.

"Don't tell me who I would or wouldn't like. I can decide that for myself. And I hate most rabbis. Is that clear enough?"

"I think you are making a mistake. This rabbi is special."

"If he is so special, have him give you a *brocha*."

"I don't need any *brochas*. I have enough money and I am not hungry for more."

"I wasn't talking about making you rich. When it comes to *gelt,* I know you are comfortable. I meant a *brocha* so that you find a good woman."

"How the hell do you know that I have money? We've never discussed my finances."

"Never the less, I know."

This comment made me curious, "But, how do you know?"

"I had you investigated," said the old man matter-of-factly.

I stopped my exercise again, "You had me investigated?"

"Absolutely. A man in my position has to be careful about acquaintances. You never know who is trying to sneak into your life."

"Who investigated me?"

"It was what we used to call a private eye. Now they call themselves 'security consultants'. We use them all the time in the company."

"And what did they find out?"

Max recited from memory, "Graduated high school at eighteen ... married Rebecca Silverstein almost immediately ... seven months later you had your one kid ... David, ... *mazel tov,*" he said with a wink. "Those first babies always seem to come a little early. College at U of M in Ann Arbor ... degree in architecture ... worked night jobs all the way. Three years at Bradford and Jenks ... then you went out on your own ... workaholic ... built up your company ... specialized in large commercial buildings ... took your son into the company when he got his degree in architecture. Looks like he was smarter than his father. He went to your old alma mater and also got a masters in business administration before he was twenty two."

"Big deal ... where is he so smart? I didn't have a dad that made a decent living. He didn't have to work nights," I said in my defense.

"I'd say that was a pretty smart move. Picking a rich father," said the old man.

"I am not rich," I insisted.

"Yeah, yeah. Anyway, you took him into the company and without coddling him he started taking more and more responsibility so that when you hit forty five, he took over and you kicked yourself upstairs in a strange sort of retirement. You finally had some time with your wife but that only lasted until she took sick. One half year later she passed away and you have been stuck in a rut ever since. You have 45 million socked away in rock solid securities ... and it is growing steadily. The salary you get for being on the board of directors of the company means you don't have to touch a cent of your savings. So cut the crap about not being rich."

"I don't believe it. You really did have me investigated."

"Of course I did. You have to admit it is kind of unusual for a forty year old to suddenly become friendly with an *alter kacker* like me. Turns out that most of your friends were actually Rebecca's friends. When she died you just lost contact and didn't make new ones," said the old man. "Actually, quite sad."

"So now you're becoming a shrink?"

"Not a shrink ... just an *aytzas gibber*."

# Good mourning

I KNOW I'M NOT BEING FAIR. But, we have an agreement. When we travel to the session at the JCC my past is to be discussed and on the ride back we talk about Mr. Lincoln's background. Of course, even if he drives very slowly, we get to the group session in less than fifteen minutes. But when we go back I pepper him with questions and it takes him much longer to answer. Sometimes we have to sit in the car for over an hour until he can finish. I know that I'm skirting the border of impropriety but this is a matter of health – mental health to be specific – almost *pikuach nefesh*. After all, the *rebbetzen* sent me to these sessions and it is my assignment to understand this man. I'm sure it is allowed. We just sit and talk and I never move from the back seat.

I've discovered that Mr. Lincoln is really a lonely man. Oh, he doesn't say that he is lonely, but the only family he has nearby is an aunt and uncle and their son, who is a private detective of all things. His only interaction with the people of the community is through the members of his *shul.* Thankfully he gets invited to people's homes on the weekends. If he had to eat all his *shabbos* meals all alone that would be dreadful. Still, the basic fact is that he has no real friends in this city. Max Rosenstein sounds like a supportive individual but he can never be a true friend because he is over forty years older than Mr. Lincoln. I learned that Mr. Lincoln's grandfather's name had originally been Levinsky before he changed it.

Funny, people don't do that much anymore. Different times.

I find it strange that he goes three times a week to a health club so that he doesn't gain weight or get out of shape. I've never needed to watch what I eat. Taking care of three young children all day will keep anyone fit.

He says that he has a full life and enjoys his retirement, but it appears to me that before he started learning with Rabbi Kalmonowitz – a very big *mitzvah* – his days seemed to have been rather empty.

Well – that is not entirely true. Twice a week he does volunteer work in the poorer neighborhoods of the Detroit inner city giving advice to the less fortunate about things related to building and contracting. Mr. Lincoln explained to me that the bureaucracy of the Department of Housing and Urban Development is a big obstacle for anyone trying to build or renovate anything in the city. If you add to that the city's codes and permit requirements it could bring even the staunchest homeowner to his knees. A simple citizen almost needs to have a full-time lawyer and contractor to add a garden shed. People without substantial resources have almost no chance. So he helps the indigent get building permits, explains to them how to do renovations, and finds contractors that are willing to do the work for a reasonable price. He doesn't think that he is doing anything special, since he enjoys helping these people. But to the poor homeowners he must seem like a *malach*. He's doing a another big *mitzvah*, and he doesn't even know it.

Apparently Mr. Lincoln built up a really impressive contracting company that specialized in doing multi-million dollar projects – malls and apartment complexes – all over the midwest and south. When he retired his son moved the whole company to Atlanta because most of his daughter-in-law's family live there and their largest customers are also located in the area. Mr. Lincoln flies down to Atlanta for two days once a month to attend the company's board meetings and to see his two grandchildren. I've learned that his firm has hundreds of employees and I guess that means that he is some sort of big shot. Probably he's quite well to do. After all, it's not everyone that can be retired at age forty-seven. But he's quite humble and plays down everything. He never shows off his wealth. Of course, he didn't get to enjoy his retirement for very long. His wife – may her memory be a blessing – took sick so quickly. He was with her all through her illness. What a dedicated man. An additional *mitzvah*.

Still, I am no closer to finding the reason why he cannot get his life back together. Mr. Lincoln seems to be – as my aunt used to say – a well put together man. He has blue eyes and wavy blonde hair and is obviously tall and muscular. I suppose most women would consider him handsome. That's something that I really should not be noticing, but it is hard to avoid. And, he is such a gentleman – I am sure there are many women that would be willing to take him as a husband. Perhaps the problem stems from something much earlier in his life.

"Did you get along with your parents?" I asked, searching for information.

"My parents? You're taking this psychology stuff very seriously," he answers. "Well ... sure. Why would you ask if I got along with my folks?"

"Because there are children that don't get along with their parents. And young people can be so rebellious sometimes. How were you as a teenager?"

Mr. Lincoln shrugged his shoulders, "I was just a normal teenager. You know TV, rock music, sports ... but a good student."

"No," I said, correcting him. "I meant, how did you get along with your parents as a teenager?"

"That's hard to answer."

"Why is that?"

"My mother died when I was fourteen."

*What?* His mother passed away when he was so young and he never mentioned this in the sessions. "What did she die of?" I ask tentatively.

He paused and then said – almost in a whisper, "Cancer."

*Just like his wife.* Somehow, I just knew that was coming. "I'm so sorry."

"What's to be sorry? That was over thirty years ago. I'm over that."

*Are you really?* "Don't you think you should mention this to Dr. Stralling?"

"Why? He will only try to make a big thing out of it. Just like you are trying to do. Believe me. My mother's death has nothing to do with what Lonnie likes to call 'my problem'."

"Do you still think you don't have a problem?"

"Not a fair question."

"Why not?"

"Because I could ask you the same thing."

"But I don't have a problem. I've told you many times I attend these sessions only because the *rebbetzen* asked me to go."

"And what about your crying all the time when no one is looking?"

*Oh my God!* I keep forgetting that he knows about that. That is supposed to be my secret. I shake my head quickly from side to side and stammer out a denial, "Don't be ridiculous ... I don't cry anymore ... where did you hear such a thing?"

"Where I heard it ... is not important. I'm just showing you that your question is not fair."

I hold up my palms in acquiescence, "Okay, truce. We don't ask that question." After a short pause I add, "So just answer me this and then we're done. When your mother ... *aleha haShalom* (may her memory be a blessing) ... passed away, did you mourn her?"

"What kind of question is that? Of course I mourned her. We had the *shiva* ... the *shloshim* ... and I of course said *kadish* for the entire year. I went to *minyan* three times a day. Missed only once, when I broke my arm."

"I wasn't talking about that. I want to know if *you* mourned her. We've had enough sessions with Dr. Stralling, so you know what I mean. Loss, despair, anguish and all those other fancy words. Basically, I'm asking, did you cry over your loss and did you heal the inner hurt?"

"My, my. Aren't you becoming the little psychoanalyst."

"You're evading the question," I demanded.

Mr. Lincoln paused and then finally said, "I was only fourteen. She was sick for over two years and almost didn't make it to my *bar mitzvah*. I remember hurting terribly when I lost her. But slowly, slowly I did heal the hurt."

"Did you cry?"

Once again Mr. Lincoln hesitated before answering, "No."

# Walked right in to it

"*REBBI* ... YOU PROMISED," I said determinedly.

"Promised what, Reb Shaul?" inquired Rabbi Kalmonowitz.

"Every time I want to ask a question about Judaism you tell me that we are in the middle of an *inyan* and can't stop. Well, we just finished an *inyan* and it is almost the end of our hour together. So, do I get to ask a question?"

"I do recall saying something like that. All right, one question." answered Rabbi Kalmonowitz putting his *Gemorah* to the side.

I closed my book as well and turned to the rabbi, "*Rebbi*, are you a *tzadik*?"

"What a strange question," answered the older man. "Why would you think a lowly person such as me would be a *tzadik*?"

"Because the rabbis of old ..."

"I assume you mean *chazal*," stated the rabbi.

"Yes, *chazal* ... they said that at any given time there are always *lamid vav* (36 – numerical value of the Hebrew letters) *tzadikim* in the world. When one dies another is born. Even though you deny it, you are still one of the greatest rabbis in the country."

"Thank you for the compliment, but I could give you a list of people who would disagree with you."

"Don't duck the question. Are you a *tzadik*?" I insisted.

The rabbi thought for a moment and began, "A *tzadik* is someone that is hard to define. So let me ask you a question. What makes one person a *tzadik* and someone else not? How do you measure it? The rabbi with the longest beard? The most students? The deepest thinker?"

I shrugged my shoulders, "I haven't got the foggiest idea."

"Neither do I," answered the rabbi. "It is almost impossible to answer. Did you ever hear of Reb Aryeh Levin?"

"The Rabbi of Jerusalem? The one that was always doing acts of charity ..."

"What we call *gemillus chesed,"* interjected the rabbi.

"Yeah, *gemillus chesed.* Certainly I heard of him. I even read a book about his life. He looked after all the Jewish prisoners during the British Mandate before the State of Israel was created."

"If there ever was a person that could qualify as a *tzadik* it was Reb Aryeh. The wonderful things he did were almost unbelievable. One day someone, just like you, came up to him and asked him if he was a *tzadik.* Do you know what he answered?"

"I have no idea."

"He said ... 'sometimes.' When the man asked Reb Aryeh to clarify his answer, he explained that he felt the *lamid vav tzadikim* that are referred to by *chazal* were not actual people but positions. Occupations/jobs that needed to be filled in this world. That there were always thirty-six *tzadik* spots open at any given time. If a person does a good deed ... then for that short period of time ... the period of time that he is doing that special act of kindness ... he is occupying a position of a *tzadik.* When he is doing something more mundane ... such as eating or sleeping ... then some other person ... who is at that time doing a good deed ... will occupy the position."

"Clever answer."

"I don't look at the answer as being clever ... I see it as a *hashkafas olam."*

"I ask again, are you a *tzadik*?"

"I think you know my answer."

"You'll say ... 'sometimes'."

"Perhaps ... only perhaps."

"So, if you are a *tzadik* ..."

"I never said I was a *tzadik,*" interjected the rabbi.

"But if you were ... could you predict the future or give me a *brocha* that would come true?" I asked.

"What do you mean?" responded Rabbi Kalmonowitz.

"Like ... whether I should make a particular business transaction, or to give a *brocha* for a happy marriage, for wealth, for health. Stuff like that."

"Who told you that a rabbi can do such things?"

"A friend."

"The concept that certain *tzadikim* can predict the future or give blessings is something the *Kabbalistic* rabbis and the *chassidim* believe in. We *misnagdim* believe that one rabbi can be wiser and more learned than another and perhaps even more 'holy'. But the idea that a rabbi has supernatural powers ... a short cut to God ... is not one of the beliefs of the *misnagdim*. We feel it is more important that each person, through his own prayers, should ask God directly for a good future and for His blessing. Jews do not need intermediaries. We feel that the prayer of one simple Jew can be as potent as the prayer of a great scholar."

"I noticed that you didn't say categorically that these *tzadikim* did not have special powers."

"No, I did not," the rabbi said with a smile. "Reb Shaul ... I have to remember your sharp mind and be careful of what I say. Why are you so interested in finding a *tzadik*?"

"My friend said that a *tzadik* could give me a *brocha* so that I could find myself a new wife."

"*Halivai* that it could be so easy to find a good wife. There are no miracles in that department. The *Talmud*, in Tractate Sotah, teaches us that a man's first wife is already determined before he is born. And since now-a-days we are only allowed one wife at a time ... if a man must take a second wife ... after divorce or death ... the type of woman he will marry is determined by the type of person he is. A partner will be chosen according to his or her deeds. If he has been a God fearing good person then his new wife will be the same. If he is a bad evil person his wife will reflect those qualities."

I smiled at the remark and joked with the rabbi, "So it looks like I'm in for big trouble."

The rabbi smiled back, "I doubt that very much. After all, in my eyes, you are also a *tzadik* ... sometimes."

On my last birthday my son, David, gave me a ridiculously expensive watch that has all sorts of fancy buttons and gizmos. I Googled the brand and was shocked to discover that its cost approached the monthly salary of the President of the U.S.A. There was little chance that I was going to test the timepiece to see if it truly was waterproof at 100 meters, nor was I ever going to need the ability to determine true north to the tenth decimal place. But there were a couple of features that I used quite often. Two of them were the heart rate and lap times and they now showed that my ticker was chugging along at a rate of 142 and my lap time was just under thirty nine minutes. I was just completing my late afternoon power walk and a 142 pulse rate was right where I wanted it.

As I rounded into my front yard and took another gander at my watch I thought to myself, 'Not bad.' I was huffing and puffing, but that is what you want when you work out. My cut-off sweat shirt was soaked through with perspiration, but that was also okay because that was another goal of power walking. Get that heart zapped up and pounding. Open all the pores to get the sweat flowing. Clean out the old poisons and build up the lungs. No pain no gain – and all the other sports metaphors that did not really make sense. In my opinion all those banal homilies were used to explain why people inflicted such cruel punishments upon themselves so that they could hopefully look and feel better. Perhaps it was all an illusion. Maybe you felt better after exercise because when you stopped you were no longer torturing your body or inflicting so much pain upon yourself.

For years I had been a devoted jogger but twelve months ago my orthopedist diagnosed the beginning of osteoarthritis and told me that if I wanted my knees to carry me for the rest of my life – without the need for reconstructive surgery – *no thank you doc* – I needed to let up a bit. So, running and jogging disappeared from my exercise schedule. It was just God's way of reminding me that I and my knees were not getting any younger. I was not one of those exercise nuts that lived to get an endorphin high from exercise. Those psychopaths practically lived at the gym and did supplemental exercise every chance they got. If I had a real choice in the matter I would limit my exposure to exercise to watching other people engaged in some sport on my 4K TV while I was ensconced in my living room couch with a bag of chips and a cold six pack. Should any pesky subconscious cravings for some personal exercise rear their ugly heads, running my thumb over the remote would suffice. But, I knew, as a retiree there was nothing in my daily schedule that required me to move my butt. If I fell victim to my couch potato urges, within one month, I would inflate up to the size of a balloon in the Thanksgiving Day Parade.

So, now I power walked and I hated it. I also abhorred going to the gym, but when I did not exercise, I hated how I felt even more. Today I was very proud of myself. Getting around my usual route in under forty minutes was pretty good. Not at the level of those kids at the Olympics, but it was darn good for an old man.

Just as I opened the front door and staggered into my house, my home phone jangled loudly and I snatched it from its cradle. I went to the fridge to get a cold drink, as I said breathlessly, "Hello."

"Mr. Lincoln ... this is Ayelet Weinberg."

"Hi, Ayelet," I said, trying to catch my breath. This was something new. She had never called my home before. I asked suspiciously, "What can I do for you? We haven't got a session today."

"I know. I have to ask a favor of you."

"Sure, if I can help," I said reflexively. *Mr. Do-Gooder to the rescue once again.*

"I need to go to a *sheva brachos,*" said Ayelet.

*"Mazel tov,"* I replied.

"My babysitter called a while ago and said she is delayed. I'm supposed to bring something over to the party before it begins and I can't be late. I called everyone I know and I am only calling you because I have no other choice. It should only be for maybe fifteen minutes or a half hour and then Marissa will get here and you can go home."

I did not know what to say, "Well, yeah ... I suppose I could ... for a few minutes ... like you said. But is it all right with you?" I inquired. Entering her house would be a huge breach of *charedi* etiquette.

"You mean our rules of *tznius*?" asked Ayelet, as if she was reading my mind. "I called the *rebbetzen* and she said that it would be okay. After all it's only for a few minutes and I won't even be home."

"Well then, all right. I just have to take a shower and change, and I'll be right over."

"No, no. No shower. I'm late already."

I looked down at my sweat soaked trainers and said skeptically, "I don't know. I just finished exercising and I really stink. I'm not fit to be among people."

"It's only for a couple of minutes and my kids will never notice."

When I arrived at the Weinberg home there was a car, with a *charedi* woman driver, waiting in the drive – obviously Ayelet's ride. There was also a good looking woman at the front door holding a large, heavy, cardboard carton in her arms.

Where was Ayelet?

It took me a moment to realize that the attractive woman with the box was actually Ayelet.

*Holy cow!!!!*

I could not help but stare. I had never seen her decked out in her *shabbos* finest – a real dress, high heels, *shaitel,* and makeup.

*The lady even had legs. And shapely ones.*

At the group sessions, Ayelet always wore scuffed gym shoes, 'burlap-sack-couture' outfits and had every strand of her hair covered up, or crammed into, some floppy hat or kerchief.

*What a difference!!!*

Ayelet click-clacked her heels down the drive towards the waiting car, and she matter-of-factly said over her shoulder, "Thank you so, so much, Mr. Lincoln. Racheli was a bit cranky before ... maybe she will want to drop off to sleep soon. Yanki is playing with his trucks and Chaim'l is doing homework. He might ask you for help. Thank you again."

I just stood there speechless as I watched the car back down the driveway and pull away with a screech of the tires.

*Okay – new facet of the Ayelet Weinberg enigma. When she dresses up – that lady can be one hot, good looking mama.*

I immediately chided myself for having those thoughts and tried to dismiss them from my mind.

*Not an easy task.*

As I walked into the house my contractor's nose reflexively took a quick sniff. I cannot help it. This was an instinctive reaction whenever I entered a building.

What did I smell in the Weinberg home?

On the good side, there was no smell of dry rot or termite damage to the wooden frame. Nor was there the acrid smell of mold growing in areas of moisture behind the drywall. There were no smells of dank and damp seeping up from the basement that could indicate foundation problems.

On the negative side, I smelled that under the ancient threadbare wall-to-wall carpeting, the polyurethane carpet pad was disintegrating with age.

I also sensed the pleasant fragrances of cleaning solutions and soap combined with cooking and baking aromas. In short, Ayelet's home was a sturdy structure that was vibrant and well maintained, but was just getting old.

I looked around as I entered and was a bit surprised by the sparse furnishings. I could only see the foyer and living room but I suspect the rest of the house would be the same. The best way to sum up the décor would be that all the furniture was in styles that screamed out 'second hand and discards'. The deep scratches and gouges on the wood surfaces of the coffee table and credenza were signs of hard usage in the past. The fabric on the couch and non-matching chairs had lost their nap and bore ancient stains. But with all that, everything appeared to be clean and the furniture sparkled from polishing. Someone – obviously Ayelet – worked very hard to keep the place tidy. Even the kids play areas were as orderly as could be expected. Anyone that has ever raised children knows that if you give three small determined youngsters a few sturdy toys and a couple of hours, they could demolish an entire city block.

Racheli – Ayelet's two-year-old – was on the floor tormenting some tiny dolls by dropping them through a chute on top of her play castle and retrieving them from the dungeon at the base. Every time a doll hit the bottom she chuckled. Yanki – the five-year-old – had a toy truck in each of his hands and was playing teamster, making loud motor sounds going up and over all the furniture in the living room.

Kids were like that. The simplest of objects could fascinate them for hours. Adults needed alcohol and wide plasma screens to keep their interest, but a child's natural curiosity allowed him to create an imaginary world out of almost anything. I once saw a really old National Geographic article that showed an Aborigine child in some God-forsaken stretch of the Australian outback, happily playing with a bit of eucalyptus bark because that was his only 'toy'. Children were terrific. When a person loses that natural childish curiosity and with it the ability to escape into a world that could be, he did not just stop being a child, he became 'old'. I hoped that I still had a little of that 'childishness' in me.

Chaim'l – age eight or so – was sitting at the dining room table with his legs tucked up under his body doing some serious homework. He looked up from his writing, "You must be Mr. Lincoln."

"That's right. And you must be Chaim'l," I said walking over.

"How do you know my name?"

"Your mother talks about you all the time. She says you're very smart."

"I suppose," said the young man shrugging his shoulders. After a moment he said, "Mr. Lincoln ..."

"Call me, Steve."

"*Ima* says it is impolite to call grownups by their first names."

"Well, make an exception for me. The name is Steve."

"Stivoo," parroted Racheli from her corner.

I turned to the little girl and laughed, "That's right Pussycat. The name is Steve."

"Stivoo," said Racheli proudly, once again.

"Mr. ... uh ... Steve ... how come you are all *shvitzy*? You smell," said Chaim'l innocently.

So much for the kids not noticing. "I was exercising. Power walking."

"I heard about that. You have to walk at over five miles an hour. Cardiac rate at 80% maximum. Exaggerated arm swing. Almost as good as jogging for cardiac toning."

What kind of kid is this? "What grade are you in?"

"Third grade."

"And they teach you that in the third grade?"

"No, we never studied topics related to exercise."

"So how do you know so much about power walking? You see that on the TV or computer?"

"We don't have those things. I read about in a sports magazine."

No TV or computer? Strange. Then it suddenly made sense. When I first walked in and saw the kids, something about them seemed unusual. Now I realized what it was. They were playing with toys. My grandchildren never played with toys. It was all screens now-a-days. It was almost impossible to detach my grandkids from their TV set or video-games or phones or tablets in order to get them to go to any kind of activity, like eating dinner or going to school. Separating Siamese twins joined at the hip is child's play compared with extracting a digital phone from the hands of one of today's youngsters. Ayelet's kids were actually playing with real, honest to goodness toys. I knew that the world of children's education was constantly progressing but it was hard to know if it was for the good or the bad.

I looked around the dining room and resting on the table was a really large, round, three-tiered chrome serving piece piled high with fluted paper cups. Each was filled with a small piece of cake or some other baked delicacy. "What's all this? Someone having a birthday?"

"No, my *Ima* made that for the *sheva brochos*."

"Who got married? A relative of yours?"

"I don't think so," said Chaim'l shrugging his shoulders. "We haven't got any relatives in town. *Zeidi and Bubbi* live in Florida."

"So why did your *Ima* make all this stuff?"

"She bakes stuff and sells them. We need the money."

I had never thought about Ayelet's financial status. I just assumed that her family had some source of income. I should have realized that her late *yeshiva bochur* husband could never have socked away a nest egg and it was unlikely that he had had any insurance. Many of the families at the yeshiva were on food stamps. "So, does *Ima* have many customers?"

"I suppose."

"If she sells her stuff, why are all these goodies here and not at the party?"

"*Ima* is very picky. If it isn't perfect she won't sell it. This is all the stuff she won't sell. Would you like one?"

I had not eaten dinner yet and I remembered the delicious treats I received after chauffeuring Ayelet. My mouth began drooling just from looking at all the inviting pastries on the different levels of the serving piece. There had to be over fifteen different varieties. Petit fours, éclairs, tiny frosted cupcakes, yeast cakes of a half dozen varieties, brownies, rum balls, mini-pies, croissants and strudel. So far, everything in my 'paper-sack-chauffeur-tip', had always tasted extremely good. This was a much larger selection. I chose a chocolate filled mini croissant and couldn't see why this was not a perfect item. It looked just fine to me.

To impress the kid I said my *brocha* for the little cake out loud.

Chaim'l was back into his books and he answered without looking up, "Amen."

*I guess I didn't impress him very much.*

I took a bite and was astounded.

The burnished crust was flakey and the dough moist and airy. They both, literally, melted in my mouth. When

I hit the chocolate ambrosia filling, tears began welling up in my eyes. It was just so good. On a score of one to ten the pastry was an easy seventeen. I had rarely savored a baked item that was so delicious.

For me, good food evoked fond memories from my past. The crunch of the flaky crust made me think of frozen snow crackling underfoot on a cold star filled evening. The sweet morsels of cake caused a sparkling sensation on my tongue and reminded me of sitting in front of a roaring fireplace watching the sparks flitting up from the flaming logs. The chocolate filling suffused my entire body with an embracing warmth. It was like coming out of a cold sea after a tiring swim and being comforted by the bright warm sun and heated sand. Her croissant was obscenely delicious. Perhaps addicting.

I felt as if I was in gastronomical nirvana and was extending my arm to take another item when Chaim'l asked, "Mr. Lincoln, have you eaten all of your supper?"

My reverie shattered, I asked, "Why do you want to know?"

"*Ima* has a rule that you have to eat all your supper before you are allowed to eat more than one cake."

It took a conscious effort to retrieve my recalcitrant arm so as not to sneak another delicacy. "So ... you are doing your homework."

"Yes, I am, Mr. Lincoln."

I shook my head, "No, call me Steve."

"Stivoo," cried Racheli with glee.

Chaim'l asked, "Steve, can I ask you a homework question?"

"Sure. What subject?"

"*Gemorah*," said the boy.

*Gemorah? That is very unusual. The kid was eight years old*, "You study *Gemorah* already? Aren't you a little young to be studying that?" When I went to Hebrew school, kids did not start *Gemorah* until the fifth or sixth grade.

"Actually, I started last year. I learn with the sixth graders."

This kid had to be super smart. "What *mesechta* are you studying?"

"*Baba Basra,*" came the reply.

I was about to make a comment when the phone rang and Chaim'l left the table to answer it. He spoke for a moment and then hung up.

"Who was that?" I inquired.

"That was Marissa."

"When will she be here?"

Chaim'l returned to the table and tucked up his legs, "She won't. Her dad's car is totally stuck and they have to wait for a tow. She doesn't know when she will get here."

*No – this cannot be happening.* Marissa has to come to take over from me. There was no way that I could babysit these kids.

I began to panic.

I suddenly envisioned myself as the endangered hero in a Class-B adventure movie stranded on the dock of a remote island populated by hostile natives. The really vicious hordes – maybe even cannibals and head hunters or worse – are closing in on him. At first the hero is not terribly worried about the milling natives because he knows that a boat will soon arrive to rescue him. But the natives are encroaching upon the dock area – perhaps all is lost. Is there no hope for him? Then, at the very last moment, the boat – his salvation – can be seen approaching on the horizon. Hooray – he is about to be saved. The attacking natives also see the ship coming towards the port entrance and they retreat a bit. The boat toots its whistle but instead of turning into the harbor, it comes about and sails off, leaving our hero, marooned on the dock. The natives began approaching menacingly. The film ends and the credits roll up on the screen. The viewer can only contemplate the cruel fate that befell the hero.

Of course, I knew that my imagination was exaggerating just a bit. The cute kids were not exactly cannibals or headhunters, but I had this sinking feeling that the 'cruel fate' part might be right on the money. I felt threatened and defenseless at the same time. "Call her back," I ordered.

"Can't. She said her cell phone doesn't work and she walked to a pay phone just to make the call."

*Where did she find a pay phone? They had to be rarer than hen's teeth. More importantly, how was I going to get out of this dilemma?* "When will your *Ima* get back?" I asked with concern.

"She said nine."

Two hours!

Was I expected to be responsible for the kids for two hours? *No way.* I had never been an uncaring dad, but my work and studies kept me out of the house when our son was little and Rebecca had always taken care of David. I was always willing to help do the dishes, vacuum the rugs, shop for groceries and even clean, but like many men I felt totally lost when it came to child care. I am as liberal as the next guy but I feel that 'mothering' is a genetic thing. The males of the species are supposed to hunt, build, and protect the nest, but the females are supposed to deal with the running of the nest and care for the kids. That was the way God made the world. Women should have equal opportunities, get equal pay, and do any job they wanted – so long as they did not expect the men to help in child care.

My world had just been turned upside down.

Racheli – cute as a button – is the major problem. I had zero experience with two-year-olds. Changing the kid's diaper might be a little more than I could handle. I said a silent prayer – 'Pussycat ... Please don't poop.'

No babysitter – that meant that I was indeed stranded on the dock and there would be no boat to save me from the hostile savages. I was on my own. I had to assess the situation from a little different angle now. Racheli was murmuring unintelligible words as she played in the corner. 'Pussycat ... Please don't poop' turned into a subconscious mantra. Yanki was making even louder car-engine noises as he attempted to get his dump truck to drive up the drapes. Chaim'l raised his eyes from his notebook, "Mr. Lincoln, are you going to be our babysitter?"

"What? Me? No ... no," I said shaking my head in a firm denial. Then after a moment changed the motion to a tentative nod and said, "Well, maybe for a little while."

"What about my question?" asked the young scholar.

"What question?"

"From *Baba Basra.*"

"Oh, that question," was my reply. "Show me the problem and maybe I can help you."

Chaim'l pulled out a well used copy of the *Gemorah* from his school bag. It was a school edition – with smaller pages and cheaper binding – but *Baba Basra* was the largest tractate in all the Babylonian *Talmud* and the volume had to weigh at least three or four pounds. This kid was going to get a hernia just from *schlepping* around his school bag. The youngster flipped through the pages and opened to page 117. "Here," he said. "I don't understand the difference between Raba's interpretation of the problem and Rav Hisda's. Could you explain it to me?"

Page 117.

Out of luck.

I was up to page thirty with Rabbi Kalmonowitz. I had no idea what the boy was referring to, "I'm sorry," I said shrugging my shoulders. "I haven't studied that yet."

"But I have a test tomorrow. I have to know it," pleaded the young man.

"Let me have a look," I said leaning over the text. All I was able to make out was an Aramaic and Hebrew jumble about an incomprehensible subject. It was impossible. Without my English translation and the internet, I was lost. "I'm sorry. I just don't know this material."

"You've got to help," pleaded Chaim'l, almost in tears.

What was I supposed to do? What was expected of me? I was just a poor male bereft of any child rearing genes. The kid looked like he was going to cry. "If I had my books ... well maybe I could help," I explained.

Chaim'l looked up hopefully, "Can you get them?"

"No, I'm afraid not. I can't leave you and the other kids without a babysitter. So, there is no way to get the books."

"Can't we go over to your house? It would only be for a few minutes."

Go to my house? I had not thought about that. Definitely a bad idea, but the young man looked so desperate. Then I remembered that kids needed special seats. "I haven't got kiddee seats in my car. So we can't do that."

"We could use Ima's car. She keeps the keys on a hook over the counter."

Chaim'l kept looking at me with his penetrating imploring stare. That, and my unrelenting paranoia, soon wore me down. I was all out of excuses. Not seeing a better solution, I just gave in, "Okay everyone out to the car."

I bent down and picked up Racheli, "Come on Pussycat ... we're going for a ride."

"Stivoo," she chirped.

"That's right, Pussycat."

As we walked out to the car Yanki looked up at me and said in all seriousness, "Her name is Racheli ... not Pussycat."

I answered with equal solemnity, "You're absolutely correct. I'm not making fun of her, but to me she seems so cute ... just like a friendly pussycat. So, I'm going to call her Pussycat."

Yanki considered my answer and then said, "Yeah ... she is like a pussycat. I'm also going to call her that."

Chaim'l turned out to be a whiz at getting the younger kids strapped into their car seats. I had to slide the driver's seat way back to accommodate my longer legs. 'Ayelet is not a midget, why is the seat so darn forward?' I thought to myself. The drive took only about five minutes and when we pulled into my driveway, the two boys let out whelps of excitement in unison, "Wow ... you have a motor home."

I had completely forgotten about the thirty-two foot long land yacht that occupied half of my front drive. It had been purchased as part of my retirement plans. Rebecca and I had only gone on one trip before she took sick. Since then the vehicle has not done more than fifty miles and most of those miles have been to get back and forth to the dealership to do the warranty work. I just have not gotten around to selling the useless behemoth.

"Can we see the inside?" the boys asked politely.

"Sure, just let me get the keys."

I held Racheli in my arms as I opened the front door to my house and the two boys rushed past me to get in. I looked beseechingly at Racheli and once again said to myself, 'Pussycat ... Please don't poop.' The boys wandered about my big living room until Yanki suddenly yelled to Chaim'l, "Take a look at this ... a swimming pool."

"A swimming pool? Inside the house? ... No way," was the older brother's response. I went over to see what was getting them so excited.

They were referring to my lap pool, in a glass enclosed sun porch, just off the den. It was only six by sixteen feet and only a yard deep. Instead of swimming over the water as in a regular pool, the water flowed from one end to the other and you swam laps against the current without really moving ahead. It was good exercise and I religiously did a half hour twice a week.

"Can we go in?" asked Yanki.

"I'm afraid not today. But you can look around the motor home while I help Chaim'l." We all went outside and I unlocked the vehicle. Yanki immediately ran around poking his head into all the doors and cupboards. He finally climbed up into the driver's seat and rocked the wheel back and forth, "This is really awesome."

"Yeah, I suppose it is," I said. "If you want to stay out here that's okay but only if you promise that when you finish you will come straight into the house and not wander away."

"All right," said Yanki.

I turned to Chaim'l and asked, "Can I trust him?"

"Yeah, he's good like that. He won't get lost."

I went in with Chaim'l. Racheli was still in my arms and I had to find some way to distract her. I pulled open the gadget drawer in the kitchen and extracted anything that had a point or a sharp edge. Then I spilled everything else out on to the living room rug. I placed her on the floor amidst all the gadgets and she immediately busied herself trying to figure out how a garlic press operated. 'Pussycat ... Please don't poop' went the mantra in my mind. Then I turned to page 117 in my English *Gemorah* and began deciphering the text. It took me ten minutes to figure out the basic heads and tails of the text and another ten to understand the logic argument. Once I got that clear in my mind I was able to explain the problematic text to Chaim'l.

"Thank you," said the boy politely. "You're pretty good, Mr. Lincoln."

"You're welcome and it's Steve," I said proudly. "You're not bad yourself."

Suddenly I heard a loud yelp followed by a resounding splash coming from the pool. I ran over and there was Yanki with his head sticking out of the water, kicking his feet for all his worth. He was holding on to the pool's edge spluttering to catch his breath, "I just wanted to touch the water."

I pulled the kid out of the pool and handed him to Chaim'l. I barked an order over my shoulder as I ran to get a towel, "Get him out of those wet clothes and shoes!"

"Don't be angry with me," pleaded a tearful Yanki.

"Yanki, I'm not angry with you ... I was just concerned," I said more softly, as I returned with a big fluffy towel. "Anyone can fall into a pool and it was my fault not to lock the access door to the pool when you got here. So you didn't do anything wrong. I spoke loudly because I was afraid that you might drown. It can be dangerous."

Yanki was out of the wet clothes and wrapped in the warm towel. "I learned how to swim at day camp last summer."

"Well, then, I'm really proud of you. But next time you want to go into the pool, we'll do it with bathing suits and with your Ima's permission."

"Can we really? Oh that would be great," said Yanki. "Pussycat ... we're going to go swimming."

Racheli looked up for a moment from her gadgets on the floor, smiled for a moment and then made a prolonged grimace. She appeared to be turning blue and did not seem to be breathing. I became concerned and rushed over to the young girl. I gently shook her frail torso and spoke with concern, "Racheli, are you okay? Do you feel all right?"

Chaim'l chirped in, "She's fine."

"So why does she look like that?" I asked with concern.

"She's just pooping. She'll stop in a minute."

'Oh my God. I'm doomed,' I thought to myself. Then I said out loud, "She can't be pooping. We haven't got anything here to change her."

Chaim'l answered matter-of-factly, "We've got all that stuff back at the house."

I ordered loudly, "Everyone ... back to the car!"

The trip back seemed to take forever. If there was any question as to what Racheli had been doing while she was grimacing on the floor, it became obvious during the short drive. Her two older brothers pinched their noses closed and complained that they could not breathe the befouled air. They insisted that I open all the car's windows widely. You could not really blame the boys – there was quite a stench.

As soon as the car stopped, Racheli's siblings scampered from the car and I was left the task of extracted the living stink bomb from her car seat. I held the squirming little girl under her arms, keeping her body at arm's length. As soon as I got into the house I yelled, "Where is the changing stuff?"

Chaim'l showed me to her room and I quickly got the young lady on her back atop the changing table. Racheli just looked up at me contentedly. I had no idea how to progress. Chaim'l apparently sensed my lack of experience and said, "First you got to open up her clothes."

I just looked down at the young boy, not comprehending the significance of his remark, "What did you say?"

"You got to open her clothes first."

*Halleluyah, there is a God that looks after the innocents.*

"Right," I said, pretending that I knew that all along.

I began following the young man's instructions blindly. In a sort of a blur, I somehow got the smelly, sticky diaper off the girl and into a plastic bag. I found the little towelettes to clean off the noisome residuals. Chaim'l explained that Racheli was going to be put to bed so she needed a bath before she could be re-diaperized, and he ran to fill the tub. I got her into the water, did a quick rinse, wash and dry, and had her back on the diaper table. Then I smeared on the diaper cream and got the little tot wrapped up in a fresh diaper. Next step, I got the child back into – no, not her clothes – into her pajamas. Finally I took a deep breath, realizing that it was very likely that I had not been breathing during the entire twenty minute diaper change and bath.

Following Chaim'l's further instructions, I put Racheli in her bed with a bottle of warm milk and got Yanki into his bath. While I helped Yanki get into his PJs, Chaim'l tossed Yanki's wet clothes in the drier and then he took a bath. Racheli was already fast asleep and I sat on the bed reading to Yanki from a thin, page-worn illustrated volume extolling the exploits of a famous rabbi – his favorite book. Chaim'l climbed into his adjoining bed and listened as I read the story. It was not long until Yanki was also in dreamland and Chaim'l began nodding off. I closed the book and headed for the door.

Chaim'l – half asleep – raised his head and said, "Mr. Lincoln ... you did very good. Thank you."

For some unexplainable reason, such praise, coming from one so young, filled me with great pride, "You're welcome ... and the name is Steve."

# 10

## *Red-hot rebuke*

WHERE IS MR. LINCOLN? Why isn't he here already? I know it's not time yet – but that is no excuse. Just when I have something serious to say to him he has to come on time instead of coming early as he usually does?

Finally, there he is pulling into the drive so I must say good bye to the kids, "I'm leaving. Be good and listen to Marissa."

His car is so high. It's so much more difficult to get into his SUV than it is to get into my car. And the seat belt and buckle are so high up on the side wall. You have to be a contortionist to secure the belt. There, I have it.

No use putting off something that has to be said, "Excuse me, Mr. Lincoln."

"Yes, Ayelet. What can I do for you?"

*Why does he always call me by my first name?* It borders on impropriety. But then again this man always borders on impropriety. "I have something to say."

"I thought when we drove to the sessions it was my turn to ask you questions."

"It is, however this is more important."

"Okay, shoot. But you owe me."

"This concerns the babysitting you did for my kids. I only found out the next morning what actually happened. I want to talk to you about that."

"Ayelet, it was nothing. You were in a bind. There is no need to thank me."

What? He thinks I want to thank him for what he did. Of all the nerve. "I don't want to thank you ... if anything, I was thinking of murdering you."

"Why in the world ...?" said Mr. Lincoln.

*What is unclear?* "You took my kids out of my home ... in my own car ... both without my permission. Then you nearly drowned my son in your dangerous pool. Yanki is nagging me all day about going over to your house to go swimming. He has also started calling Racheli ... Pussycat ... something he learned from you. I can't make him stop. Chaim'l refers to you as Steve, after all the hard work I put in to teaching him to talk respectfully to older people and Racheli keeps parroting 'Stivoo' every chance she gets. During those two short hours you put my kids in danger and turned my house upside down. That is why I want to murder you!" I said with emphasis.

He is not speaking. He just stares straight ahead at the road. His fists seem to be clenched on the steering wheel. *Could he be angry at me?* For what? Everything I said is absolutely valid. I'm right. Still I cannot have him so upset. "Mr. Lincoln? Is there something wrong? ... Mr. Lincoln?"

Still no answer.

His knuckles seem to be turning white and the muscles of the side of his face look like they are twitching. Perhaps he's gnashing his teeth like an angry dog. *Is he going to attack me?* No, any man that does so many *mitzvahs* would never attack a woman. *Why doesn't he say something?* "Don't you want to defend yourself?"

"Why? Are you planning on slamming me in the back of my head when I'm not looking?"

"I would never hit you!" *How dare him to accuse me of something like that!* Of course, for a moment I did think that he might want to hit me, but he doesn't know that.

Mr. Lincoln responded with, "Well, it doesn't seem to keep you from ambushing me when I am not looking."

"How did I ambush you?"

"Are you kidding? That night ... you called me ... I didn't call you. You were the one that was in such a hurry that you wouldn't even let me take a shower. I was supposed to be there for only a few minutes, but it turned out I was the babysitter. Chaim'l got really upset because he didn't know some little piece of *Gemorah*. Maybe it was a mistake to take the kids out of the house, but I couldn't think of anything else to do. Just remember, it was you ... intentionally or unintentionally ... that put me in charge. That also means that I get to make 'my mistakes' if problems come up. Just because you don't like my decisions ... doesn't mean you can tear me to pieces like Torquemada in the Spanish Inquisition."

"Are you comparing me to Torquemada?" I blurted out in shock.

"Hey, if the empanada fits, who am I to say otherwise."

"What is an empanada? Is that something *tref*?"

"It's like *kreplach,* only it's from Spain," he explained. "Anyway, if I made mistakes ... and you don't like them ... what you can do is not call me to babysit anymore, but that's it," he said angrily. "As far as all the rest. To me, Racheli does seem like an adorable pussycat, so the name fits and believe me it won't harm her to have a nickname. I don't mind being called Steve or 'Stivoo', so that's all right. And your son is bright enough to know that he can only get away with calling me by my first name and no one else." Mr. Lincoln seemed to calm down a bit. He took a deep breath and added more slowly, "As far as Yanki falling in the pool, well you're right about that, I should have been more careful. So, I will take the rap for what happened there. By the way, I meant it about him coming over to swim if he wants to ... but only with your permission. He'll be safe. It's only three feet deep. He can stand in the pool and reach from side to side."

"I didn't know the pool was ... what kind of a pool is only three feet deep?" I asked.

“It’s called a lap pool. I'll be glad to show you one day.”

"I have no intention of ..."

"Actually," interjected Mr. Lincoln. "I think I should get a medal for what I went through."

I started out wanting to kill him and suddenly he thinks that he deserves a medal. *For what?* "What did you do to earn a medal?"

"For duty above and beyond."

"What are you talking about?"

Mr. Lincoln hesitated for a moment and then finally said, "Racheli's diaper."

Of course, Racheli had been put to bed and her diaper had been changed. Obviously he had done that. I just never even considered it as anything special. But, of course he would. Just picturing Mr. Lincoln, with his big muscles sticking out of his sweatshirt, standing over tiny Racheli trying to cuddle, clean, and clothe my little baby, made the corners of my mouth go up involuntarily. I couldn’t stop myself from laughing. "Now that is funny."

"I don't see what there is to laugh about."

I can’t keep a straight face, "Are you kidding ... it's hilarious."

"A man who has to do ‘that’ should get combat pay."

"Women do ‘that’ five times a day every day ... no combat pay."

"That's different."

"Why is that different?" I say wiping the tears of mirth from my cheeks.

"Women know how to do that kind of stuff."

"Didn't you change your son's diapers?"

"Actually ... not even once. That was Rebecca’s job. I was not home that much."

"Apparently not," the laughter keeps coming.

"Cut that out!!"

"I'm trying, but it's hard." More chuckles escaped from my throat.

"Have you any idea how bad the stink was?"

"Of course I do. I change her every day."

He hesitated for a moment and then said seriously, "That's right ... you do."

"And I enjoy it every time. Whenever I take care of my kids it fills me with happiness. Stink and all."

"I envy you."

"If you wish, I am sure I can schedule you in to change Racheli just about whenever you want."

"I will forego that bit of happiness. But I do envy ... your kids. They're terrific. Look, I agree that maybe there were some things that were not so perfect with my babysitting job. Let's call a truce ... do you forgive me?"

"You really know how to hit below the belt. You flatter a mother by telling her that her kids are terrific and you expect her to stop being angry with you."

"You shouldn't have been ticked off at me in the first place. And yeah, I expect you to forgive me."

*It's not fair, but what he says makes sense.* It was much easier when I was angry with him. "I'll take what you said into consideration."

"What part are you considering? Forgiving me? Not yelling at me? Allowing the kids to call me Steve? Or the kids coming over to swim?"

What is he talking about? "I have no intention ..."

"Never mind. You can tell me later. We've arrived at the Jewish Center parking lot."

But I have so much more to say. I have no intention of letting him get off so easily. But then again, his explanation makes sense and what he did really wasn't so bad. He was just trying to do the best he could. This man confuses me.

It's also the first time I laughed in two years.

# 11

## *Glass houses*

ALL THE GROUP SESSIONS with Dr. Stralling had been tough, but during our last few meetings Lonnie's methods became brutal. Not in the physical sense. The shrink had never shown a penchant for corporal punishment. He inflicted his excruciating torture by playing fiendish mind games.

According to the good doctor, each person in the group was in some form of a holding pattern concerning their own personal grief. To get them moving forward again, his overall strategy was to make each of the participants somehow confront his or her problems. His current ploy was the 'name in the box' lottery. Each one of the group presented their subject's problems as candidly as possible. This made all of the participants into amateur shrinks for their own personal 'patient'. Dr. Stralling felt that there was an added advantage for us to work as amateur psychiatrists because in doing so it helped each presenter subconsciously assess their own problems. The supposed benefit for the 'subject' was that he/she could not remain in denial after hearing all their foibles, fears and phobias presented so openly. After the 'official' presentation the 'subject' had to sit through a no-holds-barred analysis of these problems conducted by the entire group of 'lay psychiatrists' in which he/she was raked over the coals. Lonnie felt that the 'washing your linens in public' method made you realize that you could not hide behind whatever denial mechanism you were using. Dr. Strallings's motto was, 'You have to tear down the old, before you can build the new.'

At last week's session I had been the 'subject'. It was me in the hot seat. Ayelet had presented my 'problems' in all of their unflattering glory. Thanks to her, everyone now knew that I had never really mourned for my mother or my wife. It was her opinion that I was in a rut and could not move on. All the group seemed to agree with her assessment.

It was a shame that she had not consulted with me beforehand about what she was going to say. I could have helped her prepare and avoid her stating a profound amount of absolute rubbish. But things like that happen when amateurs try to do the work of professionals. My plumber used to say that if he was called in to fix a leaky faucet he could charge a maximum of about $75. But give a DIY inspired homeowner a chance to fix the pipes himself – it became a gold mine. Within thirty minutes that $75 leaky faucet would be converted into a $750 major repair.

I did not have the heart to tell Ayelet how far off the mark she was.

However, her presentation did accomplish two things. Firstly it had Ayelet talking in front of the group. This was a milestone because usually she opened her mouth only when a specific question was asked of her and even then she spoke only the absolute minimum number of words. Her portrayal of my problems had her talking for over fifteen minutes. From our short conversations in the car I knew that she was actually quite clever, knowledgeable, and articulate. However, most of the other members of the group had never heard her speak freely, and since they were not familiar with the *charedi* ban on conversations, they probably thought that Ayelet was a bit slow witted. Those misconceptions were now dispelled.

Secondly, she had done me the favor of revealing to the group certain personal information that I had purposely kept hidden. After working with the other participants in the therapy sessions over the past months, I have come to realize that if the group was going to help any of the people, each participant had to feel that everyone was being open and truthful. My underlying paranoia kept signaling me that keeping secrets from the group was a tad dishonest and I was a bit ashamed of having done just that. Now, with all of it out in the open, I felt relieved. I was not better, but I was relieved.

Tonight had been Ayelet's turn under the spotlight. I laid out her problems and presented my theory as to why she continues to mourn. Amateurish to be sure – I never claimed to be a shrink – but in my own personal estimation, I thought that I had been very close to a bullseye. I explained that she of course mourned for her husband as would any wife in a happy marriage, but she was also angry with Rephael for leaving her and for not being there to fulfill their mutual dreams. Lonnie had agreed with everything I said, and even commented on my insight. Of course, Dr. Stralling – the professional that he was – said that about all the presentations. However, I thought that the doctor nodded his head much more in earnest during my talk than he had for the other presenters.

Ayelet started crying about ten seconds into my spiel. She leaned forward and did not look up from her shoes even when a small puddle began forming at her feet. Ayelet had never shown this much emotion in the previous sessions. Her bawling did not stop with the last comments of the group and the tears continued on even after all the terrible Danish had been consumed.

Ayelet was still mopping up her tears when she climbed into the back seat of my car. I empathized with her and before starting the engine I said, "I'm sorry if I hurt you in there."

She snuffled up the last of the tears and answered, “What’s there to be sorry about. That’s what the sessions are for. So we can face our problems.”

“Do you feel any better?”

“I haven’t thought about that,” she said, pausing for a moment. “Yes, I suppose I do. I still hurt. But everything seems to have a clarity it didn’t have before the session.”

I smiled smugly and said, “Chalk one up for Dr. Freud.”

“I hope you’re referring to Lonnie and not yourself,” said Ayelet, blowing her nose into a tissue.

“Um ... um ...,” I stammered. “Of course I meant Dr. Stralling.”

“But I do want to thank you about the way you presented my problems. I could see that you used a lot of consideration and kindness in the way you phrased things.”

“Yep, that’s me. Mr. Tact.”

"Thank you."

I started the engine and drove off. I had a few surprises planned for Mrs. Weinberg.

Ayelet soon realized that I was not taking the most direct route to her house. "Where are we going?" she asked anxiously.

I said in my most calming tone, "You'll see."

"I don't have to tell you that I can’t just be driving around with you. It’s not proper."

After all these months – did she think I wasn’t aware of all her restrictions? "I know ... *tznius* ... and all that. But I checked with Rabbi Kalmonowitz and he said as long as we don't go into any buildings it was okay."

"If *Rebbi* said so, then ...," Ayelet replied skeptically.

"Trust me."

"Do I have a choice?"

I drove to the northernmost neighborhood of Southfield where it bordered with I-696, until I came to an unusually large property – about four or five acres – surrounded by a chain link fence. I got out, unlocked the gate and drove in. There were no lights in the large tree-filled area but the streetlamps from the road and the moonlight gave sufficient illumination for us to see a dark Gothic three-story wooden structure looming up over the foliage. The ornate carpentry of the lower floor was somewhat obscured by the jungle of the unkempt garden but the decorative turrets and gables above could be seen climbing skywards. "This is the old Langshire estate," I explained. "They owned most of the land around here when this was all still farmland. No one has really lived in the old house for almost fifty years. A buddy of mine recently bought this whole parcel and is going to restore the house and build on the property."

"Are we here to go sightseeing?" she asked skeptically.

"Nope, get out of the car."

Fifty years without a tenant could be the death knell of any property and this place was no exception. There were weeds sprouting in what had once been a well tended gravel driveway. Unruly privet made a tall thick screen around the periphery of the main building and there were overgrown bushes and trees of various sizes all about the property. I took out a flashlight and found us a path through the undergrowth until we stood on a concrete pad at the rear of the house. Apparently there had once been a formal garden here with brick pathways and small raised beds for flowers and shrubs, but it was now a jumble of pavers, stone, and assorted weeds.

I pointed to the back of the house. "This place is sort of a classic. The Langshires made their fortune early in the 19th century by raping most of the state. They cut down every tree they could lay an axe to and made them into charcoal and timber to be shipped back east. They traded in furs and animal pelts until it was hard to find a beaver or a fox in the state. They purchased this property well before the Civil War and they had Norman Shaw, the famous Atlanta architect, come up here to build their house for them. There are only twenty or thirty of this style in the entire state. The place has been designated a Michigan landmark and that means you can't tear it down. For all the ecological devastation the Langshires caused upstate, they were good enough folks and during Civil War times they used some of their money to help runaway slaves from the South. The basement of this very building was one of the way stations for the famous Underground Railroad that helped slaves escape to Canada."

"Very impressive ... and thank you for the history lesson, but why are we here?" asked a bewildered Ayelet.

Now came the difficult part. If I said the wrong thing she was going to head for the hills.

I took a second to phrase my next words carefully, "You handled yourself okay during the session this evening. You took whatever we all dished out."

"Are you kidding? I was blubbering through the whole thing."

"But you listened and accepted what we said. I could see it in your eyes."

"How could you see my eyes, they were in my tissues all the time?"

"You know what I mean."

"So?"

"So, there is more I need to say," I said with determination.

"Gee thanks, that's what I really need ... to start crying all over again."

"It was something you said to me last week. About how I have to mourn for my mother, as well as my wife."

"What does that have to do with me?"

"You also have to mourn for someone else."

Ayelet shrugged and asked, "Who?"

"For yourself. When your husband died he took with him something else. You devoted your life to the task of Rephael becoming a *talmid chochom*. He might even have become the next *rosh yeshiva*. You would've been the *rebbetzen*. That's all gone now."

"Of course that's gone ... don't you think I know that?" said Ayelet, stating the obvious.

"Obviously you *know* that. *That* is not the problem," I said.

"Then what is *the problem* and why did you bring me here?" asked Ayelet becoming impatient.

"It's you. You are the problem. *You* feel cheated."

"That's ridiculous," stated Ayelet emphatically. "How was I cheated? And by whom?"

"I am not saying that you consciously wanted it. But you will never ... ever ... have the honor that would have come with being the *rebbetzen* of a famous *rosh yeshiva,* Rabbi Rephael Weinberg."

She seemed at a loss for words, "I never wanted honor ... ever. I run from it. I even get embarrassed whenever someone just points at me."

"That's the way true honor works. It comes to those that shy away from it," I said with empathy. "And that's what makes you doubly angry."

"How can I be angry with Rephael for dying? He is the one that truly suffered," said Ayelet, as she shut her eyes and began crying softly.

"It's not a logic problem. It's something in your heart. You have to get the anger out and crying yourself to sleep every night is not the answer."

"Crying I do very well."

I was hesitant to continue, "I know that *charedim* don't like to talk about this very much ... but I'm sure you also miss the close relationship you had with your husband. You miss having a partner ... a companion ... in the tough undertaking of raising a family. You miss having a friend to share your deepest thoughts. And ... please excuse me for saying this ... it is only natural ... you miss the physical intimacy of your husband. You won't admit it ... but you are a young woman and the need is there under the surface."

Uh oh.

Maybe I went over the line.

My last words seemed to have angered Ayelet.

I can see that she is all tensed up. Her eyes were now shut tightly and she turned her head slightly from side to side. Suddenly she said, "Oh my God," and began crying with an increased intensity. It was like a river of emotion bursting through a dam. In between sobs she raised her voice to exclaim, "Exactly just what do you suggest I do? Do you also think I can start dating again ... with three little children?"

"When the time is right ... then, yeah."

"And for now?" she asked gaining some control.

"For now, I think you should build up your life all over again. You have so much going for you. You're bright and have a good personality ... although most of the time you hide it from me and everyone else."

"That's not true."

"What's not true? That you're bright and have a good personality or that you're hiding it all the time?"

"Oh, you ... you know what I mean."

"You have a roof over your heads, you have some money to live on, and you have great kids."

Ayelet did not respond and her sobbing subsided slowly, "Where is this going?"

"You bake stuff that is out of this world," I said slowly with emphasis. I wanted to make it absolutely clear that I thought her baking skill was remarkable.

She apparently was not prepared for my strange comment. "What has that got to do with anything?"

I offered up a possibility, "You could start a business selling your baked goods."

"I already do that. But, you can't make a living from that."

"How much money do you get for a pound of your brownies?"

"Three dollars?" said Ayelet snuffing up her tears.

"Why three dollars? Why not more?"

"Because the kosher bakery sells brownies at $2.75. People won't pay more," said Ayelet assertively.

"Would you be willing to *allow* people to pay more if they wanted to?"

"If they wanted to? Of course I would, but who would ...?"

"Just leave that to me. I have a hunch that I just might know the right people that would be willing to pay a little more for your baked stuff. So I think you just went into the baking business."

"I'm not so sure about ..."

"What have you got to lose? If I don't find you customers ... you don't open up the business. Are you willing?"

"What do I have to do?"

"Two days from now, have an assortment of your stuff ready for me ... at ... let's say ... one o'clock in the afternoon so I can take them with me as samples to show people what you have to offer."

"That won't be a problem."

"Now for the second part."

"What second part?" asked Ayelet tentatively.

"We have to deal with your inner anger."

“I just told you that ...,” she retorted.

I cut her off, “I haven't got the strength to argue with you about what is making you angry. So we'll just say that you're angry about something. In your heart you'll know."

"How are *we* going to take care of my *so called* anger?"

"Simple. That's why I brought you here. Do you see that pile of broken brick and stone over there? I want you to throw a piece of brick through one of the windows. And then keep doing that until every window in the place is smashed to smithereens. Breaking something helps to vent your anger."

"I can't do that. I can't break someone's windows. It's against the law."

"It's all taken care of. I told you, the contractor is a good friend of mine. The casements and jambs are all rotten or warped and they have to be replaced. All the old glass is useless, because they're putting in triple glazing. Whatever you don't break tonight his boys will rip out later this week anyway. Go ahead pick up a piece of brick."

Reluctantly Ayelet sidled over to the pile and selected a broken paver. She looked at the piece of brick in her hand, then at the building, then at me. She did this several times as she contemplated what to do. She raised her arm to begin her throw but in mid-swing she stopped suddenly and turned to me, "I'll do it but only if you do it as well."

"I arranged all this for you. I don't need to do break any windows."

"*Kasha varnishkes*."

"What does *kasha varnishkes* have to do with this?"

"My mother would never let us say baloney, because she said only *goyim* eat baloney so it must not be kosher. Jews ate salami. So ... *kasha varnishkes* ... You need it more than me."

"Nothing of the sort."

"I didn't say it last week when we discussed your *problems* ... but you have an elaborate defense mechanism."

"I have no such thing," I said shaking my head in denial.

"*Kasha varnishkes*!! You didn't admit to or accept anything the group said about you last week. Come clean. I know you. It was like water rolling off a duck's back. *Nu* ... admit it."

Is she kidding?

Men don't admit to things like that. A man simply has to accept what he cannot change. He did not sit down and cry or feel sorry for himself. A man faced the world with chin up and head held high. He toughed it out. He bucked up. He made himself strong. He made himself impregnable. Didn't she realize that there was no way that I would admit that I had unresolved issues with Rebecca's death? Or my mother's? Or with life in general?

Never in a million years.

Never in a hundred million years.

*How could Mrs. Weinberg be so insightful?*

I could and should continue to deny everything – but what was the point? I wanted to tell her that she was way off base, but what came out was, "Okay, maybe I felt a little ... like ... you all didn't really understand ... my problems." *Did I just say that I had problems?*

"Now we're getting somewhere," said Ayelet emphatically. "I didn't say this last week, but the defense mechanism you most commonly employ is to build things. Whenever you need to escape the hurt of your grief, you build something. When your mother died you *built* yourself into an A+ student. Then you went on to become a *builder* ... how perfect. You were never at home with your son and you continued to *build* your business."

"Now, wait a second ...," I said reflexively. She was getting a little too close to a subject I did not want to discuss. Something I didn't know how to handle. If she continued, I knew that I might not be able to fully control my hidden emotions. My male ego was sending up bright red warning flares and was telling me that there was a disaster approaching. I felt threatened and was searching for an escape.

Ayelet did not allow me to think, as she continued, "Your wife died and you built up a wall that holds all the hurt in. You have never faced your losses. Not for your wife and not for your mother. And all those other things that you said that I miss ... and that I am angry about ... that goes for you too. You are angry about losing the life that was promised to you after your retirement. Growing old with the wife you loved so much. What you said tonight is absolutely right. For me ... and for you. Until we get our anger out of our systems we're going to be stuck. So, tonight instead of building something, how about you join me in breaking something," she said, holding out the piece of brick for me.

This is crazy.

I was the one that arranged all this for Ayelet. This was for her. It had nothing to do with me. I did not need to go around breaking windows.

*How absurd.*

To say that I built walls. Protective walls. Impregnable fortifications.

No way.

*Ridiculous.*

Then I realized that Ayelet was only holding up a mirror to my soul. If I did not like what I saw, I could not blame the mirror.

She was absolutely right.

I could not think of anything I could do to get out of it, so I took the rock from her hand and quipped, "Another Dr. Freud."

As if she was explaining the rules of a game to one of her children she said, "So here's the deal. I break a window ... then you break a window. We keep it up until we run out of bricks or run out of windows. Do we have a deal?"

I was not certain that breaking a window was going to help me, but I figured if that was what was needed to get her to cooperate, then I would agree, "Okay, we have a deal."

Ayelet bent over to get another brick, "Of course we might not have enough strength ... this is a big building. I don't think I can reach the third floor."

"All right, I'll take the second floor and above."

"Remember what you said. We each look into our heart and with every brick we throw we vent our anger ... that's part of the deal."

"Okay, okay, just toss a damn brick already," I said in desperation.

Most females throw funny and Ayelet was no exception. For some reason, girls rarely employed the male type, shoulder-arm-elbow-wrist, double action, side arm throw. They threw things using only the elbow, as if their arms were Roman catapults. Ayelet cocked her hand back and lobbed the stone through a side window making a resounding crash, followed by the tinkle of cascading glass shards. When the sound abated she turned to me and said with just a hint of a smile, "Wow, I'm embarrassed to say that that was fun."

"This is therapy, it is not supposed to be fun," I said in mock seriousness, as I threw my brick at an upper window. The crash was more muted and the glass fell on to the concrete. *'But it is fun,'* I thought to myself.

Ayelet moved on to the next window and her demeanor changed. She stopped talking – which, as I had learned during our recent trips back and forth to the JCC, was quite unusual. Ayelet began smashing glass in earnest. As soon as she released one piece of brick she immediately bent over to retrieve another. Her jaw became set and she stared straight ahead. After the fifth window the tears began to flow. This time, it was not her usual sedate whimpering. Now, with each throw she let out an unintelligible grunt which slowly built to a shout. Her crying was soon accompanied by loud heart rendering wails. She wiped her eyes on her sleeve as she rhythmically broke more and more of the glass.

She was not alone.

At first I simply tossed the stones in an equal cadence with Ayelet, just so she would continue. Somewhere near the seventh or eighth window – with Ayelet crying loudly

– a memory of my mother and my youth began to grow in my mind. Soon it seemed to coalesce into a continuous panoramic slide show of images that included Rebecca. I remembered all the wonderful things of our marriage and my youth and realized that it had all been ripped away from me. At first I felt a deep hurt and then I slowly became angry. With my mother – with my wife – with my life. I had built and built and built and now I was all alone. I never realized I could hurt so much or that the hurt had been there all the time.

I don't know when the tears began, but I just wiped them away so I could see the next window. We moved clockwise around the structure breaking all the glass as we circled the building. It was hard to hit the higher windows and with every miss I became angrier and angrier. As I cried I screamed curses at the building – not at my mother, not at my wife – I cursed the way life had treated me. I yelled – I cried – and I threw rocks like an automaton.

Then we ran out of windows.

All the glass in every window was shattered.

We each stood with a brick in our hands looking for another target. Slowly our crying ceased and our stones dropped to the concrete with dull thuds. Together, but as separate spirits, we walked silently to my car.

I knew that my anger was not the same as Ayelet's. My beef had been with God. Hidden deep within myself had been an intense anger for what He had done to my mother, my wife, and to my life.

I knew that Ayelet could never be angry with the Almighty. In the *charedi* way of looking at things you were supposed to welcome the bad things in life just as you welcomed the good. Her credo for life was that everything is controlled by an all-knowing God. Her anger was not aimed at God for dealing her a raw hand. When Rephael died and her universe came crashing down on her and her family – when any non-*charedi* would have felt abandoned by God – she did not blame the Almighty. She *could not* blame him. For Ayelet's life style only made sense if she accepted that God was in control of everything. If the Almighty decided that she was to be sent out rudderless in a stormy sea, then she deserved it. She reasoned that she must be at fault. Perhaps she was not pious enough. Maybe she had affronted someone. Whatever it was, she was to blame for all that had happened to her family. Ayelet was angry with herself – and she was much more unforgiving than the Almighty – therefore the anger had smoldered and grown.

The catharsis that came with smashing every window in that old house allowed each of us to confront our respective hidden anger.

During the ride back to her house we both did not speak.

When we arrived at her home, Ayelet got out of the car and said, "Thank you. Thank you for everything ... thank you."

# 12

## *Major hang-up*

SIX WEEKS HAVE GONE BY since the night we broke windows and I have not had a moment's rest. Right from the start, Mr. Lincoln returned with my first two customers. It was so clever of him to think of offering my cakes to the caterers at the sports stadiums to feed the wealthy guests in the private boxes. He sells my stuff per piece and not by weight. I make five times more than what I did when I sold it by the pound. And I cannot keep up with the demand. I have already had to hire Mrs. Leibowitz, a Russian immigrant and former cook, to help with the time consuming parts of the baking. I have converted the dining room table into a large work surface for our mixing and kneading. But there is still a limit to what the two of us can do in my small kitchen. I have never earned so much money in so short a time. *Boruch HaShem* I should be thankful, but I am so busy now.

But not tonight.

Tonight I must go with Mr. Lincoln to Abraham Tolwitz's wedding. He is the first 'successful' graduate of our therapy group. Abe was the divorcee who had mourned the loss of his son to the point where he had stopped dating. But thanks to Lonnie, and the group, he took control of his life and found someone to share his world. I really didn't want to go to the wedding but Abe insisted that the group was collectively responsible for his newfound happiness and he wanted us all to attend. To show how important it was that everyone be there, he especially hired a *glatt kosher* caterer even though no one in his family needed anything more than regular *kosher*. He did that so that I would be able to attend. Weddings are expensive and that must have added quite a bit to the cost. I probably won't enjoy the wedding because it's not going to be a *frum* affair. There will be mixed seating, mixed dancing and who knows what else, but I guess I just cannot say no.

I feel funny getting dressed up so fancy shmansy in the middle of the week. Since Rephael died I have not really gone out anywhere, except to what has been required of me. Like going to the synagogue on *shabbos* and holidays or events in our community where my presence was needed. I hope this dress is not that old looking or out of style. Rephael always liked this dress. It is *tzniusdik*, but I know that I look very feminine in this outfit. Not provocative – just feminine. Of course Rephael never said anything – that was the way he was – but I could tell. There was always that extra smile whenever I wore it and he would say that I looked very nice.

I haven't got much time, Mr. Lincoln will soon be here to drive me to the wedding. It really is amazing how with his help the baking business has taken off and seems to be prospering. Please God, may it continue. The first thing he did was make me hire a management firm to handle the books and run my 'bakery'. He said that if I tried to do it myself, I would be swamped with purchasing, paperwork, marketing, salaries, tax records and it would rob me of time to bake. I really do love to bake. I always have. My *Bubbi* Sarah explained my baking knack in two Yiddish words – '*zee ferstayt*'. The expression is untranslatable. Literally it means 'she understands', but it really means a deep instinctive ability and even that is insufficient. They say that artists are driven by their muse to create. I suppose the same is true for me. I also create, but my creations satisfy people in a way that music or art can never ever match. And my creations taste so much better. Added to that – people are willing to pay me for what I would willingly do for free.

Life is good – sometimes.

Funny, that is something that I would not have thought of saying only a few weeks ago. I guess I have to thank Mr. Lincoln for that as well.

It's getting late and I have to fix my *shaitel*. I must get all my own hair tucked up so that none of it shows. I have to look presentable but not gaudy. Pretty is okay, but not attractive. I am not trying to attract anyone. That is the fine line of *tznius*.

Where is Mr. Lincoln? Ah, here he is. It's a little cool so I will take my coat, "Good night kids. Listen to Marissa."

My, my, Mr. Lincoln is such a gentleman. He has gotten out of the car to open the back door for me. He looks very handsome in his suit. *I really shouldn't be noticing such things.*

"Good evening, Ayelet. I know you didn't want to go, so I hope ...," Mr. Lincoln had not really been looking at me but now that he sees me he paused for a split second. "... you'll enjoy the evening."

I think I shocked him with how I am dressed. Am I being too brazen? Should I ask him? No, that is impossible. I will just have to go as I am. "I'm sure I'll be fine. And you promised to take me home if I feel uncomfortable at the wedding."

"That's the deal," he said as he climbed into the driver's seat. "Ayelet, don't take this the wrong way. I just want to tell you that you look terrific in that dress and you will wow everyone at the wedding."

I can feel the color rising in my cheeks. *I did dress too provocatively*. What would the *rebbetzen* say? "Maybe I should go back in and change?"

"Excuse me?" he said in surprise. "Didn't you hear me say you look terrific in that dress? Why would you want to change?"

"A modest woman should not draw attention to herself."

"I agree 100%. Everyone knows you are modest, Ayelet. You are just about the most modest woman I know. But you can't hide the fact that you are also very pretty. I'm just stating an obvious fact. Oh, you can disguise it fairly well during the week with your baggy dresses and the frumpy headware you use to cover your hair. But madam, you are naturally pretty and there is nothing you can do about it. So you will just have to grin and bear it."

I'm so embarrassed. How can he say such things? This isn't an appropriate conversation for a man and a woman who are not married to each other. I will never be able to look him in the face. I can hardly catch my breath. "Mr. Lincoln, please don't talk about this anymore."

"Why not? We're in group therapy together. We're allowed. I'm supposed to tell you all about your strengths and weaknesses, so that you can get on with your life. Well, one of your strengths is that you are a good looking woman and any man would proud to be seen with you. I know I am."

How does he do it? He confuses me all the time. What he says makes sense, but then again is it appropriate for a *frum* woman? I'm not sure what I should do. I'll just have to go with what my common sense tells me to do. Right now all I can say is, "Thank you for the compliment."

"You're welcome," he said and pulled out of the driveway.

The King's Gardens – I remember this hall – three years ago Dr. Markowitz's affair was here. Very fancy place. Normally we never would have been invited but the doctor was a *chozer be'tshuvah* and had been coming to the *bais medrash* where Rephael learned with him in *chavrusah*. The whole family now leads an Orthodox life. He was so appreciative of Rephael's help that he insisted that we had to come to his son's *bar mitzvah*. The successful West Bloomfield Orthopedist is still one of the biggest benefactors of the *yeshiva*.

I feel chilly and I'm glad I brought the coat, but Mr. Lincoln is just like most men – he stands there shivering and pretends he doesn't feel the cold. It must go back to some caveman reflex where the male had to show the female that they were invincible.

The landscaping and the entrance foyer to the place are still stunning. At night with all the shrubs lit up you can imagine that you are in some forest glen and can forget for a moment about the fast-food restaurant and the dry cleaners just beyond the hedges.

Oh, how formal – Abe and his bride are waiting at the door to greet the guests.

"Naomi, I want you to meet Ayelet and Steve, from my group at the center," said the groom to his bride.

Abe had spoken about his fiancée at the group sessions. She has never been married before and seems to be gushing with happiness. I would guess her age to be about forty and I am happy for her. She found a good man and can finally have the pleasure of a family. I wish them both well.

The bride turned toward us and said, "Abe has told me so much about you both. Thank you for coming."

Before I could react the groom quickly reached out and began pumping my hand as he said, "Really, I thank you for coming. Especially you, Ayelet. I know the extra effort you made to be here. Thank you."

Did I just see a flicker in the bride's smile? I did. She looked me over to see if I had been or would be competition. Oh, how funny. I wish I could tell her that I have no intentions in that direction. Anyway, I am so happy for them. "My pleasure and a huge *mazel tov* to you both."

Where is the coat room? If I remember correctly, it was at the end of the foyer. Oh yes, there it is. I see that there is no cloak room attendant. I guess they didn't think they would need someone because it is usually much warmer this time of year. Abe is originally from New York and doesn't know the local Michigan adage – If you don't like the weather – stick around for five minutes, it will change.

I suppose I can hang my coat anywhere in the room. I'll put it in the back, far from the counter, so if we have to leave early I'll be able to find it more easily. What is this? Some of the threads here at the back of my coat have become unraveled. I haven't worn this coat in two years. I'll have to fix this when I get home.

Suddenly I heard someone say, "Excuse me ... if you are finished dawdling back there. Could you come and take my coat?"

It was a harsh female voice with a strong Israeli accent. Who is the woman referring to? Is there an attendant that I didn't see?

No ... there isn't anyone here.

"Are you lazy or stupid or maybe both? I'm talking to you!" said the rude lady once again with emphasis.

Does she mean me? She thinks I am the coat-check attendant. How funny. "I'm afraid you've made a mistake."

"No, mistake," demanded the woman. "I'm waiting here quite a while for you to hang up my coat."

The lady appeared to be in her forties. She wears no wedding ring and perhaps she is a friend of the bride. I must say her outfit and the way she is made up are rather inappropriate for a Jewish wedding. Perhaps for any wedding. Oh, not just in my opinion. Everyone would say the same thing. First of all, what she's wearing is not very complimentary for someone of her age and who is carrying a few extra pounds. Basically, she was wearing a strapless, form fitting dress fashioned from some sort of deep purple shiny material, with bands of fringes spiraling around her body. The hemline is up near her mid-thigh and it unflatteringly exposes her heavy legs. Her bodice is battling to contain – not too successfully – her overly abundant bosom. In addition, she has very short, out-of-the-bottle platinum hair that has been doused with hair gel, so that it is standing straight out from her head, making her look as if she is being electrocuted. And her makeup!!! Why is she wearing it so heavy? With that much makeup I could paint clown faces on everyone at the next *yeshiva Purim shpiel* and still have enough left over to camouflage an entire Israeli combat unit.

But I can understand why the lady thought I might be the attendant. She saw me hanging up my coat and thought I am employed here. From her accent I can tell she is Israeli. Let me try to explain in Hebrew. *"Gevirti, ratzeeti lehasbir ..."*

"Oh, so you speak Hebrew," said the woman mockingly. "Well, guess what? We are in America now. We don't have any of your *Charedi* stooges in *our* Congress, so you can't leverage anyone. So, speak English."

*Of all the nerve.* "Madam, let me explain ..."

"I don't want to hear any of your explanations. I just want you to take my coat already."

"If you will just listen ...," I began to say.

"I don't want to listen to you. My friend is paying you good money to do your job, not to talk to the guests. It's bad enough you people almost never work ... and when you do, you stand around and chatter all day."

What does she mean, 'you people'? What a bigot. I have a good mind to tell her off, "Madam, what you don't seem ..."

"I know all about you ultra-Orthodox Jews. I'm Jewish and I work to support myself. Your husbands never work and the women are all on the dole. I congratulate you on taking a job, instead of just sitting home on your *tuchis* and dropping litter after litter of *chassidic* brats. So what do you say, *motek,* are you finally going to take my coat."

Of all the nerve. I am so angry. Never in my life have I been so close to hitting someone.

I must get in control of my emotions. *You have met this type before.* Jews who are embarrassed by their great *Torah* heritage. Remember, it will do no good to argue with the lady. It will only fan her dislike for *frum* Jews even more.

*What to do?*

Well ... first, start by smiling. *That's better.* Take a deep breath and think of something to make this all go away. "You are absolutely correct. Let me have your coat."

"It's about time,"

I'll take the coat and hang it up for her. That will defuse the situation. I cannot help but wonder what Mr. Lincoln would have said to this lady. He is so hot-headed. Where is he? There he is.

Oh my goodness!

I think he overheard the conversation and is now approaching the lady to give her a piece of his mind. That would be terrible. It will just make a big commotion and will upset the bride and groom.

I have to catch his eye.

There, he sees me, but he doesn't understand why I am signaling him to desist. Whew – he is backing up. He could have ruined everything. "Where would you like me to hang this for you?"

"Duh!!! What kind of question is that? Some place safe. That's a $2,000 coat. An original Cinzia Rocca. But you people wouldn't know about such things."

I will put the coat right over here. “There you go ... nice and safe.”

“Where is my ticket?”

“A ticket for what?”

“For my coat, Mrs. Einstein. How will I get my coat without a ticket?”

The lady wants a ticket. What am I going to do for a ticket? Ah ha – there – under the counter, is a box filled with torn checking stubs from a previous affair. I will just get one of those. “Here you go ... number 423. Enjoy yourself.”

“I certainly hope so. But after this lousy service don’t expect to get a tip from me at the end of the evening.”

In all honesty I say, “No ma’am, you are absolutely right, I do not expect one.”

The woman now has a satisfied smile on her face, as if she were a gladiator that had vanquished all the lions in the colosseum. She made a pivot turn and began enthusiastically swinging the dark fringes on her ample hips as she walked towards the festivities in the main ballroom.

Mr. Lincoln now approached and said, "Why didn't you let me tear into that insulting woman? She had no right to talk to you like that."

“There is nothing you could have said that would have changed her mind and causing a scuffle would not add to the *simcha*. This was the best way."

"What about the ticket you gave her? She is going to go have a conniption fit when she gets back here and she doesn't find you here to give her the coat."

I nodded my head and could not help but smile, "Yes, that could very well happen. But she was the one who wanted a ticket. What could I do?"

"Ayelet ... Ayelet ... Ayelet," he said wagging his finger at me. "You have a little bit of precociousness in you. I didn't know that."

"There are many things you don’t know about me."

# 13

## Redneck revenge

"*REBBI,* THERE ARE SOME CONCEPTS that I just don't understand," I said.

"Reb Shaul, is it in something we have studied?" responded Rabbi Kalmonowitz.

"No ... no ... nothing like that. As you know I am in the grief recovery group at the Jewish Center."

"Along with Ayelet Weinberg."

"Yes," I said with a nod of my head. "At every session we deal with how people cope with the loss of loved ones. I suppose I have my own issues dealing with the loss of Rebecca ... my wife."

"*Sheh'teeheeyeh munuchasah Eden* (may she rest in the Garden of Eden)," intoned the rabbi in response.

"Amen," I said reverently. "I personally don't know how to accept her death. She was so young. There is a fellow in the group that lost a little girl. I ask myself, why? I know you can't answer that question ... but I would like to know, what is the Jewish way of looking at death and dying? Is death a punishment for what we did in life? Is it just something natural that we must accept? How do I deal with it?"

"That is a tough question. In Judaism we never ask why one person dies young and one at an older age. Why one dies in their sleep and the other with pain and suffering. That is in the hands of God. But the rabbis of the *Talmud ... chazal ...* do teach us their way of looking at life and death."

"I would like to hear it."

"One of the major sources comes from a woman."

"A woman?" I asked incredulously.

"Why are you so surprised by it being a woman?"

I hesitated for a bit, but then said, "Well, Judaism ... sort of ... puts women down. That's why."

"Reb Shaul, that is a major misconception and needs to be addressed sometime. But not today. Right now we are discussing death and dying."

"OK, and this is from a woman," I said.

"Yes, Beruriah. The wife of Rabbi Meir and the daughter of Hananiah Ben Teradion, one of the 'Ten Martyrs' that we read about on *Tisha B'Av* and on *Yom Kippur.* Beruriah was a special person. There is a phrase in the book of Proverbs, chapter 31, verse 10, 'A woman of valor, who can find.' Rabbi Meir used this phrase to describe his wife because of something she did."

"What was that?"

"Two of their sons died suddenly late on a Friday afternoon. There was no time to bury the children before *shabbos* began, and burials are never done on the holy Sabbath. Beruriah was aware of what happened but Rabbi Meir was not. She knew that the deaths would sadden him greatly. And since this would detract from his enjoyment of *shabbos,* she hid the bodies in the attic. On *shabbos* Rabbi Meir inquired where the boys were, but being the clever woman that she was, she was able to keep her secret."

"But she was sort of lying to him."

"She knew there was nothing he could do on *shabbos* so the only thing that telling him would accomplish was to prolong his suffering. When *shabbos* ended she asked Rabbi Meir a question. If one is given a *pikadone* ...," *Rebbi* stopped and looked at me quizzically, "Have we covered the subject of *pikadone*?"

I answered, "Yes, we studied that. An object given for safe keeping ... usually as a guarantee for a loan."

"Correct. So, Beruriah asked her husband, if one is given a *pikadone,* can that person delay in returning it when the rightful owner comes to redeem it? He of course answered that it must be returned immediately, even the slightest delay is unacceptable because the *pikadone* does not belong to the person who holds it. She then revealed to him that their children had died. When he began grieving over his loss she reminded him of his answer to her question. She explained to him that we are given our mortal bodies by God for use during the time we are allotted on this earth. When He, the rightful owner, comes to reclaim them we cannot delay in the slightest, since the bodies were never ours. She explained that they were given their children as a *pikadone* from God and now He has chosen to come for them. For these actions Rabbi Meir described her as a 'woman of valor'.

"It must have been very tough for her during that *shabbos.*"

"Most certainly. But remember according to our tradition the suffering each of us feels in this world is thought to be a partial redemption for the pain and suffering that we would otherwise have to suffer in the world to come. Therefore our Rabbis have taught us that just as we say a blessing when good things happen to us, we should also say a blessing for the bad, because we are being redeemed."

"I'll try to remember that the next time a subcontractor messes up a job and it has to be done again. Or a bank loan does not come through on time and delays work."

"You must also remember that not all 'bad things' are truly bad. Sometimes we just do not have the insight to know that it is really a good thing."

"I don't understand," I said.

"For instance ... a man wants to go to the airport so he can fly to another city, but on the way he gets caught in traffic and his flight takes off without him. To him ... at that specific moment ... missing his flight was a 'bad thing'. However, what would happen if he subsequently learns that that particular airplane crashed. Obviously, this too, is a 'bad thing' for the people on the plane and their families. But now, what had initially been a 'bad thing' for him ... missing the plane ... suddenly becomes a 'good thing' because of this new perspective."

"So, only God truly knows what is 'bad' and what is 'good'."

"Absolutely. Only God knows. Just as it is only God that knows how much time He has given us in *olam hazeh*. While we are here we are commanded to do *mitzvahs* to show what type of people we are. We believe that this helps determine what will happen to us in *olam habah*. We don't understand why or how people die but we accept the fact that God does things with wisdom and mercy."

It was only four months since I had found those first customers for Ayelet's baked items.

They loved her stuff. They literally ate it up.

Her business is growing by leaps and bounds, much faster than we both could have imagined. The expression: Selling like hot cakes, is entirely appropriate. So, I told her that she had to get bigger facilities for her baking for three reasons. 1 – She was baking at the limits of her present kitchen and people were clamoring for more. 2 – She needed industrial sized machines and they would never fit in the space she had now. 3 – She needed a Department of Agriculture approval of her facilities if she wanted to continue selling her baked goods to the really big time customers.

Ayelet was reluctant to move her baking out of her house because it would mean that she would not be at home with her young children for long periods of the day. She insisted that she wanted to work out of her home.

The only way to solve the problem would be to 'expand' her present kitchen.

I pointed out that there were two major stumbling blocks that had to be overcome to make the expansion. The first, was that the strict building codes of the city would not allow a commercial bakery – even a small one – with all the traffic and noise – to be built in a residential neighborhood. The second, was money. Money, that Ayelet as yet did not have.

I came up with a very creative solution for the first problem by dividing the project into three parts.

First step – Building the 'new bakery': Ayelet's home was at the periphery of the subdivision and it backed up against a small strip mall. The owners of the adjacent property had agreed to sell her the part of their back parking lot that touched her property line. The piece of land was not very large but I was able to design a structure that, although cramped, would satisfy the Department of Agriculture requirements, and it would be the official address for the commercial bakery. Thus, all vehicular traffic – the deliveries and loading – the noisy machinery – would be in a permitted area.

Second step – The kitchen build: I designed a new large 'kitchen' at the rear of Ayelet's house in what was now a large enclosed porch. Officially it had nothing to do with the unit that I was going to build on the adjacent property, but if all went well she would eventually be doing most of her baking here.

Third step – The connecting corridor: If – and it was a big if – if I got the two other units built, I would make a covered walkway to join them together. Eventually this corridor would do double duty as a storage and work area.

Only if all the units were opened and working would Ayelet have ample usable space to make the bakery feasible. So, if God favored her, and Southfield's City Planning Commission and the city inspectors were willing to turn a blind eye to a few creative interpretations of some city ordinances, she stood a good chance of getting the bakery built.

I also came up with a solution to the money problem – I offered to loan her the cash or at least co-sign a bank loan. I didn't consider my suggestion as an act of charity. Before we set out with the building plan, we asked the management firm, now running the financial side of Ayelet's business, to analyze her potential market and to see if the expansion made sense economically. Their report showed that the way her stuff was being grabbed up, after the expansion, she should be able to return the money without any problem in about 24 months. But Mrs. Weinberg, being Mrs. Weinberg, felt that she was already too indebted to me and refused my financial help. She even made me promise that I would not do anything behind her back and loan her the money in some surreptitious manner. She felt that if she needed to get a loan from the bank, then she wanted to get it on her own merit.

*Why was Ayelet so obstinate?*

So here we were, myself and Ayelet, in the spacious foyer of the Twelve Mile Branch of Amity Bank. She was all *fahrputzed* and I had even put on a sports jacket. Nowadays, for me, fancy everyday clothes sort of peaked with jeans and a shirt with buttons. In my world, sports jackets and suits were reserved for Sabbath services or catered affairs.

The loan officer, Mr. Atkins, had gone off to look for Ayelet's file and had directed us to take seats next to the large potted palm at the side of the room. His dismissive demeanor and speech made us feel that we were menial supplicants coming before an all powerful ruler.

*Not the best way to attract loan customers.*

The barely discernible muzak coming over the bank's sound system was Mozart's Eine Kleine Nachtmusik set to strings. It was supposed to be restful and soothing, but apparently it did not calm Ayelet in the least. She said in a nervous whisper, "I can't ask this man for $600,000. He will never give it to me."

I turned my head towards her and said, "He isn't giving it to you. He is loaning it to you. That's his job. He's the loan officer and he has to get the money out there working or the bank won't show a profit."

"But the way he spoke ... I think he will turn me down," said Ayelet fidgeting in her chair.

"I told you, you don't have to go through all this."

"And I told you ... no. I won't take money from you."

I noted that Atkins' large desk – made from some kind of blonde colored wood – sat all by itself in the middle of the bank's spacious atrium and not in the clerical section with all the other desks. I suppose who ever designed the layout of this place did so intentionally but I was not sure why they did it. Maybe they figured if Atkins' desk was right in the middle of the bank, any over-emotional customers would not make a big scene if they got turned down for a loan.

Strange.

Finally, after about fifteen minutes, the loan officer returned to his desk and flipped open the file as he sat down. The short scrawny man wore a dark blue gabardine suit in a style that had been popular a decade earlier. He had a gaunt face, an almost totally bald pate, and a nose that would have done the Wicked Witch of the West proud. The lack of hair made it difficult to guess his age but I suspected that he was about sixty. Over the last twenty years I had seen the man's hairline recede as he worked his way up from teller. But it looked as if he had reached the end of the promotion ladder because he had been the loan officer at this branch for quite a while. He totally ignored us as he rudely studied the papers in the file.

I had met the guy a few times over the years. He was not a native of the area and there was a certain twang to his speech that said he was raised on hominy grits and chitlins. The way the fellow was behaving right now suggested that Mr. Atkins considered himself to be the ruling monarch of the bank's loan division kingdom. This was his domain and he ruled it with his little pink fist. He wanted you to think that he alone decided who would be graced with a loan and who would be cast into the pecuniary dungeon. I guess he liked to ignore the fact that he was just a salaried employee of the bank and had to report to the loan committee. Most likely his life partner was the alpha-dog at home and this was the only place where he could play at being the king of the roost.

His Royal Highness, King Atkins, straightened the papers in the file by bouncing them on edge and then carefully replaced them in the cardboard folder. He lifted his head, smiled smugly at both of us, and twitched his fingers in the air to indicate that we could now approach the chairs in front of his desk. After we took our seats, he said glibly, "Mrs. Weinberg, after careful consideration of your request, I'm afraid we can't approve the loan. Sorry," he said with finality and flipped the file closed.

Atkins continued to smile – he was enjoying this.

*The little bastard.*

We were both shocked by the brusque manner in which the loan officer had dismissed us. I recovered first and asked, “Isn’t there a loan committee or someone we can speak to ... so that they can reconsider this loan?”

“I’m afraid not. The decision is final,” said Atkins with a nod of his head and a smirk.

Ayelet gathered her own papers and said as she rose, "Thank you anyway."

I leaned toward the loan officer, "Excuse me, could I ask you something?”

“Why certainly,” said the bank official with his ridiculous smile still plastered across his face.

Ayelet began walking towards the exit, "Come Mr. Lincoln. He said no, and his mind seems to be made up."

I was pissed off by this guy's attitude. I rose from my chair and handed my car keys to Ayelet as I said quietly, "Could you wait in the car for a moment, I'll be right out?"

Ayelet whispered in my ear, "Can't you see that arguing with him is not going to help? I will not give him the satisfaction of begging, just so he can say no again."

"I promise you, I won't argue with him. Just wait for me."

"Remember, you promised. I don't want *your* money."

I was a seething cauldron of anger, but when I returned to the desk, I exhibited an external calm, "Your name is Newell, isn't? Can I call you Newell?"

"The name is Neville," corrected the bank officer.

"Oh, it's Neville ... I'm sorry ... what a lovely name," I said with my own wide mocking smile. "Now you know me ... I have been doing business with this bank for over twenty years."

"Until your company moved out of state and closed its account with us," corrected Neville.

*So, this guy did know who I was.* "Yes, that's true. But many, many of my clients took out building loans at this bank ... at this very desk ... and they had much less collateral than Mrs. Weinberg. We've shown you the contracts for her baked goods and she will have no trouble to pay back the loan. Why was she turned down?"

"Well, let's see. Half of the money is for the commercial lot, and that is undervalued, so that is not a problem. But the other half is for the construction and equipment and all she has for real collateral is her old house. It's appraised at only $285,000, which is less than the remainder of the loan. Putting in that over-sized kitchen in her house might even bring down the property value. In this unstable real estate market, the loan might not be covered. Also, half of that money is for bakery equipment. If she defaults we might be able to sell that stuff off, but once she works with those machines it becomes used equipment and we wouldn't get ten cents on the dollar. So ... no loan. And look at her credit record. Why, she was still on food stamps four months ago. I'd be crazy to give her a loan."

"That's *kasha varnishkes*."

"What did you say?"

"I said that's bullshit. What's the real reason for turning down this loan?"

Atkins hesitated for a moment. He looked furtively from side to side and then asked skeptically, "Are you recording this or something? Are you?"

"No, Neville, I wish I was but I am not."

"You know what? I believe you. Come with me," said Neville as he rose from his chair. The bank officer took me through a door marked 'Staff Only', into what seemed to be an employees lounge. There was a small sofa and one padded chair along one wall and the opposite side had a kitchen counter with a coffee maker and a radio. At the rear there was a door that led to a rest room. Atkins switched on the radio, tuned it to a loud rock station, and closed the door. He motioned for me to approach closer and over the din coming from the speaker said into my ear, "Now I trust you even more." Atkins put the smug smile back on his face and said, "You want to know why I turned down the loan? It's really simple. The loan committee reviewed the request and determined that it was a toss-up. So they left it up to me. And I simply don't trust her kind of folks."

"Her kind of folks?" I asked in disbelief. "What kind of folks is that exactly?"

*Was this the twenty-first century in the land of the free?*

"You know what I mean."

Good old boy Neville was either one super-dumb redneck antisemite, or else he was trying to provoke me. I was pissed off enough to physically assault good ole Neville and tear him another aperture for eliminating bodily waste. But that was exactly what Atkins wanted.

There was no visible security camera in the room, nor was there a bank-cop at the door, but one signal from the loan officer would bring the Berkley municipal police down on me in under two minutes. "No I don't Neville. Explain it to me," I said loudly, trying to be heard over the bass guitar's abrasive beat.

"She's one of them holy roller Jews. Their men go around in black coats and have beards like the Amish. The women all wear wigs and stuff. I don't trust them. Everyone knows that they will cheat the gold right out of your back teeth if you don't watch them every minute."

Only with great difficulty was I was able to control myself enough so that I did not explode. If I lost my cool I knew that it would only make matters worse. All I managed to say was, "I don't believe this."

Neville's smile got even wider, "Well, you better believe it. Because, that is my decision. No loan."

I gritted my teeth and said, "Isn't there anyone I can speak to in the administration of the bank?"

"I'm an up-front kind of guy. I'm just telling you how it is. You can speak to anyone you friggin' want to ... everyone knows that you put in that letter of recommendation for the loan ... but you don't have any juice with this bank anymore."

Time to confront this guy with the truth, "Why do I have the feeling that it isn't just the holy roller Jews you don't like. I bet if you had a choice you wouldn't even give me a loan."

"As I said, I'm an up-front guy. Until I saw you with that little beanie on your head, I didn't know you were one of them. But now ... if it was my choice ... no, I wouldn't give you a loan."

I wanted to smack the smile right off of Neville's face, but I knew that if I hit the guy I would be arrested for assault and Ayelet's chances for a loan would go right down the toilet. Instead I smiled back and said, "Must bug you to hell to have to work in the one branch that is smack-dab right in the center of a predominantly Jewish neighborhood and most of your customers are Jewish."

"You are most certainly right. About the only pleasure I get is turning down the odd loan when I can," said Atkins with his mocking smile.

"Well, thank you, Neville, for this most enlightening conversation. But I hope you won't take this personally if I try to talk to some of the bank's administration anyway."

"You be my guest. And come back and see Amity Bank some time real soon."

With commendable calm and just the touch of a threat I said, "Just you hold on to that file. You might want to contact Mrs. Weinberg, if you change your mind."

Atkins shook his prominent nose from side to side and said confidently, "I don't think that will be necessary."

As I exited the bank, I was sure that there was steam coming out of my ears. To vent some of my pent up fury, I slammed my palm against the back of my car. At the sound of the loud thud, Ayelet whipped her head around in surprise and motioned to me with a rocking palm, asking what had transpired. I signaled for her to be patient as I dialed a number on my cell phone. The call was answered on the third ring, "Hello Max, this is Steve."

"Steve, *vuse macht a yid* (Yiddish for how is a Jew doing)?" said the old man over the phone.

"Max, I need a favor."

"What can I do for you? Something else concerning Mrs. Weinberg? I already gave you all the leads I've got for her baked goods."

"Yeah, I know. And I appreciate it."

"What's to appreciate? Just about every one of them called and thanked me for setting them up with her cakes. They love it ... the customers love it. I hope you are getting a crumpet or two out of this."

"I'm not doing this for money."

"I wasn't talking about money."

"You old pervert."

"Guilty as charged ... what do you need?"

"Max, do you do you have any money in Amity Bank?"

"I may have a dollar or two with them ... what's the problem?" asked the old man warily.

I spent the next few minutes telling Max about Ayelet's loan request and Mr. Neville Atkins, the bank's charming loan officer. When I was finished, Max closed the conversation by saying into the phone, "Consider it done. I have a score to settle with his kind of folks."

"That's exactly what Atkins said. But I haven't told you anything about his ethnic background."

"You don't have to. Antisemites come in all colors and races," said the old man with determination.

I turned off the phone and slid into the driver's seat. I said towards the back seat, "*Im yirtzeh HaShem* (God willing) I think maybe the bank will be reconsidering the loan."

Ayelet asked, "Who did you just call?"

I pulled out of the lot, "One of God's angels."

# 14

## *This never happened*

IT WAS AMAZING the way his men quickly tore out the rear wall of my house and put up the roof supports and then this see-through plastic wall so that I could continue working in my kitchen. Through it I can see that Mr. Lincoln is here very early this morning. He must have come directly from *minyan.* I am right – I can still see the *tefilin* marks on his arm. I already have three things in the oven and if he expects me to stop my baking just to make him something to eat, he has another think coming. No, he is just wandering around the site looking at what the crews did yesterday afternoon.

I should never have agreed to let Mr. Lincoln be the contractor for this project. It would have been better if I had found someone else to build the expansion. But Mr. Lincoln insisted that he felt obligated because he was the one that had convinced me to go ahead with all this. He also explained that I really had no choice. The loan – which like a miracle came through – I have no idea how – would never cover the cost of the land, the new building, the renovation, and the needed equipment, without him handling the contracting work for free.

I asked the *rebbetzen* and she said it would be all right. She reasoned that the work that has to be done requires an architect and a contractor. However, since most of these professionals are men, it meant that while the construction was under way there would always be some man looming around my house. So, it might as well be

Mr. Lincoln. At least we know him and – a very big and – it would save me money.

He is coming in wearing his funny construction helmet.

"Good morning, Ayelet."

"Hello, Mr. Lincoln."

"When are you going to call me Steve?"

"When it is appropriate, Mr. Lincoln. When it is appropriate."

"You're a tough case, Mrs. Weinberg."

Ouch. He is making fun of me. "Yes, I am Mr. Lincoln. What surprises do we have today?"

Slowly and seriously he said, "Today we might have a very big surprise."

What is he referring to? He never talked so solemnly before. "What kind of surprise?" I asked warily.

"Well ..." He seems to be choosing his words carefully. "Today the building inspector is making his first inspection. What we are doing is actually three separate projects with three separate permits. We're officially building your *commercial bakery* just over your property line in that little adjacent plot of *commercial land* we purchased. We are also putting in this new kitchen, which is supposedly unrelated to the bakery that we're building. Finally, we are going to be making the covered walkway that will be connecting the two."

"You have already explained this to me."

"Yes, we did it that way because of the zoning problems. But anyone looking at the plans can see that the three are actually connected ... and ... and ..."

"And ... what?"

"... and ... even though the 'official bakery' is on commercial land, it could be seen as if you are building commercial on residential property. We could be up ... a certain creek without a paddle. It's a toss-up if we are in a violation of our permits."

"You mean the inspector can stop the building work?"

"Oh yeah, and toss in a big fine as well."

"So, why did you go ahead with this?" I asked in alarm. "We've already spent a fortune of money."

"I always told you that there might be a slight problem."

"Slight? This is not so slight," I said in alarm.

"Well ... usually they look the other way."

He was not telling me everything. He was holding something back. "And ... what else, Mr. Lincoln?"

"Yeah, there is something else."

"What?"

"Well, the plans I submitted for this part of the work say it's a new kitchen build, and that is what this morning's inspection is all about. But, once the inspector arrives and gets a gander at the whole site he's going to put two and two together and know that this is not a simple kitchen construction. Especially when he sees we're going to put in a ten foot brick hearth oven ... which is adding almost 20,000 on to the cost."

"If you want good bread, you have to have a brick hearth oven," I explained.

"I'm sure you need it. It just isn't usually part of your normal home kitchen build."

"So?"

Mr. Lincoln paused and then said, "He may close us down."

"Do you mean to tell me that I have been breaking the law?" *Am I now a criminal?*

"Depends on how you look at it."

"How does the law look at it?"

"Basically, the law is whatever the inspector says it is. But ... you need Department of Agriculture approval in order to get a license for food preparation. And for that approval you need a bakery in a building that is up to code and certified by the building inspector."

Playing around with city ordinances was not how I conducted my life. "Why don't I just make do without the agriculture department approval?"

"The big time fancy restaurants and caterers can't get their baked goods from a place that doesn't have DOA approval. If one of their diners falls over dead while eating one of your pastries ... bingo ... no insurance and they would be liable. They would also probably lose their license."

"So, maybe we should just forget about the expansion and we'll stick with what we've got."

“Can't do that. The places that are buying your stuff now are all looking the other way knowing that you should be getting the DOA approval soon. No approval ... there goes the business."

Suddenly I am getting very stressed. "When is the inspector coming?"

Mr. Lincoln looked at his watch, "Any minute now."

Any minute? I could be wiped out even before I actually got started. Suddenly I’m having trouble breathing. "Why didn't you tell me sooner?"

"Could you have done anything about it?"

*How would I have been able to do anything?* "No."

"Would you have been nervous about it from the time I told you?"

"Of course I would. I’m almost sick from hearing what you said just now."

Mr. Lincoln pointed his finger at me, "There's your answer. I didn't tell you because you would only worry and it wouldn’t change a thing. This way I worried for the both of us."

Mr. Lincoln is making me more indebted to him every day. Ah, the cakes are done. Perhaps he is hungry. "Would you like a little snack?"

"I can never turn down one of your cakes ... sure. And keep a piece or two handy for the inspector. It can't hurt."

The inspector arrived ten minutes later. He carried his official looking clip board in his hand and had a set of the building plans under his arm. He was about the same height as Mr. Lincoln but was at least ten years older and much stouter. He buckled his pants belt well under his protruding stomach. The inspector put on his hard hat as he entered the site and greeted Mr. Lincoln, who then offered him a hefty slice of my cake. The man gulped it all down in three bites and then began his site inspection. Surprisingly, Mr. Lincoln left the man alone and came into the kitchen. "We're in luck. I sort of know this guy. He's fair, so we might do okay. He has this one quirk in that he likes to make the initial inspection on his own. If there are any questions he will come to ask. So for now we just wait."

"What is he looking for?"

"About a billion things. From the width of the support walls, to the access holes for the electric. There are specifications for just about everything. He wants to be sure that this building will still be safely standing and in good shape twenty years from now."

I can't stand the tension, "I wasn't this nervous on my wedding day."

"Take it easy. Everything will be fine ... take your mind off the inspection."

Easy for him to say. I can see the inspector poking his head into all the foundation holes, shining his flashlight up through gaps in the ceiling, and making little scribbly notes on his clipboard. I am never going to pass the inspection. "How am I ever going to get my mind off of the inspection? I'm on *shpilkas.*"

“Okay, let's see, what can we talk about that will calm you down?” asked Mr. Lincoln rhetorically. “I know ... baking.”

“What do you know about baking?” I asked, surprised at his choice of subject.

"Me ... I haven't got a clue about baking. But I am interested in how you know so much. I've met lots of women that have some sort of special cake or pie, but with you, everything is so terrific. It's like a miracle. Did you go to baking school or something?"

Many people have asked me that and I have always just shrugged off their question. It's so difficult for people to understand. Every time I've attempted to tell anyone what baking means to me, they just don't seem to get it. Perhaps Mr. Lincoln will be the exception. "Okay, I'll try to explain. First of all don't laugh."

"Why would I laugh?"

"I never went to any sort of *official* baking school. I just attended the normal Jewish day schools and then high school. I had a year in a *michlala* in Israel. But that's it. No special baking courses."

"So where did you learn?"

"It started with my *Bubbi* Sarah, *aleha ha'shalom* (may she be in peace). She was a terrific baker. My parents worked and I would go over to her house every day after school. From about age six I began helping her bake. She did bread as well as cakes. Her teaching methods were simple. At every step of the recipe she would explain how each ingredient contributes to the taste or texture of whatever it was we were baking. It was important to know what happens if you put in too much or too little. She would make me taste each ingredient as we put it in the recipe and then she would ask me to find that taste in the finished product. After a few years it got so that if I just tasted a baked item I could tell you all the ingredients and their general proportions. After a few more years I could even tell you at what temperature it was baked and how long it was in the oven."

"You became a baked goods blood hound," commented Mr. Lincoln.

"Are you making fun of me?"

"Absolutely not. I'm just saying how remarkable your talent is," he explained. "Then what happened?"

"Well, when I was twelve my *bubbi* passed away. She died young ... at seventy five. I inherited all her baking paraphernalia and my mother nearly had apoplexy because we did not really have room in our small kitchen for all the stuff. Every Thursday night I would bake until the early morning hours. At first I would make all the things my *bubbi* made and everyone said my baking was as good as hers. Then I started experimenting. I read cook books and I copied recipes from magazines. I baked and I baked. It got so I could look at a recipe and I could see immediately how to improve it without ever having made the bread or cake. When I tried the recipes I would increase or change an ingredient or alter the baking temperature or even vary the temperature during the baking", I said with excitement. *Am I making fool of myself?* "It's hard to explain."

"What is?"

"I can sense the finished product without making it. Just by reading the recipe I can almost taste the bread, or cake, or cookie. I can also see what any changes in the recipe will do to the finished product. Sometimes people will give me a favorite recipe and when I prepare it I make some small change in the ingredients or the method used and the stuff comes out even better than the original. Do you see what I mean?"

"Yeah, I think I do," said Mr. Lincoln with a nod of his head.

"You do?" I asked in surprise.

"Yeah," he said. "When I look at plans for a building, in my mind I can see the finished building already standing. Sometimes the architect will make a mistake in certain specifications and it will stick out in my eye. I can see where there will be problems in the construction and I see what changes are needed so that the building will get built the way the architect intended and not what the plans actually show. You do something very similar."

"Exactly," I exclaimed. He is the first person who understands my relationship to baking. *Amazing!*

"Uh oh, here comes the inspector," said Mr. Lincoln, calling me back to the reality of the moment. "He wants to talk to me. Stay here. I'll be back soon."

Through the clear plastic, I could see Mr. Lincoln as he walked about the site with the inspector, motioning with his hands explaining all sorts of technical things. The inspector continued to scribble on his clipboard.

*I am so nervous!!*

They toured around the site for about fifteen minutes until they shook hands and the inspector got into his car and drove away.

Mr. Lincoln has his hands in his pockets and he is looking down earnestly at the floor. His body language says that he does not have good news to impart. Oh well, if God did not want it to happen, then it just won't happen. I might as well get it over with, "So?"

"So ... he found at least a half a dozen things ... that he wants changed," said Mr. Lincoln solemnly.

"I knew it. I knew it," I said nodding my head in despair. "We never stood a chance. He would never ..." Did he say changed? He didn't say we failed the inspection. "If we make the changes ... do we pass the inspection?"

Mr. Lincoln shrugged his shoulders sadly and then after a pause he smiled broadly and said, "Yes, we pass the inspection! Mrs. Weinberg's Specialty Baked Goods is going to happen."

We passed! Wow! I'm going to have a baking business! How wonderful! He was pulling my leg, but I forgive him. I'm so happy. He made this all possible, "Thank you ... thank you for everything."

On impulse ... without any conscious thought ... out of sheer happiness ... I leaned forward, kissed Mr. Lincoln on the cheek, and gave him a big hug.

*Oh my God. What did I just do?*

I backed away, assuredly red as beet. I cannot speak. *What can I do?* I look at Mr. Lincoln and say earnestly, “That was a mistake. I wasn't thinking. We will never ever say anything ... about what I just did. To anyone. You have to promise.”

Mr. Lincoln held up his palm as if taking an oath and said solemnly, “I promise. Not a word.”

# 15

## *Cut to the chase*

AS I ENTERED THE KITCHEN I could hear Mrs. Leibowitz let out a sigh of relief. "Okay, okay, Mrs. Leibowitz ... stop panicking," I said to calm her. "What's the problem?"

The woman responded with, "Tank God, you angel."

Ayelet's assistant was fifty something-year-old mountain of a woman. Two or three inches taller than me and way more massive. She possessed thick muscular arms and could probably lift me clear off my feet using just one hand without even breathing hard. A bright red bandanna covered her coal black hair, which was somehow piled on top of her head and a big wide – very wide – white apron – covered with smudges of flour and fillings – was wrapped around her abundant girth. She had her sleeves rolled up above her elbows and was busy dabbing some sort of thick red gelatinous goop onto tiny squares of dough. Whatever she was making looked quite unappetizing in its present state, but I was sure that if it was Ayelet's recipe, once those blips of goop and swatches of dough got baked they would be delicious.

"I am definitely not an angel," I said. "You said you smelled gas?"

"For sure gas," she said. "You smell better over by proofing cabinet."

The proofing cabinet had been one of Ayelet's special requests for the new kitchen/bakery. She insisted that in order to get consistently good results with her yeast doughs, she needed an area which would allow the dough to rise in an environment with a controlled temperature and humidity. Commercial proofing cabinets cost quite a few thousand dollars and most were way too big for Ayelet's new kitchen. So, I designed one myself. I had the fabricator construct a large stainless steel box with a clear glass door. The temperature and humidity were regulated by circulated air over the gas heating coil located behind the unit. The cabinet was intended for the new kitchen, but it had been delivered early and my crew had jury rigged it in what had once been the breakfast nook of Ayelet's old kitchen. Mrs. Leibowitz was correct – there was a smell of gas coming from the cabinet. The only problem was that the temporary gas fitting was at the back of the unit and because the box had to accommodate large volumes of heavy dough, it was made of thick stainless steel and weighed a few hundred pounds. Two husky men working with a dolly had been needed to move the thing. If I tried to shift it on my own all I would get would be a double hernia and I still would not get a glimpse of the gas connection.

I looked around and I could see that the kitchen had at least four other gas fueled appliances and another dozen electrical units. Any open flame from a pilot light or a spark from one of the appliances could ignite the leaking gas and send everything in the house to kingdom come. It would not be a good idea to have all of the new construction go up like a Fourth of July rocket. Also, the Weinberg family would not be overly pleased when their home went into orbit. First things first. "Mrs. Leibowitz, while I shut off the gas main, you get busy turning off and pulling the plugs on all the electrically powered equipment."

"For cabinet?" she asked.

"No, for the whole kitchen," I answered.

"You can't shut gas. I am middle of baking," she exclaimed.

"Yes, I can ... shut off the gas. Because if I don't shut off the gas, the entire house, with you and me and everything in it, may explode and be blown to smithereeens. After you turn off the electrical stuff, make sure all the knobs and dials for all the ovens and burners and anything that runs on gas are on the off position."

"But you going to shut off main valve?"

"Yes, I am ... but then when we fix whatever it is that is broken ... if we leave any of the gas valves to the ovens or the burners in the open position ... when the gas gets turned back on, the room will fill with gas again and we risk an explosion once more."

"How long I be vit-out gas?"

"An hour ... maybe two. I have to get my gas man to come over."

"Mrs. Weinberg, she not going to like dis."

Maybe she would not like it at first, but it was better to shut down the bakery, than be left with a large crater where her home used to be. I made a few calls and arranged for the gas man to come out right away with his crew.

I figured the reason that the emergency call had come from Mrs. Leibowitz and not Ayelet was because she was still a little embarrassed about our little après inspection 'hug & kiss' incident. The gap that was growing between us was slowly reaching the size of the Grand Canyon. Whenever she was forced to speak with me over the phone, I could sense the awkwardness in our conversations. Even though, in my mind, nothing had really happened, she was acting as if she had committed a terrible sin and had to hide it from the world. Creating a mountain out of a mole hill. *These charedis are out of their minds.* The whole incident was a tempest in a teapot. To make anything of what had happened was simply ridiculous and I was certain that given time, the whole affair would pass into the archives of forgotten history. Until then, it appeared that Ayelet was going to use Mrs. Leibowitz as a go between. But right now she was nowhere in sight. "Where is Mrs. Weinberg?" I asked.

Mrs. Leibowitz searched for a response and finally answered, "She go ... zome place."

The way she answered made me think that she was concealing something. "Some place? What kind of some place?"

"Nahting special," she said defensively.

"Well you had better call her and let her know that all her baking is going to be delayed for an hour at least."

"Vy you don't call her," suggested Mrs. Leibowitz.

"What's the matter? Are you suddenly afraid of Ayelet?"

"No ... is just better you call."

Considering the new chasm that had developed in our relationship, I could not understand why it would be better if I was the one that contacted her, but I took out my phone and dialed the number anyway. I was immediately shunted to her voice mail. *That's strange*. Ayelet was a big stickler about keeping her phone open and available in case anything was wrong with the kids. "No luck," I said. "Did she leave any other number?"

"Yes," she said nodding towards the doorway. "Look over on message board."

There, at the top of the white board, where she wrote all her messages and reminders, was a number written in Ayelet's neat hand. I looked at the number and for some reason it seemed familiar to me but I could not immediately make the connection. I dialed the number and was answered with, "X-Ray Department, may I help you?"

I immediately realized why the number rang a bell.

A shocking feeling of déjà vu welled up inside me.

It was the x-ray Department of Beaumont Hospital where Rebecca had been hospitalized off and on during the last two months of her life. The exchange was the same.

It took a moment for me to recover so that I could stammer, “I'm ... I'm ... looking for Mrs. Ayelet Weinberg. Is she there? Can she come to the phone?”

“I'm just a volunteer here. Let me see what I can find out,” said the woman cheerfully. I heard the thumpety-bump-bump as she put the phone down on the desk. Her upbeat answer and enthusiastic response was so unexpected. Most hospital telephone greeters used a set script decreed by the public relations department. The expected response would normally have been a bland: ‘I'm sorry I do not have that information,' or ‘I cannot give out that information.' This lady seemed so much more helpful and polite. Must be because she is a volunteer.

After a minute or two the woman returned to the phone, “She can't come to the phone right now. She just went in for her examination. In about a half hour ... when she comes out ... before she goes to the operating room ... I will let her know that you were looking for her. Whom shall I say called?”

*Why is she going to the operating room? What is going on?* “Is there someone else ... accompanying her ... that I can speak to?"

"No. No one," said the volunteer with real concern. "Most people come with someone, but she came in on her own. But it shouldn't be a problem. The surgery will be in the ambulatory surgery center. After a couple of hours or so, she should be all right to take a cab home on her own."

"Could you tell me what surgery she is in for?" I inquired.

The woman did not answer.

“What kind of surgery?” I asked with concern.

She probably just realized that she had made a boo-boo and had divulged more than was allowed. The woman finally responded, "I'm sorry, sir. I don't think I can give out that information over the phone."

"I understand. Could you tell her that Steve Lincoln called," I felt more than a bit confused as I clicked off.

Most likely, the procedure, whatever it was, was some sort of simple thing and there was nothing to worry about. But Ayelet was Ayelet. She had this bee in her bonnet that she did not want to be beholding to anyone. She was always trying to show confidence and control that she did not really have.

Actually, it was a natural human response. Most folks attempted to do everything on their own and if they could, did not ask others for help. Imagine a person out on a boat or a raft, who for some stupid reason gets caught in a raging current and is about to go over a high waterfall. Any moment the guy would plunge to his death and get creamed on the rocks below. You call out to offer assistance, but because he feels embarrassed about getting himself into the mess, his typical idiotic response would be, 'Nah. I got this covered. Thanks for asking.'

Ayelet was just like that ... but worse. Before she opened her baking enterprise, her financial situation had been more than a little precarious. Yet, when you spoke with her, you would never have known it. She was a real stoic, but sometimes her yearning for independence made her do stupid things.

*I had a terrible feeling this was one of those stupid things.*

"Mrs. Weinberg ... she say she be back later in afternoon," said Mrs. Leibowitz. "She ask I stay vit kids ven come back from school until she come."

"Mrs. Leibowitz, did you know that Mrs. Weinberg is in the hospital right now?" I asked.

"I not supposed to know nahting ... but I see how she so nervous lately ... and den I vatch her make all arrangements for Racheli to be by babysitter. Den, I heard her say to cab driver she vaz going hospital."

"Didn't you ask her about it?"

"Of course I ask. I ask iz everyting all right and she say everyting iz fine. But I know everything iz not fine."

"I'm going to the hospital," I said.

"Vat about gas leak?"

"Don't go turning on any of the electrical appliances and don't strike any matches. Open all the windows and you'll be fine. My men will be here very soon."

"I be okay. You go ... take care Mrs. Weinberg."

I figured there was a possibility that Ayelet could already be in surgery so I parked in the lot adjacent to the ambulatory center. There were half a dozen people sitting in the waiting area of the surgery center but no one was manning the reception desk. I knew I might be waiting quite a while until someone showed, so I pushed open the doors marked 'Restricted – Do Not Enter'. This got me into the peri-operative area, containing the patient cubicles – where the patients were held before and after surgery.

A nurse wearing bright pink surgical scrubs was sitting at the main desk. Ever vigilant she spotted me and said, "Excuse me sir, you can't come in here."

"I'm sorry," I said apologetically. "There was no one sitting outside. I just have a question."

"Then you should have waited until someone came out," she scolded politely. "This area is for patients. Unless you are family or accompanying someone for surgery, you can't be in here."

"I am just looking for someone. Ayelet Weinberg?" I queried.

The nurse swung around in her seat to scan a large white board blocked off for the center's different operating rooms. For each room there were patient's names, doctor's names, time, and procedure. The nurse quickly turned back to me and said, “She has not come over yet from the x-ray department. She should be here any minute.”

As I left the area my terse reply was a barely civil, “Thank you.”

There was a sinking feeling of helplessness as another bout of déjà vu kicked in. I had seen the whiteboard behind the nurse and it did not take a rocket scientist to scan across the board and find Ayelet's listing. Dr. Kaufman was her surgeon, she would be in room number 4, and was scheduled for a wire-guided breast biopsy. This was exactly how it had begun with Rebecca. Her doctor told us, 'A simple breast biopsy. Nothing to worry about.' How terrified Rebecca had been and I had been at her side. Ayelet must be hysterical having to go through all this on her own. If I was the one that had to have surgery I would be having an apoplectic fit.

I knew it – she was doing something very stupid.

I had no difficulty in reaching the x-ray department because after my weeks and months with Rebecca in this very hospital, I knew my way around the institution's myriad of corridors. The friendly volunteer that I had spoken with earlier was not around and I was greeted by the regular snippy receptionist of the Medical Imaging Department.

“Mrs. Weinberg is still in the procedure room but she should be out shortly,” said the clerk officiously.

Rebecca had had this very same procedure done to her. It had been a small breast tumor – so tiny that it had only been an incidental finding on a mammogram and the surgeon could not even feel it with his fingers. Fine metallic wires were inserted under x-ray guidance to show the position of the breast tumor so that the surgeon could be sure that he excised all the suspicious areas. It was sort of like a surgical GPS system.

I waited in the x-ray reception area until I saw Ayelet come out to the waiting room. She was dressed in her normal street clothes and that included one of her bulky shapeless sweaters, so even if there were any bandages they were well hidden. I figure if drug dealers could get their 'mules' to wear this type of sweater – and if they got past the sniffer dogs – they could smuggle in tons of drugs and no one would be the wiser.

Ayelet spotted me across the room.

In the next fraction of a second her face registered a series of emotions. At first there was a look of shock, followed by the briefest smile, and ended finally with absolute mortification. She walked over to where I was sitting and in a demanding whisper asked, "What are you doing here?"

I stood to face her and asked in return, "Ayelet, why are you here all by yourself?"

"That is not your concern," she answered sternly.

"Is there someone here with you?" I asked. "If there is ... I'm out the door."

Ayelet hesitated for a moment and then said angrily, "There is no one here, but that is my business. Why are *you* here?"

"Because, I was worried that you were all alone. And I was right."

"How did you find out I was in the hospital?" she demanded.

"Nobody spilled the beans," I explained. "Mrs. Leibowitz called me to fix a gas leak in your kitchen and I saw the contact number you left on the white board and when I called they told me it was the x-ray department. I put two and two together. Then she became worried and I was worried as well."

"I'm fine," she said with a forced smile. "I don't need anyone. It's just a little procedure. The doctor agreed with me and said I can do this on my own."

"Ayelet," I said compassionately. "Don't you think you are doing enough on your own already? I went through this with Rebecca. I think I know how scared you must be."

"It's really unnecessary."

*Typical Ayelet Weinberg response.* "I know it's not necessary but I want to be here if you will let me. Remember ... we broke windows together."

Ayelet looked away from me and did not answer. She just dropped her chin and nodded her head in agreement. We sat silently in the waiting room until an orderly came with a wheelchair and took her to the reception area at the ambulatory surgical center. After a short wait, Ayelet was escorted into the peri-operative area and I was allowed to enter a few minutes later to sit at her side. She had already changed into a patient gown and was sitting on a surgical gurney in her assigned cubicle. A nurse dressed in brightly colored scrubs with a bold floral print was just introducing herself and she took Ayelet through all the steps before the surgery.

Funny, just a few years ago everyone in the operating room dressed in drab green. Now the nurses' outfits were in vivid pinks and blues and had flowers and caricatures. Anything to cheer up the patients.

Miss Springtime Flowers asked Ayelet a million questions about her health and recorded her answers on the patient record displayed on the tablet computer in her hand. *Oh so modern.* The culmination of the intake procedure was when they laid her back down on the gurney, started an intravenous line in her arm, and injected some medication. The nurse said it was to quiet her nerves before the surgery but after only a few moments it seemed to be having the opposite effect. Ayelet became restless and soon began fidgeting and turning on the gurney.

"Is everything all right?" I inquired.

Ayelet was obviously in distress. With marked urgency she requested, "Call the nurse for me."

Something was not okay, "What's wrong?"

"Just call the nurse ... quickly," she said, closing her eyes as if she was suffering.

I went to get the nurse and when she approached the bed she asked Ayelet, "What's the problem?"

"Suddenly, I feel so anxious. Like, it is hard to breathe. The air feels so cold going into my lungs. I was feeling okay before, but now something is not right," said Ayelet in discomfort. Filling her lungs seemed to be painful.

"Don't worry," said the nurse trying to soothe her. "It's probably just a reaction to the pre-med drugs. We see that sometimes." She checked the heart monitor and said, "Yup ... your heart is beating a bit too quickly. I'll have the anesthesiologist give you something."

Some fellow wearing an old fashioned green scrub outfit came over to examine Ayelet – most likely this was the anesthesiologist. He had no name tag and never spoke to us or even introduced himself. For all I knew the guy could be the night janitor playing doctor. *Not very professional.* Whoever he was, the man in green wrote something on Ayelet's chart and few moments later the nurse injected another drug into the IV line.

Ayelet reached out and held the nurse, "Don't go ... please hold my hand."

The nurse grasped Ayelet's hand and patted it gently. Ayelet put her head back down on the pillow and closed her eyes again. After a moment she seemed to relax slightly. The nurse said, "There, you go. Your heart rate is coming down. You'll be fine. I'll need to have my hand back, because I have other patients to care for."

"No ... No ... please don't go," beseeched Ayelet, still keeping her eyes closed. "Stay here and hold my hand a little more."

The nurse began to signal silently for me to move closer to the bed. I pantomimed back that I did not think it was a good idea.

Big conflict.

It was obvious that the nurse wanted me to take over in the hand holding duties. But, knowing Ayelet, if she found me holding her hand she might go ballistic. I also knew that if I did not take the nurses place, when she finally did let go, it would leave Ayelet's hand flapping in the breeze and she would have a meltdown anyway. I was definitely between a rock and a hard place. Ayelet had to be calmed at any price, because if she became more agitated it would make her surgical experience a bigger nightmare than it already was. She had her eyes closed but I did not know for how long. I was not sure what I should do. My choice bore the risk of escalating into a confrontation akin to World War III. If Ayelet found out she could very well declare me a super duper persona non grata – I would become even more of a pariah – and she would further distance herself from me – if that was possible.

The nurse's signaling became more insistent and in the end I figured I had no choice but to move my chair up close to the gurney. As expected, the nurse took my hand and placed it on the mattress. Then she took Ayelet's hand and placed it into mine. After a moment's groping Ayelet grasped my hand firmly. She had her head back against the pillow, with her jaw clenched tight.

She never opened her eyes.

*Thank goodness for that.* Her breathing was in a regular cadence but it still seemed forced.

Ayelet just lay on the bed holding my hand until she went in for surgery and did not speak or open her eyes. I knew it had to be the pre-medication kicking in. For Ayelet to knowingly hold the hand of a man that was not her husband was tantamount to a Muslim *imam* walking with a pet pig on a leash. Obviously she was totally zonked or she would never have done it. But zonked or not I could not say that I found holding her hand objectionable.

# 16

## The end of the world

HOW COULD I HAVE DONE what I did? I am so brazen and pathetic. Just reminding myself makes me feel sick. That was not me. It was the medication. But if it was the drugs, why do I still remember everything so clearly? I recall suddenly being so nervous. The nurse held my hand and that helped some, but I couldn't let her go. And then – when my eyes were shut – she put my hand into Mr. Lincoln's. I knew she did it – but I still held on. I knew it was wrong, but I needed to hold someone's hand.

No, not any someone – I have to admit it – I needed someone that cares about me – me and my family.

Perhaps I am reading too much into the episode.

It was *pikuach nefesh*. It could have been *Rebbetzen* Kalmonowitz's hand.

But it was not.

Mr. Lincoln had been the one that held my hand.

But it did not end there.

If what I did before the surgery was not bad enough, I remember waking from the anesthesia and looking around the room for Mr. Lincoln. I wanted him to be there for me. When I couldn't find him I closed my eyes – I wouldn't have been able to do what I did if I had to look at him. I took my hand out from under the sheet and just laid it out flat on the bed. Moments later Mr. Lincoln was there. He took my hand in his and sat at my side. When the nurse finally came over to discharge me he released my hand and I opened my eyes. Neither of us has said a word.

Now he comes over twice a day, supposedly to check on the work on the kitchen construction, but I know he is concerned for me. I also know that he is aware that I held his hand knowing full well it was him. But we say nothing and make believe that it was just the medication.

It simply never happened.

But now I have another problem. It is a week since the surgery and today I must go to Dr. Kaufman's office to get the results of the biopsy. I put up a good front for the kids and for Mr. Lincoln, but inside I am a total wreck.

I know myself.

I will not be able to go through this on my own. But it's complicated. This is such a personal thing and I don't want anyone to know about my operation. The entire community already takes pity on me and my family. It's hard enough just trying to get through the normal day to day conversations and encounters. If I added my surgery to their list of concerns it would be intolerable.

I know I could ask the *rebbetzen.* She would drop everything to help me but she's done so much already and she'll worry even more than me. Besides, I know that she's busy today at the *Yeshiva*'s Women's Group function. I'm not really that close with anyone else. All my school friends have families and problems of their own and I don't want to burden them further. But I do need someone. So when I think about my situation, who do I know that would come with me and already knows about the surgery? The answer I come up with is always the same. I really have no choice.

Mr. Lincoln.

But after the hand holding incident how do I ask him?

What a coincidence – Mr. Lincoln just called and said he will be here in a few minutes to inspect the building work. *M'dabrim al hamishiach* (literally – you talk about the Messiah, but means – serendipity) – I just have to steel myself to the task of asking him and be brave.

That's his car pulling into the driveway. He doesn't use the front entrance anymore because he just has to check the construction area at the rear. Being prepared never hurt. I have his favorite chocolate filled croissants and a mug of coffee just the way he likes it. The door built into the plastic barrier makes it easy for me to get from the kitchen to the construction area. "Good morning, Mr. Lincoln," I said proffering the snack to him.

"Good Morning and thanks," he said taking the coffee and cake. "Did the men finish all the tile work in the dough area and the restroom yesterday?"

"Yes, they did. And they said I didn't have to wait for 24 hours before getting it wet."

"That's great. Just what I wanted. I told them to use the new synthetic grout. It's a little more expensive but it dries almost as quick as you can put it on and looks terrific."

"Mr. Lincoln ... can I ask ... a favor?" I inquired haltingly.

"Sure, anything."

"Are you busy later this afternoon?"

"No, I'm clear," he said with a nod of his head. "I have to prepare for my *chavrusah* with Rabbi Kalmonowitz tomorrow, but I can do that in the evening. Do you need someone to babysit the kids?"

"No, I need a ride somewhere."

"Is there something wrong with your car? I know a great mechanic."

"No, the car is fine. I have to go to the surgeon and I was hoping you could give me a ride."

"If your car is fine ... why don't you just drive ..." A sudden look of comprehension crossed his face and he added. "Oh yeah ... I see ... you need a ride. Sure I will be happy to give you a ride. What time?"

"I would like to leave at three, if that's all right with you?"

"Three o'clock it is."

Mr. Lincoln, as always, is on time.

I am so nervous I cannot speak in the car. In a few minutes my world may come to an end. My children may be without both a mother and a father. Why would *HaShem* want to punish my family so? Did I do anything wrong? Was it the kiss I gave Mr. Lincoln? I cannot believe that could be the reason. God knows that it was unintentional. But, what about holding his hand before and after the surgery? That was *pikuach nefesh.* It was like holding my father's hand. *How have I transgressed?*

"I suppose you are going to get the results of your biopsy," said Mr. Lincoln from the front seat. "How are you holding up?"

Can't he see that I am a nervous wreck? I must look dreadful. I have to make the effort. "Okay, the surgery went very smoothly."

"Well, all I can say is that I have my fingers crossed for you."

"Crossing fingers is not a very Jewish way of showing concern."

"Yeah, you're right. I'll uncross my fingers. But you know what I mean."

"Yes, I do," I said with a puny smile.

"Ayelet, if I was the one going in to get the results of a biopsy, you could be assured that I would be wetting my pants. So, if you are a little nervous it's absolutely normal."

He does really understand. Thank goodness. "Well, yes I am ... just a little."

Mr. Lincoln turned his head towards me, "So ... it's just a little."

"To be perfectly honest ... no, it's not just a little. I am going out of my mind worrying." I looked up at the roof of the car to hold back the tears, "I think that at any moment I might just break down and cry. It's even hard for me to breathe. That's how nervous I am."

"First of all calm down. Worrying about the result is not going to make things any better."

*He does not understand what I am going through.* "Easy for you to say," I answered impatiently.

Mr. Lincoln did not speak at first, but after a moment he said, "I've had some experience with this."

*How could I have forgotten?* His wife died from breast cancer. How stupid of me to bring him into this. It must be very hard for him. I am totally selfish. "I'm so sorry. I forgot."

"That's okay, just remember I am a certified *mavin* in this field. The odds that you have anything serious are very small."

"You're just saying that to make me feel better," I said, trying to control my emotions.

"No, I'm not. You're young and luckily the tiny tumor was picked up on a routine mammogram in an area not suspected of any disease. It's a one in ten thousand chance that it's cancer. And even if it is cancer it is so small that surgery will be curative in over 95% of the cases."

"How do you know how small it was?"

Mr. Lincoln looked sheepishly over the seat back, "I peeked at your chart when you were knocked out by the anesthesia. Sorry."

I was happy that he had. In his own way he is now helping me. "Are you sure? Is the information correct?" I asked anxiously.

"What did your doctor say?"

"He said the same thing."

"There, you go. If two geniuses say the same thing ... it's gotta be right."

"So tell me Mr. Genius, my doctor went to medical school ... where did *you* get your knowledge?"

"From the internet ... where else?"

"You're right," I said. "I know all those statistics. But my mind says one thing and my emotions tell me another. I guess I'm just going crazy."

"Ayelet, you're anything but crazy. A little *mishugah* ... maybe, but not funny farm crazy. So try to relax ... you're gonna be just fine."

I took a deep breath, "Okay ... I'll try to relax."

We pulled into the parking area of my surgeon's office and Mr. Lincoln asked, "Would you like me to wait in the car?"

"Thank you for being so discreet, but I have to be a little bit more honest," I said surprising myself with my sudden courage. "We both know that I didn't ask you to come here just because I needed a ride or for you to wait in the car. I'm so worried about what the doctor might tell me and I would appreciate it if you would come in with me." There, I've said it. I cannot believe I was brave enough.

At first Mr. Lincoln did not answer but then he smiled, "You know if you need my help ... any time, any place ... I'll be there. Let's go in."

The modern décor of the doctor's office featured muted earth tones on the walls, carpeting, and curtains. As in all waiting areas there were seats strategically placed about the room, but these were large padded wooden chairs of an ultra modern design and had strange angles and abutments. None were alike. Last time I was here, I tried a seat made for two people and found it remarkably uncomfortable. Today I took a single seat and once again did not find the experience enjoyable. There were low tables of matching wood that held the usual assortment of home and garden magazines with all the interesting recipes torn out by previous patients. Mr. Lincoln sat opposite me and every once in a while looked up from his magazine to give me an almost imperceptible encouraging smile.

There were two patients ahead of me and after fifteen minutes we were escorted into an examination room. I was told to go behind the curtain, don a patient gown, and then sit on the exam table. Mr. Lincoln sat on a low stool near the door and we both waited for the doctor. After about five minutes Dr. Kaufman entered the room along with his nurse. He was wearing a white laboratory coat over a light blue shirt and red tie. The doctor had his name prominently embroidered in red above his left breast pocket. He took a quick peek at my chart – I suspect to remind himself of my name – and said, "Mrs. Weinberg, how are we doing? Is there any problem with the surgical wound? Let's have a look."

All his questions were said in a rapid staccato that did not allow me to answer. I was totally bewildered. I pulled up my patient gown for him to inspect my breast. This is such an embarrassing moment for a religious woman. I am happy that the gown covered my face and he cannot see me blushing.

"The wound looks terrific. Whoever did this surgery is a really talented surgeon. Wow, I am totally impressed with my own work," he said jokingly. "All the sutures are internal and will dissolve by themselves, so there are no stitches to remove. It will be a bit sore for another week or so. I expect the scar to be almost invisible. What a great surgeon I am," he added with a nod and a self satisfying smile.

When Dr. Kaufman took a break in his well rehearsed patter, I said, "Doctor ... about the results of the biopsy. Could ..."

He interrupted me with, "What are we ... a week since the surgery?"

His nurse checked the chart and said, "Yes, it is a week."

"Pathology should have the report already. Ask Denise to contact them to send a copy over." Then to me he said, "Why don't you get dressed and I'll speak with you in my office."

I sat in front of the doctor's massive mahogany desk in his spacious consultation room with Mr. Lincoln at my side. The entire wall behind the desk – floor to ceiling – was covered with framed diplomas. To keep myself occupied I began deciphering the calligraphy on some of the more ornate certificates. Besides the obligatory medical school and residency diplomas there were quite a few certificates that attested to the fact that the good doctor attended some two and three day courses or meetings on some arcane subject. His grade school diploma is probably somewhere on the wall, although I haven't found it yet.

My chart is resting on his red Moroccan leather desk blotter and after a few minutes the secretary came in with a sheet of paper and added it to the file. *That had to be the pathology report from my biopsy.* It's all I can do not to jump up and reach into the folder to read my verdict.

Finally, Dr. Kaufman came in, and sat down behind his desk. He opened my chart and said, "Let's see."

He seems to be mumbling to himself as he studies my chart. My heart is now beating a mile a minute and it's hard to breathe. I don't know how it happened or why I did it, but my hand moved over towards Mr. Lincoln and he took it in his. I could feel his concern through his touch and it calmed me slightly. It was enough so that I could start to breathe again. I looked at the doctor and we waited.

The concerned look on the doctor's face can mean only one thing. It is cancer and my life is over. I must prepare my family for the worst. I wonder if Mr. Lincoln can feel my despair through my fingers. All is lost.

Doctor Kaufman flipped the chart closed and broke out in a smile, "Good news. It was just a tiny fibroadenoma ... a benign tumor ... everything is clear. You are completely healthy."

I can't believe my ears. I'm okay. All my morbid thoughts and fears were for naught. Suddenly, I realize that Mr. Lincoln is squeezing my hand. I know he's doing it out of happiness. I don't have to look – I can feel it.

Mr. Lincoln chimed in, "Great news. That's terrific. Thank you, doctor."

"Mr. Weinberg, I didn't really do anything but perform your wife's surgery," said the doctor.

Mr. Lincoln answered, "I'm not Mr. Weinberg. I'm just a friend."

I could see Doctor Kaufman eyeing our grasped hands when he said, "Oh, just a friend. That's great."

I pull my hand from Mr. Lincoln's and say, "Thank you doctor. Thank you for everything."

"No problem," he said. "Just keep healthy, and don't come to see me anymore except for routine stuff."

The doctor rose and left the room. I turned to Mr. Lincoln and said, "Thank you. Thank you for everything."

"It was nothing. I'm just glad I could be of help."

But it was not nothing. It was something. Something that could become a big problem if I was not careful.

We both knew it.

# 17

## Outdated

I CLOSED MY *GEMORAH* and turned to Rabbi Kalmonowitz, "I have a tough question today, *Rebbi.*"

"Your questions are easy, it's the answers that are tough," replied the rabbi.

"That's what I meant."

"So into what realm of the *halachic* world do you take us today, Reb Shaul?"

"In the group sessions I attend with Mrs. Weinberg, a few people mentioned how their loved ones suffered before they died."

"The person who is on his *eres dvai* is not the only one that suffers, their families suffer as well," said the rabbi with empathy.

"I would like to know if euthanasia is allowed under Jewish law."

"That *is* a tough question," said the rabbi with a nod of his head. "But before I even attempt in answering, please define euthanasia."

"You know ... mercy killing," I said matter-of-factly.

"I think the term 'mercy killing' is what you would call an oxymoron. Is there such a thing as mercy killing? That is also a term that needs definition. Try giving me an example."

"Okay" I said thoughtfully. "Let's say there is a person that has terminal cancer ... a few months to live ... and right now he barely functions ... the man knows that in his final days he will be a terrible burden on his family.

He wants to end his life now ... with respect. Is this allowed?"

"If you mean by euthanasia giving a drug or treatment that will cause such a man to die ... the answer is definitely no. This would not be allowed."

"How about if he was in terrible pain ... would it be allowed then?"

"The answer is still no," said the rabbi with finality. "Let me tell you a true story to help clarify what is allowed and what is not."

"Okay"

"This case occurred in Israel about thirty years ago and it is interesting because both civil and rabbinic authorities were consulted."

"I'd like to hear about it."

"The case involved a child who just after he was born was diagnosed as suffering from a rare disease. The condition caused the boy's brain to stop developing and his mental age remained at about six months. The child's body grew ... more slowly than healthy children ... but it grew none the less. However, mentally the boy remained like a six month old. That meant that he could not feed himself, or control his urine or bowels. He could not walk or stand and was even unable to turn over on his own. He would react to pleasurable things with a smile and even laugh ... but it was all at the level of a six month old. The doctors said that there was no hope that the child would ever improve. The parents of the child were very devoted and even though they had two other children they faithfully cared for the child as best they could. The father carried him everywhere he had to go and the mother fed him and changed his diapers as needed."

"What a sad story," I commented.

The rabbi continued, "When he was eight years old, the child developed kidney failure and was immediately started on dialysis using a tube placed inside his abdomen. This was done as a temporary measure until an operation could be performed to prepare blood vessels in the boy's leg so that he could have blood dialysis. The parents were asked to give their consent to perform the operation."

"That's standard procedure even here."

"The problem was that the family situation had changed. The father was now under treatment for advanced cancer and he had only a few months to live. There was little chance that the mother ... on her own ... would be able to properly care for their son. The parents asked the child's doctors what would happen if their son did not get the surgery. They were told that eventually the abdominal catheter would become plugged and without functioning kidneys, the poisons would build up until their child died. The parents asked specifically what kind of a death the child would go through and were told that after a few days the child would lose consciousness and after a few more days he would die. When asked if there was any pain involved with the death, they were informed that he would pass away painlessly. The parents then made a conscious decision not to give permission for the surgery. If and when the abdominal catheter ceased to function they would allow their son to die.

"I completely understand them," I said.

"Understanding is one thing, but the question is ... is this allowable?" said the rabbi making a point. "The doctors of the hospital were faced with a legal and moral dilemma. They took the case to a civil court asking the judge to rule as to whether the child could be left to die based on the wishes of the parents. The courts decided that the parents had no right to make this decision and ordered the hospital to do the surgery and save the child."

"That family must have been devastated."

"The story does not end there. Four years later, the child was now twelve years old and the father had passed away. The boy now needed surgery to make a hole in his abdomen so the he could get proper nourishment. Without it he would die. Once again the mother refused to give permission and once again the doctors went to court and once again the court ruled that the doctors should do the surgery and save the child."

"Oh my goodness," I said sadly.

"The end of the story is that one year later the boy developed pneumonia and passed away."

"What a relief for the family."

"My question to you is ... how would you have ruled? Were the parents right in refusing to give permission for both surgeries? Did the civil courts make a mistake?"

"Personally, I agree with the parents. The courts should have let the child die."

"And why is that?" asked the rabbi.

"That poor kid was never going to get better. What kind of life was that? Better he should be put out of his misery."

"So you think the child was suffering?" asked Rabbi Kalmonowitz.

"Most definitely," I said with confidence. "Growing physically ... but staying like a six month old ... my goodness. That is definitely suffering."

"First, let me tell you that the rabbinic authorities were consulted on this case and their ruling was that they agreed with the civil court. Would you like to know why?"

"Of course."

"The key to this case is in understanding who is suffering. Is it the child or is it the parents and family? The answer is obvious. Remember the child has a mental age of a six month old ... and I would not wish that on my biggest enemy ... but this child also enjoyed life as a six month old. He was not really suffering. If he was suffering he would have been crying all the time. This boy laughed when he was tickled. He enjoyed the food he received. He smiled when things were good and cried when things were bad. He reacted and functioned as a six month old. Jewish law says that we are not here to judge why one person enjoys life on one level and another on a different level. That's the decision of *HaKadosh baruch hoo*. If we make a decision that people that have a mental development of a six month old should not get basic medical care, then what's to prevent us from deciding to withhold care from someone with an IQ of 20? Or an IQ of 40? Or an IQ of 60? Or from someone that does not have blonde hair and blue eyes? If God has decided that a particular *neshama* should reside in a brain with the mental capacity of a six month old ... then, so be it and we must make the best of it. The key is in the suffering. In this case it was not the child that was suffering ... it was the parents."

"So if the child had been suffering it would have been all right to allow him to die?" I asked.

"Now we are getting closer to understanding what is permissible and what is not. Once again it is the suffering. The basic tenant is that if a person is alive we are not allowed to do anything to kill them. It is one of the Ten Commandments. However, we sometimes are allowed to withhold treatment and allow people to die."

"In what case?"

"There are three factors that are necessary. One ... the person must be dying ... or what is usually defined as terminal ... and short of a miracle there is no chance that he will recover. Two ... the person has expressed the desire that his life should not be prolonged. Three ... the person is truly suffering. An example would be someone with end-stage cancer who is in severe pain all the time and now has developed breathing problems. We know that there will come a time when his lungs will not be able to support his bodily functions. When this point comes his lungs will give out and he will die. However there is the possibility of giving him all sorts of drugs or putting him on a respirator and this will allow the person to live longer. The problem is that this longer life will bring with it more pain and suffering. If this person has expressed the wish that he does not want this added agony and would rather die, then we are permitted to withhold the treatment and allow his life to end. So the rule is, if the three factors are present, we may passively participate in the person's death by withholding treatment. But in no case can we actively participate in ending life."

"Thank you, *Rebbi*," I said.

"May we be blessed so that we never have to face these dilemmas," said Rabbi Kalmonowitz as a blessing.

"Amen, *Rebbi*. Amen."

Max Rosenstein stopped his exercise machine and straightened his scrawny body for dramatic effect. Then he turned to me to ask in disbelief, "What did you just say? You're dating? When did you start? *Mashiach is gekimen* (the Messiah has come)! What made you finally get back on the horse?"

I knew exactly why I had started dating again, but there was no way I was going to tell Max. It was something that Ayelet and I would never talk about. *The little kiss at the inspection and then the hand holding when she had her surgery and at the doctor's office.* I realized that at the inspection she must have reacted instinctively from happiness and when she went for surgery I just happened to be the closest human being at the time. To her it must have been like kissing and holding hands with her brother and I had no right to think any more of it than what it was.

But, it was more than that to me.

I rationalized that much of the feelings I was having towards Ayelet stemmed from my long period of sexual abstinence – or as Max liked to say – I was probably just overly horny. So I decided that the time had come to start looking for someone to share my life. I had to be at the construction site numerous times each week and I did not want to ruin the relationship I had with her and her children. This was becoming more difficult every day, because Ayelet's house was now in a topsy-turvy state and it was getting impossible to live there. Out of necessity her kids were coming over to my house a couple days a week to swim in the pool and to have a place for Chaim'l to do homework. I even set up an improvised changing table to handle any emergencies with Racheli. She was now almost three and was calling me Steve most of the time – as did the other two – much to Ayelet's consternation.

My son, along with his family, had come to town for a visit and Ayelet's kids had played with my two grandchildren. They got along all right, but the difference between the two sets of kids was obvious. I love my grandchildren fiercely but I noticed that my grandkids were always glued to their video games, cell phones, laptops and internet. In contrast, the Weinberg kids spent most of their time playing with each other or reading. I am not trying to be overly judgmental but it seems to me, that Ayelet's way of raising kids was not bad.

But Max did not have to know any of the factors that were motivating me to start going out with women and I said, "I don't know why ... I just started dating."

"Whatever the reason ... it's about time. Okay let's have all the juicy details. How many women so far?" said the old man.

"Three, but why do I have to tell you anything?"

"It's the rules of the game. You got to tell someone or it doesn't count. Did you nail them all?"

"You *are* a pervert."

"As always ... guilty as charged," said Max in all honesty. "So, tell me."

"All I can say is that I am definitely rusty in the dating business."

"So, you screwed up," said Max shaking his head slowly from side to side. "I am very disappointed in you."

"I didn't say I didn't ... you know what," I said in my own defense.

"I'm glad to hear that. I was getting worried about you. So, what's the problem?"

"I'm just not used to the new dating protocols."

"What's not to get used to?"

"It's weird," I said in an exasperated tone. "You gotta understand that when I spoke to these women to set up the date, I told them that I'm a practicing Orthodox Jew. That I try to follow the *Torah* rules rather strictly. They knew that I was looking for someone who might eventually become my wife. I was not looking to just have some fun with nothing serious in mind. I wanted to find a life partner for a religious Jewish home. Do you get the picture?"

The old man rubbed his palms together and exclaimed with glee, "I get the picture ... a strange distorted picture ... but I get it. Now get to the good parts."

"So the first one was maybe forty years old. Very nice Jewish divorcee. A lawyer."

"Was she a looker? A blonde with a great body?" asked the leering old man.

"What difference does it make?"

"I have to have a visual to fully enjoy the story."

"Yes, she was pleasant to look at," I explained.

"I'm asking if she was blonde and *zoftig*."

"She was blonde and sufficiently endowed. Is that visual enough for you?"

"Not really enough, but continue."

"So, we went to an exhibition at the Cranbrook Institute and afterwards we sat in the cafeteria having coffee. She seemed nice but I could tell right off that we had no chemistry and I was trying to figure out how I could end the date gracefully. Then she puts down her coffee cup and says to me, 'You seem like a real nice guy, but I don't think this is going to work out so let's stop wasting time.' I think to myself, this lady is a mind reader. Then she says, 'So that this day will not be a total loss ... let's go back to my place and ... and ...'" I am unable to complete the actual quote.

"And what?" enquired Max.

"And ... you know," I said.

The old man nods his head and says knowingly, "Ah, have sex."

"She says, 'Why don't we have ...'"

"Sex."

"Thank you. I didn't know what to say and I think I stammered something. I'm not sure what. Then she says, 'If I thought that we had a future I would hold out until the third date, but since that is not going to happen, why don't we just enjoy ourselves. From what they tell me you can use it and I know I certainly can.'"

"Please don't tell me you turned her down," beseeched Max.

"No ... I can't say I turned her down," I said slowly, knowing that I was not being completely truthful.

The old man gave a wicked snicker, "At a boy!"

Liar, liar pants on fire.

When the woman made her proposition of a romp in the sheets, I didn't know how to react ... so at first I just kept my mouth shut. I was torn between two conflicting urges. On the one hand, having noncommittal sex after such a long period of abstinence would not be a bad idea. It would be pleasurable and would give me a chance to see if the old equipment was still in working order. Also, having not dated for almost thirty years, I was concerned that I might be a bit out of touch with modern dating etiquette. Perhaps, in this new age, with the new independent women, the old dating rules were obsolete. It could be that now, when a man agreed to go out on a date, if the woman so desired, he was obligated to be a willing sexual partner. To do otherwise, would disappoint the woman. Perhaps having sex had become the new responsibility of the Wi-Fi – digital – Facebook age. On the other hand, I was not looking for a one night stand. I was seeking someone with values similar to my own to share my life. Having a quickee – the old 'biff-bam-thank you ma'am' – was not part of my value system.

So there I was with my paranoia 'devil', of never disappointing anyone, gnawing at my resolve. It could have gone either way, but I reached a decision – I turned her down – politely.

When I dropped her at her home her exact words were, 'You don't know what you will be missing.'

There was just no way that I was going to tell Max the truth about this part of the date. The old man would never let me live it down. Funny thing was – I actually did want to discuss my dating encounters with the more experienced octogenarian.

Talking about dates is a natural part of the typical male showoff – notch-on-the-gun – bravado – 'Let me tell you about the one I nailed.' But, in my situation it was more about 'The ones I could have nailed.' I was suffering pangs of guilt about something I did not even do. It was crazy. Here I was, a warm blooded male, in good health, considering having consensual sex with warm blooded females – and I was feeling guilty. Worst of all, I was telling him all this because I hoped that Max – who was probably the most lecherous old man in the western world – would somehow absolve me from my feeling of – of – of – almost committing a 'sin'.

Christian ethics considers sex out of wedlock – even by two consenting single adults – as fornication – a mortal sin. Jewish law does not. Judaism does not condone it and considers such a relationship to be lewd behavior and therefore should be scorned, but it is not a *mortal* sin. I also knew that I did not, in any way, feel as if I would be cheating on Rebecca's memory. After all our years together, I knew that if she could come down from heaven to give me advice, she would most definitely have been encouraging me – even more than Max – that as a widower, it was perfectly all right to relieve my sexual tensions with an appropriate partner. The guilt I was feeling was not a logic thing – it was more on some sort of abstract ethical level. I apparently believed that when men and women seek each other, with the intent of forming a long lasting relationship, hopping into the sack right out of the gate was a no-no.

My emotions on the subject were a mixture of remorse, guilt, and a strange feeling of sullying my soul – and was most difficult to explain. I needed someone to help me sort out my 'almost-fornication' depression. It was not as if I could go to Rabbi Schlussel, spill the beans, and ask for absolution. The good rabbi was not a confessor type clergyman. He delivered sharp pithy sermons, he made compassionate visits to the sick, and he could ignite the congregation's conscience to donate to charities. He could even goad most people on to the path towards repentance. But personal stuff was tough for Rabbi Schlussel. If I tried to talk to him about this problem, the rabbi would squirm in his seat as he listened, turn a bright red, and break out in a sweat.

Rabbi Kalmonowitz was also out of the question because I would be too embarrassed to bring up the subject before the *rosh yeshiva*. So Max, with his anything goes, liberal attitude on life, was going to be my confessor. That meant that I would have to embellish the truth a bit or Max would make my life a living hell.

"That's my boy. And did you have a good time?"

"I did ... of course ... but only on a physical level," I lied with a straight face.

"Physical is good. That's the way sex works."

"What I'm saying is I don't understand such women," I said with concern.

"From that I am to understand that you had similar success with ladies two and three. Is that correct?"

I could not bring myself to also lie about the other two, "Well, yes and no. Each, in their unique way, tried to get me into bed."

"Are you joking with me? You didn't *shtup* the other two?" asked the disappointed old man.

I ignored the question, "When I was young it was the man that chased after the woman, now it is just the opposite. It seems the ladies nowadays won't take no for an answer."

"Isn't life a bitch sometimes," said Max mockingly. "What about the other two?" the old man insisted.

"I have another date tonight," I said sadly, evading the question.

"What's with the *Tisha B'Av* face?"

"At my age I'm not sure if I'm cut out for this dating business."

"Your heart is still beating ... there is blood circulating in your veins ... you are not brain dead ... so you are cut out for this dating business," insisted the old man.

I realized that society looked at the sexual act, between a man and a woman, in a number of ways. Some referred to it as hooking up. Some described it as having sex. And some referred to it as making love. For me the sexual act was more than just semantics. All three of the woman I had dated preferred the expression 'sex', or something similar. One of them had said, 'What's the big deal – it's only sex.' To me, it was a big deal. Sex between a man and a woman was also more than just 'making love'. Although that term was an improvement on the word 'sex', because it implied a bit of mutual respect – affection – consideration – between the couple. But it still did not define what I felt. For me the true meaning of the coming together of a man and woman was intimacy.

Being intimate implied that each one of the partners was completely vulnerable but at the same time completely confident in their partner. You were naked in every aspect of the word – totally defenseless. For that short period of time you were able to attain pleasure without fear or need to guard yourself, because you had someone that shared the intimacy with you. Someone that very often put your welfare before their own. So for me, sex was a big deal. "Maybe my kind of woman doesn't exist anymore," I said.

"What kind of bullshit are you handing me?" said Max. "I know what your problem is."

"You do? What's my problem?"

"Ayelet Weinberg ... that's your problem," said the old man emphatically.

What was Max suggesting? What did he know? "What are you talking about?" I said defensively.

"You got the hots for little Ayelet and you keep comparing your dates to her. You gotta know none of them are going to measure up."

"How would you know?"

"Born Ayelet Krantz, in Sinai Hospital 32 years ago, the youngest of six children of a Detroit man and a woman from an Israeli family ... that explains Ayelet's modern Hebrew name. Her folks retired to Florida and all her siblings have left the state. Her birthday is next week ... don't forget to wish her a happy birthday ... and she went to the local 'holy roller' Bais Yaakov Girl's School. Super bright kid, skipped two grades and finished high school at age sixteen and a half. She spent one year in Israel and got married within six months of returning to the city. At the end of high school she took the SAT exam on a whim, with no preparation and got an almost perfect score. She was offered scholarships to the best colleges in the country but turned them all down to marry her *yeshiva bochur* husband. She had some trouble getting pregnant but after a few years the doctors got that sorted out and she now has three kids. Her rabbi husband was a pedestrian killed in a motor vehicle accident ... drunk driver ... almost three years ago now. She is bright, smart, witty and also very, very beautiful. Do I know enough?"

My mouth had dropped open, "How the hell do you ...?"

"I had her investigated."

"Why did you ...?"

"Because when you asked me to help with that Amity Bank loan business, there were two problems. One was that *shmuck* of a loan officer, and it was a pleasure to handle that. But there was also the problem that making that loan for your lady really was a financial risk for the bank."

"But they came through with the loan."

"Sure they did after I co-signed the loan. So you made me part of the Ayelet Weinberg Specialty Baking Company. I like to know something about the people that get my money and I had her investigated."

*Oh my God. If Ayelet finds out she will kill me.* Still, what was the old man's take on Ayelet? "So, what do you think?"

"I think ... that I don't blame you for falling for her."

I could feel color rising in my cheeks, as I said in denial, "I have not fallen for her. I just enjoy helping her and her kids. They've had a hard time."

"You are a regular Santa Claus," said the old man derogatorily. "But I'm not buying that. You like her ... so why not just tell her? You're available ... she's available?"

"I'm not saying I like her," I said turning my head aside and holding up an index finger to make a point. "But she is fifteen years younger than me. She needs someone more her age. I'm not getting younger and she doesn't need to wind up a young vibrant woman taking care of an old decrepit man."

"Am I an old decrepit man?" asked Max.

"I am not referring to you. I'm just not going that route."

"Suit yourself, but as long as you are going to hang around with Mrs. Weinberg ... none of your dates are ever going to measure up."

"Maybe I should just stop dating."

"Are you nuts? I just said they won't measure up. Not that you shouldn't date. These modern women are just dying to meet a guy like you. So why not? You're a religious man. You believe God controls everything on this earth. So, if God puts a tender morsel on your plate ... why shouldn't you partake and enjoy it? It's *ba'al tashchis* (law against destroying anything useful). So it is against your religion not to date."

"Suddenly you're a big *talmid chochom,"* I said.

The old man looked up to the heavens, spread his palms, and said, "God moves in mysterious ways."

# 18

## Matchmaker, Matchmaker

ONE OF THE BIGGEST SURPRISES I've had since opening the bakery enterprise has been the popularity of my bialy rolls, and that is what we are making this morning. The small flat roll with roasted onions in its center was named after the city of Bialystock in Poland where it originated. My big trick for it to come out extra special is to have the dough rise several times and then during the last rise selectively suppress the process in the center part just before the dough goes into the oven. It required quite bit of kneading and elbow grease to come out properly. Mrs. Leibowitz was pounding and kneading the dough trying to get the right texture, when she asked innocently, "Zo how vas fellah I saw yoo vit yesterday?"

God Bless her – she has been in the U.S.A. for over fifteen years – but her accent still drips borscht with every syllable. It always takes me an extra moment or two to decipher whatever it is that she is trying to say. But I have no difficulty this time. Perhaps after five months of working together, I am getting used to her Russian-English, or perhaps the reason her question is so clear is because I am overly sensitive about having started dating. I saw how she gave me that nod and a smile, when my date picked me up yesterday.

I moved some hot scones from the oven to a cooling rack and tried to keep my voice calm as I said, "Just a date."

"Date is good. Ver you meet young man?"

There are some folks that think I am overly talkative.

That my lips are always in motion.

Thing is – when I am doing something – I like to talk to the people around me. I will talk to strangers when I go shopping and if there is no one close by I will sometimes talk out loud to myself. I know that behind my back people say I talk too much. But, as much as I am known to bend an ear, compared to Mrs. Leibowitz, I am a Trappist monk in the middle of Lent. For over twenty years, before emigrating to the U.S.A., she had been the head cook of a huge Moscow medical facility where she and four other women prepared lunch for three thousand workers. She once told me that the only thing that kept them all sane during their grueling work day was the laughter and conversation. When Mrs. Leibowitz is around there was always plenty of both.

She is a big, tall, heavy woman but is surprisingly light on her feet. Always flittering around the kitchen like a humming bird. Her previous cooking experience gives her an uncanny knack for organizing the baking process. Amazingly she can work on multiple recipes at the same time. She also has a remarkable ability to determine how to do a particular task in the simplest way possible. If there is something new in one of the recipes you only had to show her once and after that she could do it perfectly. You did not feed an army of hospital workers if you wasted your time. Her massive arms are at home kneading large quantities of dough and doing the most delicate of decorations on the cakes. She is terrific and I know that the business could never have progressed so fast without her.

But now she is asking me some very personal questions. "Zo ver you meet?" she asks again.

"We met yesterday when he picked me up," I answered, starting to put frosting on a batch of cup cakes.

She carried the large crock with the bialy mixture to the proofing cabinet and brought some risen dough back to her table. She cocked her head to the side and asked, "You never meet him before dat?"

"No," I answered honestly.

Mrs. Leibowitz nodded her head in understanding, "I hear about dat ... a nosey date."

I did not have the vaguest idea of what she was talking about. What is a 'nosey date'? What does a nose have to do with a date? What is she trying to say? Does she mean that she should not be nosey about my affairs? I must have made some gesture that indicated my bewilderment because she added, "You know ... nosey ... no see. Vat you call it ... blind date?"

Oh – she thinks it was a blind date. "No, no ... it wasn't a blind date."

"But you said you never meet before."

"It was not a blind date. It was an arranged date," I try to explain.

Mrs. Leibowitz was punching down the new batch of bialy dough with vigor when she asked, "Vat difference blind date ... arranged date?"

This is not going to be easy to explain. The whole *frum* dating process will seem strange to her. I guess it would seem strange to anybody outside the community. I am sure she never saw anything like it back in old Mother Russia, but I will give it a shot. "A blind date is where a fellow gets a girl's number and then calls her up without seeing her or knowing her. The girl has to decide ... almost on the spot ... whether she will go out with the fellow or not."

"And by you, vat vas? Fella didn't call you?" said the large women squeezing off a ball of bialy dough.

"No, no ... he called me. But that is just a formality, to tell me when he would come. It was already agreed that I would go out with him."

"Who agreed?"

"The *shadchan*."

"Who iz dat?"

"The matchmaker."

"Der ver tree of you on date?" asked the woman in surprise, as she carefully placed the rounds of shaped dough onto the baking tray.

"No, no ... there was just the two of us."

"Glad to hear. Vit tree people ... difficult to ... you know vat."

What is she referring to? I do not understand. "I don't know what," I stated in confusion.

"You know. You being vidow for so long. You get lonely. All women need man for ... you know vat," she said with a wink of her eye.

She means sexual relations. Oh my goodness. I can feel my face getting red. "Mrs. Leibowitz, I'm surprised at you. You should know that in our community, we don't have relations without marriage. We just went out together."

"If no ... *you know vat* ... vy you go date?"

"To get to know each other. To see if we might want to marry."

Using both hands she was simultaneously rolling small balls of dough on the counter as she said earnestly, "But you go out vit fella you not spoke to ... you not meet. Vat if fella ... sick in head ... ven you in dark place? Could be dangerous."

That made me laugh. She thinks someone in our community would go to a secluded place on a *shidduch* date. "Very little chance of that. Way before we ever met ... someone investigated this man. Just like he probably had someone check me out before he called me. So, no one is sick in the head."

"Who iz someone?"

"For the young kids just going out for the first time, it would be the parents. A *shadchan* would propose a possible match. Then each family would get their 'Jewish FBI' to investigate the candidate. Way before the boy calls the girl the families have already decided that if the couple hit it off, they have agreed to the marriage."

"Vat iz 'Jewish FBI'? Like KGB?"

How do I explain this to her? "I know someone ... who knows someone ... that lives in the same community with the boy or girl. Then I get them to tell me all about the candidate and the family. By the time they are finished I will even know the boy or girl's shoe size."

"Vy do dis vay? Vy not boy meets girl? Dey go out ... dey like ... dey say hello to family ... den make vedding? Vat wrong vit dat? Old fashioned vay. Very good."

"Because a boy might become attracted to a girl that is not right for him. And then they would have the problem of having to split up. There would be all sorts of arguments. It wouldn't work."

"Vy vouldn't vork? Been doing like dis many years. Okay"

"For us it wouldn't be okay," I try to think of a way to explain the problems that could occur. "Suppose a young man meets a young girl ... at a public library or someplace else ... they go out and they like each other. But he is a very good *yeshiva* student who is going to be a rabbi, and she is someone that is not very religious. They feel they love each other and want to get married. The problem is that their match would have terrible problems from the very beginning. They might get over them, but then again they might not. There could be children and if the marriage fails, a family would be destroyed."

Mrs. Leibowitz squeezed off two more balls of bialy dough, "So vid de *shachdan* der is no love?"

"Not *shach-dan.* That's *shad- chan.* Oh definitely we want to have love in the marriage, but we don't leave matching of our children to pure chance. Instead we screen the candidates beforehand so that the boy or girl will fall in love with someone appropriate for them."

"Who does screening?"

"As I said before, usually it's the parents. After all, they are the ones that know their child best and want only good things for him or her. They can be trusted to pick someone appropriate."

Mrs. Leibowitz seemed to be extremely curious and stopped forming the rolls to ask, "Who pick date for you?"

"My parents are old and live in Florida, so for me it was *Rebbetzen* Kalmonowitz."

"I saw fella," said Mrs. Leibowitz shaking her head. "She not see so good? Vy she not pick good looking guy?"

"By us, looks are really not that important."

She resumed forming balls of dough and asked, "Vat not important? Dat very important. Vat do she check?"

"She checks to see that the boy is as religious as I am. And since I have three children ... if he can make a living. Most important if the man's family has a good reputation in the community. Things like that."

"So young people don't date just to have good-time."

"Absolutely not. They date until they know if they want to marry. That's it."

"How *shad-chans* get names of boys and girls to make matches?"

"You have to understand that there are many professional *shadchans* and even more amateur ones."

"I saw dat vonce in cinema ... in Moskva ... in movie 'Fiddler on de Roof'."

"Yes, like that."

"Vy vould someone vant to be a *shadchan*? Sounds like big headache to me."

"Some do it for the *mitzvah* of helping people find a match, but a large number do it for a very basic reason. If the match works ... and there is a marriage ... they get *shadchonus gelt*. A matchmaker's fee."

"Dey do it for money?"

"And some of them make a good living at it. The better ones have ways to find out the names of all the boys graduating from the big *yeshivas* and using their own 'Jewish FBI' they know which are the strongest students and are destined to move up in the *yeshiva* world. These are the most in demand."

"Not doctors and lawyers?"

"Not in our community," I responded. "Anyway, these names are then circulated to the *shadchans* for the girls and the bidding starts."

Mrs. Leibowitz stopped squeezing off the bialy dough again and looked at me incredulously, "You sell dese boys?"

"No ... no. The various *shadchans* put in the names of different available young ladies. These girls are then presented to the boy's family to be considered for their son to date. A good *bochur* may have three or four hundred female candidates."

"Can't believe so many," she said in surprise.

"Believe me it's true. I know this from personal experience with my nephew in New York."

"So vat do day do? Do day line dem up and boy picks prettiest?"

"No, never like that. The boy's family checks out the various girls by looking into the important things."

"Vat are *important tings*?"

I am surprised Mrs. Leibowitz is so interested in all this, but obviously she is, "For an up and coming *yeshiva bochur* that would either be *yichus* or money."

"Vat is *yichus*?"

"It basically defines how close the girl's family is related to some famous rabbi. Like a granddaughter of a great rabbi would move to the head of the list in trying to snag a particular boy. And if the family is reported as being not so reputable she would drop way down the list. But I have found that if the girl's father is rich enough that can overcome just about everything else." I suddenly thought to myself how odd it was that I had managed to get Rephael. He had been such a brilliant student and my folks were not wealthy. Perhaps it is because his parents had died when he was very young and Rabbi Kalmonowitz had selected me as his first and only *shidduch. Boruch HaShem.*

"So girl's father buys him?" asked Mrs. Leibowitz.

"He doesn't buy him really. He just offers to support the family during the years he must sit and study."

"Vat does fahder do? He gives bread and vahter?"

"Hardly. It usually means he buys them a house or apartment. A car and supplies a cash payment every month for a number of years ... possibly for a lifetime."

"So, like I said ... girl's fahder does buy him."

"No one is sold."

"Okay, not sold ... but how does girl vitout rich fahder get husband?"

"She settles for the not-so-top-of-the-line *yeshiva bochur.*"

"And if she is lovely, brilliant girl ... but no money?"

"The same thing."

"And you tink dis good system?"

"I don't know if it is a good system, but it's the system we use."

"So vat kind man does young vidow lady vit tree little children and struggling business get? How vas fella from yesterday?"

Ouch, she is hitting below the belt. I have to be honest. "She also settles for someone that is not-so-top-of-the-line."

"So no *yichus* and no money, you take damaged goods. Like bialys and cookies from yesterday."

The fellow from last night was not damaged goods. He was a nice man, thirty six years old and never been married. He has been learning in a *yeshiva* since he was sixteen years old and has no profession. Mrs. Leibowitz is right – he was not as good looking as Rephael had been – but that is not important. I cannot really say anything about the man's personality, because he had been so shy he hardly spoke to me all evening. There was also that strange smell about him that suggested that he and his shower were becoming strangers. Maybe Mrs. Leibowitz is more objective than I am. "I wouldn't say 'damaged goods' ... let's just say 'not-so-top-of-the-line goods'."

"So you go out vit fella again?" she asked relentlessly.

"No, I won't," I replied.

This was one of the nice things about a *shidduch* date. Part of the *shadchan's* job is to call both the girl and the boy the next day and find out if they wanted to see each other for another date. If they both agree, she notifies the boy and he will make another date. If either says no, then the *shadchan* just stops the process – *oise shidduch* (the match is broken). No big let downs, no hassle. The *rebbetzen* called this morning and asked. Almost reflexively I told her that the man was not my *beshert.* She did not argue – I guess at some time she had also been downwind from the fellow.

She told me that she had my next *shidduch* all lined up. He was a fellow from Cleveland, who would drive in to see me next week. He divorced his wife two years ago.

Perhaps this is more damaged goods?

# 19

## *Just perfect for you*

IT WAS QUITE OBVIOUS to me that ever since the little peck on my cheek and the hand holding, things had become more than a bit awkward between Ayelet and me. She was still making a mountain out of a mole hill. Anyone with half a brain could immediately see that there had never been any romantic connotations. But Ayelet had her *charedi* way of looking at things. She probably felt that what she had done was tantamount to being the starring participant in a Roman orgy – nudity, whips, and ravished goats galore.

Things came to a head when a few weeks after the visit to her surgeon Ayelet called me at home, "I am very worried about something."

"What something?" I inquired innocently.

"I am very afraid that what we did will become public knowledge. You have to promise me that under no circumstances will you ever speak of what happened to anyone. And I mean *anyone*!"

Obviously she was referring to what she considered to be problematic 'incidents' and that was what she was trying to squelch, so, I said in nonchalant manner, "Ayelet, what are you talking about? Nothing happened. It was nothing. One day you will look back at all this and laugh."

Ayelet responded angrily, "I will not laugh. Not now. Not ever. Can't you see what happened between us was wrong?"

"We didn't do anything so how could it be wrong? When I was a kid, our family used to have a playful puppy and when he wanted attention he would hold out his paw. When I grabbed it the dog would give me affectionate licks," I said in explanation. "It's the same thing."

"Now you compare me to a dog?" exclaimed Ayelet in exasperation.

*When can you ever win with a woman?*

"Of course I'm not comparing you to a dog," I said in my defense. "What I meant was that no one would think that I was ... was ... you know ... close with my little dog. Same thing ... between you and me."

"It is not the same thing," said Ayelet in earnest. "Can't you see that?"

Obviously, to Ayelet what had occurred was significantly more important than me holding a puppy's paw, but at the same time, to me it was not.

*Well – maybe it was.*

Of course whatever I thought about the 'incidents' was not the issue. The whole problem was what Ayelet thought about the whole thing. To her it was a cataclysmic catastrophe. I had to say something that would calm her. So, I changed my tone and said solemnly, "You're absolutely right. I wasn't thinking." I paused for a moment and then added with mock contrition, "Yes, this is a big problem. What do you suggest we do?"

"Good. I am glad you now see the seriousness of the matter," said Ayelet gravely. "First, we must stop the familiarity that we've had between us."

I said skeptically, "But, we're in the middle of the building project. That could be kind of awkward,"

Ayelet was ready for me and said, "If we must speak about the project it will only be in the most proper manner and only when absolutely necessary."

I could not see how this would change anything but I went along with it, "Agreed, Ayelet."

"Second, I wanted you to know that *Rebbetzen* Kalmonowitz has officially started making *shidduchim* for me. It is important that *nothing* happens that will interfere with that."

Suddenly things became crystal clear and I said in total acquiescence, "I understand."

Just as she said, in the weeks that followed, Ayelet successfully distanced herself from me. Funny thing though – circumstances caused an almost opposite dynamic with her kids. She was now extremely busy running her baking business with only her two small ovens – in desperation she had added a second. From the time she awoke until she went to bed late at night she was working like a whirlwind. Most of the time, she looked like a one-armed wallpaper hanger whizzing around her kitchen from one task to the next.

It became almost impossible to find enough time in the day to devote proper attention to her kids and the guilt weighed heavily on her. Someone had to help Chaim'l with his homework, read stories to Yanki, and play with Racheli. She knew that her kids were looking everywhere for the attention that they were not getting from their mom. Whenever I visited the construction site, her kids would flock to me and would find all sorts of reasons to prevent me from leaving. On one visit Chaim'l asked me to help him with a homework problem and I asked Ayelet – in a perfectly formal manner – if it was okay to assist her son. Since at that very moment she was up to her eyeballs in a huge baking order, she reluctantly agreed. Over the next weeks, her work load became even heavier and it was not long before I was devoting an hour here and an hour there to help with the kids. When things got particularly hectic in Ayelet's house I took them to my home so they could have a little peace and quiet.

Soon I was doing it twice a week.

Much to the consternation of Ayelet, I was having a ball. Yanki was becoming a proficient swimmer in the lap pool, and the *Gemorah* sessions with Chaim'l were very enjoyable. The kid was brilliant. I even raided the local toy store to purchase some toddler toys and made the corner of my living room into a play area for Racheli. The toys kept the cute child busy for hours at a time. The price of children's toys nowadays had amazed me. The money I spent on those few toys probably equaled the GNP of a small third world country.

In a nutshell – Ayelet barely spoke to me but I was getting along just fine with her kids.

Then I made my infamous suggestion of going on an outing and barbecue.

It all occurred just before the weekend when the electricians were hooking up the heavy electric power mains that would energize the new bakery and the large addition to her house. Ayelet would not let them work on the Jewish Sabbath and they had to get the job done from Thursday afternoon until late Sunday, minus the twenty-five hours of *shabbos*. Since all the power to the house would be turned off she would not be able to bake or cook during this period. It also meant that for those three days the Weinberg family could not live in their home. They planned on spending the entire weekend at Rabbi Kalmonowitz's house, but Ayelet learned that *Rebbetzen* Kalmonowitz had an important fund raiser brunch planned for her home on that Sunday and had hidden that fact from her when she invited them. Ayelet knew that her family's presence there on Sunday would be a huge imposition. So, she told the *rebbetzen* that she had other plans for Sunday and would leave in the morning. Now Ayelet was faced with the problem of finding a way of keeping the kids occupied all Sunday without a roof over their heads.

When I heard about her Sunday difficulties I made a spur of the moment suggestion, 'Hey, Rabbi Kalmonowitz is busy that Sunday so he canceled our lesson. Why don't we all just go out to one of the state parks for a barbecue and make a day of it?' Even though I am sure she knew this could be a perfect solution to the problem, the idea was met with an immediate refusal – I had not expected any other response. It should have all ended right there except Yanki overheard me make the suggestion and he told Chaim'l. Once they both knew about my idea they started pestering their mother. She was a good mom and normally she could deal with any pressures her kids made upon her – but with all the accumulated guilt of practically ignoring her family over the previous weeks and not having an alternative solution – she had agreed.

As soon as it was decided that the day trip was a go, certain *halachic* technicalities cropped up. At first I planned on taking them in my SUV but soon realized that it would not work. Michigan law required special car seats for young children and this equipment had to be fastened in the back seat of the vehicle. Chaim'l didn't need a safety seat but he was still too small for the front seat, so all three kids would have to sit in the back and Ayelet would have to ride up in the front seat with me. There was snowball's chance in hell that she would go along with that. For the same reason we could not use her car – and that put a damper on the plans. So, when I suggested using my motor home the kids went ballistic and even Ayelet ran out of excuses.

Although I rarely drove the motor home, I kept it in good repair and Sunday morning it started right up. On the way to the Weinberg home I made a stop at the 'super-Kosher' supermarket to pick up all the meat for the barbecue. Since I was already there I also did my weekly grocery shopping, instead of waiting for my regular shopping day on Tuesday. I stowed the perishables in the motor home's fridge and put the rest in the cupboards before heading over to Ayelet's house.

As I drove I could not help but reflect on my weird relationship with Ayelet. I knew that I enjoyed being around her and her kids. I was not sure if it was a 'father instinct' expressing itself or perhaps something more. I was pretty sure that she enjoyed my company as well – but that was not important. She was convinced that if we attempted any kind of relationship it would never work. I was not the right sort – not *frum* enough and I am sure our age difference made her wary.

The week before Ayelet had complicated things even more. It happened on Tuesday when I came over to check the carpenter's work of the previous day, she nonchalantly mentioned that she had a *shidduch* for me. This caught me totally by surprise and it took a moment for me to gain my equanimity. With a mask of outer calm I asked for the details of her proposed *shidduch.* Ayelet wanted me to go out with a woman named Victoria Schwartz, a widow from Bloomfield Hills. She was an Orthodox woman and a long time customer of her baked items. Her exact expression was, "She's just perfect for you."

I did not know what to do. There was no way that Ayelet had the slightest inkling as to what type of woman would be 'just perfect' for me. But, I did not want to insult Ayelet or her good customer Mrs. Victoria Schwartz. In addition, I was extremely curious to find out just what kind of woman Ayelet thought was appropriate for me. So, I had gone out with the woman.

The date turned out to be very interesting.

What Ayelet did not know, and I was not about to tell her, was that Mrs. Schwartz is one crafty woman.

I took Vickie – she hated being called Victoria – to an early movie and then we stopped at the snack bar at the

Jewish Center for something to eat. The woman was a good looking petite brunette who obviously took very good care of herself. I was only a year older than her but she appeared to be much younger. She proudly informed me that her taut trim physique was the result of her thrice weekly sessions with her personal trainer and some costly visits to her plastic surgeon or one of his associates.

She was actually a very charming person and an excellent conversationalist. I enjoyed her company, but there was no *spark*. When the date drew to a close I just wanted to drop her at the curb in front of her home. However, Vickie insisted that she was very safety conscious and asked that I accompany her to her door. She further requested that I wait there until she was sure that everything in her home was okay before I left.

Being a good Samaritan - as always - I of course complied. *It never crossed my mind that it was all a ploy.*

Vickie unlocked her door, stepped inside her home, but when she hit the light switch, nothing happened. No lights went on. She looked to me - with what I now know was a feigned vulnerability - and asked for my help. I quickly assessed the situation and stated the obvious. Since all the power to the house was out, I suggested a look at the fuse box. Mrs. Schwartz found a flashlight in a kitchen drawer and showed me the way down into her dark basement. The main circuit box was on the wall at the foot of the steps and all the switches seemed to be in working order. Mrs. Schwartz, conveniently remembered a secondary box higher up on the wall and brought over ladder so I could inspect it. All these breakers also looked good and then she said that sometimes you had to fiddle with them just a bit. Vickie then suggested that she should get up on the ladder to try it herself.

*What a sneaky lady.*

Things happened very quickly after that.

I held the ladder as Vickie climbed up and properly averted my line of sight once the hem of her skirt went above eye level. The woman jiggled her behind in front of my face for a moment and then the lights went on. The sudden illumination seemingly frightened Vickie and it made her lose her balance. She slipped from the ladder right into my arms.

*Miracles do happen.*

*Pshaw – it was all planned.*

I never really stood a chance.

Vickie was a determined woman who knew how to use her wicked wiles.

She started by telling me that she felt in my debt for saving her from a bad fall and to show her gratitude she was going to reward me by giving me a demonstration of her expertise as a masseuse. I tried to refuse but she was adamant.

"It's only a massage and you will be fully clothed," she stated matter-of-factly.

*Yeah, right.*

We went up to the living room and she pulled out a folding massage table. Once again I tried to get out of it, but was unsuccessful. I suppose part of the reason I acquiesced was that I subconsciously didn't want to offend Ayelet's friend and customer.

*How dumb can you get?*

I got on the table – face down – fully clothed. *Hey, what could be bad?*

To be truly fair to Vickie, I have to admit she really is a talented masseuse. Ten minutes into the massage she had all my muscles relaxed and quivering to the point where I felt like a huge bowl of jiggling Jello. At that point I don't think I could have gotten off the table unaided.

Then she innocently suggested an improvement in the massage experience by progressing up to an oil massage. I expressed my concerns about removing any of my clothing, but she shushed my negative comments by saying, "You'll still be in your undershorts. That's just like a bathing suit, ... so it's not inappropriate. Right?"

I tried to voice further reservations about the idea – but that did not stop her.

Out came the heated scented oil. She help me shuck off my shirt and pants and then she slipped out of her dress to don a loose fitting robe – she said she did not want to stain her good clothes with oil.

*Yeah, right.*

The crafty woman sloshed warm scented oil on my body and started massaging areas that rarely saw sunshine. It was more than pleasurable. I felt like I was floating in a warm comfortable bath. I have to admit it was terrific.

The sex advice columns of the ladies magazines usually define 'foreplay' as activities that stimulate the erogenous zones prior to sexual relations. Vickie meticulously avoided these zones – but came awfully close. I suppose what we were doing should probably be classified as three play. Maybe even three play-ultra.

Slowly but surely the little lady very effectively employed a *kvetch* here and *kvetch* there, lots of gentle stroking, soft purring, and more and more suggestive touching.

She definitely aroused some primitive reflexes and they were responding appropriately. My no-sex-on-the-first-date resolve was crumbling before my eyes because three things were coming into play. The first was my two years of abstinence. I was feeling things that I had not felt since my wife took sick. Good feelings. *How could this be bad?*

Second, my *yetzer ha'rah* was suddenly out of control. This was the Jewish rationalization that we are all naturally good and only when the *yetzer ha'rah* – a person's evil inclination – rears its ugly head do we do bad things. *It was not me – it was the yetzer ha'rah.*

Third, an extremely lewd Mrs. Schwartz. Obviously, this was not the first time the electricity had been 'on the blink' and a massage had been offered as a reward. No question about it –Vickie had lots of experience. The lady also had a way of turning up the ‘energy in the room’ to make everything very intense.

*One sexy lady.*

I was holding out pretty good against the first two but when number three kicked in I could feel my resolve dissipate rapidly.

Vickie was all over me and I must admit she was successfully arousing the primitive side of my being. For about twenty minutes – an intense twenty minutes – she engaged in some very – very – intense massaging in all sorts of exotic positions. Did I mention that Mrs. Schwartz was very athletic?

Oh, how sneaky.

The sleeveless robe she was wearing was also part of the plan. It was more like a smock and didn’t really close in the front. Whenever Vickie moved about – and she did that a lot – I would get a glimpse – actually a heck of lot more than a glimpse – of her underwear and taut trim physique.

Years ago Rebecca had explained to me that there were four types of ladies undergarments. The first was the utilitarian comfortable kind. They were low cost and easy maintenance. Then came the frilly-feminine stuff with lots of lace, ribbons, bows and embroidery and made the women wearing it feel good about herself. They were high cost and required delicate washing. Then there were the ‘miracle’ underwear that enhanced and/or restrained and/or corrected certain physical imperfections so that a woman could look good in the clothes she wore. These were even more expensive and higher maintenance. Finally came the ‘display’ lingerie. This stuff was designed so that a woman could look good when she was no longer in her outer clothes and specifically triggered prurient musings in men. They were ridiculously high priced, poorly constructed, very uncomfortable, and not made for long term use.

Vickie's undergarments were definitely of the 'display' variety and were quite effective. No doubt about it, they were definitely evoking salacious thoughts in me.

This lady was an icon of the Jewish community, president of the local Hadassah group, vice-chairman of the ladies organization at her synagogue, and was also quite a vixen. She was quite proficient in effectively using her feminine wiles and supple curves.

Then she suggested moving it all up a notch and transferring the massage to her bedroom. This was the first time I ever met anyone in the Orthodox community that proudly announced that they had a large locked cupboard in their boudoir closet chock full of 'bedroom items'.

This new information made something in my brain go 'click'. I suddenly realized that this was not what I really wanted and somehow I had to escape the lady's clutches. This was no easy task since Vickie's previous ministrations had already turned my brain to mush. I have no idea how I accomplished it, but I was able to get up off the massage table, retrieve my clothes, and go home. I made it to my house feeling just a bit guilty and more than a bit tuckered out. One good thing did come out from the night's events – I now knew that my equipment was definitely out of mothballs and was responding just fine.

I had to laugh when I recall that it was Ayelet that felt Mrs. Schwartz was 'just perfect' for me.

*So much for Ayelet's matchmaking.*

When the motor home pulled into the Weinberg driveway the kids piled out the front door and clambered aboard. Ayelet followed in their wake toting the various bundles and bags that are required whenever a family leaves the safety of their home – snacks, toys, and clothing changes. I showed Ayelet where to stow all her 'emergency' equipment and then introduced her to all the accoutrements of the vehicle. The large living room in the front, the spacious bedroom in the rear and the well equipped kitchen, including the double sink for *kashrus* reasons. Orthodox Jews never mixed milk and meat food or utensils so that required two sinks for maximum observance. "Do you have two full sets of dishes, pots, and cutlery in the motor home?" she inquired.

"We did ... but not now. I gave all that stuff to the Goodwill last year. We'll be eating off of disposables today," I answered.

With all the usual kid's bickering it took about a half hour to decide where everyone would sit. Once we got the kid's safety seats connected to the upholstered chairs, I pulled away from the curb.

We were just getting on the Southfield freeway when Ayelet asked loudly, from her seat on the living room couch, "So, did you go out with Mrs. Schwartz?"

*God, how do I answer that question?*

It took a moment for me to collect my thoughts, "Yes, I did."

"And?" inquired Ayelet expectantly.

"And what?"

"Will you be seeing her again?"

"No ... I had a lovely time ... but no ... I will not be seeing her again."

She asked in alarm, "Did you do something to offend her?"

"Offend her?" I said, straining to keep from laughing. "I doubt very much if I could offend her."

"What did you do? Did you do anything that I wouldn't be proud of?" scolded Ayelet.

"Let me assure you ... concerning Mrs. Schwartz ... you can be very proud of me." Then added under my breath, "Hell, I deserve a bronze star for valor under fire."

"What did you say about fire? What does that have to do with Mrs. Schwartz?"

"Nothing ... simply nothing."

We merged on to I-94 and drove west. As we cruised down the road the children used every excuse they could think of to get out of their seats and roam around the motor home. Kids will be kids. Each one went to the bathroom at least three times in the first half hour – and that included little Racheli – and she was not even toilet trained. Ayelet was busy with her children so that allowed me to let my mind wander and think a little more about my dating situation.

I had no idea if there was a bull or bear market for middle aged single Jewish men but once the community found out that I was on the block, people who had not spoken to me for ages began calling to offer names, phone numbers and intimate histories of available Jewish ladies. The attributes of each of the thirty two 'perfect' women offered were almost unbelievable. They were all unattached women – widowed, divorced, or single. Ladies that were separated (but still officially married) were excluded off-hand. Most were touted to be as pretty as Miss America – were as smart as Madame Curie – were as devoutly religious as the Dali Lama – and all had the disposition of a pussy cat.

I did my part and called them all. I discovered that twelve of the women could be eliminated at the get go because they were not really religious enough. Modern Orthodoxy allowed for a wide range in levels of religious observance, but these women were well below the lowest standard. Either they did not keep kosher, did not observe the Sabbath, or had some other basic religious deficiency. The politically correct term would be, 'religiously challenged'.

That left twenty possibles.

Two declined my offer for a date stating that they were presently unavailable. Traveling? Sickness? New boyfriend? I had no idea.

So in the end, I had diligently gone out on eighteen dates with supposedly 'religious' women. About the only thing they all had in common was that they all were interested in finding a man. But they differed in other ways.

I can divide them into three general groups. The first was a group of four women with whom I found absolutely no chemistry whatsoever. Perhaps a better term would be that there was an anti-chemistry. Luckily, I was able to recognize these women the moment I met them or when I entered their home. I tried to make these dates short and sweet. One was recuperating, not so successfully, from an acute psychiatric aberration. Another let me in on her closely guarded secret. She had absolute proof that aliens had possessed the President of the U.S.A. and the responsibility for stopping them had fallen to her. The woman was about to enter under the care of a shrink – none too soon. The two others had personal habits that left something to be desired. One admitted, superfluously, that she was a naturalist and had an aversion to using soap or deodorant. And the last one had twenty-seven cats and was interested in having that number grow. Unless I develop an acute masochistic psychosis, I would toss myself under a train rather than have a second date with any of these women. There was absolutely no chance of me developing any sort of serious relationship with any of the four, now or in the future.

The second group, made up of six women, wanted a man, for all sorts of self-satisfying reasons, but were not interested in matrimony. Unfortunately, all six let me know that wedding bells were not an option late in the date. This disturbed me quite a bit since I always prefaced my request to go out with them with a statement about the seriousness of my intentions. When

I confronted them and asked why they did not admit that all they were looking for was a temporary sexual companion – they all said, in one form or another – 'That's what all the men say.' Sex on the first date was considered de rigueur and expected by these women. I politely refused the sex offered by five of these ladies (the woman from Cranbrook was in this group) and this – no doubt – had offended all of them. The only one that almost broke through my no-sex bulwark had been Vickie Schwartz. But she probably could have seduced the Pope.

The last group of eight ladies was made up of women that were interested in a relationship and marriage – very much. Unfortunately, with many of these women I had this unsubstantiated feeling that their interest was sparked by my Dunn & Bradstreet credit rating and not because of some overwhelming intellectual or physical attraction they felt for me. Sex on the first date was offered circumspectly by four of them and I was fairly certain that if I was interested, the other four would have capitulated as well. It was as if they were at an audition. If they did not show everything they had right then and there they would not get the part.

I had not met my *beshert* – I was batting zero for twenty.

I knew that somewhere out in the vast wasteland of the Jewish dating circus there was probably some nice Jewish woman who shared the same values that I did and was interested in joining with me to set up a respectable Jewish religious home. Unfortunately, up until now our paths had not crossed.

I knew that Ayelet was also dating and for all the restrictions of the *charedi* way of dating it did have some benefits. The prospective couple knew that whoever was waiting at the other end of the line was someone that had been screened by their careful selection process. Almost all the thrill seekers and weirdoes were eliminated. All monetary considerations were laid out on the table before the couple ever met. It went without saying that there was no first date sex.

Maybe I should go to a *shadchan*?

"Where are we going?" asked Ayelet, rousing me from my thoughts.

I had to think fast to determine if there was any connection between what I had been mulling over in my mind and her question. *Had I accidently said something out loud?* I quickly realized that there was no way that Ayelet could know what I was thinking. She also had no idea about our destination, because I had kept it a secret. All I told them was that we would be making a day of it and there would be a barbecue.

I glanced over my shoulder and said, "Used to be when my family went out this way towards Battle Creek, we would go visit the Kellogg's factory. David loved it. But they closed down the tours. So instead we are going to see an alpaca farm. I have never been there but some friends said it was great."

When the kids heard where we were going they went bananas – Ayelet just frowned.

# 20

## *Well done*

I MUST SAY MR. LINCOLN handles his motor home quite skillfully. I would be petrified driving such a big vehicle.

The seats in the motor home are extremely comfortable – it is almost like the chairs in my living room – and I am trying to relax but it is difficult because I am still apprehensive about going on this trip with Mr. Lincoln. I know that there are people that would look askance at me for being out for an entire day with a single man – even if it is with my entire family. But he did say that we will be going far from the city and it is extremely unlikely that anyone in the community will see us.

Still I worry.

The kids seem delighted with the trip. It must be because it has been so long since we have been able to go anywhere together. My business has occupied almost all of my time. With the bakery closed these last few days – it seems almost like a vacation.

*I guess I worry too much.*

My kids are mesmerized by the rural scenery with all the passing farms, trees, and little streams. They are constantly chattering away about the new sights that they are seeing. A cow here and a tractor there, and everything in between. Mr. Lincoln surprised them when he suddenly turned off of the blacktop highway on to a well maintained gravel entrance road. There is a large sign welcoming us to the Sunrise Alpaca Farm.

*It looks like we have arrived.*

He explained that he read on the internet that this farm had once been a dairy operation and now had over three hundred head of alpaca, which was considered pretty respectable because they had only started fifteen years before with a handful imported from South America. The alpaca, it turned out, were hardy beasts and tolerated the harsh Michigan winters quite well.

"Why is it important for my children to see these creatures," I asked skeptically.

"No reason ... it's just interesting," he said.

*We'll see.*

There were a surprisingly large number of vehicles in the small parking lot and at first I did not think the large motor home could get between the rows of cars. But Mr. Lincoln navigated through without difficulty and was able to park in the area designated for larger vehicles. As soon as he stopped the motor home the kids unbuckled their belts and eagerly piled out to start their adventure.

Without asking me Mr. Lincoln paid our entrance fees – *I must remember to reimburse him.* We all visited the restrooms and then passed through the alpaca educational center to begin our walk along the marked gravel paths that took us out to see the alpaca grazing in the pastures.

The sign said that the closest grazing area held forty head and there were also large blue signs telling one and all about the interesting animals. However, before we reached the first sign Chaim'l was already spouting his unbelievable knowledge of alpaca. *He is definitely an ilui – and not just in Torah subjects!* His explanation began by giving their scientific name and then went on to describe the difference between alpaca and their cousins, the llamas and vicunas. Other visitors to the farm stopped to listen to my Chaim'l's guided tour.

He gave an interesting explanation about the grazing characteristics of the alpaca, especially about the part where they all got rid of their waste products in one specific area of the field and none of them would graze in that area.

*That was Chaim'l.* I just accept my son's ability as something expected and normal but I can see that Mr. Lincoln is astounded by Chaiml's erudition. He asked Chaim'l, "Did you get all that information by just walking through the alpaca education center?"

"Oh no," my son said in all modesty. "It's from an old encyclopedia we have in the house."

"But how did you know to look up stuff about alpacas?" he asked in surprise. "I didn't tell you we would be coming here."

"I didn't look it up," said Chaim'l. "It's just something I read a couple of years ago."

"When you were six?" asked Mr. Lincoln. "I have trouble remembering things I read on the same day."

Chaim'l told us that the young of the alpaca are not called calves like with cattle, but are called cria. The cria stay in the herd and nurse from their mothers until about eight months. After that they move the younger animals to start new herds. He stated that he read in the encyclopedia that because there is only one dominant male in each family unit, some of the males are castrated. He stopped his dissertation and looked up at Mr. Lincoln to ask, "What does it mean to be castrated?"

I smiled at his innocent question. *That's my Chaim'l.*

Mr. Lincoln seems to have been surprised by Chaim'l's query and he turned his head slowly trying to figure out what he should say to my son. After a moment he began to stammer, "Well ... castrated ... is where ... they take the males ..."

Obviously, Mr. Lincoln was about to educate my son by describing the intricacies of this surgical procedure. *Not a good idea.*

This was not the first time my son had delved into subjects that I felt he wasn't ready to tackle. I came to the rescue and stopped Mr. Lincoln from continuing – with what I am sure would be an overly informative reply – by saying, "Chaim'l, that is something I will explain to you when you are older."

As usual my son trusted me and simply accepted my answer with a smile and said, "Okay." Then he rushed ahead to join his brother and sister at the main grazing area.

Mr. Lincoln looked at me in relief, inclined his head, and mouthed a silent, 'Thank you.'

A number of the shaggy beasts began to drift towards us. I noticed the signs that cautioned the people to keep back if the animals approached, but I could not see any reason for the warning since the animals seemed so docile.

When I first saw the herd from a distance I was sure I would not find these beasts interesting, but as the big creatures lumbered slowly towards us I began to be intrigued. The animals seem to be a cross between a camel and a cow. *How unusual.* I tried to get a closer view of a large brown animal that was now up against the wire barricade.

Mr. Lincoln suddenly said loudly, "Ayelet, get back. It's dangerous."

"This fence seems plenty sturdy. I don't think there should be a problem," I answered leaning even closer.

"It's not the fence, that's the problem," he said. "It's just that they ..."

Chaim'l completed the warning, " ... spit."

The word left the my child's lips at about the same time as a sloppy green glob left the brown alpaca's mouth and caught me bullseye right between the eyes.

*Oh my God.*

"Gaaaaaaaah!" I exclaimed, wiping my face.

I heard everyone in the area burst out laughing. I just stood there frozen in my embarrassment. At first I remained absolutely mortified and did not know how to react, but when Racheli piped up with, "Ima ... spit ... Ha ha ha ha!" That was it! I realized that I must look a sight – and to everyone around me it must seem quite hilarious. I couldn't keep myself from cracking a smile and then laughing along with rest of the crowd.

I saw Mr. Lincoln smile and nod his head in my direction as if to say, 'Good sport.'

He stayed with my kids in the information center while I went back to the rest room to wash off as much of the alpaca goop as I could.

Okay – I will admit that alpacas are interesting, but I have reached my saturation point. In more ways than one. So, when I came out I tried to convince my children that it was time to conclude the Alpaca experience. Unfortunately, my family thought differently and Mr. Lincoln didn't help. They insisted that they wanted to go into the farm shop to see the items made from alpaca wool. The sweaters and scarves were nice but the prices were unbelievably exorbitant. The cost of a small scarf – the cheapest item in the place – was equal to what we paid for a month's rent when Rephael and I first got married. *Almost like spun gold.* Luckily the children did not find anything that interested them. Mr. Lincoln then told them that it was time to go to our final destination – his 'secret place' – and they reluctantly said goodbye to the South American beasts.

Apparently his 'secret place' was not much of a secret to the people in the Battle Creek/Kalamazoo area but for anyone else in the state – including me – it was fairly unknown. After driving about thirty minutes through a heavy drizzle we reached our destination – the entrance to the Fort Hauling State Park and Recreation Area.

Chaim'l asked, "Why do they call it Fort Hauling?"

"I don't know," Mr. Lincoln said with a shrug. He explained that in all the years that he had been coming to this place he never once asked that question and maybe the locals knew the story. He had no idea if the park was named for a military bastion somewhere nearby or for some momentous thing that Mr. Hauling had done to have a fort and a park named after him. He was sure that it must have been something significant because he was certain it was very unlikely that anyone would ever name a park after Steve Lincoln.

It was three o'clock in the afternoon when we stopped at the park office to pay the entrance fee. The park ranger gave Mr. Lincoln his receipt and said, "You've got the park pretty much to yourselves. What with the cold weather and now the drizzle, we had only a few people today and most of them have already gone home."

Mr. Lincoln responded, "We're just here to see the lake, have a barbecue. Maybe the rain will stop and we can also watch the sunset. Then we'll head home as well."

"No problem if you want to spend the night," said the attendant. "We don't have any hook-ups but the campsites are all available. If you want to you can pay the over-night fee in the morning."

"Won't be necessary ... but thank you," he answered. "By the way, why is this placed called Fort Hauling?"

The ranger smiled and said, "A lot of people ask that. This land was purchased at the beginning of the last century by Mr. Alworth Fort ... he was a local resident from here in town ... and in his will he donated it to the state to be a park. He stipulated that it be named after his freight company, 'Fort Hauling'. Have a good day."

It was now obvious that the man got the park named after him because he was a famous author. He wrote some monumental things. A check to buy the land and a will giving the park to the state.

"What's a hook-up?" I asked.

"A hook-up is a campsite where we can attach the motor home to electricity, water, and sewer connections," answered Mr. Lincoln.

"Doesn't a motor home have all that?"

"Yes and no. We have water tanks and separate holding tanks for the sewerage. We get electricity from three sources. From the engine when it is running, from the generator, or from batteries. But without a hook-up we are limited somewhat and we will eventually run out of water, sewerage capacity, and electric power.

"Are we okay now?"

"For a short barbecue?" he asked rhetorically. "Yeah, we're fine."

He drove the vehicle right up to a picnic area situated on a slight rise above a beautiful body of water. The sign identified it as Eagle Lake. The shores of the lake were surrounded by lush second growth forest. The drizzle muted the colors and made a blur of all the sharp edges. The view from the front window was almost like an impressionist painting of a lake in the French Pyrenees. It was lovely.

It stayed cool and drizzled off and on over the next three hours, but I knew that it would not stop my kids. They put on their raincoats and went down to the lake to play ball and dig in the sand. Mr. Lincoln showed the boys how to skip rocks and they were soon busy exploring all the other natural wonders of the deserted lake and beach. The only other vehicle at the lake left at about five o'clock.

To give us shelter from the sporadic rain, Mr. Lincoln rolled out the side awning of the motor home and was able to set up the portable barbecue grill. He started the charcoal and unfolded some chairs and a small table. When the coals were hot enough he put the hotdogs, hamburgers, and rib steaks over the fire – all were 'extra' *kosher* items – *glatt kosher* – that he had specifically purchased this morning. He also threw on a few ears of corn and grilled some marinated vegetables.

Very nice.

Behind the rain clouds the sun was getting lower in the sky and daylight was slipping away. Since there was no *minyan* in the area, Mr. Lincoln said his afternoon prayers to himself while the meat cooked on the barbecue.

I am usually not a *kibitzer,* but at first I tried to tell him how to grill the food. I reasoned that he practically doesn't cook at all, so how would he know what to do? However, he obstinately ignored everything that I said and insisted that he considered himself to be a barbecue *mavin.* He stated that he had been grilling well before I was born – literally. I was a bit miffed that he was not taking my advice, but one hour later I sampled the food and had to admit that everything was cooked to perfection.

We called the kids back from the beach to eat but now the rain was falling harder and a chilling breeze had kicked up and that made it too cool to eat outside. So, Mr. Lincoln started the generator to power the lights and we set up the meal in the dining area of the motor home. With the elements beating at the windows it was all comfy and dry inside, and the kids tore into the food with a vengeance. The youngsters kept up a lively chatter as they enjoyed the tasty victuals. Everyone was joking about the happenings of the day, and at my expense the alpaca spitting incident was mentioned once or twice – maybe more. The atmosphere was absolutely delightful.

With the meal over we all said grace and organized our waste to be thrown into the park's trash receptacles at the entrance gate. The smoldering charcoal was dumped into the fire pit and doused with water from the lake. Mr. Lincoln turned off the generator, repacked all the barbecue paraphernalia, and rolled in the awning. With everyone back in their seats, ready for the return trip to Detroit, he turned the ignition key. The starter motor revved up but the engine would not turn over. The starter seemed to be working fine, but even after a number of attempts the engine just would not catch.

"What's the matter?" I asked nervously.

"Won't turn over."

"Well, keep trying," I insisted.

"That's what I was doing but if I continue I'll just run down the battery."

"So what are you going to do?"

"I'm an architect ... not a mechanic. So I better get some assistance," he said taking out his cell phone. He punched in the emergency road service number but got no response.

"What's the matter now?"

"The screen is flashing 'No Service'."

"That's not good," I commented.

"You can say that again,"

"Maybe you're out of gas," I suggested.

"I'm not out of gas. I barely drive the thing and I ..." he began to say and stopped.

"When was the last time you filled this thing with gas?"

"I don't remember," he responded.

"As I said before ... that's not good. What does the gas gauge show?"

Mr. Lincoln turned the switch to power up the dashboard and he looked down at the gas gauge.

"What does it say?" I asked apprehensively.

"Empty."

My heart sank.

# 21

## *Out of gas*

"SO JUST LIKE I SAID, we are out of gas," said Ayelet with satisfaction.

I did not know what to do next but then I remembered one of the special attributes of the vehicle, "It won't be a problem. This motor home has dual gas tanks. I remember that I filled both, so all I have to do is flip the switch to the reserve tank and we'll be fine." I found the toggle and moved the switch to the second tank, but the needle refused to budge. I stared in disbelief for a moment and then rapped on the gauge trying to get it to move.

*This is not a good omen.*

The indicator remained on the empty mark. I reluctantly decided to check the tanks manually. I crawled under the vehicle and pounded with my fists on each of the fuel tanks. Both gave back a hollow echo. I returned to the motor home defeated.

"No luck?" asked Ayelet.

"Ima, how will we get home?" asked Yanki.

"Don't worry," said Chaim'l. "Steve knows how to fix everything."

'Thank you for that vote of confidence,' I thought. This kid is the perpetual optimist, but I did not have a clue as to how I was going to get out of this. "I can't figure why there is no gas in the second tank."

"That's easy," said Ayelet.

"Besides being a baking genius have you suddenly become some sort of mechanical whiz?" I asked sarcastically.

"Nope ... not at all. Your gas was probably stolen."

"Stolen? Did you see anyone come sneaking up behind our backs to steal the gas?"

"Not now. Last week ... last month ... maybe last year. You keep this big motor home parked in your driveway all the time. Everyone knows that these things are gas guzzlers so they have got to have big gas tanks. If I was a gas thief looking for a vehicle to siphon gas from, I would pick a motor home parked full time in a driveway. Wouldn't you?" asked Ayelet.

What she said made sense. "Yeah, you're right. That's probably what happened," I admitted nodding my head. "I suppose there is nothing for me to do but hike the mile or so back to the park station and ask the ranger for some help."

"You don't have to do that," said Chaim'l.

"Why not?" I inquired.

"Because it won't do any good. The sign said that there is an attendant from 7 AM to 7 PM. So there is no one there now," said the child.

"What sign?" I asked.

"On the side of the station, when we drove in."

Of course – the kid's photographic memory. "Thank you." I thought for a moment and said, "So I guess I'll hike the eight miles down to the main road ... should take me about two hours ... and try to get a ride to the nearest gas station."

Ayelet shook her head, "No you won't ... it's not a good idea. We're at least fifteen miles from the nearest town out here. It's pouring rain and the odds of anyone coming down these rural roads are fifty-fifty at best. Even if you got a ride you'll be gone for hours. You aren't going to leave me here with the kids when I haven't got the vaguest idea of how anything on this motor home works. So you're not leaving. Think of something else."

I thought about my options and none were good. It did not take me long to figure out what we had to do but I also knew that Ayelet would have a conniption fit if I even mentioned it. I tried to figure how she would react and what came to mind was a volcano blowing up in a furious eruption. Following the explosion I visualized fiery molten lava shooting into the sky and flowing down the slopes insidiously destroying everything in its path.

A very appropriate metaphor.

Nodding my head I said, "I don't think I should be the one to suggest how we solve this problem."

Ayelet said angrily, "You want me to think of something? You're the one with the brilliant idea to go to some God forsaken place for a barbecue."

"I wasn't thinking of you," I said.

"Then who?"

*Great, she fell for it.*

"Why, Chaim'l of course."

"Chaim'l? He's only eight years old."

"But a very smart eight year old," I said, as I held up an index finger to make the point." I turned to the boy, "Chaim'l ... you see our situation. What do you think we have to do? Handle it like a *Gemorah* problem."

The young boy barely hesitated before he began, "We are here in a motor home without gas. The phone does not work and there is no place that can be walked to, within a reasonable distance. And even if you could, *Ima* won't let you. Is that it?"

"The problem in a nutshell," I agreed. I turned to Ayelet, "Don't you think that he has a full grasp of the situation?"

Ayelet agreed by nodding her head reluctantly.

The young boy thought for a moment and then finally said, "The real problem is not that we are without gas. That is merely the cause of the main problem. The real problem is that we cannot go back to our homes. That is what makes this situation problematic."

"Chaim'l what are you saying?" asked his mother.

"If we were at our home, or Steve's home then this would not be a problem," offered the child.

"That's obvious," said Ayelet.

Chaim'l smiled and said, "Problem solved. We are at our *home*. We are at a *motor home*. We can stay here for the night until the ranger comes back in the morning. It's obvious."

"Oh no, we're not," she said, shaking her head.

I knew exactly what was bothering Ayelet, but I shrugged my shoulders and said, "He's right and we really haven't got a choice."

"We can't stay out here," scolded Ayelet.

I had to make her see that they really did not have any other option, even though she would be furious about it, "But we can. The place is water proof and wind proof. We have food and water and a toilet and electricity."

"Won't we run down the battery to the engine?" she asked.

"Different battery. If need be I can restart the generator. We have all the comforts of home. There is a full bedroom in the back and there's room in it for all the kids," I said pointing to the rear.

Yanki chirped in, "Can we sleep here, *Ima*? Oh *Ima*, please!"

Ayelet was in a state of shock and kept shaking her head repeating, "We cannot stay here. We cannot stay here. We cannot ..."

I motioned for Ayelet to join me at the rear of the motor home. Then in a low voice so that only she could hear I said earnestly, "We really do not have a choice. If you have any other ideas that I haven't considered, now is the time to throw them into the pot. If not, then let's think about how we're going to arrange this and make the best of it."

"But we can't sleep here," she insisted.

"You mean you can't sleep here with me," I whispered. When I saw Ayelet nod her head, I continued, "I realized that immediately. But you've been to my house before. This is just another house. The kids will be here and we're wearing our coats for God's sake."

"What will people say if they find out?" she countered.

"Who's going to tell them? Not me. Did I tell anyone about that little kiss on my cheek you gave me? Or the hand holding?"

In an instant Ayelet's face turned bright red as she spit out vituperatively, "Why did you just bring that up? We agreed not to talk about that ... ever."

"Ayelet ... stop," I commanded. "You are in a difficult situation. A situation that you have no control over. You can make this into a big problem and the kids will go nuts, or we can just play this like two adults and make the best of it."

Ayelet contemplated what I said and after a moment responded, "Okay but this place is freezing. Do you have any heat in this *home?*"

"Actually I do, but it won't do any good. It has two heaters. One works off the engine ... so that's out ... and the other is a gas furnace like in your house."

"So turn it on. It's cold."

"I can't. I have no propane. I vented all the gas for safety reasons."

"So now we do have a real problem. The kids could freeze to death if the temperature drops any lower."

I looked upwards in thought, "I'm sure we have some blankets in one of the cupboards." I searched a bit and after a few minutes returned with two rolled up sleeping bags, "These will do just fine."

We all went to the bedroom at the back of the motor home. The kids took off their shoes and climbed on to the bare mattress. I unzipped one of the sleeping bags and opened it like a large comforter and covered all three. It took a while for all the kids to go to the toilet one at a time and then quiet down. After all the excitement of the day, it was only about twenty minutes until they all began closing their eyes.

While she watched over her kids as they fell asleep, I returned to the front of the vehicle and turned the driver's seat towards the living room area. Soon Ayelet came to join me and sat on the couch. I unzipped the second sleeping bag and spread it over her. "What are you going to use?" she asked.

"I'll be fine. Don't worry about me," I said giving my head a nod to confirm what I said. "By the way, the couch unfolds into a bed when you are ready to sleep."

"Are you really going to sleep in that chair?" she asked skeptically.

"I've slept in worse places."

"What do we do now?"

I rubbed my shoulders and arms through my light windbreaker. I could hear the rain beating with a drum like rhythm on the roof, "Now we wait for the morning."

# 22

## *Ladies & Gentlemen*

I FEEL BAD for Mr. Lincoln. He must be freezing sitting in that chair with only his light jacket.

But then again, it's his own fault. Bringing us out here to this wilderness – and not bothering to check the gas. Why am I worrying about him at all? He deserves whatever he gets.

But what about me? If anyone hears that I was caught out here alone with Mr. Lincoln I will never be able to live down the shame. Well – not exactly alone – but close enough. If anyone finds about this the chances of me getting a *shidduch* go right out the window. Why did I ever agree to this? This – situation – however unintentional – could ruin my life. I don't know what I'm going to do.

"You shouldn't be worried that any of this will get out," said Mr. Lincoln.

*Is he a mind reader?* "What makes you think that I'm worried about anything?" I ask innocently.

"Are you kidding? I know you. Things like that bother you."

"No they don't," I insist, wrapping myself in the folds of the sleeping bag.

"Oh, really? You nearly had apoplexy, because you thought I might tell someone that you accidentally gave me a little peck on the cheek. I won't even mention the holding hands business when you had your surgery. I know how tough that could be for you."

I know my face is turning fire engine red and it suddenly is getting so hot. The nerve of him mentioning that again. "We talked about that and you said you would never bring it up. You promised."

"That's right I did. And I haven't told a soul."

"You promised never to say a word about those ... occurrences. And a few minutes ago you agreed once again that you would never mention it. But just now you did it again."

"Are you totally nuts? We both know what happened with that the kiss on the cheek and the hand holding. They were spur of the moment reactions. They did not mean anything. So what's the harm in talking about it between ourselves?" he asked.

What's wrong with him? "You are talking about it again!" I point out emphatically.

Mr. Lincoln held up his hands in acquiescence, "Okay, I'm not mentioning anything ... about any occurrences ... ever again. But you will admit that certain ... things ... do worry you ... an awful lot ... and yet you also know that I keep my promises. So, I will never mention ... to anyone ... including you ... anything about those certain things." Then added, "You have to admit that I do keep my promises?"

"Okay, I'll admit that."

"Fine, then don't worry what people think. You didn't do anything wrong then ... when and if certain things might have occurred ... and you are not doing anything wrong now. This time it was totally my fault that there is no fuel, not yours. We're here because you wouldn't let me go for help, so that really left no options."

As if I would let him walk down these rural roads – in the rain – to help me. Doesn't he realize that my conscious is already burdened with the death of one man who walked down a road for me? If another man died because of me – especially one that I – especially one that is my friend. Someone who really is trying to help me – I don't know how I could bear it, "There was no way I was going to let you walk to get help. It's pouring out there."

"I know," said Mr. Lincoln dourly.

*Doesn't he realize why being caught out here together is such a problem?* "But, you do understand that there are people in my community that would make a *shmatah* of me if they ever heard that I was here with you all night. They couldn't care less what the extenuating circumstances might have been."

What I said seems to have agitated Mr. Lincoln greatly. After sitting there for a moment shaking his head angrily, he suddenly leaned in my direction and asked loudly, "So why do you accept this ... their closed minded way of looking at things?"

I looked towards the rear of the motor home to see if his loud outburst had aroused any of the kids. "Would you please be quiet, you'll wake the children," I scolded. It appeared that no one had stirred so I said softly, "I accept it because I really do not have a choice. Just like I'm spending the night out here because I really don't have a choice."

"But you do have a choice," said Mr. Lincoln tentatively. "There is the more lenient Modern Orthodox way of doing things."

The Modern Orthodox way? He's got to be kidding. "Does the Modern Orthodox community condone a man and a woman who are not married to each other being out all night together?"

"No, but ..."

"And in the Modern Orthodox community there are no *yentas* who would make a mountain out of a mole hill?"

"Of course there are *yentas*, but ..."

"So why do you think that Modern Orthodoxy is better than my brand of Judaism?"

"Well, feminism. For one."

"When you say feminism, does that mean that all Modern Orthodox women go without ... support garments? That they never get married?" I asked.

"That's not what I meant," he said in his defense. "I am talking about the fact that a woman can decide not to cover her hair. To wear pants. To study *Gemorah* if she wants. She can be the bread winner in the house. Or even be a single mom."

"Are these things important in your eyes?" I asked.

"Well, yes. Doesn't it bother you that in your community the woman are ... are ... I haven't really got a better term ... oppressed?"

*What is he talking about?* "Oppressed? How am I oppressed?"

"Are you kidding?" he asked. "Look at you. You're a young vibrant ..."

How can he talk to me like that? I stared at him in shock, "Mr. Lincoln!"

He gave me a scoffing smile, "Don't give me that look. You are pretty ... we both know it ... and you are young and vibrant. But I'll try to be more ... careful with what I say ... you're an intelligent woman. But your rules say that you have to cover your hair so that not a strand sticks out. You have to give in to everything your husband says. You have to take care of the children ... lots of them ... and still keep up the house, cook, and very often hold down the only paying job in the family. Meanwhile many of the husbands in these households sit in their *yeshivas* and basically do nothing constructive to support their family."

How am I to answer him? Has he progressed far enough in his lessons with Rabbi Kalmonowitz to understand what I want to tell him? "I take it from your tone, that you believe that in our *frum* world the woman is assigned to an inferior position. Is that correct?"

"You hit the nail right on the head. We believe in more equality."

"Equality? Is that something good?" I inquired earnestly.

"Of course it is. It's at the basis of modern society," he answered.

"So do you think that when men and women are equal it is a better situation?"

"Of course."

I cocked my head to the side and asked, "Better for what?"

He looked at me perplexed, "What are you talking about?"

"You said that by having men and women on an equal footing it will be better. In what way? Will they live longer lives? Be more successful financially? Have more to eat? Be better parents?"

Mr. Lincoln appeared confused, "What are you getting at?"

As if I was talking to Chaim'l – well maybe not Chaim'l – perhaps some of his classmates – I explain, "In the medical world, if doctors want to scientifically prove that a certain drug is effective, they must first define what specific symptoms or disease they are trying to treat. Then after using the drug they check to see if this symptom or disease was improved."

Mr. Lincoln shook his head from side to side, "We're not talking about a disease."

"Aren't we? For instance which would you rather take? A drug that tastes good but doesn't cure the disease or one that tastes bad but makes you better?"

"The answer is obvious."

"Of course it is," I said nodding my head. "I once had a long discussion with my husband on this subject and he told me his personal way of looking at this problem. Would you like to hear what he said?"

Mr. Lincoln looked at me reverently, "Of course I would."

"Rephael said that the inequality of men and woman in *halacha* is based on the simple fact that men and women are different. Oh, they share a good many things, but there are definite physical and mental differences. They are two related sub-species of the same 'animal'. God did not create them equal. A woman will never have the muscle brawn of a man and a man will never be able to get pregnant and bear children. A man can never understand the love a woman has for her children and her home. And a woman will never understand why a man has distinct urges to hunt and join or watch sports teams. Yet, God has deemed that man and woman should marry, create a family and raise ... hopefully ... happy productive children. In the end the problem we want to solve is ... what is the best way to have happy families? Which way is the 'tasty but ineffective medicine' and which one is the 'bitter cure'?"

"How can you know?"

"Simple ... look at the end results. In which community do you think the odds are in favor of creating happy families? In the open material world of equality or the cloistered spiritual ... un-equal ... *frum* world."

"You can have happy ... and unhappy ... families in both groups," insisted Mr. Lincoln.

"Of course you can ... but in which group do the people seem happier? Have less drug addicts? Fewer criminals? Have more people with good values?"

"Okay, I'll concede the point, but the women are still oppressed."

"Do you really think we are?" I asked.

"Of course you are."

"Rephael did not *think* we are oppressed, he said we are suppressed."

Mr. Lincoln seemed perplexed by my statement, "What's the difference? It's just semantics. Oppressed? Suppressed?"

"Suppression is where you limit or control something."

"That's the same as oppression."

I wonder if he can see the difference, "No. Oppression is when you control or limit something out of cruelty or in a harsh manner. When you oppress someone you are not interested in their well being. It is almost always done to benefit the one that is oppressing."

"I don't get it," said Mr. Lincoln. "Give me an example."

"Okay. My kids love my cake and cookies ..."

"Who wouldn't?"

"That's not the point. They love my cake and if I would let them, their sweet tooth would have them gobbling cookies all day. They would never eat any healthy food. So I have to *suppress* their desire for sweets. But, if it were a different situation ... in some cruel world ... and there was someone ... someone official ... that was responsible to give out cakes to all the children in the neighborhood and this someone decided that he wants to single out my kids so that they would never get any cake, that would be *oppression.*"

"I think I follow."

"Or let's take traffic laws. You might have a desire to speed. The problem is that if you exceed the speed limit you might have an accident and injure yourself or others. So the city or state puts up speed limit signs and road bumpers and gives out speeding tickets. They do this to *suppress* your tendency to speed. But if the city made a racially biased law ... let's say ... that any Black person that drives in the city can only drive at 15 miles per hour. That would be *oppression.*"

"But for the person being *suppressed or oppressed* it is the same thing. They are being limited and they usually don't know the reason," Mr. Lincoln said, extending an open palm.

"That's true. But a child trusts his parents and he knows that if they set limits it is for his ... the child's ...

benefit. And one can only hope that governments do the same."

"I wouldn't count on that," he said.

"The big difference between suppression and oppression is defined by the person being limited. If he can understand the reason for the limitation ... if there is logic behind the suppression ... it can be easily accepted. Oppression is never acceptable. It may have to be tolerated, but it is never accepted."

"So you say that *halacha suppresses* women, but does not *oppress* them."

"Exactly," I said.

"But why do you have to *suppress* women at all?"

"I'll try to explain. Bear with me, my husband could explain it so much better than me."

"I doubt that," he said with a chuckle.

"Rephael was of the opinion that *halacha* specifically and intentionally suppresses women. Not to create an inequality, but to attain an equality. He said the suppression is necessary because men are defective creatures and so much more inferior to women. The rabbis must put constraints on the superior women in order to attain some sort of equality, otherwise women would outshine the men just about all the time."

"Stop, stop. This goes against all feminist logic. I can't believe you're saying this," he said holding up his palm like a traffic policeman. "No woman could really believe that."

"Believe what? That women are superior to men?" I asked.

"No. The part about women accepting that it's okay to attain equality by *suppressing* them. No woman would fall for that."

"Oh, really? And what am I? A portion of chopped liver?"

He looked at me in surprise, "Did you just make a joke?"

"I'm not allowed to make jokes?" I asked. "People say I have a very good sense of humor."

"You could have fooled me."

"What does that mean?"

"You're just always so serious," he responded.

"Yes I am. So, what about *my* beliefs?"

"You don't count. You've been brainwashed."

I stopped for a moment to decide how to answer him. I was insulted and hurt by his comment. How do I explain the difference between brainwashing and *chinuch.* I began slowly by saying, "First of all it is a cheap shot to say someone has been brainwashed just because their viewpoint on life differs from your own."

He seemed to realize his poor choice of words and said, "OK, not brainwashed, but you have to admit that most modern women won't accept or justify suppression in any form."

"You are correct, but most Jewish women and men have no understanding of *halacha.* Unless you study the *Torah* thoroughly it can be hard to understand the genius in the rabbi's decrees down through the ages."

"So, you say that the rabbis decided to suppress women to achieve an equality."

"Correct."

"That's ridiculous. If women are superior ... why not just let them reach their full potential?"

"Do you remember that I said that you have to define the problem you are trying to solve?" I asked.

"Yes."

"Remember the traffic laws? Why do we have such laws? Why not just let everyone drive any which way they want? Go for their maximum potential. If you want to drive on the left ... that's okay. If you want to speed along like a rocket or go slow as a snail ... that's okay as well. So why do we have traffic laws? It's simple ... because without them people would never be able to reach their final destinations. There would be traffic jams and people would even lose their lives. In dealing with traffic, the goal is to safely and efficiently reach our final destinations. So in order to reach the goal I have to put up with all sorts of inconveniences ... like traffic lights, speed limits, vehicle safety equipment, and other constraints. But it's worth it."

"I understand that. It's obvious," said Mr. Lincoln.

"Good, so what's our problem in the '*women's inequality*' situation?" I said, emphasizing the point by making air quotes by twitching my second and third fingers on both raised hands. "Is the problem how do we help women reach their maximum potential? Or is the problem how do you maximize the number of happy healthy families?"

"What's the difference?"

"If I help women reach their potential but by doing this I lessen their chance of having happy families, have I really done these women any good?"

"Why should that happen?"

"Because of the weak link in this equation. Men. Remember what Rephael said ... men are defective. Most, but not all, feel that they must be the boss in the family. They also believe that their purpose in life is to care and protect their families and the 'weaker women'. It's built into their chromosomes. They can't help it. Such men cannot tolerate women who boss them around and certainly they won't tolerate it in a family situation." Mr. Lincoln is grimacing. "Don't you believe this is true?"

He is squirming in his seat but finally says, "Okay. Some men."

"I think it is most, but we won't argue the point. Also, if both husband and wife work, but the woman is the major bread winner, you can count on difficulties ... with *some* men. The male of the species has certain built in buttons that if stimulated will make him ... explode."

Mr. Lincoln rejoined with, "Then he should learn to control himself."

"Spoken like a true liberal. Oh, some men can control themselves ... but *halacha* does not deal only with those special few. It has to deal with the average man. The manual laborer, the bank clerk, and the employee in a retail shop. These are good men but most of them are simply not able to control these primal urges. They are the ones with the 'explode buttons'.

"What do you mean explode?" he asked.

"Men are basically different from women in two aspects. One - they have more muscle mass. They can carry heavier loads and hit harder. Two - men like to solve their problems with aggression." I lowered my voice to a bass level, and mimicked a typical male bully, "Let's step outside and settle this."

He smiled and said, "Cute."

"Women will almost never do that. Do you agree?"

"Well, yeah. Those things are true."

"So if a woman in a family situation triggers one of those explode buttons it could be extremely dangerous for her and her children." I see he wants to respond and I cut him off with, "And don't tell me he should control himself. You know as well as me that it simply doesn't work. Just look at the statistics of wife abuse."

"Once again, I agree."

"But it is not only abuse that is the problem. Not too long ago I read in a magazine the results of a large study of American families in which the woman was the major breadwinner in the family. They found that there was a significantly greater incidence of men that would need psychiatric help, and there was also much more infidelity in those marriages. Obviously, these are families in great danger of falling apart. If you look at these studies you can see that Judaism's way of preventing problems in the family makes sense. *Halacha* does not want to jeopardize any families. So Jewish law *officially* places the man on a higher pedestal in his home. That's the *official* position ... but you know from everyday life ... and there are numerous citations in the *Gemorah* ... that the true ruler of the home is the woman. They basically make all the household decisions and determine just about everything in raising the children." I got up from the couch because I wanted to check the kids in the rear bedroom. The floor of the motor home felt cold under my stocking feet, "Think about what I just said until I get back."

When I returned Mr. Lincoln was nodding his head in agreement, "Okay, I'll also accept that women do rule the home, but what about the restrictions with clothing? That's certainly oppression. Why can't you wear what you want?"

As I rewrapped myself in the sleeping bag I asked, "Who says that I don't wear what I want?"

"Oh come on now," he responds, shaking his head from side to side in apparent disbelief. "You have to keep your hair covered all the time. Every inch of skin covered. No pants. No tight clothing."

"Exactly. *Tznius.* And why do you think *halacha* wants women to dress modestly."

"What's the difference?" he asked. "It is a form of ... of ... involuntary servitude."

"There you go again. Thinking *tznius* is involuntary. When will you realize that that the opposite of modest clothing is provocative clothing? And what is it supposed to provoke? The answer is obvious ... a response from people."

"Obviously."

"What women wear delivers a message. I'm not talking about cleanliness or the state of repair. Nor am I talking about ethnic or stylistic differences. Clothing can be clean, neat and proper. Or it can be revealing, suggestive or even erotic. Did you ever ask yourself why a woman would wear something that would specifically draw a man's attention?" I asked rhetorically. "Simple ... to attract a man."

"That's what it means when you say, 'You look very attractive.'"

"Exactly. Attracting ... men," I emphasized.

"Oh, come on now," he answered in exasperation.

"We had a non-Jewish housekeeper who taught me a phrase that was often used in her church and I think it's appropriate. 'If you're selling something you should advertise. If you ain't selling you shouldn't advertise.' *Frum* women ain't selling."

"Women don't necessarily dress up fancy just to *sell* something."

"No they don't. They dress up to feel good about themselves. If they know that they are looking good. Good enough to attract a man ... or a woman ... "

"Yes, there is that as well," he said in agreement.

"They feel empowered. That's what makes them feel good."

"What's wrong with that?" he asked.

"The *yetzer horah,*" I said pausing for dramatic effect. "Both men and women have it ... but men can be more easily tempted and fall. Rephael once told me that if a woman offers herself to a man ... any man ... long enough and hard enough ... and she's not repulsive ... the man will fall to the temptation almost every time. At first I couldn't believe it but he said it was true. What do you think?"

Mr. Lincoln seemed to be mulling something over in his mind and finally said sheepishly, "There might be some truth to that."

"I know that it is not so with most women. A man can throw himself at a woman for days and even years and she can take him or leave him as she sees fit. It is not by chance that the man woos the woman, but ... unless the man uses sheer force ... physical or otherwise ... it is always the woman that decides."

"So where does that leave you?"

"*Rebbetzen* Kalmonowitz told me a story once. When she was a young woman and Rabbi Kalmonowitz was studying in the great *yeshiva* in Lakewood, New Jersey, the hemlines of women's dresses were well above the knees. And because that was the style, all the women in the *yeshiva* went around with high hemlines. One day her mother sent her a skirt in the new 'Empire style'. This skirt went all the way down to the floor and covered her legs entirely. She wore the skirt on *shabbos* thinking that she was in strict observance of all the rules of *tznius.* On Sunday, the *rebbetzen*, the wife of the rabbi who was the *rosh yeshiva* in Lakewood, called her. She told her to stop wearing the long skirt and go back to the shorter one. The *rosh yeshiva's* wife explained that women's clothing should not draw attention. When she wore the new style ... even though it covered more of the body ... it drew attention and that went against the spirit of *tznius.*"

"But why do *you* ... Ayelet Weinberg ... agree to cover yourself entirely?"

"We have to go back to what I said before ... men are different from women. Men are much more visual. They see a pretty woman in provocative clothing and they become attracted. They can't help themselves. It's their *yetzer horah.* Some rabbis say they must strive to overcome this attraction and some rabbis believe it is impossible to overcome. Over the years *halacha* ruled that in order for men not to fall prey to their inborn weakness, Judaism must rely on women to take charge and to dress modestly at all times so as not to stir up immodest thoughts in men. They must sit in the back seat if a man gives them a ride to the JCC."

"Touché," he commented.

I nodded my head at him and continued, "Rephael taught me to see that whenever I cover my hair or wear modest clothing, I am overcoming a *koach* that I have within me. A power that could upset men and their families. And families are what Judaism is all about ...

remember? What I wear directly helps Judaism. When I dress modestly I feel empowered. I feel good and I do it because I want to."

Mr. Lincoln nodded his head a few times and then said, "So, to summarize ... you disagree with all the feminist movement."

"On the contrary," I insisted. "I agree with most of the goals of the feminists."

"But you just said ..."

"I believe that society mistreated women in the past and this must change. Women should not be objectified." I stopped for a moment. "What was the most important sociological change that affected women in the last fifty years?"

He thought for a moment and then said, "Birth control?"

"That certainly affected women, but it was not a sociological change. The big change was in day care. Up until fifty years ago women were expected to give up their plans for having a career and be stay-at-home-moms to raise the family. A woman who put her kids in day care was considered a bad mother. Only when day care was available and truly accepted could women really begin to make an impact on the work force."

"Yes, that was a big factor," he agreed.

"I firmly believe that a woman should receive equal pay for equal work. Women should not be abused or victimized. Women should have equal opportunities compared to men. They should be free to decide their destinies and not be under the rule of men if they so choose."

"So, where do you differ?"

"As I said before, I don't think that men and women are equal. They have many many things in common but there are still major differences in their physical makeup and in the way they behave. There is proven scientific evidence that shows that they will react differently in times of stress. All types of stress. If you try to ignore this fact, and say they are totally equal, you are just asking for trouble. I believe that over the last two thousand years *halacha* has been able to refine and implement the best strategy for dealing with the difficult problem of men interacting with women. I think our way makes for better relationships and happier families. Don't you agree?"

He nodded his head as he said, "I don't know if I agree ... but I have a better understanding of your position."

# 23

## Three star shovel

MISERABLE IS A TERM that is insufficient to describe how I feel.

All through the night the unrelenting cold only allowed me short fitful spells of sleep and in order to conserve body heat I kept myself curled up in a ball. Even with the driver's seat reclined back to its maximum, when I rolled to either side, the arm rests and buckle apparatus poked my body in the most tender of places. As the night progressed it became obvious to me that the designer of this chair had insidiously planned it just that way. Anyone that was foolish enough to attempt to use this chair for sleeping purposes, would soon discover that all the protuberances and bumps would constantly press painfully into their flesh and convince them that it was not such a good idea. After only a few minutes in one position, it was necessary to turn again. Certain body parts were already throbbing with a chronic dull ache that continued to vex me even after I turned to a new position. All the signs indicated that it was going to get worse.

I even tried sleeping on the motor home's carpeted floor, but that was not any better. The ice cold hard flooring drove me back to the uncomfortable seat. I was now convinced that the chair needed only minor modifications to become a certified torture apparatus.

Every hour or so I had to get longer periods of respite from the chair-of-pain, so I would get up and walk the length of the motor home. On these patrols I made sure that the kids and Ayelet were well tucked in under the sleeping bags and that the vehicle was secure. On my last look around I noted a lighter cast to the eastern sky, indicating the approaching dawn. That was a bit of encouragement. Once the morning light shed its grace upon the earth we could all get up and I would not have to remain on this accursed seat.

Yes, now there definitely is more light in the East. It was time to rise and shine and say my morning prayers. I suddenly realized that I did not have my *talis* and *tefilin* with me. Oh well, God would forgive me.

I also had to get some sort of breakfast going. Luckily, I had purchased my weekly groceries the day before, so I had the fixings for a morning meal and the kids would not be hungry. Strange – I almost never did my grocery shopping on Sundays, but God moves in the strangest ways. The rabbis of old say that the Almighty shows special compassion (i.e. luck) to widows, orphans, and idiots. Since I was not the first two, I guess I knew where my luck came from. An idiot that did not check his gas before taking a long trip.

The vehicle was as silent as a tomb and I gingerly climbed out of the driver's seat. As I stood there flexing and straightening my groaning joints, I thought to myself, *'When should I waken the Weinberg family?'*

Suddenly – without any warning – Ayelet shot up from the couch like a bat out of hell. She was flailing her arms and screaming hysterically at the top of her lungs, "Oh my God! Oh my God! Oh my God! ... It can't be! It can't be!"

The unexpected outburst scared the crap out of me.

Unless Ayelet was in the habit of waking every morning behaving like the chief lunatic in the asylum, something was obviously wrong.

I tried to think of a rational reason for such an uncharacteristic outburst. My mind, when confronted by an unknown emergency situation, could become a strange quagmire of conflicting thoughts. In the next split second my brain came up with a myriad of possible reasons for Ayelet's strange behavior. Just as quickly I excluded the more exotic scenarios. She had not suddenly developed an acute psychosis nor was there a band of terrorists threatening her life. After all, the door was locked and why would terrorists want to come specifically to central Michigan? I excluded quite a few of the other possibilities, including a dinosaur attack and an approaching tsunami. But I could not completely shake off the one about a large rattlesnake curled around her leg. I knew that all the weird possibilities were figments of my deranged imagination but just to be safe I looked around to see if there was anything at hand that I could use to defend myself and found a long handled ice scraper under the driver's seat. Ayelet had her back to me but it was quite apparent that she was still extremely agitated. I asked with concern, "Is everything all right? Did something happen?!"

Apparently my voice surprised her because she spun around quickly – obviously totally disoriented and utterly confused. She snapped her mouth shut and stopped her caterwauling. Ayelet pointed an accusing finger at me and asked loudly, "What are you doing there?"

I had my snow scraper in hand and was now wafting my menacing weapon aloft, "This is my motor home. We got stranded without gas. Don't you remember?"

"But ... but ... but ... under the cover," stuttered Ayelet, trying to catch her breath. "I was sleeping ... and I suddenly felt ... someone was with me ... under the cover ... and I remembered." She stopped for a moment and then seemed to calm slightly, "I guess I must have panicked."

I noted that there was some sort of lump under the sleeping bag. With my less-than-lethal ice scraper in hand I approached the couch warily and stood poised for a moment. Then I tore back the sleeping bag to reveal

Racheli curled up in a little ball sucking her thumb. The commotion had roused Yanki and Chaim'l and they came forward to investigate. I lowered my weapon and looked at Ayelet, "I guess this was your nighttime guest. I think you can calm down now."

"I was so frightened," she said holding a hand to her chest to quiet her thumping heart. "You have no idea."

"Yeah, I do," I said nodding my head knowingly. "I think I figured out what you were frightened about."

With everyone up, the crisis passed – but I knew it was not going to be easily forgotten. It was almost six o'clock in the morning – and since no one wanted to go back to sleep – we just began our day. At six thirty the morning sun began to peek its way over the horizon in earnest and that made us all feel more cheerful. We each took turns in the bathroom and helped arrange things in the motor home.

The rain had stopped around two o' clock in the morning and I went outside to start a fire in the nearby fire pit. It was still quite chilly and I figured that after spending the night in the cold motor home the flames would get everyone warmed up and also give us something to cook on. I explained to the boys how to find dry wood from the dead branches on the trees around us and sent them out to gather fuel. When they returned we all stood around the warm blaze. Chaim'l said his morning prayers by heart – of course. But I had to use the *siddur* I had on my cell phone. *The wonders of modern technology.* Since my own groceries were not geared for kiddee food, Ayelet searched through the packages to see what we could serve the children. She found bread and jam so at least we were assured we would not starve. I took out a carton of fresh eggs and a package of butter and headed outside. Ayelet looked up and asked, "What are you going to do with the eggs. You said the stove doesn't work and you haven't got a frying pan?"

"You're right."

"So how are you going to cook the eggs?"

"Come to the fire pit and see."

Ayelet picked up Racheli and joined the boys who were toasting bread over the fire. I went to the back of the vehicle and began rooting around in the tool box. After a few minutes I returned with a small collapsible shovel. I washed off the steel blade and then stuck it over the hot coals in the fire. After a minute I blew the ash off of the shovel blade and threw on a dab of butter. The butter sizzled and popped and I re-positioned the shovel over the coals. When the butter was all melted I opened an egg onto the blade. Within a minute I had a sunny-side-up egg. I slid the egg on to a paper plate and asked, "Anyone hungry."

"Aren't you the amazing boy scout?" said Ayelet appreciatively.

"I have three merit badges in shovel cooking," I boasted.

Chaim'l and Yanki were delighted. I made a variety of eggs, including over easy and even French toast. The kids sat on one of the picnic tables and gobbled it all up as fast as I could make the grub. Good thing I had purchased two dozen eggs. Racheli was soon sated and sat to the side playing with some twigs, but the two boys were still hungry. I made a large pile of scrambled eggs and the boys began devouring it.

Ayelet joined me by the fire and said softly, "I'm sorry for acting like a crazy person in there."

I nodded my head and said, "It's okay, I know why you panicked. You thought that that someone in your bed might have been me. I'm sorry I make you feel that way."

Ayelet did not respond for a moment, but then said, "First of all, there is no *way* for me to feel towards you. You are a friend to me. A good friend. And I will always appreciate what you did for me and my children."

"Thanks a lot ... but the very thought of me ... in your bed ... or couch ... or whatever ... was so revolting that you shot out from under that sleeping bag like a red hot cannonball exploding out of a Howitzer."

"That's not what happened."

"What are you talking about? I was there. I thought that someone had started World War III."

"You only saw the end of what happened."

"What do you mean the end? It was all over in five seconds and I was there the whole time," I said emphatically.

Ayelet looked away into the distance and said softly, "What I'm going to tell you remains between us. You will never ever repeat this to anyone ... not even to me. I just don't want you to think that I find you ... revolting. Do you promise?"

I could not imagine what she was about to say, "I agree."

"Promise," she demanded.

"Promise."

Ayelet began slowly, "What happened this morning began almost fifteen minutes earlier. Surprisingly I had slept amazing well. For a change, none of the kids woke me during the night. I felt a warm body next to mine in the comfortable bed ... something I had not felt in a long time ... I did not know it was Racheli and I reveled in the feeling. To me it was a blissful sensation. I guess ... as I lay there ... I began to remember the events of the night before. I thought of how I had felt sorry for you sitting by yourself in the uncomfortable freezing seat while I was in the warm bed. I tried to figure out whose warm body was up close to mine and the two thoughts mingled. In my confused semi-awake state I assumed that the body next to me ... must be yours."

I could see that Ayelet was having a difficult time confiding all this to me so I did not rush her.

She paused for a moment and took a few deep breathes, "Suddenly, everything changed. I realized that if it was true ... if you were really under the sleeping bag with me ... I could be ruining everything. I would ruin our friendship. Ruin my chance for a *shidduch*. Ruin my children's future. That's why I woke up screaming. I have never found you revolting. Far from it. I know that I have gotten where I am today mostly because of your efforts. I am so far in your debt I don't know how I will ever repay you. To me you are a *tzadik*." Silent tears started down Ayelet's cheeks, "How could I ever find a *tzadik* revolting?"

I did not respond immediately. I finally said, "Thank you. I know how hard it must be for you to say what you just did."

Ayelet snuffed up her tears and said, "No you don't. You have no idea. And if you ever tell anybody what I said I will carve your heart out with a dull knife and feed it to the vultures," she said half jokingly.

I answered with mock solemnity, "You do know that there aren't too many vultures in Michigan."

"I will import a flock just so you know I mean business," she said with a nod of her head between tears.

"What about the dull knife business. Isn't that a little cruel?"

"I can be a cruel person when I have to be."

Chiam'l looked up from his eggs and asked, "Ima, are you okay?"

"Yes, I am," she said wiping away any residual tears. "Couldn't be better. We're having such an adventure."

Chaim'l got up from the table and approached, "Steve."

"What?" I asked.

"When you go back home make sure you mark the shovel," said the boy earnestly.

"Why would I want to mark the shovel?" I asked in bewilderment.

"So you won't confuse it with other shovels," said Chaim'l.

"How will I confuse it? It's just a shovel."

"Yes, but you fried eggs with *butter* on this shovel. Now it's a *milchig* shovel."

Of course – how did I not see that?

# 24

## White knight

WE PASSED THE FINAL INSPECTION and about two weeks after that the Department of Agriculture came through with a certificate for the bakery. I am officially in business. The hearth oven makes such a difference. Now I can make all the specialty breads that people have requested. I am already supplying twelve ethnic restaurants with the bread they need. They require their fresh baked goods for the heavy evening crowds so I am able to bake their breads in the mornings. It is all working out beautifully and my staff is terrific.

It's hard to believe that there are now twelve of us working full time in the bakery. Added to that were the four part-timers that help out on Sundays. The management company that I have been working with did all the hiring and chose people that are totally compatible with the business and each other. I now have a full time plant manager and business manager. Antoine comes in early each day and he heats all the ovens and does all the heavy lifting. His son, Albert, and another three men, go out to make the first deliveries at noon. I found that if we prepare the various types of dough the day before, Mrs. Leibowitz along with Anna, can handle almost all of the bread and rolls all by themselves. That leaves me, along with Alice and Jimmy, to do all the cakes and sweets. Everyone multi-tasks and by three, we are cleaning up and preparing the dough for the next morning's work.

Mr. Lincoln planned the bakery perfectly and with all the special ovens we can bake over a dozen different things at the same time. Over this past year we developed creative ways to supply 'fresh' baked goods to our customers seven days a week even though we do no baking from Friday afternoon until Sunday morning. People like our products and business is good. We are handling just about all we can. God willing, if things keep up I will be able to pay off the bank loan – what seemed a huge amount of money – in less than a year.

God has indeed been good to me. He sent me Mr. Lincoln and he has done so much. But the expansion work is finished and now he rarely comes by. The kids miss him – and to be honest – I miss him as well. He is a true friend. One that I could talk to – even if we had to use stilted methods of conversation – on just about any subject. He's a good man. I've heard that his dating efforts have not been going so well. I hope he finds his *beshert* soon. My luck has also not been good. Today will make the eighth *shidduch* date. Still no match. I am hopeful. The *rebbetzen* assures me that she will find the perfect match soon. The fellow I am to see tonight is supposed to be a well sought after man from Toronto. Thirty nine years old, excellent family and works in real estate.

I purchased a new dress just for this date. Something I have not done since Rephael's death. I was never in the mood until now and money had been scarce. The outfit is very feminine but still proper.

It is getting late and I must put on my *shaitel* and do my makeup. He will be here soon and I don't have time to waste. Marissa has already arrived and is now taking care of the kids so that's one less thing to worry about. I'm just about ready.

There's the door bell. One last check – everything seems in order, "Kids, come to the door, to meet Mr. Horowitz. He's from Toronto."

I put on my widest smile and open the door but surprisingly it is not Mr. Horowitz standing on the porch, but Mr. Lincoln. How awkward, "Oh, it's you."

Mr. Lincoln seemed puzzled by my less than enthusiastic welcome and said, "And it's nice to see you as well, Ayelet. Hi kids," he said over my shoulder to my children who came rushing to the door.

"What are you doing here?" I asked.

Mr. Lincoln greeted my three kids, who stood at his side trying to get his attention. He shushed them and turned to me to say, "You left a message for me this afternoon. Something about one of the gas lines to the hearth oven not working properly. I called you back and told you I'd come over to check it."

"Yes, but I thought you would come tomorrow ... in the morning."

"Don't you have to bake tomorrow morning?"

"Of course I do."

"Well I've discovered an amazing fact. When you bake things in an oven, it gets kinda hot. And that makes checking gas lines extremely difficult and dangerous. You gotta do it when the oven is cool, so I came over," he said stepping through the doorway and going towards the kitchen.

"Yes, of course. Come in," I said running after him. "It's just that I have to go out on a date and I won't be here."

"That's fine. I know my way around. And whatever I don't know, Chaim'l will show me. Have a good time."

He went through my kitchen to the bakery extension – with my three children following behind him – and began moving equipment away from the side of the large oven to get at the gas lines. Meanwhile the door bell rang once again. *Oh my goodness, my date is here.* The kids along with Marissa stood watching Mr. Lincoln work, "Kids, come with me to the door to meet Mr. Horowitz."

Yanki said, "But *Ima*, we want to stay here with Steve."

Mr. Lincoln put on a stern expression, "Kids, you listen to your *Ima*."

Amazingly they obeyed him immediately. They never do that for me.

To the door.

The kids are in a formal line. Okay here goes. The fellow standing in the doorway wore the official uniform of the *frum* world. Black suit, black shoes, black fedora, and a white shirt. But there was one unusual thing in the way he was dressed. He had a bright yellow print tie and a matching pocket handkerchief. Very strange. "You must be Mr. Horowitz," I said with a smile.

"Yes I am ... in the flesh. But please call me Moshe."

Best to get the awkward stuff over with, "I'm Ayelet. I'd like you to meet my children ... Chaim'l, Yanki, and Racheli. Kids this is Mr. Horowitz."

The fellow leaned down and formally shook my children's hands one after the other. Then he brought out a package of chocolates he had kept behind his back and offered it to them, "I hope you don't mind. I brought something for them."

How considerate and thoughtful. "Sure, why not? But only one piece each. Save the rest for tomorrow."

Chaim'l grabbed the package and took the others over to the side to give each their share and then Marissa ushered them into the living room. When Moshe took off his hat I made another unusual discovery. His dark hair had been tinted with blonde highlights. That was definitely not something you would commonly see on a *frum* man and certainly not a man almost forty. Oh well, you shouldn't judge a book by its cover. I have to be patient. This might be my *beshert*.

"Let me get my coat and we can go," I said.

Just then Mr. Lincoln came in from the kitchen rolling down his sleeves, "Everything will be just fine with the oven. One of the valves has an automatic shut off and it popped. I think I set it properly now ... I'll have the gas man check it tomorrow. But you should be all right."

Moshe stared at Mr. Lincoln and then cocked his head to the side pantomiming the question, "Who's this?"

I can understand his bewilderment. I'm sure the grapevine let him know that I have no living relatives in the city and yet, it is night time and a man just came out of my kitchen. "This is Mr. Lincoln. He's the contractor that did my bakery enlargement. Came by to fix something."

"In the evening?" asked Moshe.

Mr. Lincoln turned to me and asked, "Ayelet, aren't you going to introduce me to your date?"

*Why did he request that?* I have no choice but to say, "Mr. Lincoln ... this is Mr. Moshe Horowitz. He's from Toronto."

Mr. Lincoln leaned towards Moshe and extended an open palm, "Hi, nice to meet you ... Moshe from Toronto. You have a great gal here."

Moshe shook Mr. Lincoln's hand, but looked at me and asked, "You discuss your dates with your contractor?"

Mr. Lincoln pushed past us walking out to his car and said over his shoulder, "I'm a full service contractor. I do whatever is needed. You two have a good evening now,"

"Strange man," said Moshe, shaking his head.

"You don't know the half of it," I said under my breath.

We went out to his rental car and very gentlemanly, he opened the door for the passenger seat. When I date I'm allowed to sit up front. We're supposed to get to know each other. After almost a year of driving around in the back seat of Mr. Lincoln's car, being in the front still felt strange.

The venues for *frum* dates are quite limited. For *tznius* reasons you could only go to public places. Most movies were taboo. Live shows were definitely out of the question. So it was an interesting surprise when he took me to the Detroit Motor Home Show at the Northwest

Armory. Very original and creative. There were over 700 exhibitors and almost two hundred recreational vehicles. They ranged from folding tents on wheels to huge land yachts with all the luxuries of home and then some. Moshe did not recognize some of the weird gizmos that the vendors had for sale or were fitted to some of the vehicles, but after my experience in Mr. Lincoln's motor home I knew what most of them were and offered an almost running explanation for him.

"Where did you learn so much about motor homes?" he asked.

I was not eager to tell him about my evening stranded with Mr. Lincoln and simply said, "It's just something that interests me ... so I keep up."

We spent about an hour and half wandering the aisles of exhibits. He's a decent conversationalist and keeps referring to his big real estate deals and all his commissions to impress me. He doesn't realize that things like that are not important to me. So far he hasn't mentioned a single thing that sets him apart from any other man in the *shidduch* market. Not one word about his *Torah* study – which is something that is very important to me. Nothing about his attitude towards family and especially my children. What is he waiting for? The date will soon be over.

After the show, we stopped at a small brightly lit coffee shop on Woodward Avenue and he ordered orange juice for the both of us. When we were served, he pulled a small flask from his pocket and poured some of the contents – I assume some sort of alcoholic beverage – into his juice and then offered me some. What strange behavior. He drinks and drives. I suppose this was all a waste of time. He's talking about his future plans for travel and opening his own agency. Obviously he's still trying to impress me – but it's not working. Perhaps I should just say that I have an important appointment in the morning or that it's late.

Finally, we're back in the car returning home. I really have nothing in common with this man. I will just have to tell the *rebbetzen* that he was not right for me.

Why did he pull into this parking lot in the industrial area? It's dark here. Not a proper place for us. "What are you doing?" I ask suspiciously.

"I just thought we could park for a bit and get to know each other a little better," said Moshe with a smile, as he switched off the engine and dimmed the lights.

"I don't think this is proper. Would you please start the car and take me home," I demand.

"Just a minute. Hold on. I'm not going to do anything. I just want to talk," he said, as he unbuckled his seat belt.

"Why did you open your belt?"

"I'm just trying to get comfortable. Why don't you do the same?"

"Take me home right now," I insist.

"What's your rush? You want to hurry home to spend another night ... alone?"

"I don't like where this conversation is going. Please start the car."

"It's not as if you don't know what I want. You do have three children. Women say that they have a good time with me. So just relax and enjoy yourself."

"Mr. Horowitz, this has gone far enough. Take me home right now."

"I know your type. You have to hold out ... always insisting that you don't do this kind of stuff. Who are you kidding?" he said with a smile as he slid a hand up around my shoulder.

I push his hand away but his other hand came up and grabbed at my breast. I pushed that away as well. Suddenly he was an octopus grabbing and squeezing as I fought him off, "If you don't stop ... you will regret this."

"Oh, really," he said trying to pull my face close to his so that he could kiss me. "What's a little woman like you going to do?"

"I will scream," I was able to say, as I fought him off.

"Go ahead ... no one will hear you," he said laughing.

Suddenly his car door flew open and he was dragged from the car. A voice outside said, "But, I will hear her, you little creep."

Oh my goodness! That's Mr. Lincoln. What is he doing here? I unfastened my seat belt and climbed out of the car to see what was going on.

Moshe was standing about three feet from Mr. Lincoln, "Well, look who's here. It's the friendly contractor. How cozy. I get it. You and she are ..."

"Shut your mouth you dirt bag. You're a disgrace," said Mr. Lincoln. "How can you call yourself religious?"

"Me a disgrace? What about you? I'm not the one who's *really friendly* with the bakery lady," said Moshe tauntingly.

"Why you little ..." said Mr. Lincoln, as he pulled his arm back to take a swing at Moshe.

The punch never reached its mark.

Mr. Lincoln stepped forward to put a bit of momentum into his thrusting arm. Unfortunately there was a small pothole in the asphalt of the parking lot and when his foot sank into it his leg gave way. He toppled forward like a felled tree to land squarely on his face and then he just lay there.

I tried to rush over to Mr. Lincoln to see if he was hurt but Moshe grabbed me by my arm, "Leave him be. Let's just go back to the car and get out of here."

Mr. Lincoln stirred just a bit and was making unintelligible sounds. I turned to Moshe and said, "He could be hurt."

"Look. He's moving and breathing. And he started it. I never laid a hand on him."

I tried to free my arm but he held it tight. "You can't just leave him here," I said beseechingly.

"Why not? It's his own fault. Let someone else take care of him. He's coming around. He'll be fine."

I could see that Mr. Lincoln was blinking his eyes but it was also clearly evident that he was still out of it. "He's not all right," I insisted.

"Yes he is. In a couple of minutes he'll be up and around. Meanwhile, now that your little contractor friend is out of the way, what do you say that you and me go back to the car, find another spot to park, and really get to know each other better?"

I couldn't believe my ears.

I turned towards Moshe and looked directly into his eyes as I faked an innocent smile, "You want to get to know me better?"

"Now you're talking baby," said Moshe taking hold of both my shoulders. "I sure do."

"Good. Try this on for size," I said, just as I lifted my knee rapidly and directly into his groin. Exactly the way my *Krav Magah* instructor had taught me. He went down clutching his aching private areas. Once he was on the floor, I gave him a sharp kick to the side of his head and he was out cold. I checked to be sure that he was still breathing and that I had not killed him. I looked down at Moshe and said ironically, "You're breathing so you should be fine and you were the one that started it." Then I turned my attention back to Mr. Lincoln.

He was still face down on the pavement. I never realized how big a man he was. Only with great effort am I able to turn him over. He is bleeding from a cut lip and from his nose. I used my scarf to staunch the flow of blood and got him to sit up but he said he was dizzy. After a moment I was able to pull him up on to his feet but then he said he could not stand on his ankle, "Where is your car?" I asked.

He was obviously confused but still could point a wobbly finger across the street, "Over there."

"Give me your car keys."

"But it's night time," he said spitting blood. "You can't drive at night."

He hasn't left me any choice, "Just give me the keys."

I put Mr. Lincoln's arm across my shoulder – and keeping as much pressure as I can off his injured leg – we somehow got across the street. I propped him up against the car and unlocked the doors. Why are the seats so high in his car? It is like climbing Mt. Everest. By some miracle I got him into the passenger seat and buckled his belt. The car's engine started up just fine. I wait apprehensively for the crippling fear to develop within me that always keeps me from driving at night, but it doesn't happen. Before I can drive away I've have to do something. I got out of the car and said to Mr. Lincoln, "Sit in your seat and don't move."

"Don't worry ... I'm not going anywhere," mumbled Mr. Lincoln, spraying blood on to the windshield.

Moshe Horowitz was still sprawled on his back groaning in pain and holding himself between his legs. I kicked his shoulder with my foot to get his attention and asked, "Are you okay? Do you want me to call an ambulance for you?"

"Are you kidding? If I get an ambulance everyone will know that I just got whupped ... and by a woman? You're some piece of work, lady. No, thank you. Just leave me alone and let me go home."

"Just so you know. Maybe some of the women you went out with were desperate enough to fall for what you just tried to do and never said anything. But you met the wrong woman. I will be filing a report with the police in the morning so I suggest you skedaddle back to Toronto and I wouldn't plan on coming back to the U.S.A. for a while. I'm also going to do something much worse. I'm going to tell *Rebbetzen* Kalmonowitz. Believe me, once she spreads the word you're finished on the *frum* dating circuit. So good night and good riddance."

With a grunt and quite a bit of effort, Moshe got to his feet and hobbled over to his car. He drove away even before I was able to return to the SUV.

When I got back into the car Mr. Lincoln was pinching his nose closed to slow the flow of blood. He said very nasally, "Please, just take me home."

"I'll take you home, but first we're going to visit the emergency room," I said.

"What for?" he asked.

I looked at him and objectively assessed the damage he had sustained with the fall, "Let's see ... your lip is gashed open, your nose is bleeding and it appears to have been relocated to about three inches to the left of where it is supposed to be. You can't walk on your ankle. That's what for."

"I'm fine," he insisted with bravado.

I pulled the SUV out into the street, "I'm sure you are an excellent diagnostician but if you don't mind I would much prefer to hear a doctor say that."

It took four hours in the ER and x-ray department. All during that time Mr. Lincoln didn't make things any easier. He kept falling asleep and even in his moments of wakefulness he was not too lucid about where he was or what he was doing in the hospital.

First the doctors injected his lip with local anesthetic and began sewing. Even as they did their embroidery his lip continued to swell up. Now he looked like he belonged to one of those African tribes where they have those incredibly large lips.

Luckily, an Ear, Nose, & Throat specialist happened to be in the ER, and with a little more local anesthetic they got Mr. Lincoln's nose moved back to where it belonged in the center of his face. They placed a plastic splint on the surface of his nose and packed the inside with Vaseline gauze to stop the bleeding. His whole face was now bluish-purple, bloody and swollen – really looked terrific.

They did a CT exam of his head – apart from the broken nasal bones everything was fine – and an x-ray of his ankle – which showed a tiny chip fracture. The doctor explained that it was basically a very bad sprain but in order for it to heal properly he would need a walking cast. They informed me that Mr. Lincoln's insurance only covers plaster casts and I had to decide if they should put on the more expensive lighter plastic cast or go with the free plaster. I tried to ask Mr. Lincoln what he preferred but it was like the old Yiddish expression: *Mir ret tzu dem vant* (you were talking to the wall – i.e. nobody home). I figured he had the money so we splurged on the lighter plastic.

Finally they put Mr. Lincoln in a wheel chair and the ER doc began giving him the discharge instructions. Actually he was giving me the instructions because Mr. Lincoln kept nodded off to sleep. He told me what to do with the lip, the nose, and the leg. Then he threw in the monkey wrench. "He keeps going off to sleep because he has a slight concussion. The CT exam was fine so you have nothing serious to worry about, but there could be some brain swelling so he needs to be watched."

"If he needs to be watched why not admit him to the hospital?" I asked.

"Because there is no medical reason to admit him and therefore his insurance won't pay for it. All he needs is to sleep it off and for someone to check him every hour," said the doctor.

"Check him for what."

"To wake him and look at his pupils to see if they are equal."

"What do you do if they're not equal?"

"Then you bring him back here as fast as you can."

"So it could be serious?"

"Oh, yeah, sure. But it is highly unlikely. This is just a precaution ... but a necessary precaution."

Mr. Lincoln lived alone – who would watch him? *Oh no. I can't.* "If it's so necessary why don't you just admit him and you can watch him?" I said, barely controlling the panic I felt within.

"I told you the insurance won't cover it."

"That's okay, he's very rich. He can afford it."

"The insurance problem is not the only issue, we are overcrowded and only admitting real emergencies. Look, Mrs. Lincoln. Your husband is really okay. All he needs ..."

"I'm not Mrs. Lincoln."

"From the way you were caring for him ... I just assumed."

"No. I'm just a friend," I corrected the doctor.

"Well, then be a friend," the ER physician scolded. "Help take care of him. It's only for tonight. He should be fine in the morning."

The attendants helped me get Mr. Lincoln into his car. I knew that I could not just take him to his home and leave him there alone. He needed someone and at two in the morning I was the only one available. This was truly a case of *pikuach nefesh* and according to Jewish law it superseded just about every other *mitzvah* that there ever was. I really do not have a choice.

Luckily, I had spoken with Marissa earlier and she told me that she would be able to stay for the rest of the night to help watch the kids. When I got near my home I called her on my cell phone and she came out to help me get Mr. Lincoln into Racheli's bedroom. Thank God she was there because he could not walk on his new cast and I would never have been able to move his massive frame on my own. He is semi-lucid and is blathering away, insisting that he could get into the house on his own, but with every step he let out a howl of pain. I got Mr. Lincoln's other shoe off and somehow got him under the blankets. As soon as his head hit the pillow he was out cold.

Other than having a man sleeping in my little girl's bed, everything else in the house was under control. Marissa was with Racheli in my bedroom, the boys were fast asleep in theirs and I dragged a big hard wooden chair up next to the bed. This was my most uncomfortable chair – but that was good. If it was comfortable, I might fall asleep and I had to stay awake to check on Mr. Lincoln every hour.

I changed my clothes and began my vigil. I looked at Mr. Lincoln with all his handsome features all bruised, swollen, and battered. His nose was packed with bloody gauze and that made him breathe through his mouth with a sonorous rattle. Not a very enticing picture. I should be angry with him for disrupting my personal life but I'm not. I feel good being able to help him. Why is that?

"Ayelet? Is that you?" someone said.

I must have dozed off. Yes – that's it. The morning light is coming in through the bedroom window.

"Ayelet? What are doing in my bedroom?" the nasal voice asked.

As my mind cleared the cobwebs I realized that the voice belonged to Mr. Lincoln. He was awake and he sounded lucid. Oh my God – I just realized – I had not checked him these last few hours. Thank goodness, he was all right. I wiped my eyes and said, "Unless your room décor also has a strong predilection for Winnie-the-Pooh, you will notice that you are not at home. Perhaps you recognize Racheli's bedroom."

"Were you here all night with me?"

"Guilty as charged."

"What happened?"

"Don't you remember?"

"It's coming back a bit at a time," said Mr. Lincoln shaking his head slowly.

"Do you remember my date ... the little scuffle ... the emergency room?"

"Yeah, now that you mention it. This explains why I feel as if I was run over by a steam roller. My whole face hurts. Did that guy hit me?" said Mr. Lincoln in a nasal tone.

"Nope," I said. "That's just what happens when your foot slips into a hole and you plop down straight on your *punim."*

"Ouch," he said wincing slightly. "I remember ... you told me what happened."

"Can I ask you a question?"

"If I'm able to answer it I will," he said.

"What were you doing there last night?"

Mr. Lincoln raised his head from the pillow to explain, "He was trying to take advantage of you. So I was trying to protect you ... I didn't do a good job ... but I tried," said Mr. Lincoln in his defense.

"You did a great job. He never laid a hand on you and you wound up in the emergency room. Just imagine what would have happened if you two actually had fought."

"By the way ... I remember you also told me what you did to that guy. Right in the cajones! Is that what they teach you in *Bais Yaakov*?"

"Rephael made me take three years of *Krav Magah* training at the Jewish Center. He said I would never know when it might be useful."

"What is that ... like Karate?" he inquired.

"It's from the Israeli commando training program. Basically there are no rules and it teaches you to use whatever you can against an attacker. I still do the basic exercises a couple of times a week. That was where I first met Mrs. Schwartz, that woman you dated. Did you know that she is very athletic?"

"Is she? ... Really? ... I hadn't noticed," he stammered.

*Is he blushing?* I can't tell with all that swelling and bruising. "But you're changing the subject. I want to know, why you happened to be where I was, just when I needed you."

Mr. Lincoln's eyes looked about the room, but he did not answer.

I added, "I'm waiting for an answer."

He squirmed about uncomfortably for a moment and then said, "I followed you."

"You followed me? Why in the world did you follow me?" I inquired.

He said in his defense, "I saw that guy in your house and I knew right away that he was no good."

"And just how did you know that?"

"He's a grease ball. Guys can recognize them a mile away. For some reason many women can't."

"What's a grease ball?"

"It's a guy that thinks that he is God's gift to women. They strut about bragging about their exploits and use just about every devious trick they can to get women to have sex with them."

"You could have been making a mistake. After all, it was the *rebbetzen* that set up the *shidduch*."

"What are you talking about. He was all over you. I saw. I don't care if these guys are dressed up like a *tzadik*. They are all dirt bags. I couldn't believe that you couldn't see him for what he was."

"And you noticed this during the one minute that you met him?"

"Actually that just aroused my suspicions. After I left your house I drove around the block and waited. When you came out ... then I knew for sure."

"What convinced you?"

"When he helped you into the front seat ... he ogled you. He craned his neck to get a look at your body and legs from every angle. That's a sure sign of a grease ball."

I feel the color rising in my cheeks, "So then you followed me the entire evening."

"Absolutely. I figured if I was wrong I would just keep my distance and you would never find out. But I knew that the guy would make his move sometime. And I was right."

"Even if I concede that you were correct in your evaluation of Moshe Horowitz ... who gave you the right to be my protector? Did I ask you to do it? You weren't in the car ... maybe I encouraged that kind of attention? Maybe I was trying to trap him into marrying me? Perhaps your meddling cost me my *shidduch*."

"Don't be ridiculous. You're not that type of woman."

"Maybe I am and maybe I'm not. But who gives you the right to butt in without my permission?"

"Do you mean to say that you want to be pawed like that?"

"I don't have to answer that and it's not your business."

"It is my business," he exclaimed loudly. "I care for you. For you and the kids. I don't want to see you getting hurt."

"I'm sure you didn't want to do anything to hurt me. But what happened last night may have ruined my reputation forever. It may have destroyed my chances for a *shidduch* completely."

"But you didn't do anything wrong," he pleaded.

"It doesn't matter. I sat here for the last few hours and had nothing better to do than think about our ... situation. It's not healthy. You're a wonderful man and I will always be in your debt. I know you care for us and ... I care for you as well. But we both know that because of our differences nothing can really develop between us. It's so obvious. But instead of moving apart as we should ... we have been hovering around each other for months. It has to stop."

"Why?" he asked innocently.

"Because even though you never told anyone about our night in the motor home, my kids did. They bragged to all their school friends about their adventure. Just a few weeks ago one of the women from *Bais Yaakov* asked me if there was any truth to the rumor that the two of us had gone out camping in the woods. My kids are going to see you here in a few minutes and Marissa knows as well. Your spending the night here is going to get out for sure. My reputation is going to be dragged through the mud very quickly. If I don't get a *shidduch* in the next few weeks ... before all the *yentahs* get the story ... I probably never will."

"But Ayelet, can't we talk about this?"

"I already told you that I think you are a terrific person and will hate to lose you as a friend, but I have my kids to think about. So, I'm making some new rules. If you have to check the construction related to the bakery don't come over unless you call me first and get permission. My children have loved having you as their honorary uncle, but they are not to go over to your home any more. And finally, don't call me for any reason other than business. I'm sorry, but I have no other choice."

# 25

## In the dumps

"*REBBI*, I HAVE A QUESTION," I said.

"*Mah nishtanah hayome hazeh* (Why should this day be different [from all other days] – a paraphrase of the line from the Passover *seder*)," commented Rabbi Kalmonowitz.

"We just read in the *Talmud* that a person should not go into a deserted building for fear of *ayin horah*. I also heard that for the same reason, we do not call close relatives up to the *Torah* reading one after the other. And you once showed me that the rabbis state that for every one hundred people that die, only one dies of natural causes and all the rest die from the 'evil eye'. But the whole idea of the 'evil eye' seems foreign to the way the *Torah* looks at God's place in world. The idea that someone can do harm to another by simply looking at him seems a little strange."

"So what is your question, Reb Shaul?"

"What is this whole 'evil eye' business all about?"

"Interesting question," said the rabbi collecting his thoughts. "First you must understand that the 'evil eye' is not the same as *kishuf* or black magic. There are cases cited in the *Talmud* of magicians and witches who apparently were able to do many unbelievable things. However, today we have almost no understanding of what *kishuf* ... as mentioned in the *Talmud* ... really was. On the other hand there are Orthodox rabbis who indeed believe in the 'evil eye'. These are mostly in the mystical, Kabbalistic, and *chassidic sects*. But I have adopted a different way of looking at the 'evil eye'. I learned this from the teachings of Rabbi Shalom Mashash, who was the chief rabbi of Morroco and then became the chief *Sephardi* rabbi of Jerusalem, about fifty years ago. He wrote that the 'evil eye' does indeed cause great harm, but the harm is not to the person receiving the 'evil-eye', but to the person that gives the 'evil eye'."

"What do you mean? He gives the 'evil eye' to himself?"

"No, it is not black magic that is transferred from one person to the next," explained the rabbi. "If you look at the cases of 'evil eye' in the *Talmud* and in *Torah* law, almost all involve situations where particular individuals raise unfounded suspicions about the actions of others."

"I don't follow," I said.

"Take the cases of a father and son, or two brothers, who receive the honor of being called to the *Torah* one after the other. Theoretically it should not arouse any comment, but unfortunately there will always be someone in the synagogue who might say to himself, or to others, that the two brothers don't deserve the double honor and the only reason they are only getting it is because they must have bribed someone or used influence. This dark side ... always thinking the worst ... is the 'evil eye'. The very thought corrupts the person who thinks it. You also gave the example of not going into a deserted building."

"I see," I said with a nod of my head. "Someone could possibly see him enter and say, 'That fellow must be up to no good.'"

"Exactly."

"So the 'evil eye' is not some sort of magical curse, it's just a normal human behavioral defect."

"Exactly. It perpetuates unnecessary suspicion and this corrupts and spoils the beauty of the inner Jewish spirit of the person who thinks in this manner. For this reason we do whatever we can to avoid situations that could arouse the 'evil eye'."

Over three months have gone by since my chip fracture and I'm almost two months without my cast. Six weeks ago my orthopedist gave me the green light that allowed me to get back to the gym. I am now exercising regularly and I've gotten the orbital stepper up to a decent rate. It is still slower than the speed setting I used before the 'accident' but I am improving at every session. There is only a modest sliver of pain with every cycle but I can tolerate that with ease. No pain no gain. But – ouch!

I had already worked up a good sweat and was getting ready to quit.

I rationalized that the leg injury was God's way of punishing me for acting like a total *shmuck.* What was I thinking when I tried to swoop in like a proverbial white knight to come to the rescue of a damsel in distress – aka Ayelet Weinberg – from the cruel and sadistic black knight – aka Moshe Horowitz of Toronto? Yes – a total *shmuck.*

To top it all off – I have never been a confrontational person. I am not even skilled in any of the martial arts. If I had not fallen on my face, there was a good chance that Mr. Horowitz would have beaten my *tuchis* to a pulp.

Ayelet was right. It was not my business and has never been my business. And, although she never said it, I have come to realize that the source for my sudden urge to act as Ayelet's savior was fueled by a bit of subconscious jealousy. She made her feelings quite clear that there was no possibility of any kind of relationship and it was time to move on.

So I shall move on.

But not too quickly, because I still get that slight twinge in my ankle when I walk and there is just a hint of a limp.

"I can't stand looking at you like this," said Max Rosenstein rotating the pedals of his machine at his much more sedate rate.

The old man had been riding me at every session since my return to the gym, "I'm hot and sweaty. What do you want from me?"

"I'm not talking about hot and sweaty. You look like something the cat dragged in and then dragged right out again."

"I'm just getting over a broken ankle," I said defensively.

"What kind of B.S. broken ankle? You told me it was a little chip fracture ... sprained ankle. Are you looking for sympathy? Well, from me, you ain't gonna get it."

Typical of the old man, I thought. "And all along you said I was your friend."

"You are ... and that's why I'm not going to cut you any slack."

"You're a heartless son of a gun," I quipped.

"Never said I wasn't. But you and I both know that it ain't your ankle that's bothering you."

"I don't know anything of the kind."

"When did you go out on your last date?"

Ouch!!! A stab wound to my self esteem. *Why is he bringing that up?* "None of your business."

"Need I say more?" said Max holding up open palms to indicate victory.

"My dating has nothing to do with how I feel."

"We're making progress. You just inadvertently admitted that it isn't your ankle. Correct?"

"Okay, okay ... it's not my ankle," I said holding up my hands in acquiescence. "But it also has nothing to do with my dating."

"That's where you're wrong. It has everything to do with your dating ... or more correctly with your lack of dating. It has to do with Ayelet Weinberg."

I stopped my exercise and looked at Max, "Is it that obvious?"

"Obvious? Of course it's obvious. Even a blind man can see it."

I reflected for a minute and said softly, "I miss her kids."

"Another *bubbah mysah,*" said Max in exasperation. "And what about her? Do you miss her as well?"

"Well, yeah sure. They go together you know."

"More B.S.!" exclaimed the older man. "You are still smitten with Mrs. Weinberg."

"I am not," I insisted, trying to find the words. "I just grew very attached to her and her family. I really enjoyed helping them."

"You say 'very attached'. Like when she walked into a room your heart grew happy all of a sudden ... kind of attached?"

"Yes," I admitted sheepishly.

"And when you just remember her laugh, you sort of smile to yourself ... kind of attached?"

"Yes," I admitted once more.

"And when you run out of excuses for keeping her around and she leaves the room, the place grows dim ... kind of attached?"

"Okay, okay, I get your point. I suppose I kind of like her."

"Kind of *like* her? What's the matter with you?" said Max disappointedly. "Are you in the sixth grade?"

Score two points for the old man's team. My behavior is quite immature. Time to act my age. "You want me to say I ... have a thing for her? But how can I? She told me under no uncertain terms that she wants nothing to do with me. Besides, we haven't even held hands, for goodness sake ... I mean ... not romantically."

"So what? You have a good imagination. If you and she did hold hands or even kissed ... what do you think would happen?"

I contemplated the question for a moment and then said with a smile, "It would probably be terrific."

Max tilted his head to the side and spread his arm with palms upward to indicate victory once again, "Your honor, I rest my case."

I interjected, "But only if she felt the same way. And for now ... she is pushing me away."

"So why don't you ask her how she feels about getting serious?"

"Because it's too late."

"Too late for what?"

"She's going to be married soon and it won't make a difference."

"You didn't tell me she was engaged. I see you every two days ... you never said a word ... when did it happen?"

"She's not officially engaged yet, but she's been out with this same fellow eight times and in the *charedi* world that can only mean that they will announce any day now."

"*Yetz farshtay ich* (Yiddish for now I understand). That's the reason you're in the dumps."

The heartless old codger figured it out. "So now, are you going to give me some sympathy?"

"Not on your life," said the old man emphatically. "What are you doing about this situation?"

"Me?" I asked in surprise. "What am I supposed to do?"

The old man got off his machine and approached me with his index finger extended. As he got close he began thumping me on my chest while he said scoldingly, "The lady you love is about to tie the knot with some other guy ... you have got to convince her that you are the better choice."

With every painful jab I moved a bit further away from the thrusting digit, “How can I be a better choice? We’re from two different worlds. And there is a fifteen year age difference. How many happy years could we have together?”

“Her last husband was nearly the same age as she was ... how many happy years did they have?”

“That’s a completely different situation.”

"What about all the middle age men that get divorced and marry women half their age? That's pretty common."

"And I think it looks ridiculous."

“Why are you being so judgmental? It's not up to you. It’s all up to the big man in the sky,” said the older man pointing skyward.

“Suddenly you are becoming *frum*?”

“No, but you are. You know that if God arranged it that you should fall in love with a woman much younger than you. He must have a plan. But you’ve got to do your part.”

“What can I do?”

“Talk to Ayelet, you *fahrshtupta* idiot!” the old man exclaimed loudly.

“I don’t even know this guy’s name. All I know is that he comes from New York.”

“How did you get the information you do have?”

“From Mrs. Leibowitz, Ayelet’s baking assistant. We have become ... sorta ... good friends. She’s on my side. She lets me know what’s happening.”

“It sounds to me that Mrs. Leibowitz is also of the opinion that you should take a bit more interest in the bakery lady.”

“I suppose.”

“Look, just give me Mrs. Leibowitz’s number and let me see what I can do.”

“You’re going to call Ayelet?”

"Don't you wish?" said Max. "No, I'm going to get this guy's name and have him investigated."

"I don't think you should do that. Ayelet would be furious."

"Do you know the expression, 'All's fair in love and war'?"

"Yes."

"Well you're in both," said the older man. "Besides, what have you got to lose? If you do nothing, you lose Mrs. Weinberg. If this guy turns out to be Prince Charming on a white steed, you'll lose her anyway. But ...," Max paused for dramatic effect. "... but if he turns out to be a jerk, you would feel miserable about it. You wouldn't want her to make a terrible mistake and ... it would give you an opportunity to win her over."

I thought this could be a very dangerous thing to do, "I don't know."

"What's not to know?"

"Ayelet is a terrific woman ... but the age difference ... just has me worried."

"I know what's bothering you ... but that's why God created Viagra."

"I can't go into a relationship that is based on chemicals."

"And why not?"

"It's just not proper?"

"You mean religious-wise?"

"Exactly."

"Rabbi Kalmonowitz told you this?"

"No, of course not. We never talked about the subject."

"Well, it's time you did."

# 26

## *Mister Perfect*

I HAVE TO GET READY – Aryeh just flew in from New York and we have a date this evening. That doesn't leave me much time. There had been a problem with the temperature in the hearth oven. That's what slowed me down and the reason I'm late. The batch of focaccia bread ordered by the new Italian restaurant needed to be baked properly. The small loaves, made with a pungent rosemary and spiced yeast dough, have to go directly into an extremely hot oven in order to get the crunchy crust.

"Mrs. Leibowitz, is the sourdough ready to go in?"

"Just two seconds and dey in de oven," she said easily swinging the heavy board laden with the loaves. "Don't you vorry about dem. Me and Alice vill take out and I vill see Albert deliver dem. So you quit and get ready your date vit Mr. Rappaport."

"Thank you Mrs. Leibowitz," I said taking off my apron heading for the bedroom.

I love this work. The new bakery is such a godsend. Even the long walkway going from the house to the 'official bakery' is a blessing. Mr. Lincoln planned cabinets and closets for the entire length and this makes a perfect storage and pantry area. It's so easy to stock the shelves and find everything. *Boruch HaShem*, the business is thriving. I'm so thankful. Financially, I've never been in better shape. My private life – well that's a different story.

Tonight will be my eleventh date with Aryeh and he has also asked me to go to New York next weekend to meet his parents. That can only mean that he wants to make everything final and we will probably talk about it this evening. I should feel so happy about this *shidduch*. He is everything that a woman in my situation could ask for. He comes from New York and is forty years old. That's a seven-year age difference but he is tall and handsome and so charming. Every single time we go out he comes around the car to open the door for me. He is so considerate and always knows just the right thing to say. The man also has such illustrious *yichus.* Before the war, one of his great-grandfathers was the *rosh yeshiva* at one of the biggest *yeshivas* in Poland and another was the chief rabbi of Manheim. If it was not for the fact that he is divorced, there is no way that a man like him would look at a woman like me.

Even though he doesn't like to talk about it, I know that he went through a nasty separation. In the end the courts felt his children would be better off in his home and not hers. That's very unusual – there must be something terribly wrong with his ex-wife. He tells me that his computer business is very successful and he travels all over the U.S.A. much of the year. When he's home he sits and learns in the *bais medrash* three times a week. A real *talmid chochom.* He has also agreed to move his entire business here to Detroit so that my kids will not have to leave school and I won't have to give up the bakery that I love so. This is very important for me.

I should feel very lucky.

My only problem is that I do not feel towards Aryeh what I felt when I dated Rephael. There is no real spark between us.

I do not love him.

There, I said it.

I spoke to the *rebbetzen* and mentioned that I was having my doubts about Aryeh, but she kept telling me about all of his better points. That he is such a catch. That I have to realize that my children need a father. And then she added that in a second marriage one can only hope that love will eventually grow.

I don't think I will ever be able to have an honest conversation with Aryeh. He always seems to distance himself from me. It's not like my conversations with Rephael or even Mr. Lincoln. Oh yes, Mr. Lincoln. What a wonderful *neshama.* I really hated cutting him off from the kids. They liked him so much. He was more than an honorary uncle to them. He was more like a father. Always there to help and always doing it with – love. Yes, love. The kids miss having him around.

I had no choice but to push him away. I'm afraid that he was beginning to think that there could be something between us. That was all an illusion. Those months together were fun, but I have to be realistic and think about what's best for my family.

I think I'll wear my new grey dress this evening. I've had to buy all new clothes for this dating business. For the upcoming weekend in New York I'll need almost all of them to impress his parents. Aryeh thought it would be better if only I came without my children. So, Marissa will babysit the kids Thursday and Friday and then they will be by the Kalmonowitz's for *shabbos.* On Saturday night Marissa will return to babysit until Monday morning when I return from New York. Even though everything is all arranged, I know that I will still worry.

When we made the extension, Mr. Lincoln put in a new boiler and now I have all the hot water I can ever use. No more lukewarm showers. *Ah' mechaya.* Thank you Mr. Lincoln – once again. Cannot stay in the shower too long. Aryeh will be here in fifteen minutes. He is also a big stickler for punctuality.

Everything seems to be in order. I'll wear one of my two new *shaitels.* They look good on me – not as nice as my own hair but he'll see that after the wedding.

*Oh, my goodness. Did I just think about our wedding?* My wedding with Aryeh Rappaport? That was the first time I thought of him that way. As my husband. Is that good or bad?

I don't know.

There is the door bell.

One more quick glance in the mirror. Everything seems to be in place.

I have to put on my biggest most welcoming smile as I open the door, "Hello, Aryeh, I am ... Mr. Lincoln? What are you doing here? You didn't call."

"No, I didn't, but I had to speak to you. It's important."

"What's the problem?"

"Steve!!!" came the sudden scream from behind me as Yanki zoomed past leaping into Mr. Lincoln's arms.

"Where is Steve?" screamed Chaim'l and he too rushed past me to greet Mr. Lincoln. "Steve ... where have you been?"

"Are we going over to your house to go swimming?" asked Yanki excitedly.

"Are we, *Ima*?" chorused Chaim'l.

I have to get control here, "Mr. Lincoln has been busy."

"But he's here now. Can we go to his house ... please, *Ima*?" beseeched Chaim'l.

"I'm sorry kids," said Mr. Lincoln. "Like *Ima* said, I've been really busy. Can't take you today. Maybe some other day, when *Ima* says it's okay."

*Mr. Lincoln, thank you for the help.* "You heard Mr. Lincoln. Now get back to your homework. Marissa will be here in a little while, until then Mrs. Leibowitz will look after you."

"Are you going out with Steve?" asked Chaim'l hopefully.

"No, Chaim'l," he said. "I just came over to talk with your *Ima*. You listen to what she says."

Chiam'l reluctantly went back to the dining room table and his pile of books. I turned to Mr. Lincoln, "So what is it that is so important that you had to come over unannounced?"

"It's about your new friend, Aryeh Rappaport."

"How do you know about him? Have you been spying on me again? After I specifically told you not to?" I asked angrily.

"It doesn't make a difference how I know about him. Let's just say I didn't have to do any spying to know about your New York friend."

"Okay, we'll leave that for now. What could you possibly tell me about Aryeh that I don't already know?"

Mr. Lincoln took a moment to answer and then said, "It's about his business."

"What's wrong with his business?" I asked. "It's a respectable computer business. They sell programs for managing private schools. Many *yeshivas* and parochial schools use his products."

"It's not the type of business. It's the way it's being run. Your Mr. Rappaport may be a crook."

"A crook? What are you talking about? When you say 'may be', does that mean that you have no proof?"

"I'm worried that you may have problems if you get involved with this guy."

"Knowing you ... that means that you do not have proof. Is that correct?"

"Okay, I don't have proof ... yet."

"So you have not been spying on me ... you have been spying on Aryeh."

"It's not exactly spying."

"What would you call it? Do you like the word espionage better?"

"This fellow could be a big fake."

"What is he faking about? Being tall and handsome? Being the grandson of famous rabbis? Being a *talmid chochom*? Being a gentleman at all times? What is he faking?"

"He could be faking that he cares for you," said Mr. Lincoln seriously.

Of all the nerve. "Suddenly at the eleventh hour you come in here to tell me to be careful. Why now?"

"Because I know that in the *shidduch* business when a couple gets up to ten plus dates, it means something."

Of course everyone knows what that means. It means that I am considering Aryeh for my husband if he will have me. The nerve of him coming here now to make these accusations just when I have to make such an important decision. "Who gave you the right to meddle in my affairs?"

"Ayelet, you know I care for you and your family. I don't care what happens to me. I just don't want you to get hurt."

I can't let him interfere.

He has to leave me alone.

In the past when I've been with him I did some very foolish things. I can't deny that he helped me greatly when I needed help. But he confuses me. I must distance myself. "How did you get this information?"

"Do you remember my friend, Max Rosenstein?"

"The one who helped me with my loan?

"The very same."

"Why would he investigate Aryeh?"

"I never told you this but you got the loan because Max co-signed it at the bank."

"How could you do this?" I said in anger. "I told you I didn't want to get the money from you."

"You didn't. Honest," said Mr. Lincoln holding up a hand as if swearing an oath. "Max, did that on his own. I had nothing to do with it. I didn't even know about it at the time. He has been following your business ever since and is very happy with your success."

"I suspect he is very happy that the loan is almost repaid."

"That too. Anyway, when he heard you might be marrying this guy he had him investigated ... just to protect his investment. I had nothing to do with it."

"How did he know that I was going out?"

"He is always asking about you and I guess I sort of mentioned it."

"So you're spreading information about me to strangers."

"He's not really a stranger ... he's sort of a silent partner in your business."

"He's someone I don't know, so that makes him a stranger."

"Anyway, Max's investigator checked out Mr. Rappaport and gave a preliminary report."

"And what did this preliminary report say?"

"Basically, it said 'don't buy a used car from Mr. Rappaport' and that he is continuing to investigate."

"What am I supposed to make of that?"

"All I want you to do is hold off on making any major decisions about Mr. Rappaport until we get the final report."

Of all the nerve. If Aryeh asks me to marry him on the weekend in New York, how can I put him off? Why did Mr. Lincoln have to come just now and throw this monkey wrench into the works? Why does God want to try me with so many tribulations? "I must repeat what I've said to you in the past. Stay out of my business. I'll ignore what you have told me here today because it is pure *loshon horah.* You have no proof of anything. I'll continue to go out with him and in my eyes he is as near perfect as can be for me and my family. I'll make my decisions about Aryeh Rappaport as I see fit."

"Did I just hear my name mentioned in vain?" said Aryeh striding up my driveway. He looks so handsome in his dark blue suit.

"Aryeh, you're just on time," I said. *How much did he hear?*

"As always," he said with a smile. "And who is this gentleman?"

That's right. They have never met. "Mr. Lincoln, please meet Aryeh Rappaport."

They shook hands and Aryeh said, "Mr. Lincoln, Ayelet has told me so much about you. You were a real help to her in her time of need. You did a big *mitzvah*."

"Yeah, that's me. The big *mitzvah* man," said Mr. Lincoln sarcastically. "Well, I have to be going. Nice seeing you and the kids again. Aryeh ... take care of her. And Ayelet, you think about the information I gave you. It could be important. If I hear any more I'll get back to you."

What *chutzpah.* "I told you that I don't think I will be interested, so you'll be wasting your time."

Mr. Lincoln walked out to his car and Aryeh asked, "What was that all about?"

"He had some ideas involving a partnership ... for my business ... but I told him I wasn't interested."

"Seems like a very nice man. Do you see him much?" he inquired.

Oh, Mr. Lincoln is a nice man – he really is. But he is also a man that confuses me and best that I stay away from him. "I told you he was the contractor that helped me with the bakery construction but now I almost never see him."

"That's good," said Aryeh.

What did he mean by that?

# 27

## *Tummy ache*

FROM MY SUNDAY MORNING SESSION with Rabbi Kalmonowitz, I went directly to the Dunkin' Donuts shop to meet Max Rosenstein. The older man chose this venue because he was a confessed doughnut addict. His ability to down the fried pastry was astounding. When I arrived, Max was just getting his order of two glazed creamed filled doughnuts and a double shot cappuccino into which he was shoveling three heaping teaspoons of sugar.

I just ordered decaf because ever since I tasted Ayelet's baked goods, I could not bring myself to go back to the lack luster stuff they served here. I also knew that if I ate what Max was eating – the greasy crullers and the extra strong coffee – my stomach would be upset for hours. The old man had to have the intestinal fortitude of a horse.

Max bit off a mouthful of a glazed donut and a large glop of the custard cream filling squirted out on to his napkin. The old man reflexively gobbled up the extruded sweet gooey cream – waste not want not. In between swallows of coffee he said, "I've been drinking strong coffee for the past eighty years and it hasn't hurt me yet."

I blew away the steam from my own decaf and took a tentative swig, "So what have you got for me?"

"For you, I have nothing. You said you weren't interested in knowing about this Aryeh Rappaport. You just wanted to let your Mrs. Weinberg slip through your fingers."

"I told you how she cut me off at the knees. To her, this guy is Mr. Perfect. She doesn't want to know anything bad about him."

"She should," said Max taking a long pull from his Styrofoam cup.

"She should what? Think that he is Mr. Perfect or know about the bad things?"

"The latter."

"Did your guy discover anything?" I asked eagerly.

"Did he ever," he said nodding his head. "I told you something was fishy with that guy. He was too squeaky clean. *Yeshiva bochur* ... *yichus* ... handsome ... terrific personality ... hard worker ... financially successful ... big family man. So I asked myself, why was he divorced? Why is his company going down the tubes?"

"His company is in trouble?"

"Chapter 11 any day now. But here is this guy still traveling first class to all his destinations and staying at the most posh hotels. I knew there was something rotten in Denmark."

"So he is a bad businessman. That doesn't necessarily mean that he's a bad person."

"No it doesn't," agreed Max. "But this guy is not just a bad person ... he is *drek."*

"That's a pretty harsh statement. From what Ayelet told Mrs. Leibowitz, he sounds like a very considerate person. The guy is even willing to move his company here to Detroit so that Ayelet does not have to uproot her family."

"Well, I would also be willing to move if I was already six months behind in the rent."

"It's that bad?"

"It's worse. His whole company was given to him."

"By whom? Who would give him a business?"

"His former father-in-law purchased the company from the previous owners for a ridiculous sum of money and gave it to Rappaport as a wedding present. He has been living off of the company's resources for the last twenty years. The well is about to go dry. It's time to look for a new source of income."

"Ayelet's baking business."

Max pointed his index finger at me, "You're not as stupid as you look. He knows enough to recognize a potential goldmine. The way her business has grown she will have the initial loan paid off any day now. She has more requests than she can fill. Even though I love these doughnuts, you and I both know that her baked goods are so much better than this greasy stuff."

"You can say that again."

"It won't be long until she will have to expand again and maybe go national. And he wants to be in on that."

"Sneaky son of a gun," I said angrily.

"But that's just the half of it. And that's the better half. It is almost good news compared to the rest of the stuff we learned."

"How did your guy get this information?"

"It wasn't difficult to figure out your boy's out-of-town itinerary. He has a pretty set pattern. My man got the first class seat next to his on his flight to San Francisco. Rappaport is a teetotaler while he is in New York. That's all part of his façade. But once the plane leaves the tarmac he belts down the booze like a *shicker* with a hollow leg. A couple of drinks down the road he became really palsy with my man and when he heard that they would be at the same hotel, they shared a cab. He goes by the name Leo ... his English name ... when he is out and about. One thing lead to another and it wasn't long before they were spending the night with a couple of San Francisco's most expensive ladies of the evening. Turns out he is a regular and is known for being a big tipper. He has similar arrangements in another six cities across the U.S.A. His wife divorced him when she found out."

"But he keeps hinting that his ex was the one that was fooling around. After all he got custody of the kids."

"Leo got custody after he threatened her that he would not give her a Jewish divorce and she would never be able to remarry. He also said he would use his *yichus* to ruin her father's name in the *charedi* community. They had four kids ... all teen agers. Two were old enough to leave his house and move in with mom and the other two will both be able to move out within two years. One this year and one the year following. She knew what good old Leo was capable of and figured it was best to keep her mouth shut about the whole affair."

"Has this stuff been verified?" I asked.

"My man has it all recorded."

"How come no one knows these things about him?"

"In New York ... everyone thinks he is a *tzadik*. His company still makes big donations to all the right charities. He is a big shot in his *shul*. *Supposedly* he learns in the *bais medrash* a couple of times a week. The learning is just an excuse to have free time for Leo to visit his various girlfriends that he has spread around New York City. I'll bet that even now, with Ayelet in New York, he is still making the rounds."

"Your man was able to pry all this out of him?"

"He didn't have to pry out anything. Once Mr. Rappaport is in his cups he boasts about it. You can hear the recordings. And there is one more thing."

"What can be worse than what you have already told me?"

"When he doesn't get his way, he can be very violent. Although his wife never made a formal complaint, there are hospital records that show that he beat her. And more than once. My investigator saw him slap around one of the women in his hotel room and Rappaport had to pay her a thousand dollars to keep it quiet. Like I said ... he is *drek*. You have to tell Ayelet. She can't marry this guy."

I suddenly had a feeling that I was the captain of the Titanic telling everyone to abandon ship, all the while knowing that there were not enough life boats. It was hopeless. "I'm afraid it's too late. She is in New York this weekend meeting his folks and you know what that means. Last week I told her not to commit to anything until you gave me the full report but I don't think she is going to listen to my advice."

"Do the best you can. I hate to think what will happen if you don't succeed."

I sat in my den for almost two hours until I worked up the courage to dial Ayelet's cell phone. She answered on the third ring, "Hi, Ayelet, this is Steve Lincoln."

"Mr. Lincoln? Is there something wrong with the kids?"

"This has nothing to do with the kids. I suppose they are fine. I wouldn't know."

"Then why are you calling me here in New York?"

"I told you I would get back to you when the final report came in."

"So you have more *loshon horah,*" said Ayelet angrily. "I told you I didn't want to hear it."

*This is not going to work.* "But you have to, Ayelet. Your friend Mr. Rappaport is not what he seems. I have proof that he is a fraud. His company is going bankrupt. He just wants to rob you of your business."

"That's your proof? Aryeh already told me that he is having a cash flow problem right now, but he said the company is recuperating well."

"He's a liar."

"So you say that he's the one that's lying. Have you any idea how well respected he is in his community? The people here don't agree with you."

"It gets worse. He's also a heavy drinker and he goes to see women during the time everyone thinks he is in the *bais medrash.*"

"You must have the wrong Aryeh Rappaport. My Aryeh is considered the most eligible religious divorcee in the New York area. I have never ever seen him take a drink."

"That's because he hides his drinking when he's in New York. He does most of his *shtick* when he's on his business trips. He can also be violent ... so be extra careful."

"Aryeh wouldn't hurt a fly."

"You're wrong. He beat his wife. Even if you don't believe me ... at least don't commit yourself to marrying this guy until you look at the report and you listen to the recordings."

"Now you also have recordings?" she asked in disbelief. "Have you lost your mind? I have to make one of the most difficult decisions of my life and you fabricate some fake report just to make me miserable. How dare you do this to me?"

I didn't know what I could say to convince her, "Ayelet, I'm not doing anything to you. I'm just trying to help."

"You're ruining my life," she exclaimed in desperation.

"Why would I do that?"

"Is this your way of getting back at me?" asked Ayelet. "Is it because I told you there could never be anything between us?"

"You're right ... there is a reason for me to lie, cheat, and sneak just to be with you. But I didn't do any of those things. Do you know why? Because you told me to stay away and I did."

"How do I know that you aren't lying right now?"

"You don't ... but deep down in your heart you know that I would never do anything to hurt you. Believe me, keep away from this guy. He's bad news."

Ayelet interjected, "Mr. Lincoln. This conversation is over. Please don't call me anymore. If you call I will not answer. Let me get on with my life."

I heard the click that disconnected the call.

For the next few hours I just sat in my den staring at the walls contemplating what to do. I felt like I was watching a train wreck about to happen and there was nothing I could do to stop it. She did not want to believe my warnings. I had done the best I could.

My whole world was shot to hell.

A little after five in the afternoon I decided that it would be a simply terrific idea to break open my new bottle of Glen Fiddich single malt and see if an ample sampling of some Scottish ambrosia could give me a little more optimistic slant on life.

I went to the freezer and filled a heavy glass with ice cubes but changed my mind and tossed them into the sink. I figured that diluting the scotch would only delay the desired effect. I poured off a good four fingers of the amber liquid and had the glass half way to my mouth when my phone rang.

"Mr. Lincoln, is that you?" said a young girl's voice.

"Yeah, this is Mr. Lincoln. Who is this?"

"Mr. Lincoln, this is Marissa. You remember me. I babysit for Mrs. Weinberg. You used to take me home."

"Sure Marissa, of course I remember you. What's the matter?" I asked with concern.

"I'm babysitting this weekend for Mrs. Weinberg. She's in New York."

"I know."

"Racheli has been complaining about her stomach since the morning and she just threw up. I think she has a fever and I don't know what to do. My folks are also out of town and I didn't know who to call. Chaim'l suggested you ... so I called."

"Gee, Marissa, I would like to help, but I'm not family. I can't do anything without Mrs. Weinberg's permission. Why don't you call her cell phone and ask her."

"I tried that already. There was no answer and I left a message. I'm afraid Racheli might be really sick."

I looked at the glass of 18 year old Scotch in my hand and dumped it down the drain, "I'll be right over."

I hit the speed limit twice getting to Ayelet's house. Once when I set out and then again when I slowed to a stop in her driveway. I found the little girl curled up in a ball and moaning softly. Any attempt to move her caused load wails of pain. Racheli was definitely not well. This was more than a tummy ache. I flipped open my cell phone and called Ayelet. Thankfully, she answered on the eighth ring, "Ayelet, This is Steve Lincoln."

"Why are you calling me again?" she asked angrily.

"No, Ayelet, you don't understand. This is something else."

"I understand perfectly. I am busy here with someone who really cares for me. Don't call anymore."

I heard her click off.

I dialed her number again but she did not answer and the call was eventually shunted to voice mail.

This was an emergency – *pikuach nefesh* – and I had ever right to use whatever means that were at my disposal to get through to her. Obviously her call identifier would tell her that it was me and so she would not answer if I tried to call her again. Marissa was totally shaken by what was going on and couldn't make the call. So I decided I would try using Ayelet's home phone to call her in New York. She would have to answer that. I got through to her cell phone again and a man answered.

"Is this Mrs. Weinberg's phone?" I asked.

"Yes, it is. She is busy right now. Can I take a message?"

"Yes, this is Steve Lincoln. Would you tell her to call her home as soon as possible."

"Steve ... Steve ... what sort of game are you playing?"

"I am not playing at anything. This is an emergency."

"Ayelet told me about all those false accusations you made about me. You see ... we have no secrets."

"You mean, she has no secrets from you. But what about the secrets you keep from her?"

"I don't know what you're talking about."

"About your drinking and the whore you beat up in San Francisco last week. And the whores that you have all over the U.S.A. And the whores you visit when you're supposed to be in the *bais medrash*."

"I still don't know what you are talking about," he said derisively.

"Ayelet will never marry you," I declared defiantly.

"That's where I think you are wrong. She's crazy about me and even if she wasn't ... there are reasons she won't be able to say no. In a couple of years I'll be able to sell off her company for quite a few million dollars and it will be smooth sailing from there on."

"She'll never sell her business. She loves it."

"She won't have anything to say about it," he said matter-of-factly. "Just like any good *frum* wife, she has already agreed to sign the company over to me when we get married."

"You thieving rat."

"I hope you don't mind if I don't give this message to Ayelet. And don't try to call again. Just to be certain ... I'm taking the battery out of the phone. Good night, Steve. As always, it was a pleasure talking with you."

I added quickly, "Wait ... wait ... I have to tell her ..."

Click.

I could not waste any more time – Racheli was very sick. She needed medical care. An ambulance would take at least twenty five minutes and the hospital was only five minutes away. I turned to Marissa, "First, put a big blanket in the cargo area of my SUV. Then move the car seat for Yanki from Mrs. Weinberg's car into mine and have Chaim'l strap him in."

I went to Racheli's room and picked up the little girl as gently as I could. Trying not to jostle her more than necessary, I moved her to the cargo area of my car.

"Marissa, get in and hold her while I drive to the hospital. I'll try to avoid all the bumps in the road. You just watch her."

The emergency room staff whisked Racheli into the treatment area and Marissa accompanied her. Meanwhile, the boys and I went to the admitting area to get her registered. I was giving Racheli's information to the admission's clerk when one of the doctors came out into the reception area. He was dressed in wrinkled, green surgical scrubs and had a stethoscope draped around his neck. The unshaven medic appeared to have had a long day and probably needed some sleep. He looked inquisitively around the reception room as he asked, "Where are the parents of the little girl that just came in?"

I approached the doctor and answered, "She only has a mother, but she is in New York right now."

"She's going to need an emergency appendectomy and we need some next of kin to give permission for the surgery."

"There may be a problem in contacting her mother. She has phone trouble. How much time have we got?"

"Well let's see," said the doctor sarcastically. "The little girl's appendix is about to rupture ... if it hasn't already ... and she has fever and signs of peritonitis. How much time do you think we've got?"

"I see your point," I said.

The doctor looked at me and asked, "Are you a relative? Can't you sign?"

I was about to explain that I was just a sort-of family friend, when Chaim'l chirped in, "Yes, he can sign."

"And who are you," the doctor asked Chaim'l.

"I'm Racheli's older brother."

"And who is this man," asked the doctor pointing at me.

Never batting an eyelash, Chaim'l looked up at the doctor and said, "He's our uncle."

I thought to myself – perhaps I was an honorary uncle, but the kid was out and out lying.

I was suddenly smack dab in the middle of a major ethical dilemma.

According to Dr. Spock's written in stone rules of child care, it was my responsibility to discipline Chaim'l and tell the doctor to disregard what the kid had just said.

But after all my months of studying with Rabbi Kalmonowitz, I knew that the Jewish way of looking at things was different from the cut and dried 'according-to-the-law' modern outlook. *Halacha* analyzes legal problems by trying to determine why any rule was made in the first place. If a situation arose where the general good was in conflict with a less than logical rule, then certain accommodations could be made to get around the rule.

Chaim'l was a smart kid. It was obvious to him that had his mother been there she would have consented to surgery. In the present situation the rule was protecting the best interests of the hospital a lot more than it was protecting Racheli's best interest. His sister needed to have the surgery, so the kid had lied.

I kept my mouth shut.

The doctor spoke decisively to the reception clerk, "This surgery can't wait. Let him sign and I'll attest that it was an emergency."

# 28

## The bubble bursts

THIS PAST *SHABBOS* in New York has been like a fairy tale. So many important rabbis introduced themselves to me over this weekend. I couldn't believe it – they came to meet me. It was as if I was on display. Each one had such good things to say about Aryeh. It started on Friday when I arrived and just did not stop. They told me how he is such a *tzadik* and that I am so lucky that he is considering me for his wife. There were twenty people for dinner at his parent's home in the evening and Aryeh delivered *divrei torah* during the meal. Everyone was greatly impressed.

The next morning in *shul* he received the most coveted sixth *aliyah.* He told me that he would have given a *kiddush* after the services but that it would not have been proper since we are as yet not properly engaged.

All day on *shabbos,* people came and went. It's impossible to remember all of their names or positions. Each one was more *mechubad* than the one before them. It was almost as if it was choreographed that way. I think almost every *rosh yeshiva* and every *dayan* in Borough Park came by. When nightfall arrived and *shabbos* ended I was totally exhausted, but it did not end. Because then people started arriving by car from other parts of Brooklyn, Manhattan, Staten Island, and even New Jersey. The last people left around midnight. Luckily, I was staying with the family that lived next door to the older Rappaports and I had just enough strength to climb into bed.

The hectic *shabbos* left me so tired that this morning I woke only at about ten for my breakfast with Aryeh's parents. He wasn't home because Sunday mornings was one of his regular times to be in the *bais medrash.*

It is hard not to be impressed with Aryeh's family and friends. They must be one of the most influential families in the entire Jewish community. What an honor to be considered to join their *mishpocha*.

Mr. Lincoln called me a little after noon and that put me in a bad mood. Why did he do that? Thankfully Aryeh came back from the *bais medrash* and took me out for a lovely tour of the city. If not for that I would have been miserable all day.

First we went into Manhattan and he drove his car right onto the Staten Island Ferry. The Statue of Liberty looks so much larger when you get up close. Then we returned to Brooklyn via the Verrazano Bridge and went to see the Japanese Garden in the Brooklyn Botanical Gardens. It was so lovely, with the beautiful lake, waterfalls, and streams. Almost like *Gan Eden*. I wanted to stay longer but Aryeh said we had to go back to the house in time for his folks 'official' reception. Although I've been with Aryeh's parents all weekend, I must 'officially' meet them at a special dinner they have organized for me tonight.

I changed my clothes for perhaps the umpteenth time this weekend and I was resting on the bed in an upstairs bedroom, waiting for the reception to begin, when Mr. Lincoln called again. Did he think I would fall for all those lies? How dare he say all those things about Aryeh? Why did he do that? It was so unlike him. Maybe he does feel something towards me, but it would simply never work and I refuse to even consider it.

Look at me. It is an hour since the call and I am still a basket case. Here I am about to consent to marry Aryeh and I am thinking about Mr. Lincoln. *What is the matter with me?* Well, at least I know not to answer any more calls from him.

Speaking of phone calls, where is my phone? Perhaps I should call the kids before the reception just to see if they are okay. Marissa is a responsible girl and she would have called if there was any problem. Here is my phone deep in my pocket book. I will just make a quick call.

That is odd. It does not light up. The buttons aren't working. What a bad time for my phone to be out. I had better call home and give them my number here just to be safe. I must find Aryeh – ah, there he is, "Aryeh ... could you come here?"

Looking as handsome as ever, Aryeh came into the room – leaving the door open as is proper. "It's like a zoo out there. You have the right idea to just lie down and rest for awhile. I could use a rest myself," he said, as he removed his jacket, threw it on the bed, and collapsed into an upholstered chair. "What's the problem?"

"Can I borrow your phone? I want to check in on the kids and mine doesn't seem to be working."

"Sure," he said pinching the bridge of his nose from exhaustion. "My phone should be in my jacket pocket. Help yourself. Let me see your phone ... maybe I can get it to work."

I handed him my phone and went over to his jacket. In which pocket would he keep his phone? How odd – I knew where Rephael kept his keys and his phone. But this man is a stranger to me. Oh well. I will learn. There seems to be something in the inside pocket. Ah, here's the phone. There's also a piece of paper around it. There, I got the phone open – which button do I press to make the call? Each phone is somewhat different. Ah, there it goes.

*That's very odd.* No one is answering. I get the answering machine. Why is Marissa not picking up? Maybe I should call her parents – No, that would not do any good, she told me they are out of town. "I'm very worried."

"What's the problem, Ayelet?" he asked.

"No one is answering at my house," I said anxiously.

"I'm sure everything is fine with your kids," he said.

"Maybe Marissa tried to call my phone when it wasn't working?"

"I doubt if anything serious happened to the kids in the last hour."

"How do you know how long my phone has been broken?"

"Well ... well ... you told me you got that call from Mr. Lincoln an hour ago ... so it must have been working then."

"That's right, and then I took it to the rest room ... no wait ... I didn't ... I gave you the phone. Did something happen to the phone when you had it? Did it fall or something?"

"Okay, look Ayelet. You might as well know. When you gave me the phone Mr. Lincoln called again and he started telling those lies once more. I saw how disturbing his call was for you and I knew he just wouldn't stop."

"So, what did you do?"

"I took the battery out of your phone so he couldn't bother you anymore."

*Why in the world?* "You took the battery out ... without telling me? What's wrong with you? I have little children at home. I can't be without a phone. Give me the battery please," I demanded.

He closed the door to the room, handed me the battery and said sternly, "It was my decision to make and I decided you should not talk to him."

I opened the back of the phone and inserted the battery, "How is this your decision to make? You are not my husband yet. And even if I was married to you, you haven't got the right to just arbitrarily do something like that without my consent."

"In a Jewish household it is the man's right," said Aryeh firmly.

The phone powered up and it indicates that I have an SMS message from Mr. Lincoln's phone. Aryeh was making me angry and I could not remember the access numbers to get the message. "What right are you talking about?"

"The *Torah* states that a woman must defer to her husband's wishes at all times."

"Not in my *Torah*. Mine says she must honor him. But not if he dishonors himself," I said.

Oh my goodness, the SMS message is from over an hour ago. Oh my God. "Racheli is in the hospital!!!" I said out loud. Does Marissa have a cell phone? Yes here it is. There were three missed calls from her and one from Mr. Lincoln, before the call from my home.

It suddenly hit me. The last call to my phone was from my home. But that did not make sense. "Didn't you say that the last call was from Mr. Lincoln?"

"Yes, it was, and then I took out the battery."

*Oh my God! Oh my God!* "Mr. Lincoln was in my house. Marissa must have called him. Something terrible must have happened to Racheli."

"Calm down, Ayelet. I'm sure everything will be just fine. They aren't in a remote village in the deepest jungle. Besides, how can you be of any help?"

I started to think of what would be the fastest way to get back home, "I can be there, that's how. I have to go back right now. My child is in the hospital."

"It's a two hour flight and I don't want you to go."

"Aryeh ... my baby is sick and I am going to her."

"My parents went to a lot of bother to make this reception for you and I will not let you embarrass them or me by walking out."

*What is he talking about?* "Why aren't you backing me up on this?"

"I forbid you to go."

*What did he say?* "You forbid me? How dare you?" *What kind of person is Aryeh?* Doesn't he understand? This is a side of him I have never seen before – he is a stranger to me.

Somehow I have a crumpled paper in my hand. Oh my goodness – this was in Aryeh's pocket with his phone. I forgot I had it. Perhaps it's important – I must straighten it out. What's this? A computer receipt for a motel near here. "Who was at a motel? And this morning?"

"Where did you get that?" he asked striding over to me.

"It was in your pocket," I said handing him the receipt.

"You snooping little bitch," he exclaimed loudly.

Suddenly my head exploded!

My cheek and jaw were just a mass of stinging pain and I was literally seeing stars. It took me a moment to realize that he had hit me. I must have been knocked down because I found myself on the floor looking up at him standing over me. I could not speak.

"You will never, ever, look through my pockets or complain to me again like you did a moment ago. If you do, what I just did to you will seem like a pat on the cheek. I'm very easy to get along with so long as you do as I say. Your kids won't like it if something happens to their *Ima*. Do you understand?"

Who is this person? What is he? Oh my goodness, Mr. Lincoln was not lying. Things began to fall into place. I grabbed the edge of the bed and began to rise from the floor, "You're right. I understand perfectly. This will never happen again. I just figured out what you were doing in a motel this morning. And then you had the gall to come back and take me out for the day. I'm leaving and don't try to stop me. Thank God I was saved from marrying you."

"Ayelet, it is not so simple," said Aryeh threateningly. "I will not be embarrassed by you. Not now, not ever. I have told people that we will marry ... so we will marry."

The anger seemed to boil up in me, "Not while I'm breathing."

"You've seen the *yichus* my family has and all the people I know and how they respect me. If you walk out on me I will spread the word that you are the biggest slut in the whole *frum* community. I know all about your escapades with Mr. Steve Lincoln. You can deny it all you want, but who will they believe? You or me? When I get through with you, it goes without saying that you will never get a *shidduch*, but I also guarantee that none of your children will find one. I will also destroy your baking business if it is the last thing I do. You have a choice. Stay here and agree to marry me or you will ruin your family's future for ever. The choice is yours."

Oh my God – Mr. Lincoln was right – he is a monster. What am I to do?

# 29

## *I'll take it from here*

SINCE I WAS NOT ALLOWED to be with Racheli while she was in the operating room, I used the time to shuttle Marissa and the boys back to Ayelet's home. Then I returned to sit on *shpilkas* in the O.R. waiting room reading old magazines and drinking vile machine coffee. Finally, the doctor in the green scrubs came back out and said that everything had gone as expected. He insisted that most of the time was spent getting Racheli ready for the anesthesia and that the surgery itself was quite short. The medic explained that the infection had been contained around the ruptured appendix and that the rest of the abdomen seemed to be clear. The next twenty four hours would tell them if she was out of the woods.

I still remained apprehensive.

From my experience with Rebecca, I knew that there were doctors that coddled their patients and their families. They figured that for the patient's own good they were allowed to – embellish the facts and/or withhold some of the gruesome details. The physicians would say that everything was going just as expected when in fact the situation had already turned into a disaster. I just hoped for the best.

From the moment Racheli got to the recovery room, I was at her side. My heart just melted looking down at the helpless little girl. Every few minutes her eyes would flutter open but for the most part she just dozed peacefully and did not seem to mind the intravenous antibiotics that were running into the IV line attached to her leg. When the recovery room doctor thought she was sufficiently stable, she was transferred to her room. A private room. I was springing for the extra cost – even though I knew that Ayelet would never have agreed to that. The surgery made me into an 'honorary' uncle, and 'honorary' uncles were allowed to pamper little girls.

While I was in the recovery room the nurses made me switch off my cell phone – they said it interfered with some of the monitoring equipment. Now that we were in Racheli's room, I turned it back on and saw that Ayelet had replied to my SMS message with a cryptic, "I am on my way back home." I tried to call her phone but now it was her line that was unavailable. I called Marissa, who was back at the house with the two boys, "Hi, this is Steve."

"Oh, Mr. Lincoln ... is Racheli okay?" she asked with concern.

"She's out of surgery and sleeping now. The doctor thinks everything will be all right."

"I am going crazy. Mrs. Weinberg is going to be so angry with me," she said, almost in tears.

Poor kid – she thinks she did something wrong. "Marissa ... none of this is your fault. Ayelet should be thankful she had such a responsible babysitter to handle this. You were terrific."

She answered warily, "You're just saying that."

"No, Marissa. If they gave out medals for babysitting above and beyond the call of duty ... you would get one. So stop being hard on yourself. You were terrific and *boruch HaShem* things look very good here."

"Thank you so much for calling ... I was so worried. I have to tell the boys. Neither of them has been able to sleep."

"Tell them everything is fine and they shouldn't worry. Mrs. Weinberg sent an SMS that she is already on her way back from New York. I not sure if she'll stop at the house first ... I just wanted you to know."

"I knew that ... she called from Chicago."

Chicago? *What was she doing in Chicago*? I hunkered down in my chair to keep my vigil on the tiny little girl dozing peacefully in the bed.

At two o'clock in the morning, the nurse came in to check Racheli and said the vital signs looked good. There was no fever or evidence of continued infection. Thank God.

About a half hour later, with the ward quiet as a tomb, I heard the approaching staccato clatter of high heels on polished tiles and something being wheeled down the corridor. A drop dead gorgeous woman entered the room dragging a large suitcase behind her. It took a moment for me to realize that the good looking lady was Ayelet. She was wearing a new *shaitel* with a really modern hair style and was decked out head to foot in chic new clothes. She looked like a stunningly beautiful movie star on the red carpet of a Hollywood premier. Wow! I had never seen her like that before.

Ayelet rushed to the bedside and stood poised over Racheli's tiny body. She began to bend over to pick her up and hug her but hung back. Instead she paused and turned in my direction, "Tell me what happened."

It took less than two minutes to give Ayelet a synopsis of the evening's events. Then I waited for her to begin berating me for stepping in when she had asked me to stay away, "If you want to yell at me ... go ahead. It's just that Marissa called me when she couldn't find you. When neither you nor your boyfriend would listen to me ... I couldn't think of what else to do but bring her here. I know I had no right to say that I was a relative," I paused and did not mention that Chaim'l had lied as well. That would be between me and Chaim'l. "But they couldn't get you and without me giving permission it would have delayed surgery. So I became an 'honorary uncle'. I was just trying to help."

She pulled back her shoulders and said calmly, "I am not going to yell at you."

Thank goodness for small favors. "Now that you're here I'll just butt out of this whole situation and you and Aryeh can take over."

Ayelet said matter-of-factly, "Mr. Rappaport did not come back with me."

*That is odd.* "So is a *mazel tov* in order? Did you guys set a date?"

She paused before answering and said, "I will not be seeing him anymore."

"Until the wedding?" I asked tentatively.

"There will be no wedding. It's *oise shidduch,*" she said with finality.

I could not believe my ears. She was not going to marry the guy. I had to contain my emotions – it definitely would be inappropriate to show my happiness with Racheli lying there on her sick bed. "I'm sorry to hear that."

"Don't be sorry," she said sadly. "I was the one who was a fool. You were right ... right about everything."

She seemed reluctant to elaborate further and I wondered what she meant. Then I noticed that one side of her face was more heavily made up than the other, but it did not completely hide the bruise on her cheek. I stood and gently pushed aside the hair of her wig – she did not stop me, "What happened to you?" Suddenly it dawned on me, "Did that son of a bitch hit you. I'll kill that bastard with my bare hands," I said vehemently.

She stepped back and looked at me, "It's nothing. I'll be fine. My face will heal. And don't you go trying to beat up anyone. Remember what happened the last time you picked a fight. I haven't got time to take you to the hospital again. But I have a bigger problem ..."

Before she could continue, Racheli began to stir. She opened her eyes and looked up at her mother, but did not show any signs of recognition. Instead, she turned to me and held out her arms as she said loudly, "Stivoo!!!"

I didn't know what I should do, but instinct took over. I bent over to be close to her and the little girl got me in a bear hug. "Hi pussycat. Everything is all right. Shhh Shhh."

Ayelet stood at the side of the bed and began sobbing, "Oh my God, I wasn't there when she was sick and now she doesn't want me."

With the Racheli's arms clamped tightly around my neck I had a hard time turning towards Ayelet. "Are you crazy? Of course she wants you. She just doesn't recognize you all made up like that. You look like a fashion model. Just say something."

Ayelet sucked up her tears and said tentatively, "Racheli ... hi, it's *Ima*. How are you feeling?"

The little girl relaxed her death grip ever so slightly in order to search for the source of the voice. It took her a moment to figure out that the gorgeous woman was actually her mother, but once she got that sorted out she began screaming over and over again, "*Ima* ... *Ima* ... *Ima* ... *Ima* ... !!!!!"

Ayelet immediately bent over to hug her, "I'm here *zeiskite*. *Ima* is here. I will always be here."

They hugged and kissed for over five minutes.

Ayelet sat down on the bed with Racheli's little head up against her shoulder. With all the anesthetic drugs in her system, it did not take long until the little girl dropped off to sleep again. Ayelet laid her down gently on the sheets and pulled another chair up to the bed.

I moved my chair to the opposite side of the bed. "Is it okay to sit over here? It won't violate any of the *tznius* rules? The door is wide open."

Ayelet actually smiled for a brief moment and said, "Don't be stupid. Just sit down." The smile vanished from her face and she looked down at her baby girl. After a few minutes she began crying silently and the tears began streaming down her face.

At first I did not say anything and let her cry in silence. But from across the room I could sense the pain. "Ayelet ... you could ask me to shut up ... but maybe you would like to tell me what happened in New York. It might help. You know I'm a good listener."

She did not respond at first and just kept looking at her daughter, but then she sucked up the tears and turned to me, "Yes, I would."

Without any emotion in her voice, Ayelet told me all the objective facts concerning her trip to New York. It was as if she were filling in a police crime report. She described the time she spent in Aryeh's house and with his parents. All the important people that had been there. The *shabbos* meals and the *divrei torah.* Then she elaborated on what had transpired between her and Aryeh on Sunday. The Staten Island Ferry, the Japanese Garden, the phone calls, and then the motel slip, the confrontation and the way he hit her. She never raised her voice and never expressed a hint of anger. She summed up her description of Rappaport with, "He is the most despicable human being I have ever met. He is a *rasha* and a walking *chilul HaShem*." She ended by telling me about the warning he had given her about what he would do to her if she did not marry him.

I said angrily, "That's exactly what he did to his wife when they got divorced. But that's not going to happen to you. So don't you worry about that. Not even for a minute."

"But he said he would use his influence to ruin me and my family and the business."

"If Mr. Rappaport dares open his mouth with any of those lies, he is going to find a full page ad in the New York papers describing his life style for all to see. He is not stupid and knows that it will totally ruin him. And don't think he is off the hook for what he did to you."

"I don't want you to harm him physically. You might get hurt," she said with concern.

"I won't go near the guy. I have something worse in store for him. I will make sure that every major *shadchan* in the U.S.A. will know about good old Aryeh. If he's lucky, maybe he will get a *shidduch* with a blind *klaftah*."

"Thank you Mr. Lincoln. For everything. I mean it," she said.

"Think nothing of it. I was happy to help."

"Well, I'm here now. I relieve you of your 'honorary' uncle status and all its responsibilities. You must be tired. Why don't you go home and get some rest."

I could sense the dismissal. "Well ... yeah ... good idea. I could use a little sleep. Just remember ... you can call me at any time."

# 30

## *No more shidduchim*

I AM GLAD MR. LINCOLN took my hint and left the room last night – I needed time to think. Is he to be my eternal nemesis or my eternal savior?

The morning has not shed any light on my problem. Objectively, I know that he is not the man for me. He is too old, not *frum* enough, we do not share the same values. I also know that if we ever tried to get together it would most assuredly lead to disaster. But subjectively – that is a different story. Look what just happened here at the hospital. When I came into the room I thought that my whole world was in ruins. My daughter had emergency surgery and I did not know what was happening with her. I lost my *shidduch* and with it perhaps my entire family's future. But after a few minutes with Mr. Lincoln everything changed. He instilled within me a feeling of confidence that my daughter will be fine. Then, like a magician he was able to make me talk about what happened in New York. I can never talk so openly with anybody else. He even convinced me that Aryeh won't be able to harm me or my family, when I was sure that I had ruined everything.

He listens and he cares – but what am I to do about him?

As I sat there contemplating my relationship with Mr. Lincoln, *Rebbetzen* Kalmonowitz came charging through the door like an express train entering a local station, "Ayelet, is that you?"

As she always did, the *rebbetzen* had arrived gushing with energy and exuberance. She was a short woman but her strong personality made her dominate any room she entered. The *rebbetzen* was wearing her standard weekday uniform of a dark colored mid-calf length dress and a plain brown *shaitel* topped by a hat that matched her dress. Most people estimated her age at about sixty, but there was no way to tell because she did everything with the verve of a teenager.

"It is you Ayelet. You look so good, I hardly recognized you," said the *rebbetzen*, in her rapid fire way of talking. "That Aryeh Rappaport is an idiot. No, he is more than an idiot, he is a criminal. Best you are done with him and don't worry about a thing. I spoke to *Rav* Kalmonowitz ... he will take care of everything."

How did she know about what happened? I had not told a soul other than Mr. Lincoln and he promised not to say a word. "*Rebbetzen*, you know what happened in New York?"

"Of course I do. What kind of a *shadchan* would I be if I didn't know that?"

"But how did you find out?"

"That's not important. I'm just sorry that I was the one that arranged the *shidduch.* Please forgive me," beseeched the *rebbetzen*.

"There is nothing to forgive. He had everyone fooled."

"Just know that Aryeh Rappaport will not harm any more women. He is a criminal in many more ways than you know. He is in for a surprise and it is not another *shidduch,"* said the *rebbetzen* with emphasis. "But forget about him. How is Racheli? That's what's important. Did you speak with the doctor?"

"Not yet ... because the surgeon had to go back into the operating room again ... but Mr. Lincoln filled me in on what happened and he said that the doctor told him that Racheli should be fine."

"I heard that Mr. Lincoln was here in the hospital."

"Yes, he very generously gave of his time to help my *mishpocha* and he was here most of the night so I sent him home to get some sleep."

"Oh ...," said the *rebbetzen* knowingly. "And when did you get here?"

"I just got in from New York early this morning and came ..." Suddenly I understand what she is hinting at. "Oh no, it is nothing like that. I didn't spend the night here with Mr. Lincoln," I insisted. "You have to believe me."

"Of course, Ayelet. When have I ever not believed you?"

"Thank you, *Rebbetzen*. I would never do anything to violate your trust in me."

"I trust you completely."

"And I trust you as well. After all you are the one person looking out for me and arranging *shidduchim* to help my family."

"Yes, the *shidduchim,*" said the *rebbetzen*, looking up to the ceiling for a moment. "Perhaps we will take a little break with the *shidduchim* ... until the Rappaport thing dies down. You understand?" she asked.

Of course I do. It looks like Aryeh has started his vicious rumors and it will take some time to repair my name. No – it probably was too early for that. Perhaps I've done something wrong. I don't know what it is but I guess I'm being punished. *What could it be?* I can't believe that what I did was not what any other woman would have done in a similar circumstance. Still, without *shidduchim* my prospects are quite dim. *Boruch HaShem*, my business is still good, so I don't have any immediate financial problems. But my children need a father. I have to know. "How long do you think it will be until you could begin making *shidduchim* for me again?"

"Oh, this was not my idea. The *rosh yeshiva* suggested it should be so. We will just have to wait until he thinks differently."

What could Rabbi Kalmonowitz have in mind? "Did he say I should not accept all *shidduchim* or just your *shidduchim*?"

"He was quite specific. He said no out-of-town *shidduchim* whatsoever."

It definitely sounds like some sort of punishment. "That's okay I need to devote myself to developing my baking business and taking care of my children."

"The *rosh yeshiva* did make an exception ... he mentioned that if some appropriate local person wanted to go out with you ... so that you could get to know each other ... it would be okay."

*What did Rabbi Kalmonowitz mean by that?* He is a real and true *talmid chochom*. His mind sees things that most people cannot. They say that such great men can often see things before they occur. What does he see? Does he know what the future has in store for me?

*When he said someone local – what could he be suggesting?*

# 31

## *Edifice complex*

THE LOUD CHIRPING RINGTONE of my cell phone woke me from my deep slumber. I glanced at the bedside clock and it read 9:35. Ayelet had been correct last night – I really did need sleep. I shook the cobwebs from my brain and picked up the phone, "Hello."

"*Shalom Aleichem Reb* Shaul," said the familiar voice of Rabbi Kalmonowitz.

*Why was he calling me? "Alaychem haShalom, Rebbi.* What can I do for you?"

"I heard you had a hectic night."

How did the *rosh yeshiva* know about that? The man was amazing. The Jewish FBI strikes again. "Yes, I suppose you could say it was hectic."

"I know that Ayelet has returned from her little disaster in New York."

*He really is informed.* "Yes, and the last I heard she was at the hospital with Racheli."

"The *rebbetzen* told me that she is. I have to give you a hearty *yasher koach* for what you did. *Pikuach nefesh* is a big *mitzvah.*"

"Anybody would have done the same."

"I am not so sure about that. Ayelet is most definitely in your debt."

"It was nothing ... really. Her kid was sick ... what else was there to do?" I said belittling myself.

"Ayelet owes you for your help in transporting her to the group sessions ... which seems to have done her wonders ... you helped build up her baking business ... and now this."

"She doesn't owe me a thing."

"Be that as it may ... are you sufficiently rested now?"

*Rested for what?* "I don't know. What did you have in mind?"

"Oh, just a little building job," said the rabbi.

"*Rebbi*, unless you need help to put up a shelf or two, you know I'm retired and my company is no longer located in town. I won't be able to handle any kind of contracting work right now. I can recommend someone to you ... that should work."

"I'm afraid that would ... not work. I need to explain this situation to you in person. I know you have not had much sleep but could you come over to the *yeshiva*? I would like see you face to face so that we can discuss this with you."

*Who is the 'we'?* "I don't know what there is to discuss ... but if you're asking me to come to the *yeshiva* ... of course I'll come. When would you like me to be there?"

"How about right now? Would that be convenient?"

The urgency of the request took me by surprise, but after a moment I said, "Well ... yeah, sure. I just have to get dressed, say my prayers and then I'll be right over."

What I found when I entered Rabbi Kalmonowitz's cramped study knocked me for a loop and I think my jaw dropped open. It definitely stopped me in my tracks. *Rebbi* motioned with his hand to indicate silently that I should sit in the empty chair in front of his desk.

Seated next to Rabbi Kalmonowitz – as if it was the most natural thing in the world – was none other than Max Rosenstein. The incongruity of the situation was enormous. If I was asked to pick the least likely person to find sitting next to *Rebbi*, it would be Max Rosenstein. It was like seeing Yassir Arafat come back from the grave to be the keynote speaker at an Israeli Bonds Function.

There was an open *Talmud* volume in front of them and they were obviously discussing something when I made my entrance. Rabbi Kalmonowitz looked up for a moment and indicated for me to wait patiently. After listening to their exchange for a few moments I figured out that they were in the midst of a heated argument about a small point of scholarly minutia in the Talmudic text. Each man quoted extensively from other sources in the *Talmud* or the commentaries without once opening any other books. Everything was from memory.

Max Rosenstein?

*The man that went out of his way to eat proscribed food on Yom Kippur?* It was surreal. I could barely follow the conversation but it appeared that after five minutes, Rabbi Kalmonowitz succeeded in defending his position and Max acquiesced. But it was not a scene of victor and vanquished. Both had smiles on their faces for having participated in the enjoyable mental joust.

Rabbi Kalmonowitz now turned to me. "Thank you for coming so quickly. I believe you know *Reb Mordechai* (Hebrew for the name Max)."

I extended my hand to my gym partner. "Max, good to see you as always. I must say that this is just about the last place in the world that I would expect to find you."

"That's the way of the world ... expect the unexpected," said Max wagging his index finger.

"I thought you said you didn't know Rabbi Kalmonowitz," I stated.

"When I said it ... I didn't know the good rabbi. But you kept on talking about him every time we met. Rabbi Kalmonowitz said this and Rabbi Kalmonowitz said that. I got curious."

"But I thought you said you hate rabbis?"

"Most of them ... I still do."

"Then why are you here?"

The octogenarian nodded his head toward the rabbi. "Rabbi Kalmonowitz has been good enough to answer some *Talmud* questions that have been bothering me."

"Bothering you from when?" I scoffed. "You told me the last time you studied *Gemorah* was seventy years ago."

Rabbi Kalmonowitz said, "I believe it was closer to eighty years."

Max nodded his head in agreement and then looked at me with disdain, "A man can't ask questions anymore?"

I answered back defiantly, "I wasn't commenting on people asking questions ... I was commenting on certain *particular* people."

Rising from his chair Max asked angrily, "Are you implying that only *you* should be allowed to learn *Gemorah*?"

I also stood and responded testily, "I said nothing of the kind. What I said was ..."

"... that you didn't think I should be learning *Gemorah*. My hearing is still good," the old man said excitedly.

I looked Max in the eye and said loudly, "Don't put words in my mouth!"

"Then keep your mouth closed," Max responded heatedly

Rabbi Kalmonowitz interjected, *"Rabbosai,* this is ridiculous. What are you arguing about? Why should there be any disagreement about someone ... anyone ... learning *Torah*?"

I was the first to concede, "You're right."

Followed immediately by Max saying, "Of course Rabbi, you are correct as usual."

The words 'as usual' took me by surprise. Obviously this was not Max's first encounter with Rabbi Kalmonowitz. *What was going on here?*

"Good, now that we have that settled ... would you both care to sit down again? *Reb* Mordechai, perhaps it would be best if you could explain to *Reb* Shaul why we asked him to come here," said the rabbi.

Max Rosenstein pulled a large roll of building plans from under the table and said, "Take a look at these."

I slid off the elastic band and rolled out the large sheets of paper across the table. The legend at the base of each page of the plans said '*Yeshiva* Project'. I quickly flipped through blueprints and saw that they were plans for a major expansion of the *yeshiva*. It included a new, huge *bais medrash*, a larger dormitory to handle the increased number of out-of-town *bochurim* and many new classrooms to supplement the crowded ones now in use. It took me only a moment to make a rough estimate of the building costs (without contractor commission) at about $14-17 million, depending on the materials used and finished stone and carpentry work. The architectural firm that had designed the project was just about the very best in the area. I now recalled that about a half year earlier Max had asked me so innocently to recommend someone to design a building he was planning. *Has he been meeting with Rabbi Kalmonowitz since then?*

"So what do you think?" asked Max.

"What do I think about what?" I replied.

"Will you build this for me?" inquired the old man.

Rabbi Kalmonowitz interjected, "Reb Mordechai has generously offered to help solve some of the problematic physical constraints of our present building. The new *bais medrash* will be called the '*Ohel* Moshe Study Hall' in memory of his late father who died in the holocaust ... *HaShem yikome es damo* (may God avenge his [spilt] blood). I thought it should be called the '*Ohel* Mordechai Study Hall' but he wouldn't hear of it."

"My father's name is more appropriate. You and I both know that my name doesn't deserve to be on a *bais medrash*," said Max.

"We're making progress," exclaimed Rabbi Kalmonowitz. "This is the first time that you admitted that you have been a sinner. Have we started on the path of repentance?"

"Don't you go reading anything into what I do. You don't know my reasons ... I don't even know my reasons," said Max with a shrug of his shoulders.

"So if you don't know the reason ... it could be repentance. We'll make a *yireh shamayim* out of you yet," said the smiling Rabbi.

Holding out his palm like a traffic cop Max said, "Enough, Rabbi, I don't want to talk about that subject right now. Also ... we haven't heard Steve's answer."

Rabbi Kalmonowitz looked at me. "So will you take the job?"

I looked from the plans to the pair seated in front of me, "I assume you want me to be the general contractor for the job. But I told you that my company is no longer in town and I'm retired."

Max asked sarcastically, "What does that mean 'retired', you retired your brain?"

"It means that I haven't got the resources in town to oversee the project properly. I make a rough estimate at $16.5 million ..."

Max interjected, "Closer to 18."

"So it's a big project. It will take at least nine months to a year to complete ... and that is once the plans get approved by the city."

"Taken care of ... ," said the old man.

Rabbi Kalmonowitz said, "To be fair, there are a couple of factors that have not been mentioned. Mr. Rosenstein made two stipulations for funding the project. Without them there is no building. One ... only you can be the contractor for the job; and two ... you have to take the normal contractor's commission for the work."

"I don't want you working for free. People who work for free ... give you shoddy work," commented Max.

*That sneaky old codger.* If I turn down the job then the *yeshiva* expansion will not get built. He wants to force me to do it by making me feel guilty if I refuse. He also does not want me to donate my services. "So you're saying that if I did this project for the *yeshiva* ... and did not charge for it ... I would do a crappy job? Pardon the expression *Rebbi*. That's what you think of me?"

"It's only normal," insisted Max. "Either you get paid or we don't start the project."

"So you want to be stubborn. I can be stubborn as well. If I do the job for free ... I don't get to do the job? Is that it?"

"You want it to be for free ... it will be free. No money," said Max raising his voice. "There will be no money because the whole project is called off. Finished. *That's* it."

"That's it? That's it?" I stated angrily. "Well, then I'll ... find some way to raise the money and I'll build the darn thing without you ... and until then I will put up a big sign saying that you were too cheap to fund the project."

Max leaned over the table and said directly into my face, "I was too cheap? It has nothing to do with me. It is all *your* fault. I am going to put up an even bigger sign saying that because of your stubbornness the project did not get built."

"Oh yeah?" I answered getting red in the face.

"Yeah," said Max spitting out the answer.

I pushed my face up close to Max's, "Well, we'll see."

Rabbi Kalmonowitz rose from his chair, "*Rabbosai* what are you arguing about now. This is possibly an even more ridiculous argument than the one you had before. I'm sure we can find a reasonable solution."

Max Rosenstein said accusingly, "He's the one that is being stubborn. I just want him to take his money."

"I'm being stubborn? You won't let me work for free. You want to arrange things so that you're the only one that can do a *mitzvah.*" I said angrily.

"Don't accuse me of doing *mitzvahs.* Whatever I do, I do out of 100% self interest," insisted the old man angrily.

"Reb Mordechai, but if this building gets built it will be a big *mitzvah,*" corrected the rabbi.

"Purely an accident," commented Max.

"I think we've made some progress," said the rabbi tentatively. "Reb Shaul, it appears that you have agreed to be the contractor for the project and the only problem is whether you get paid for your work. Is that correct?"

I suddenly realized that I had inadvertently done just that. I really could not help myself. The plans were indeed beautiful and the moment I laid my eyes on the drawings I was attracted to the project. I envisioned the completed building and could see that the architect had done his research very well. The various rooms and halls were planned to perfection. The designers had given great thought to just about everything, from the copious shelving around the periphery of the main study hall to the acoustics in the sanctuary. It would be a privilege and an honor to build what would probably be one of the finest *yeshiva* buildings in the country. I nodded my head and said, "I guess so."

"And you Reb Mordechai, I think you would agree to let Reb Shaul oversee the project if instead of taking the money, he returns his commission to the project as his personal donation."

"I suppose," acknowledged Max sheepishly. "But he has to get recognition for the donation."

"I think that would be acceptable ... how about we put back those stained glass windows for the entire eastern wall of the main sanctuary. The ones I made you drop from the plans because of their exorbitant price. Now, we have a new generous donor. We could dedicate them to the loving memory of Reb Shaul's wife, Mrs. Rivkah Bilhah Lincoln. How does that sound?"

Wow. That would be something. I knew that Rebecca would be honored to have her name shining down on future generations of Jewish scholars. It was a fitting memorial for her.

Max and I nodded our heads simultaneously, "Okay, okay."

"Why don't you two shake hands, so we can get this project on the road," said the rabbi.

I reluctantly took Max's hand and shook it in a slow movement that lasted longer than a normal handshake. I looked into his face and said with a smile, "You tricked me ... I'm going to get you for this."

Max smiled back, "Never thought you wouldn't."

Rabbi Kalmonowitz interrupted us with, "We'll have to drink a little *le'chaim* to celebrate but not today. Mr. Rosenstein, if it is not a problem, could you leave us for a few moments. I have something I must discuss with *Reb* Shaul ... not related to the project."

"Of course Rabbi, I have to be going anyway," said Max. "Steve, take these plans with you. Look them over and call me tomorrow. We'll start working out the details."

Max left the room and when the door closed Rabbi Kalmonowitz began, "So you will be doing more *mitzvahs,* Mr. Lincoln. Before long we will be making you into a *tzadik."*

"Hardly, *Rebbi.* I'm still not entirely sure of what just happened here. But I guess I am back in the construction business ... at least temporarily."

"I wasn't aware you ever left."

"I'm retired ... I told you that almost a year ago."

"Just like you were retired when you built Ayelet Weinberg's bakery."

"That was different," I said defensively. "She had zero cash and she needed the expansion to get her business going."

"What did I tell you ... a regular *tzadik."*

"Well ... I worry about Ayelet ... for her and her family."

"That has been obvious to both me and the *rebbetzen*."

"Rebbi ... I'm worried about her now," I said with concern. "I know that the *rebbetzen* is very close with Ayelet."

"We both are."

"So you know that I think very highly of Ayelet and her family. She is a very brave woman."

"Sometimes too brave for her own good. The *rebbetzen* made a mistake with that Mr. Rappaport from New York, but Ayelet's mistake was even greater. What happened to her was a result of not letting her heart search out to see if he was her *beshert*. Instead she only saw someone that might be a father for her children."

"I'm just worried that she has not learned her lesson." I paused and then said, "And what's to prevent her from making the same mistake again?"

"I couldn't agree with you more. So, for a short while she will be taking a break from her *shidduchim.*"

"She agreed to this?" I asked incredulously.

"I suggested it to her."

"Knowing her ... that means she's following what you said. Does that mean she's totally grounded?"

"Not totally. I only suggested that she should stop all out-of-town *shidduchim.* However ... if some local fellow should ask her out ... and if he is appropriate ... then she should consider ... on her own ... whether or not she would like to get to know him."

"*Rebbi*, that sounds a lot like the way we Modern Orthodox do things. We call it 'dating'."

"*Chas v'shalom*. It just seems to me, that in this particular situation, it would be the best for Ayelet."

I thought to myself that it was highly unusual for Rabbi Kalmonowitz to do something like this. *Also – why was he giving me such personal information?* "*Rebbi* ... you're a *misnaged* isn't that right?"

"If you mean did I study in a *yeshiva* that was not *chassidic* ... then, yes, I am. But the boundaries of the various sects have become rather blurred in recent generations."

"So do you believe that certain ... *talmidei chochomim* have the ability to predict the future?"

"We've talked about this in the past. You are referring to those individuals who are purported to perform miracles. Heal the sick. Give business advice. Things like that ... is that what you mean?"

"Yes ... things like that. But I'm more interested in the ones that can see things before they happen."

"It is reported that there are those who can do such things."

"So do you believe in them?"

"Let's just say that I do not ... *not believe* in them."

"Okay, I'll settle with that answer for now," I said with a slow nod of my head. "Then, I have a question for you. When you stopped Ayelet's *shidduchim* ... but allowed her 'dating' ... did you make those changes based on something that you ... as a *talmid chochom* ... saw or felt?"

"If you are asking me if I saw into Ayelet's future, then the answer is a definite no. But I will say that none of the *shidduchim* that the *rebbetzen* offered to Ayelet ... felt right to me. Not the way I felt when she was matched with Rephael, *zaycher tzadik livracha* (may the memory of the righteous be a blessing). When they went out on their first date I could ... feel ... yes, feel ... that they were meant to be together."

"Maybe you should be a *shadchan?"*

*"Nore doos failt mir* (Yiddish expression meaning - that is all that I am missing in my life)," said *rebbi* wryly. "I'll let the *rebbetzen* take care of that."

"So, you didn't feel anything with this Rappaport fellow."

"Unfortunately, no. Ayelet has always been special to us, so the *rebbetzen* would tell me about the men she was considering for Ayelet. None felt right."

"Could it be that none felt right because you *know* she is meant for someone else?" I asked tentatively. "Someone local?"

"I don't *know* anything of the kind," said the rabbi cryptically.

The rabbi was choosing his words just a bit too carefully. "Let me back up a little bit. I'm going to take a big chance here. What do you feel about me and Ayelet getting together?"

That took the rabbi by surprise, "I told you I am a *misnaged* ... we don't make those kinds of predictions."

"And I'm just asking a simple question. If you feel nothing ... just tell me so. My question is do you get a good feeling or a bad feeling when you consider Ayelet with me?"

The rabbi thought for a few moments and with a nodding of his head said solemnly, "It feels good. Very good."

# 32

## *Definite maybe*

RACHELI IS SLEEPING PEACEFULLY – thank God. Her room is on the eleventh floor and as I stand here looking out of the window I can see for miles. From this height all the surrounding homes and lush gardens look beautiful. Everything appears so orderly and tranquil. But my thoughts have been anything but peaceful. What was the *rebbetzen* hinting at? I have been pushing away Mr. Lincoln for so long that it is difficult to think of him in any other way.

*Do I have feelings for him?* Of course I do. But is it gratitude or something deeper? He has been so good to me and my family and all I ever do is scold and complain. *What does he think of me?* That I'm just an ungrateful bitch.

*Did I just use that term in my thoughts?* How could I? *What is becoming of me?*

I feel better now that I had the opportunity to change my clothes and scrub all the makeup from my face. This is the real me and this is who and what I am. I am not really comfortable playing at being one of those New York City painted dolls. Mr. Lincoln said I looked like a fashion model. At first his words made me angry but I have to admit, in the back of my mind, it made me feel good that he liked the way I looked. Him. Not any other man.

I have a problem.

Any relationship with Mr. Lincoln will mean difficulties. There is the age difference, he is not *frum* enough, and he has a different *hashkafas olam*. It would never work. Then again, Aryeh Rappaport did not have any of those problems and it would never have worked with him either. I am so confused. Now is not the time to make such decisions. Perhaps it would be best if I completely cut off Mr. Lincoln from having any contact with me or my family and simply wait for the *rebbetzen* to allow me to receive out-of-town *shidduchim* again. That way I can take the time to sort out what I feel for Mr. Lincoln. That is it. I will make a clean break as soon as possible.

My thoughts are broken when someone says behind my back, "Hi, Ayelet."

I immediately recognize Mr. Lincoln's voice. I guess I'll get my opportunity sooner than expected. I turn to him and say, "Hello, Mr. Lincoln."

"Just dropped by to see how Racheli was doing."

"The doctor is very pleased with her progress and said if there is no temperature, we can go home tomorrow."

"*Boruch HaShem*. Glad to hear that," he said with a smile. "When she was sick, I was so worried."

I can feel his sincerity. He was truly worried for my child and he is truly happy that she's getting well. What a perplexing man. Funny how he answered with the expression *'Boruch HaShem'*, just like we do. He is not that much different from us. "Thank you for all your concern and for what you did. I am very grateful."

There was an awkward silence and then he seemed to remember something. "Oh yes, I have some news. I'm not sure if it is good news or bad news, but it's news none the less. Max Rosenstein ..."

"The snooping Max Rosenstein?" I asked.

"One and the same," he said. "He's donating practically a whole new building to the *yeshiva*."

"That's amazing." I was truly surprised. From Mr. Lincoln's stories, Max Rosenstein was just about the last person you would ever expect to build a *yeshiva.* "What a great *mitzvah."*

"He's not the only one doing *mitzvahs.* In a really sneaky way I got roped into donating my services to be the contractor for the project," he said sheepishly.

"You should be even prouder than Mr. Rosenstein. He is just donating money ... you are donating your knowledge, time, and expertise. I saw what you did with my bakery and I know that you are ... an artist ... yes an artist ... in transforming the drawn plans into reality. If you build the new *yeshiva* ... I for one will be very proud of you," I said enthusiastically.

Did I just say that?

*This is certainly not a good way to make a clean break with him.*

"Thank you Ayelet, I appreciate that," he said.

Once again there is a pregnant silence in the room. I finally decide that now is as good a time as any to broach the subject. I take a deep breath and say, "Mr. Lincoln."

"Yes, Ayelet."

"We've been through quite a bit together over this past year," I say haltingly.

"The good, the bad, and the ugly," he said.

*What does that mean?* "What was that?"

"I'm sorry ... that's the title of a famous movie. I forgot that you *charedis* don't go to films ... so you wouldn't know what I am talking about."

Another facet of our different life styles. Yes, a clean break is needed. "Please don't interrupt," I command brusquely.

"Yes Ma'am," said Mr. Lincoln snapping off a smart salute.

I suppose he thinks that was a humorous response. *We have nothing in common.* "Allow me to finish."

"Go right ahead," he said extending his arms palms upwards.

"We have been through quite a bit and as I said many times I am extremely grateful ... but for some unknown reason, *HaKodesh baruch hoo* has seen fit for things to occur when I'm with you, that have threatened the well being of my family. I'm sure I don't have to enumerate them for you. So, I've decided to ..."

"No need to continue," interjected Mr. Lincoln. "I understand perfectly well. You think it would be better if we didn't see each other anymore and you want to cut off all contact. It's something you have been saying for months ... but I just didn't want to listen. Well, I'm listening real good right now. You know I want only the best for you and your family so I'll save you the effort. I propose that in two minutes I leave this room and from this day onwards I'm out of your life. Does that fulfill all of your requirements?"

How did he read my mind? I hear him say that he will be out of my life forever and I cannot shake the feeling that I don't want this to happen. I do not want him to leave. I am speechless. I want two opposing things. My heart is beating so fast right now. What should I do?

"Nothing to say?" he asked. "Well, I guess I really didn't need the whole two minutes." He turned and headed towards the door, "Have a good life and hug the kids for me."

I whispered, "Where do you think you're going?"

He stopped at the door, "What did you just say?"

"You heard me ... but if you didn't ... what I said was, 'Where do you think you're going?'"

"Why? You have everything well in hand ... you don't need me so ..."

"Who's says I don't need you?" *Did I just say that?* How did everything get turned around so quickly? I guess it's because I am speaking from my heart and not worried about what everyone else might be thinking.

Mr. Lincoln looked at me quizzically, "Well ... for one ... you said you don't need me. I mean ... that's what you told me the last time we talked ... about twelve hours ago."

"That was twelve hours ago. Women are known to change their minds. Things happen."

"They sure do," said Mr. Lincoln nodding his head in agreement. "Like right now. I don't really understand what it is you're trying to say. Do I take it ... that you would like me to stay ... for a few minutes?"

"Yes, please ... for a few minutes."

He took a seat and sat quietly.

"Steve, Steve, Steve, what am I going to do about you?" *Did I just call him Steve?*

"I don't know ... what do you want to do with me?" he asked with a coy smile.

"First off, you have to stop playing the role of my kid's honorary uncle," I said seriously. "I won't have that anymore."

The smile disappeared from his face when he sensed my serious demeanor. "I'm sorry. I think I misread the signals you were sending. But I read you loud and clear now and I won't be a problem. You just want to clarify the nuts and bolts of your little break with me. That's fine. These last couple of days were an exception and it was only because I was afraid for Racheli. From now on, I'm out of your life for good."

*Am I so frightening a person?* He doesn't understand what I am trying to say. I begin again slowly, "From the first day I met you at the Jewish Center I knew you were a good person. Someone I would like to have as a friend. But in my world, women do not have male friends other than their husbands. So, like a good *frum* woman I tried everything in my power to push you away. But you wouldn't go."

He cocked his head to one side and admitted openly, "Guilty as charged."

"It was you, more than anything else that got me out of my depression over Rephael's death. You set me up in business and made me independent. I know you love my children ..."

"They are wonderful kids."

"And ... I think you feel something for me," I stated cautiously.

He hesitated for a moment and – choosing his words said softly, "I told you that I did."

"When I was seventeen and the *rebbetzen* told me to start dating I was very worried that I wouldn't know how to recognize my *beshert.* She never used the word 'love' that everyone throws around so freely nowadays. Instead she told me that if I truthfully answered five questions about the person I was considering, I would know if he was right for me. One ... Would I feel good if I did things to help this person? Two ... Would I feel bad if something bad happened to this person and would I do everything in my power to correct this bad thing? Three ... Would this person make a good partner to raise my children? Four ... Could I talk freely to this person about any subject? Five ... Would I enjoy just being in the person's company even if we were not speaking or doing anything special? She told me that if I answered yes to all five questions that I couldn't go wrong. " I paused and looked at Steve. "What do you think about the questions?"

He nodded his head and said, "The *rebbetzen* is a wise woman."

"I wasn't talking about the wisdom of the questions. I want to know how you would answer them."

"About whom?" he asked.

"Steve ... you are so dense. About me."

He must have heard me call him Steve again. *Have I been too brazen?*

He looked at me in earnest and as he nodded his head he said, "Do I enjoy your company? Well let's see. Every chance you get you chew off my *tuchis* for doing something in an improper manner or not according to *tznius*. Every two weeks or so you tell me you can't stand the sight of me and that I should stay away from you and your kids ... that's always pleasant. What else do we have?" he added with a smile.

"Steve ... seriously. How would you answer? This is important."

He looked at me so intensely, "You know my answer. The answer is 'yes' to all five. What are your answers about me?"

I never expected he might ask me to answer those questions in return. I'm so embarrassed I can't speak. Finally I say, "Yes ... to all five ... for me too."

"What about our age difference and the fact that I am not part of the *frum* community?"

"I can't do much about our age difference ... but I don't see it as a problem. As far you not being *frum* ... well, I'm sure that after your year of *chavrusah* with Rabbi Kalmonowitz, you must have learned that there are always appropriate compromises if people are willing to work together."

"Are we going to be *together*?"

"I don't know. First, we have to start looking at our relationship in a different light," I said surprising myself.

"I need a *peirush Rashi* on that statement. What do you mean when you say 'a different light'?"

"I mean we should start seeing each other to find out if we are right for one another."

"Do you mean go out together?"

"Exactly." *My God, I am such a hussy.*

"Does this mean that I have to go through a *shadchan* or something?" asked Steve.

Ouch!!! He likes to see me squirm. "I think in this case it would be superfluous. You can just call me up directly."

I think he realizes that I have practically said that if things work out on our dates I would consider marrying him. For a *frum* woman to come out and say such a thing is unheard of. *Doesn't he realize what I'm doing here?*

Why is he sitting there with that smug smile on his face? He has turned his head away and now is looking down at the floor as if he's weighing the pros and cons of my offer. *Of all the nerve!*

As he raises his head to look up – I can see that he has this stern continence. Perhaps he came to some onerous decision.

"All right, I'm willing to date you ... but I have one condition."

Oh my God, what did I get myself in to? What kind of condition will he set? "What is your condition?" I ask with trepidation.

He put on a playful smile and said, "If we go out ... you have to ride in the front seat with me."

I smiled back happily, "No problem ... the front seat."

## *AUTHOR'S BIOGRAPHY*

Born in London, England, Melvyn Westreich was raised in New York City. He attended Yeshiva University and completed his medical degree and residencies at Wayne State University, in Detroit. After completing his studies he moved to Israel and eventually became the chairman of the Department of Plastic Surgery at the Assaf HaRofeh Medical Center of Tel Aviv University, Sackler School of Medicine, the President of the Israel Association of Plastic Surgery and the Chairman of the Board of Plastic Surgery of Israel. His interests include travel, photography, gardening and he has a *mishigas* about Japanese Gardens. He presently lives on Kibbutz Yavne, with his wife, Ada.

# Glossary of terms

(y) = Yiddish

| | |
|---|---|
| Ah' mechaya | life giving (sheer bliss) |
| Aliyah | honor of being called up for the reading of a portion of the *Torah* |
| Alter kacker | old codger, crotchety old man (y) |
| Amidah | lit. to stand – the central prayers of the three required daily prayer sessions - aka *shemonah esreh* |
| Ayin horah | lit. bad eye - evil eye |
| Aytzas gibber | one that gives advice, usually unasked (y) |
| Bais medrash | *yeshiva* study hall |
| Beshert | soul mate, predestined marriage partner (y) |
| Bocher | young man or student |
| Boruch HaShem | blessing to (thank) God |
| Brocha | blessing |
| Bubbah mysah | grandmother's story [prevarication] (y) |
| Bubbi | grandmother (y) |
| Charedi | someone that practices Ultra Orthodox Judaism also called *frum* |
| Chassidim | Ultra Orthodox mystical sects that were started by Rabbi Yisroel ben Ze'ev, the famous Baal Shem Tov in the early 18th century |
| Chas v'shalom | God forbid |
| Chavrusah | study partner |
| Chazal | the rabbis (sages) of old - acronym for ***Cha****chamaynu* ***Z****ichronum* ***L****ivracha* |
| Chazan | person leading the prayer service |
| Chilul HaShem | denigration to the name of God |
| Chinuch | education |

| | |
|---|---|
| Chozer be'tshuva | one who repents |
| Chutzpah | audacity (for good and bad) |
| Daven | to pray (y) |
| Davening | praying (y) |
| Dayan | judge in Jewish court |
| Divrei torah | short *Torah* vignettes |
| Drek | feces (y) |
| Eres dvai | death bed |
| Fahrputzed | dressed up fancy (y) |
| Fahrshtupta | blocked or dense (y) |
| Frum | Orthodox Jews - term used by *charedi* Jews when referring to themselves (y) |
| Frumies | slang for Ultra Orthodox Jews (y) |
| Gan Eden | Garden of Eden (heaven) |
| Gemorah | The *Talmud*, also refers to main text of the tractate |
| Gelt | money (y) |
| Gemilus chesed | good deeds |
| Glatt kosher | food prepared under stringent observance of Jewish dietary laws (usually referring to meat) |
| Goy | lit. nation - refers to non-Jew |
| Goyish | not Jewish |
| HaKodesh Baruch Hoo | lit. blessed holy one - Almighty God |
| Halacha | Jewish religious law |
| Halivai | God should only make it so, if only it were so |
| HaShem | God |
| Hashkafas olam | viewpoint on life |
| Ilui | prodigy, genius |
| Ima | mother |
| Im yirtzeh HaShem | if God wills it |
| Inyan | subject for discussion or chapter/subtopic, usually of the *Talmud* |

| | |
|---|---|
| Kabbalistic | related to Jewish mysticism and study of Kabbala and the book of Zohar |
| Kaddish | special memorial prayer |
| Kavode | honor |
| Kasha varnishkes | bowtie pasta with buckwheat groats – a traditional East European Jewish food (y) |
| Kashrus | Jewish dietary laws - *kosher* |
| Kibbitz | to offer off the cuff advice (y) |
| Kiddush | blessing over the wine at start of festive meal, also food served in synagogue after *Shabbos* or festival services |
| Kiddush HaShem | sanctification of God's name |
| Kipa | skull cap – aka *yarmulka* |
| Kishuf | black magic |
| Klaftah | nagging woman or harridan (y) |
| Koach | power |
| Kosher | food prepared according to Jewish dietary laws. |
| Kreplach | dumpling usually filled with meat, similar to ravioli (y) |
| Kvetch | lit to pinch or press, vernacular for complaining (y) |
| Le'chaim | lit. to life – used as a toast when drinking alcoholic beverages |
| Loshon horah | lit. bad tongue - idle gossip |
| Malach | angel |
| Mavin | expert |
| Mechubad | honored personage |
| Mensch | (good) human being (y) |
| Mesechta | tractate of the *Talmud* |
| Michlala | religious college for girls |
| Milchig | Foods containing dairy products or utensils used to prepare milk products (y) Foods containing meat |

| | |
|---|---|
| | are termed *fleishig* (y). The two are never mixed in the *kosher* diet. |
| Minyan | prayer quorum of at least ten Jewish men |
| Mishigas | craziness (y) |
| Mishna | Opening text of segments of the *Talmud* |
| Mishpocha | family |
| Mishugah | crazy or quirky |
| Misnagdim | sects that disagree with *Chassidism* |
| Mitzvah | religious requirement or meritorious deed |
| Motek | sweetness (often derogatory) |
| Neshama | soul |
| Noodge | to pester (y) |
| Nu | an exclamatory word, used similarly to the word 'well' in English, that has no definitive meaning but can change its meaning by specific inflection or repetition. 'Nu, are you coming?' 'Nu, that is unusual', 'Nu, nu, who would have thought?' (y) |
| Ohel | lit. a tent, also a gathering place |
| Olam habah | the world to come – heaven |
| Olam hazeh | present world |
| Peirush Rashi | Rashi was the most eminent commentator of the holy books and the expression means that a clarification is needed |
| Pikuach nefesh | life threatening situation |
| Pishka | cup for collecting donations (y) |
| Punim | face (y) |
| Purim shpiel | (costume) party during Purim celebrations (y) |
| Rabbosai | honored gentlemen |
| Rasha | evil person |

| | |
|---|---|
| Reb | version of the word rabbi, often used as an honorarium |
| Rebbetzin | a rabbi's wife |
| Rebbi | version of the word Rabbi, but usually signifies one's teacher or a rabbinical authority |
| Rosh yeshiva | head rabbi of a *yeshiva* |
| Sechel | intelligence |
| Seder | special celebratory meal, conducted according to the *Hagadah* book, on the first night of Passover. Also on second night for those outside of Israel. |
| Sephardi | relates to Jews that came from North Africa and the Middle East |
| Shabbos | the Jewish Sabbath - Saturday |
| Shacharit | morning prayers - There are three prayer sessions in the Jewish day; *shacharit, mincha*, and *maariv*. |
| Shadchan | matchmaker |
| Shaitel | woman's wig (y) |
| Shemonah esreh | lit. eighteen (prayers) – aka *amidah* |
| Sheva brachos | lit. seven blessings. Also term for special festive meals during the week after a wedding which culminate in the recital of the *sheva brachos* hence the name. |
| Shicker | drunken individual |
| Shidduch | match - usually matrimonial |
| Shiur | teaching session or class |
| Shiva | seven days of mourning after the death of a close relative |
| Shlep | to carry with effort (y) |
| Shloshim | mourning period of thirty days after the death of a close relative. |
| Shlump | inept person (y) |
| Shmatah | rag (y) |

| | |
|---|---|
| Shvitzy | sweaty (y) |
| Shmooze | non structured conversations (y) |
| Shmuck | lit. gem – also euphemism for penis (y) |
| Shomer Shabbos | one who keeps the Jewish Sabbath as a strict day of rest. |
| Shpilkas | lit. sharp points - pins and needles (y) |
| Shtick | trickery (y) |
| Shtup | lit. to push or pack – also slang for sex (y) |
| Shul | synagogue (y) |
| Siddur | prayer book |
| Simcha | happiness or celebration |
| Talis | prayer shawl |
| Talmid | pupil |
| Talmid chochom | great scholar |
| Talmud | The Oral Law given to Moses on Mt. Sinai. There are two *Talmuds*: The Jerusalem *Talmud*, written in the Land of Israel and mostly in the Hebrew language, and the Babylonian *Talmud*, written down by the rabbis of Persia, where the language was Aramaic. The latter was bigger by far and is the main body of material studied in *yeshivas* around the world. |
| Tefilin | phylacteries - worn on the arm and head during the *shacharis* prayer |
| Tisha B'Av | A somber fast day on the ninth day of the Jewish month of Av – date of destruction of both Jewish temples |
| Torah | The holy scroll containing the first five books of the Bible. Also refers to all aspects of religious Jewish life and study. |
| Tref | unkosher |

| | |
|---|---|
| Tuchis | buttocks (y) |
| Tzadik | righteous person |
| Tzitzis | small prayer shawls worn under the shirt, also refers to fringes at the end of the prayer shawl |
| Tznius | modesty |
| Tzniusdik | follows rules of modesty |
| Yarmulka | skull cap – aka *kipa* (y) |
| Yasher koach | salutation for a job well done |
| Yentas | gossip spreaders (y) |
| Yeshiva | academy teaching religious Jewish subjects |
| Yeshiva bocher | student in a *yeshiva* |
| Yeshiva gedola | highest *Torah* study center |
| Yichus | rabbinical lineage |
| Yireh shamayim | a person who holds God in awe, religious |
| Yom Kippur | holiest Jewish fast day |
| Zeidi | grandfather (y) |
| Zeiskite | sweetness (y) |
| Zoftig | female pulchritude (y) |

Read the prologue and the first chapter
of Melvyn Westreich's next book:

**The Murders of Zion – A Lincoln/Lachler Mystery**

# *Prologue*

IT HAD BEEN STOP AND GO along Highway 1 for the last twenty minutes as people from Jerusalem and Tel Aviv left their places of employment. All these commuters were now competing with each other trying to get to their homes as quickly as possible and the road was clogged in both directions. Meir was so nervous that he barely was able to concentrate on the heavy rush hour traffic. *'Something is wrong,'* he thought to himself. *'The Doctor has never called for an urgent meeting like this. Normally he scheduled things well in advance.'*

His Toyota was doing less than thirty and he worriedly glanced at his watch. *'If this gets any worse I will be late for the meetup and The Doctor is a stickler for punctuality.'*

With his mind so preoccupied he almost missed the Latrun interchange. At the very last moment he was able to swing the wheel hard to the right. With horns blaring all around him, he managed to weave between the cars, and veer across two lanes of angry motorists, to take the exit onto Highway 3.

Meir kept trying to figure out what The Doctor might possibly want and could not pay attention to the scenery.

The picturesque Trappist monastery, the British Tegart fort – now a museum – and the ruins of the Crusader fortress hardly registered as he drove past. The only visible greenery were the patches of irrigated farm land and the hardy trees and shrubs that had adapted, over the millennia, to the Holy Land's harsh dry season. All the other plants lining the road had all been scorched to shades of gold and brown in the summer heat.

As per The Doctor's instructions he turned right a few miles up the road at the entrance to the Ayalon Canada Park. He took the first left onto a serpentine road that soon led him to a parking lot located adjacent to some ancient ruins. At the base of a crumbling wall there was a tiny waterfall – fed by the natural springs of the valley – which trickled and splashed its way down into a modest sized pond. The water's edge was adorned with a random assortment of olive trees, gnarled with age, and stately palms. The only car in the lot was The Doctor's, but the man was not in it.

When Meir stepped out of his air conditioned Toyota the inferno like heat of the Israeli *chamsin* hit him like a fist. *Not too smart to be outside on day like this.* He knew that once the sun was completely below the horizon the temperature would drop a few degrees, but that was a while off. For now, there would be no relief from the hot winds coming in from the Arabian Desert, far to the South. Beads of sweat began forming on his brow. Meir spotted The Doctor sitting off all by himself, at one of the picnic tables overlooking the pond.

The older man – who seemed impervious to the searing heat – kept his gaze on the waterfall as Meir approached and when he was a few yards away he heard him calmly say, "I have always liked this park. Very restful. Never has any crowds and it is right off the highway."

"It's my first time here," said Meir, mopping his forehead as he looked around. "Yeah ... it's nice."

The Doctor had as yet not glanced in Meir's direction and after a few moments of silence said, "We will not be going ahead with the plan."

"What changed? We went to an awful lot of trouble." said Meir in surprise.

"They have now become a liability. And *Hamifakade* cannot have liabilities," said The Doctor sternly.

"After all that work?" asked Meir.

"Can't be helped. Things have changed. *Hamifakade* decided to handle things differently from now on. You'll have to deal with both of them."

"I kinda liked them. Do you want me to warn them to keep their mouths shut?" he asked.

"That will not be sufficient," said The Doctor succinctly.

Meir nodded his head in understanding, "You want us to add a little demonstration? How bad should we hurt them?"

The Doctor continued to look off into the distance and said, "That won't be necessary."

"So, what should we do?"

The Doctor turned slowly towards Meir and gave a knowing nod of his head, "You have two days and make it look like an accident."

# 1

# Early Warning System

POOF – JUST LIKE MAGIC – we went from being 'newlyweds' to a plain old 'married couple'.

All because Dafna uttered those four little words.

Up until that point we had been in the lovey-dovey stage of our marriage. Our wedding had taken place a scant two months, one week and three days before. So we were still in that goofy period where you smiled when that unbelievable person – who had made a commitment to tolerate you for the rest of their lives – entered the room. The place lit up when they came in and dimmed when they left. *Gan Aden.* Paradise.

That life changing conversation had started out so innocently but because of what transpired that morning it was still burned into my memory. I had just come back from *minyan* and Dafna surprised me with one of her out of this world cordon bleu breakfasts. On most mornings her mother, Shaindel Kalin, did the cooking – Dafna was always so busy with her data retrieval business – but my mother-in-law was out in California visiting her son's family and Dafna's two teenage girls, Aliza and Suzie, were away at a sleep away camp. We had the house to ourselves and she was showing off her phenomenal cooking ability. I can still visualize the dish she put in front of me. It was a large peach colored ceramic plate with a red floral pattern and was laden with a huge fluffy mushroom/cheese/onion omelet – prepared exactly the way I like it. Complimenting the eggs were a large pile of crispy savory hash browns and some sliced fresh vine ripened tomatoes with a honey-garlic dressing. Yummmmm. To accompany that gustatory delight there was a crunchy fresh bialy sliced open and slathered with butter. It was all way beyond delicious and she was just handing me my cappuccino when she said those four little words that changed our lives forever, "Let's go to Israel."

At that exact moment I did not fathom the impact that simple statement was going to have on our lives because I naively assumed that her words were just an innocuous part of one of our routine mealtime conversations.

Retrospectively I now realize that the brouhaha that developed that morning came about because my EWS had been in the *idle* mode. EWS is an acronym for the **E**arly **W**arning **S**ystem that husbands are required to develop in order that they do not fall into the hidden matrimonial traps that wives sometimes spring on their spouses. This subject had been part of Rabbi Friedman's lectures in the 'young husbands course' that I had only recently completed at the *yeshiva*. Perhaps a more appropriate name would be '*Shalom Bayis* for Dummies *shiur*'.

Rabbi Friedman never came out and clearly said it but – by reading between the lines – I was able to decipher the messages he was trying to deliver; Modern Orthodox Jewish women were very different from the women of only a few decades ago and we should be aware that the divorce rates in the *frum* world have skyrocketed. Our mothers and grandmothers may have been willing to put up with a domineering or abusive spouse in order to save a marriage, but modern women were not playing that game anymore. These new young women were much better suited to face the world. They had a better all around education and were well versed in Jewish philosophy, *Torah*, and *halacha*. They were also better equipped to make a living and could more easily get along in a secular society. Thus they were no longer economically dependent on their husbands and they did not fear the stigma of divorce. If a young married couple wanted to successfully navigate the stormy waters of matrimonial existence and establish a good Jewish home, the men needed to get with the program and learn to live in a partnership without any strife. Little disputes could snowball into irreconcilable differences. The trick to survival was learning ways to avoid the little stuff. Thus the need for the EWS alarm.

Rabbi Friedman said that one of the most common pitfalls was when a man made inappropriate comments after a totally innocent – or not so innocent – statement or question posed by their wife. If she felt the response was; 1 - offensive, 2 – inane, 3 – sarcastic, 4 – belittling, or whatever – we were in trouble. Such a faux pas could set the couple on the slippery slope leading to civil war. He explained that one of the typical questions – that required the EWS to give warning – was when the wife asks, 'Does this dress make me look fat?' Another was, 'Do you think this dish (one that she had prepared) tastes good?' In addition, certain combinations of words should also trigger the alarm: 'Don't you' linked with verbs such as 'think, agree, or want'. Or 'I and we' in the same sentence, 'I think we should ...' or 'I believe we can ...'. Or the variation of this, 'you and we' together, 'Do you think we should ...' Also any sentence with, 'How can you sit there and ... ' was very ominous. There were many more.

Although we all laughed when the rabbi gave these examples he emphasized in all seriousness that if they were not handled properly, they could be real threats to marital harmony. He told us that in general, honesty is the best policy but when it came to things related to *shalom bayis,* you were allowed a little leeway. So, in order not to wind up in the proverbial doghouse – or be banished from the bedroom, house, or planet – when your EWS signal went off, you had a choice of skipping town or treading extremely carefully when you responded to these tricky questions or statements.

Married life is difficult.

Do not get me wrong, without a doubt the smartest move I ever made in my almost thirty-eight years of life was marrying Dafna, and I would do so again in a heartbeat. But at that point in time I had yet to learn the intricacies of married life or how to fine tune my EWS.

Dafna's four words – the statement that altered our lives – were actually in answer to her own question that she had posed when she got up from the table to get my coffee. She asked so innocently, "What do you think we should do during *bain hazemanim*?"

This Hebrew term translates into 'the interim period' and was the three weeks at the end of the summer just after the Jewish fast day of *tisha ba'av* and the beginning of the Jewish month of *Elul*. The major *yeshivas* would all be closed during this time and the *bochurim* then had time to travel near and far. Up until six months ago I had also been a *yeshiva bochur* – albeit a very old *yeshiva bochur* – in my three year journey back to Judaism. We are still affiliated with the *yeshiva* but now I was devoting most of my time working to build up my client base for my re-opened private investigation firm. Before becoming a *chozer b'tshuva* I had been a detective on the Detroit Police Force for over fifteen years and a private investigator for two.

So, my business and Dafna's media retrieval company were not really linked to the *yeshiva's bain hazemanim*, but her question was appropriate. The house was now empty and at the end of the summer my business was usually very slow. In addition during that specific time my administrative assistant, Mary Lou Evans, would also be in the Holy Land as part of a mission organized by her church and the Archdiocese of the Greater Detroit area, so things would be extra slow.

Maybe that was where she got the idea.

Whatever the reason for her travel plans, there was no escaping the fact that I got myself into this predicament – I totally missed the fact that she had used the words 'you and we' in her question. Most likely I was not sufficiently alert because Dafna's outstanding breakfast had put me in a post-prandial stupor and the warning system was turned off.

My mistake.

I did not have the sense to keep my mouth shut.

In searching for a response to her question I naively thought about our situation. Here we were – newlyweds who never really had a honeymoon. We would be completely on our own for three weeks. Not surprisingly my mind naively wandered to thinking of things of a romantic nature. I responded with a sly smirk, "I don't know. What do *you* want to do?"

Retrospectively, that was the wrong answer.

I left myself wide open.

That was when she fired back those four words, "Let's go to Israel."

In order to understand the significance of her remark I must explain the unique relationship that the Jewish people have with Israel. It is not just some vacation spot in the exotic Middle East. For millennia Jews have referred to the Land of Israel as the Holy Land. After the holocaust and the decimation of almost all of Europe's Jewish communities, Palestine – which in 1948, was transformed by the League of Nations into Israel – naturally became the homeland and safe haven for the Jewish race around the world. Even my folks, who barely had any connections with the Jewish religion, were staunch supporters of the United Jewish Appeal and the Jewish National Fund – organizations that help Israel's growth and development. Jews went to Israel to touch base with their roots. So even though I had never personally been to the Holy Land – and I am totally ignorant about things concerning Israel's geography, history, politics and culture – I understood why Dafna wanted to visit.

Still, to travel to Israel was an unexpected answer. But being the loving considerate person that I was, I responded with, "Sure, why not? Maybe next year."

My reply was based on the wrongful assumption that when she said, 'Let's go to Israel', it was on the same level as 'Let's order a pizza some night' as opposed to getting take-out hamburgers for a dinner next month. I was soon to learn that her words were not a suggestion. She had already made a decision on this matter. In her mind her utterance was on the level of 'Let's support motherhood, apple pie and goodwill to all men.' Anyone opposing these ideas should be eliminated from the ranks of humankind for all eternity. Those fateful words – 'Let's go to Israel' – were meant to be inscribed on tablets of stone and held aloft for the masses – meaning me – to heed. No dissent was expected.

She looked at me with her tolerant smile. The one she used to explain simple facts to the learning impaired and said slowly, "No, not next year. Let's go to Israel for *bain hazemanim*."

At that specific moment I thought to myself, 'What an absurd idea.' After all it was obvious to anyone with half a brain that it was not appropriate for us to go meandering off to the other side way of the world at this juncture. I was sure that with a short discussion I could convince her of the folly in her statement.

I was utterly and totally wrong because I did not realize that we had already gone from the newlywed stage to the married couple stage.

A big difference.

And thus began our first marital disagreement – or perhaps a better term would be 'intense discussion' – on the subject.

Of course it was not really a level playing field.

My lovely wife, Dafna, is way out of my league on so many different levels. Most of her friends simply call her Dafna – although there are some that call her Dafnaleh –

which she hates – but she is too polite to correct them. However, now that we were married she is officially known as Dafna Lincoln – I am Simon Lincoln – and so it says in her recently renewed passport – I checked. Her business associates still call her Dafna Lachler, because her company is called 'Lachler Data Retrieval', and she runs it out of our home. She was a child prodigy and received her PhD in computer science when most kids got their high school diploma. Besides all that she is a great mom to her two daughters, and is smart and beautiful.

No, that is not correct.

She is a genius and gorgeous.

Dafna presented her side of the argument in a logical manner. Simply stated: My investigative company would be limping along anyway, and with the rest of our immediate family and my administrative assistant absent, it was a perfect time to go.

Very succinct.

I did not see things the same way and offered my way of looking at the problem. First of all *bayn hazemanim* was only one week away. Second, Israel was 7,000 miles away in the dangerous Middle East. Third, I already suffer from the intense heat of the Michigan summers. If we visited that part of the world during the summer months I would turn red as a beet, melt away like a Hershey bar getting zapped in a microwave oven, and die of heat stroke. Not a good idea.

In addition I pointed out that even if she could guarantee air conditioning in every vehicle and building, there was no way such a vacation could be planned in such a short period of time. I also felt that my business might suffer much more than hers. She could close her company and get away with it. The services Dafna's business supplied were in high demand. All the major disc repair companies referred their tough projects to her and law enforcement and government agencies sent her stuff all the time. She was known in the trade as the 'Disc Lady'. If she suspended work temporarily, people would just wait patiently for her return.

In my company things were different. Even though it was a slow season, if I closed up, there was a good chance that if any of my regular clients needed something done, they would just go to another investigator and I might lose their business permanently. Very risky.

Our *intense discussion* became – for want of a better word – heated. Retrospectively I realize that my reaction was fueled by a subconscious feeling that my position as the man of the household was being threatened and reflexively my testosterone levels began rising. Anyone familiar with male physiology knows that when these hormones are on the rampage brain function dwindles.

In my impaired status I almost made a colossal blunder. That miscalculation would have plunged me headfirst into one of those traps that Rabbi Friedman had warned us about. By sheer chance I was spared.

I had been tempted to put my foot down and take a stand and say something foolish like, "Absolutely not. And that is final."

That would have been a disaster.

Luckily, I never made that ultimatum, but I stayed steadfast in my beliefs and was confident that I could retain my position no matter what.

I should have realized that I might have exaggerated just a tad about my confidence level.

That half a brain statement I made before – refers to me – not Dafna.

My gorgeous genius wife out maneuvered me.

After 24 plus hours of *intense discussion* we were able to sum up our disagreement: Her position was that we were going to Israel during *bayn hazemanim* and mine was that we were not. A' la the advice I received in Rabbi Freidman's course, we decided the best solution to the problem was to compromise.

So, the compromise we came up with was – that we would be going to Israel during *bayn hazemanim.*

I wish to inform you that I did not knuckle under, since I – as the official wearer of the trousers in our family unit – imposed some very stringent conditions before I agreed to this little jaunt.

First condition: Only vacation stuff.

Second condition: Dafna does all the heavy lifting.

Third condition: Safety first.

Let me explain these rules.

First: Our activities, while in Israel, would be restricted to only doing vacation type stuff. That meant the three vacation S's: Scenery, swimming and spa. I made this stipulation based on my previous experiences with Dafna. I knew that if she happened to stumble upon another cyber geek she had a tendency to get side tracked. My wife could sit and speak computer talk for hours. I would hear the words arrays, strings, code, and who knows what else. It was all gibberish to me. Therefore, only vacation stuff. In addition I required that each of us had to totally close down our businesses for the entire three weeks. To insure this I demanded that both of us would not take any business calls starting 48 hours prior to our flights. I left a little wiggle room and allowed people to leave voicemail and text messages in case some real emergency did come up.

Second: Since I had many open cases I would be running around like a one-armed paper hanger trying to tidy them up before we left. I could not share in the responsibilities of planning this vacation. Dafna had to make all the preparations for the trip: Arranging airline tickets, making hotel reservations, finding transportation, getting us an itinerary and a tour guide, etc. The only thing I was expected to do was pack my own luggage and Dafna was even responsible to get me a suitcase.

Third: Since Israel is known for its heightened security tensions – you never knew when missiles might rain down on your head or a *jihadi* terrorist would spring up – we would avoid any areas in Israel that could possibly be dangerous.

It took me fifteen minutes to present and explain the intricate particulars of these restrictions to Dafna. She listened carefully to everything I said and when I finished she immediately responded with, "Fine by me. Let's get started."

From that moment on Dafna swung into gear and began making her preparations. Without letting up in her work in her data retrieval business, she plunged into our vacation planning like a demon. She contacted dozens of companies to organize the itinerary and make all the reservations. Dafna was phenomenal. She was able to conduct convoluted phone conversations even when she sat in front of her computer console writing code. The lady could multi-task like crazy. Me, not so much.

Walking and also chewing gum at the same time were about the limits of my multi-tasking abilities.

So we were going to Israel just as Dafna had proposed, but I rationalized that I had not become a simpering wimp. I was not going simply because she had made a unilateral decision and I had nothing to say in the matter. No sirree – we were going only because she had totally acquiesced and agreed to my stringent conditions. I was still wore the pants in our new family.

Right?

Made in the USA
Monee, IL
10 March 2022

92679255R00204